THE PURSUIT

CHRONICLES OF THE DAWNBLADE BOOK 7

ANDREW CLAYDON

The Pursuit

By Andrew Claydon

Published by Andrew Claydon

Edited by Danielle Fine

Cover Design by MiblArt

ISBN 978-1-0685190-2-4

Manufactured by:
Produced and bound by IngramSpark Australia: Ingram Content Group AU Pty Ltd, Melbourne, Victoria. US: Lightning Source LLC, La Vergne, Tennessee / Allentown, Pennsylvania / Jackson, Tennessee, United States. UK: Lightning Source UK Ltd, Milton Keynes, United Kingdom. Europe: Lightning Source UK Ltd, with facilities in Germany, France, and Spain.The authorized representative in the European Economic Area is Lightning Source France, 1 Av. Johannes Gutenberg, 78310 Maurepas, France. compliance@lightningsource.fr

Published by:
Dawnblade Publishing
61 Bridge Street
Kington
United Kingdom
HR5 3DJ
andrew@andrewclaydonauthor.com
ISBN – 918-1-0685190-2-4
This book was manufactured using paper and ink products in accordance with commercial standards.

Just because you're chosen, doesn't mean you want to be...

An ally has gone rogue, stealing a magical amulet entrusted into Nicolas's care.
Not about to let this betrayal go unanswered, Nicolas and his companions set out in pursuit of their former friend.
Though that will be no easy task, for winter has come to Etherius.
The very thought of a chase through the snow would be enough to put off all but the most stalwart adventurer, but Nicolas will soon learn that the conditions aren't the deadliest thing about winter...by far.
Facing the elements, fierce predators, and the occasional barbarian horde, Nicolas could have parts of him frozen off, bitten off or simply hacked off as he pursues his wayward companion.
Yet, amongst even all these dangers, one stands out.
For winter means the coming of the Visitor.
He'll be knocking on doors. And Deities help you if you aren't in a hospitable mood.

Dedicated to Bea. An awesome human being who should never stop
pursuing her dreams.
(Even if the dream is just getting the kitchen to yourself in the morning).

And to everyone who loves a good adventure.

Orc Wastelands
Golthorak
Ivilar
Nalbina
Babylon

CHAPTER 1

With a gasp, Nicolas opened his eyes, only to reveal pitch blackness around him. Looking left and right, he was met by more of the same. It was hard to move, but he couldn't understand why. The strong smell of wood was a strange one too. All he really knew for sure was that he was stood in the most awkward position imaginable. He was almost in a half squat, but his legs were at odd angles to each other. He was definitely leaning against something, but due to the darkness he had no clue what.

What's going on?

Trying to force himself to focus proved a difficult task, like wading through a swamp. He could've sworn that he was drunk, but if that was the case, why was his throat so parched? Why were his lips so dry? Opening and closing his mouth was an unpleasant experience. The taste made him wince.

What happened?

His mind still refused his summons to provide him with a full account of the events that had led him to...wherever he was. All it did was tease him with vague recollections. There was a green flash. A feeling of betrayal. Choking, maybe? Actually, was the colour that'd flashed by green or red? Frustration boiled at the fruitlessness of his efforts.

Okay. Let's focus on moving, so I can get out of here.

Tentatively, he commanded his legs to straighten. They ignored him. Frowning, he bent his will to getting them to move. The sum result of his effort was some slight shaking.

Dammit.

His arms weren't much better. They felt heavy and floppy, but they were more obedient than his damnable legs. But the minute he did move them, his elbows struck solid wood, creating a thud that echoed around him.

Where am I?

Carefully, he began to probe his surroundings. He already knew he was leant against something, maybe wood, and that there was wood to either side of him. Reaching forwards, he soon found his motion arrested by yet more wood. It was smooth to the touch, so not the bark of a tree. Was it varnished? Panic gripped him. It took some careful manoeuvring, but he managed to position his hand so he could reach upwards. Above him was another wooden wall.

Possibilities ran through his mind as he tried to figure out what sort of place he might be in right now. His mind was becoming sharper by the second, most likely due to the fear-induced adrenaline rushing through his body, and those options cycled down to one.

I've been buried alive...

Screaming turned into a farce as the single high-pitched note became a fit of hacking and coughing. He wondered briefly why his throat wasn't working properly, but, he couldn't really give the problem too much attention right now. There was a long pause, the silence only broken by the pounding of his heart which, in his confines, sounded like the footsteps of a running giant. His eyes darted from left to right as sweat beaded on his brow. Then panic told him to act. With a wail, he began to thrash, flailing as best he could in attempt to break out of wherever he was. There were impotent thumps as his body still refused his commands to move properly, and he banged ineffectually against his prison.

Stop, Nicolas. Think.

That was easier said than done. His breathing was coming out as desperate gasps, even though he knew his air may be scarce. The notion that he was buried alive shouted down any attempt at logical thought. A tear ran down his cheek as his head shook slowly from side to side, trying to deny what he saw as the inevitable outcome of his imprisonment...he was going to die here.

Dammit Nicolas. Stop it. Pull yourself together. Channel your inner Auron. Anything. But calm down. Right now!

Closing his eyes, he began to get his breathing under control. Panic fought back, trying to make him gasp for air like a drowning man, but gradually he got his lungs back into a regular rhythm. His mind soon followed, albeit against its will. Wherever he was, he wasn't getting out of it by having a fit. That was the old Nicolas...or the younger Nicolas, really.

Instead of focusing on what could happen next, he began to focus on where he was.

I'm in some sort of wooden box. But I can't be buried alive. I'm upright, for one thing. And I don't think the wood would make such hollow thuds if it was covered in tons of dirt. So where am I?

Think, man. Think...

As he couldn't really move, he had one recourse. With several coughs, he cleared his throat and took a deep breath.

'Heeeeeeeeeelp.'

His voice was hoarse and croaking. He got the impression he hadn't used it in a while. But he pushed that concerning thought aside for the more concerning one. He hadn't put himself in this box. Whatever else, he was sure of that. So therefore, someone else had put him in it. Calling out could end up summoning said person...but right now, it was his only option.

'Heeeeeeeeeelp.'

Three more times, he tried. Silence was his only answer.

Shit.

Then he began to get angry.

All the crap I've been through, and someone puts me in a bloody box? I did not fight demons and monsters to end up stuffed in some damned wooden prison.

Pouring his fury into his defiant limbs, he forced them into action, bucking and thrashing furiously against his confines. Each movement became stronger, more violent as his coffin—poor choice of word though that was—began to shake with every blow he landed on it. There would be bruises when he was done, but to the Underworld with them...and whoever had put him in here.

Thump. Thump. Thump. Thump.

Suddenly, he stopped, his eyes flicking to his right. Something had moved. He'd struck the side, and it had moved slightly, causing a brief flash of light. Hope manifested into an idea: there was a door.

With determination, he shuffled his body around so he was facing what he really hoped was a door. As he did, he somehow managed to bang his forehead, causing a sharp stab of pain. He quickly suppressed a growl, forcing his annoyance down inside him, and adding it to the ball of fury that had already been building up inside him. He'd need every ounce of it to give him the strength to get out of here. Planting his legs firmly, he tensed his muscles and readied himself, glaring ahead.

Bang.

The deep thud resonated around him as he threw his shoulder against the door. It moved slightly under the impact. Glaring at it as if it were his archnemesis, he threw himself against it again.

Bang.

Another slight movement.

I will not be stuck in here forever. You will open, damn you.

He began a regular rhythm, throwing himself against the door, backing up as much as he could and then repeating. Each time, the door gave a little more, the light peeking around its edges increasing. His hope grew. Bracing himself again, he pictured the rage inside him as a fiery meteor waiting to be unleashed. With a cry he launched it, and himself, forwards.

Rrrrrrraaaaaagggggghhhhh.

With the sharp cracking of wood, the door gave way, and sudden, bright light blinded him as he fell forward. There was nothing he could do to stop himself as he tumbled down like a tree after the final blow from the lumberjack. Luckily, the blinding light had instinctively caused him to bring his arms up to shield his stinging eyes, and he landed on his forearms instead of his face. His whole body shook from the impact. The loud, metallic clang reminded him that he was wearing armour.

Groaning, he moved his arms away from his face—not a pleasant experience as pain flared in them both—and felt cool marble beneath him. He blinked until his eyes adjusted and could make out a swirling, cloudlike pattern of greys and blacks in the artistic flooring he lay on.

With one last groan, he pushed himself over so he wasn't facedown, which took a tremendous effort. His body was limp with exhaustion. But at least he was free, and he was alive. The worst was over.

Isn't it?

Shock that he hadn't thought to check whether he was alone or surrounded by violent men with pointy weapons reinvigorated his muscles in an instant. Raising himself up painfully to a sitting position, he quickly scanned the room. At first glance, he appeared to be the only one in the room.

But just in case…

Sighing with relief, he found he still had the *Dawn Blade* sheathed at his side. Happy as he was about it, it was also pretty surprising.

Why confine me but not take away my sword?

Wherever he was, it was fancy. The ceiling high above him had expertly carved patterns in it that he really couldn't be bothered to focus on. The walls were decorated with works of art of many serious and official-looking folk.

Would it hurt to smile when you had your portrait done? Dignity is all well and good, but when you're immortalised as a sour, humourless fellow, does it matter?

The room itself was filled with small podiums upon which valuable-looking vases sat.

Turning his head caused a lance of pain to run from his neck to his brain. He had no idea how long he'd been confined, but his neck had evidently been crooked all that time and suffered for it. Looking in the direction he'd fallen from, his face set in a scowl.

I was in a bloody cupboard.

It was one of several lining the back wall of the room, each made of thick, dark wood. They looked valuable. Maybe heirlooms? They could've been antiques, though one had certainly lost its value now that some vandal had broken the door from the inside. It currently hung on a single hinge. As he watched, the wood around said hinge splintered and, with a loud crack, the door fell away and crashed to the floor to his left. He winced at the sound of the impact. The vases on the podiums nearest him shook a little.

'That's not my fault,' he muttered angrily. 'Blame whoever put me here.'

But who *had* put him here? And where was *here*?

Focus, Nicolas.

Closing his eyes, he summoned his last memories.

The citadel. I was in the citadel.

He frowned and checked the room. It looked like he still might be.

What was I doing?

Cloudy images came into focus. Governor Morrow. She'd given him that healing amulet for safekeeping. And then...

Garaz!

Emotions flooded his mind: confusion, anger, hurt, betrayal, surprise—that was a big one. But he couldn't deny his memory. Now it was back it was vivid. His orc companion had smacked him in the face with his staff then choked him. And then apparently stuffed him in a cupboard. Instinctively, he brought his hand up to his jaw, instantly regretting it as he pressed the tender area too hard.

Garaz. Garaz? But...it's Garaz...

He knew the truth, but he couldn't understand it. It was Garaz. They'd been through so much together. Why would he turn on Nicolas?

We were talking about...

Quickly, he patted himself down. His arms moved slower than his urgency demanded, the price of being immobile for Deities knew how long.

No. No. No.

The amulet was gone. Garaz had taken it. Correction, Garaz had attacked him and stolen it.

I need to find him. I need to get it back. And by the Deities, I need some answers.

He wasn't going to achieve any of that sitting on the floor. But pursuing the orc wasn't going to be easy, because his stupid legs were still being stupid.

Determined, confused, and furious, he crawled on his elbows back toward the cupboard he'd been stuffed into. Holding the frame the door had once rested in, he pulled himself to his feet. Finally, it seemed as if his legs would obey.

Okay then. Here we go.

Nicolas took a single step and stumbled forward like a newborn deer just learning to walk. His body swayed left and right as he half walked and half fell, his arms flapping at his sides as if that would somehow help. It took four whole steps for his legs to give out and send him tumbling into one of the podiums, which collapsed under the weight of his armoured body. Nicolas, the podium, and the vase crashed to the floor. The podium thudded. Nicolas grunted. And the vase smashed into hundreds of pieces.

Shit...damn, bugger, bastard, shit, crap.

With a growl, he rolled off the podium. He glared at the smashed vase. One of the heroes of old that had been painted on it, who'd been fighting some monster or other, looked back at him. That was Garaz's fault too, so he could pay for it.

He's got a lot to pay for.

Lying on the floor, again, he realised there was really only one course of action left.

'Heeeeeeeelp.'

Within moments, multiple boots stomped urgently toward the doors to the room.

Please don't be villains. Please don't be villains.

The doors burst open.

CHAPTER 2

'*Two days?*' he cried again. '*Two bloody days?*'

The healer glanced at him nervously before getting back to finding the potion he'd promised would numb the pain. He was clearly worried he'd be the one suffering Nicolas's wrath for revealing that he'd been in the cupboard for...well, two days.

He attacked me and stuffed me in a cupboard.

Nicolas's mind whirled with possible reasons Garaz had turned on him. They ranged from the fantastical—being mind-controlled by an evil wizard—to the mundane—he'd been drunk. None of his imagined explanations seemed authentic. The way the orc had spoken to him had been measured. Calm. Garaz.

'Excuse me.' Tentatively, the healer held Nicolas's head and examined his eyes. The strong smell of herbs from the man made his nose tingle. 'Still a little cloudy,' he said finally with a nod. 'But I believe the main effects have worn off.' Nicolas found a vial held in front of his face. 'Drink this, please.'

Apparently, his *companion* had drugged him as well. Some sort of potion to keep him in a deep sleep for his two-day holiday inside a cupboard. The guards who'd found him had already given him some water, which had been very welcome. He just needed some food now. Lest he forget, his stomach rumbled at regular intervals to remind him.

He held the vial to his lips and downed the contents. It was sweet and fragrant, enough so that he winced as he swallowed it, but he didn't question it. It was doubtful the healer was any kind of poisoner. And if he was, he'd be stupid to do it in front of the four citadel guards in the room with them.

Never mind the guards. Where are the bloody cleaners? Fine job they do, not checking the cupboards when they work.

Whatever the healer had given him worked a treat. The last of the disorientation—and slight nausea—vanished.

'Better?' the elderly man said, reading his expression.

'Yes, thank you.'

'Now, let's give those bruises some healing magic,' the healer continued, rolling up his sleeves.

'No, thank you,' he said quickly but firmly. 'Don't trouble yourself.'

I really don't want to explain why I start going ow *when he uses it.*

A couple of servants entered the room with brushes and walked over to the podium he'd knocked over. The moment they saw the shattered vase they both sucked their teeth in shock.

Very expensive then. I hope Garaz can afford it.

But that wasn't the most pressing concern, which was finding the orc and figuring out what in the Underworld was going on. In his mind, he played through every interaction he'd had with Garaz since they'd first met as neighbours in a necromancer's prison. Did anything give a hint of the future betrayal? It was difficult to focus, his mind throwing itself from memory to memory in a desperate bid for answers. He wanted to be furious with the orc, and part of him was, but a bigger part of him was worried about Garaz. And hurt by his treachery.

The guards suddenly standing at attention caused him to look up. Governor Morrow and Chancellor Basch had entered the room. Basch stared at him with concern. Governor Morrow had the same neutral face she used for any and every occasion.

With little to no grace, he stood up, using the wall he'd been leaning against for support. His legs were still not quite in synch with his brain. But two days stuffed awkwardly in a cupboard will do that.

'Are you well?' Basch asked, taking him gently by the arm.

'I think so,' he said wearily, before collecting himself and standing up straighter. 'I am.'

'The amulet?' Governor Morrow asked.

His mouth became a thin line to protest to giving an answer that it really didn't want to give. 'Gone.'

The irony of this wasn't lost on him. Governor Morrow had given him the healing amulet—used by a demon to disguise its true form—as she couldn't entirely trust all those around her. His task had been to see it to the vault in the Academy of Magic, where it would be safe. He hadn't even made it out of the citadel.

How could I have known?

He cursed himself. He should have known. All his paranoia and worry and the number of times he'd imagined terrible things happening, or things going wrong, and he hadn't accounted for *this*. Was it obvious? Garaz was an orc, after all. They got their reputation from somewhere. Just because Garaz could speak politely and...

Dammit. I wish I had an answer.

'Sorry,' he said.

'Did you see the thief?' the governor asked. He had no idea whether his apology was accepted.

Taking a deep breath, he prepared himself to say words that didn't come easily But they had to be said. 'It was Garaz.'

The silence that suddenly fell on the room was uncomfortable.

'Explain,' Governor Morrow said.

His lip curled slightly. Going over it again was going to make it even more real, and he was quite happy with it being surreal. Though he knew it had happened. Invisible pins and needles jabbed his muscles as blood flowed to them after being held captive in a piece of furniture, proving that this was not a stupid dream or delusion.

'After you gave us the amulet, we were leaving the citadel,' he explained, doing everything possible to avoid direct eye contact with the governor. 'Garaz was talking then said he needed to sit down. We went into a side room.' Briefly, he glanced around. 'Probably this one. He hit me with his staff, choked me until I was unconscious, stole the amulet, drugged me and stuffed me in a cupboard.' He hadn't even realised he'd clenched his fist halfway through his retelling until it started to shake. Quickly, he flexed his fingers open and shook them.

'Did he say why he was doing this?' Basch asked, clearly struck by the revelation.

'No,' he answered quickly. 'Or I don't think so anyway. That bit is still fuzzy. He said something about the greater good, or doing what's right, then attacked me.'

Governor Morrow turned to one of the nearest guards. 'Contact the city watch. I want the orc found.'

'Yes, ma'am,' the guard said with a nod, before hurrying out of the room.

Closing his eyes, he tried to play back his last conversation with Garaz in his head, to find some kind of clue or tell he'd missed. The orc had said some strange things before his betrayal.

'It is sad that sometimes we must all do things for the greater good. They may seem bad, but only because others cannot understand their reasons.'

'You have a good heart, young Nicolas. It is just a shame it sometimes blinds you to the necessity of life.'

His jaw set in a scowl, which caused his bruise to complain. How do you compliment someone before knocking them out? It made what had happened even more confusing. If Garaz had said, *'Ha, ha, fooled you, human. Now take a staff to the face,'* that would've made more sense.

And why can't I just be angry at Garaz? Why am I not smashing every vase in here in outrage that someone close to me turned on me? What am I missing?

Pondering and questions had to be set aside as Shift strode into the room with the force of a storm.

Oh no.

Green eyes furious, they walked up to him and punched him on the arm, hard.

'Ow.'

'No,' Shift snapped. 'No *ow*. You don't get to go missing for two days and then just...' The shapeshifter stepped back, frowning as they searched his eyes. 'What happened?'

Silva and Auron walked in right behind the shapeshifter. They were both clearly about to express their relief at finding him but stopped dead at whatever expression he was making that had doused Shift's fury.

'I need to tell you something,' he said quietly.

CHAPTER 3

The others stared at him in stunned silence. He'd known it would be difficult for them to take in. He was still struggling with it, and it'd happened to him. So, he kept quiet and gave them time to come to terms with what he'd told them. As his eyes flicked between them, he found himself searching their faces for signs of betrayal too.

No. Stop it. Paranoia is a steep slope once I start rolling down it.

'No, kid,' Auron said with a laugh. 'It can't be. You must be mistaken. The orc betraying us, it's too...obvious.'

'Easy for you to say.' Nicolas couldn't contain the growl in his voice. 'You weren't the one he choked and stuffed into a cupboard.'

There was no real argument behind the spirit's words. The—now-deceased—legendary hero had learned to trust Nicolas's opinion. All it took from Nicolas was a lift of his eyebrows, and there was no further protest from Auron.

Worse than the spirit's denial, though, were Silva and Shift's reactions. The warrior said nothing, but it was clear that anyone who crossed her right now would suffer greatly. Shift was much more obvious with their emotions than Silva. Their eyes darted from side to side, as if Nicolas had written down the events and they were reading them over and over again. At least Governor Morrow and her people had left them alone to talk it through. Though search parties were no doubt being organised to find Garaz as they spoke.

'Rrraaggghhh,' the shapeshifter snapped finally, grasping the air as if choking it. 'I knew it. I *knew* it. I told everyone there was something off with that orc. But oh *no*. I let myself get sweet-talked into ignoring it. All my years with the Thieves Guild, learning to pick up on cons and tricks, and I let the orc—an orc, of all things—play me for a Deitie's damned fool.' Finishing choking nothing, Shift threw their hands in the air. 'I should've trusted my instincts after the freighter.'

Maybe I should've listened then too?

Though he hadn't seen what Garaz had done on the freighter—he'd been busy fist fighting then killing a faun—he'd heard about it. The orc had grabbed the toad creature the faun used as a bodyguard and tore it in half. Granted, it was in the process of beating the sense out of Garaz, Shift, and Silva all at once, but it had seemed like overkill. When Shift had first told him the tale he'd assumed they were over exaggerating. Now though...

Auron stood in front of him, a hint of pleading in pupilless eyes that ought not to have been that expressive. 'Okay, kid,' he said softly, apparently not quite giving up on his denial just yet. 'I know you've just been through something traumatic. And that can play tricks on the mind, especially with...well, you.' *Cheers for that.* 'So, talk me through it again.'

He understood his companion's reluctance to believe the truth. 'Garaz hit me across the jaw with his staff then choked me until I was unconscious.' Nicolas shivered as the vivid memory replayed in his head. 'We were talking only seconds before. And he's big and green. It was definitely him.'

'Did he give you any clue why?'

That part was completely clear to Nicolas. Well, the base reason was. The thinking behind it was much more mysterious.

'He wanted the amulet,' Nicolas said quietly. 'And he knew I wouldn't just hand it over, so he just took it. Why he wanted it so badly...' *That he'd throw away our friendship.* '...I have no idea.'

'Maybe he's been biding his time since we met him,' Shift said, staring at the nearest vase as if they wanted to smash it. 'You meet a civilised orc in a necromancer's dungeon. That's a bit convenient, by any standards. Maybe he lulled us all into a false sense of security for just this moment.'

'I can't believe that,' Nicolas said quickly. *After all we've been through: vampires, gangsters, monsters, bards...* 'I won't believe it was all some grand setup. Garaz was trapped, just like the rest of us. He risked his life with us, for us, so many times. He—'

'Turned on us when it suited him,' Silva said coldly. 'And now he must pay for it.'

'Pay?'

'He dies.'

'Whoa,' Auron said quickly, holding up his hands. 'That's a knee-jerk reaction. He could've been being mind-controlled by magic.'

'Then he would have killed Nicolas, not *stored* him like a second-hand rug,' the warrior spat. 'He betrayed Nicolas. Attacked him. And he will pay for it.'

'Of course, murder's your first reaction,' the spirit shouted back. 'But we need to find out why he did what he did. Like you said, he could've killed Nicolas, but he didn't.'

Silva looked as if Auron had struck her. 'Murder is my first reaction?'

From there, communication between Auron and Silva devolved into a stream of curses and insults. Shift just looked away from them all. Nicolas wanted to go over to them, but there was a clear wall around them with a sign on it that said *bugger off*. Instead, he thought about Garaz. The orc was wise, genial. With those big red eyes.

Nicolas frowned to himself.

Garaz's eyes are yellow.

His frown deepened.

Are *they yellow, though?*

'Hey,' he shouted, clapping his hands to get everyone's attention. When he had it, he continued. 'What colour are Garaz's eyes?'

'Red,' Shift answered.

'They're yellow,' Silva corrected.

'Yel… Red…' Auron scratched his chin in confusion. 'They're… Dammit, I'm suddenly not sure. I thought they were yellow, but now you've said red, I want to agree with you.'

For a long moment the group stared at each other in confused silence.

'They're yellow,' Shift said, finally and firmly, glaring as they did. 'Except when he's angry. Then they go red.'

Nicolas stared at his companion—more than that now, in all honesty—and thought it over. Shift was right. Garaz's eyes went red when he was angry. How had he not noticed it before? Okay, that was a silly question. How had the others not noticed it before?

'That…is right,' Auron admitted. 'Well, I'll be damned. I had no clue.'

'None of us picked up on it,' Nicolas said with sympathy.

'Well, of course *you* didn't.'

'Up yours,' Nicolas retorted dryly, glaring at the spirit. 'But that's not natural, right? People's eyes don't just change colour.'

'Other than mine, no,' Shift answered.

'We will have our answers when we find him.'

Following the sensation of pure fury, he looked at Silva. Nicolas shuddered. To those who didn't know her well, she probably looked her usual self, but there was a fury in her eyes that could've burned the citadel to ash. Her knuckles were white as she gripped the hilt of her sword. Nicolas began to pray that Garaz had a good explanation for this, because he wasn't sure even *he* could keep Silva from killing him if he didn't.

'You're right,' Nicolas said. 'We can stand here pondering the whys all day long. We need to find him.'

And I really don't want to be in this room anymore.

'And get the amulet back,' Auron added.

'That doesn't sit right,' Shift huffed to themselves. 'I steal things. I don't retrieve things that have been stolen.'

'But it's a healing amulet,' Nicolas replied. 'What harm can it... Actually, never mind.'

He knew well what harm it could do in the wrong hands. It had only just been used by a demon to prevent its latest host body from burning out whilst it conducted its foul murder spree. Even things designed for good could be turned to evil with the proper application of imagination.

'We need to get it back,' he said firmly. 'We need to find Garaz.'

But it was more than just the amulet. He needed answers. A single answer, really, to a very simple question: *Why?*

But before that, another question needed to be answered: *Where?*

Babylon was a huge city when you were looking for a single person who didn't want to be found. Even an orc.

CHAPTER 4

Nicolas whistled as the parchment was rolled out, covering Governor Morrow's desk. Upon it was a map of the city of Babylon. Lines and squares marked various districts, streets, and places of interest, in any of which Garaz could be hiding. But it would be even more complicated than that. There were cellars, lofts, and all sorts of nooks and crannies in which to hide that were not marked on the map. Finding the orc would be a daunting task.

And we need to find him.

Nicolas wished he could just be angry with his comp...the orc. That would make this whole thing easier. But the conflict, the love he still felt for Garaz, made everything confusing. When they caught up to him, Nicolas was as likely to hug him as punch him.

He stuffed me in a cupboard.

Hunting bad guys was much easier.

'Where do we even start?' he asked as his eyes traced the streets.

Any of them could be concealing Garaz. Well, maybe not *any* of them. He highly doubted the orc was hiding out in some well-to-do family's dining room or beneath a market stall.

'We can cross a few places off the list already,' Silva said as she studied the map.

'Oh?'

The warrior's eyes flicked to his. 'We have been searching for you for two days. Between us and the city watch, a lot of ground has already been covered. Someone would have noticed Garaz.'

'Maybe he has friends in the city,' Chancellor Basch suggested. 'Do you know anyone he would go to?'

Nicolas imagined he looked as sheepish as his companions. It was awkward to admit, but he didn't really know Garaz that well at all. There was the obvious bond forged from surviving mutual danger, and he knew the orc had a brother, but beyond that, facts about his life were thin on the ground. Maybe that had been a warning sign?

He doesn't like witches or brothels. But that doesn't help... Actually, we can cross brothels off the search list.

Or could they? Maybe Garaz would know they knew that and so hide in one? Inwardly, he sighed. The betrayal was making him second-guess everything.

Sat in her chair of office, Governor Morrow steepled her fingers thoughtfully. 'Has anyone considered the option that he isn't in the city anymore?'

Nicolas certainly hadn't. And the others had been studying the map so intently he guessed they hadn't either.

'While our city welcomes any and all who come here peacefully, having orcs visit is a rarity. I can guarantee he's the only one in the city, and therefore, he stands out. For us to find no trace of him after our rigorous searching suggests he isn't here anymore.'

'She's right,' Auron agreed. 'Even if Garaz went to ground, someone would see something eventually. He does stand out.'

'But surely someone would note him leaving the city?' Nicolas replied. 'There can't be that many leaving now?'

With winter setting in, traffic to and from the city was slowing as people prepared to bed down. When they'd destroyed the false heating system created by Professor Shaw, Nicolas had worried the city would freeze. But Governor Morrow had proven herself prudent. The city had prepared for winter as it would come, whether or not they had a heating system.

And a good job too. The city could end up a giant icicle otherwise.

'Not necessarily. There are ways to go in and out of the city unseen.' Shift, who'd been at the back of the room all this time, pushed themselves from the wall and approached the map. 'I've made sneaking in and out of places an art form. There are always ways if you look hard enough.' They ran their hand over the map. 'But Garaz doesn't strike me as the sneaking type. And like the governor said, he's too conspicuous. He would've needed help.'

His heart froze in his chest. *Help.* Did that mean Garaz wasn't working alone? Had this all been planned? Was he somehow an ally of the Maestro, and this was all a plan within a plan stored in another plan wrapped in one more layer of another plan before being hidden in plain sight?

That's how the Maestro works.

He shook himself. That didn't make sense. Garaz had helped foil too many of the Maestro's schemes to be in league with him. And if he was, somehow, he doubted the orc would get a welcome reception when he returned to his master.

'Do the Thieves Guild have ways in and out of the city?' Silva asked.

Shift winced. 'Possibly, but I can't go to them.'

'Why?' Nicolas asked with a frown.

'I might've recently robbed one of their stash houses...then reported it to the city watch,' they admitted. 'I heard on the grapevine they might know it was me.'

'You've been stealing?' he asked quickly.

Instantly, Shift became defensive. 'I *am* a thief,' they replied sharply. 'And do you know how much you all eat on the road? And the inns? It doesn't pay for itself, you know.'

'Was that the orphanage I heard had been raided by the watch?' Basch asked with a frown.

'You robbed an *orphanage*?' Nicolas cried.

'I liberated the money stolen by orphans pressganged into becoming thieves then ensured those poor children would never be used again,' Shift corrected with a cold smile.

'And you gave the money back to those it was stolen from?'

'No.' Shift scoffed. 'I invested it in the *High and Mighty Nicolas Carnegie Adventurers Fund*...' There was a loaded pause. 'Just like I always do. And you're welcome.'

He was about to reply when he caught Silva and Auron's expressions. 'And I'm the only one who didn't know how we get our coin. Brilliant.' He held his hands in the air. 'For the record, if you're stealing from thieves, I don't care.' He realised he still sounded like he was on his high horse, so he brought the tone of his voice into check. 'But nice work ensuring that the orphans are safe.'

Shift gave him a sarcastic curtesy.

'I don't think Garaz knew either,' Auron admitted thoughtfully. 'He'd find it distasteful.'

'Moving on,' Shift interrupted quickly. 'Smuggling people out of cities is more of the Criminal Guild's thing anyway. Chances are, Garaz would've gone to them.'

'Can you please call the sergeant in?'

At Governor Morrow's request, Chancellor Basch walked to the door of her office and opened it. As he walked back into the room, a familiar figure followed him.

'Are you okay?' Nicolas asked as he took in the faded bruising on Sergeant Tallith's face.

The awe in the young sergeant's eyes made him wince inwardly. As did the beaming smile the watchman quickly tried, and failed, to suppress. Tallith looked up to Nicolas. Apparently, there was a fan club.

'Um, yes, sir,' he replied as he snapped to attention at the desk. 'Nothing that won't heal, sir.'

Sir? Yuk.

The sergeant had gone missing when the Maestro's minions had ambushed the convoy taking Professor Shaw to the city jail. Tallith had vanished at the time, leading Nicolas to assume he was the demon murderer plaguing the city—at least for a few minutes until he realised who the real culprit was. It appeared the sergeant had been given a thorough working over in his captivity.

'He was kept at Professor Shaw's manor as bait for a trap for us,' Silva informed him, giving Tallith an uncharacteristic look of sympathy. 'I tracked him down.'

'The trap?' he asked.

'All dead.'

All? I suppose it serves the silly sods right for crossing Silva.

'We found evidence at the scene leading to the location where the professor was taken,' Tallith cut in. 'The city watch surrounded the place. It seems the perpetrators had a fire mage with them. Things went wrong, and the place burnt down. Professor Shaw is dead.'

The man who opened a portal to the demon realm to heat a city died in a fire? How ironic.

Though he'd been an arrogant fool, the professor hadn't been an evil man. Just very, very misguided.

And manipulated.

Quietly, he said a prayer for the professor's soul. If it turned out Nicolas had misjudged him, and he was evil, well Sha'then would be having his fun right now.'

'Sergeant,' Governor Morrow began, 'who is the Headman of the Criminal Guild in Babylon?'

Tallith mulled this over for a moment. 'It's changed several times recently, sometimes daily. Since the High Chair died, the Guild's been a mess. And all the other Guilds acting up hasn't improved matters. But I believe Maxas Thrall is the current Headman. Until he dies or is arrested, anyway.'

'I doubt we can just ask for an audience with the Headman of the Criminal Guild,' Silva said. 'Even if we could find him.'

'Everyone knows where he is,' Tallith said. 'It's finding evidence of his wrongdoing that's the problem.'

'And I can get us through the door.' Shift smiled knowingly. 'Maxas owes me a favour.'

Don't ask for details. Don't ask for details. Don't—

'How do you two know each other?'

Dammit, Nicolas.

CHAPTER 5

'So, you never said how you know Maxas?' he said casually.

'Oh, didn't I?' Shift replied with faux confusion. 'I'm sure I'll re-member to tell you at some point.'

The fact that Shift still wasn't answering his question was driving him insane. He already had enough unanswered questions. He needed to start trimming the list. Problem was, he'd shown his hand about how badly he wanted to know, so Shift was now having a good old time denying him.

They'd recently left one of the main pedestrian areas of the city and were moving into what almost seemed its own section, closed off from the rest of Babylon. Clearly a rougher area, the buildings were all a little dilapidated, with many needing repairs. Instead of looking like they welcomed customers, each street trader watched them pass as if Nicolas and his companions would suddenly grab what they could and run.

We aren't thieves.

Well, Shift was. But they wouldn't grab and run. The trader would simply turn around and find all his stuff missing.

Most of the passersby wore knives prominently, as visible deterrents to whatever pickpockets might be roaming around. Coupled with how naturally shadowy it was, and the sheets purposefully placed to stop people seeing dirty or illegal deeds in action, this was a very unsavoury place.

'Why does Greer tolerate this place?' he whispered, ensuring his hand was very obviously on the hilt of his sword. It was a futile gesture. Silva's seething at Garaz's betrayal would've given an approaching dragon pause.

'Every city has a level of corruption,' Sergeant Tallith answered, ignoring the foul glances his uniform was gathering. 'Greer is happy to have it contained here. I know he and the governor have plans to deal with this place in the future, but those who dwell here are excellent at hiding their illicit activities whenever we come here in force.'

In force.

They weren't exactly in force right now, and they clearly weren't welcome. Tough. They needed to find Garaz, and he wasn't about to let a group of street thugs put him off. Still, he knew to tread carefully. His last experience of the Criminal Guild had been less than pleasant—if you could even have a pleasant experience with a group of criminals—thanks to the dwarf who called himself Big Boss. Suddenly, it occurred to Nicolas that he'd been right there when the head of the Guild, the High Chair, had been assassinated by said dwarf. That could make their potential reception a deadly one.

Still, I got some armour out of it. And I'm not about to be intimidated by some ruffians. After you face a demon, gangsters aren't a great worry.

Still, it was best to be prepared and not show fear.

'What are you doing?' Shift asked, looking at him askew.

'What?' Nicolas stopped and checked himself over. He wasn't doing anything.

'I think Shift's referring to *the walk*, kid,' Auron offered.

'What's *the walk*?'

'You had your arms away from your body and were puffing your chest out.' Shift helpfully demonstrated, just in case he didn't have the imagination to picture it.

'I wasn't doing that,' he nearly cried, checking himself quickly and lowering his voice. This wasn't an area in which to show weakness.

'He also had his head tilted up slightly,' Silva added. 'And some kind of forced scowl.'

'Of course he did.' Shift smirked. 'I forgot that. Is this better?' They mimicked his walk again, this time with an upward jut of the chin.

'Yes, that's it,' the warrior confirmed.

'I wasn't doing that,' Nicolas protested. 'But if I had been, it was to show strength. This is a shady area, and I don't want to come across as prey.'

'That does make sense,' Sergeant Tallith said.

Nicolas tried to ignore the fact that Tallith was doing his own version of the walk.

'So this one time, there was a warrior called Zelos Gell.' Auron seemed to gain some perverse enjoyment from their collective groans. 'He did a big tough guy walk like that. Trouble was, he didn't have any sort of skill to back it up. But when you spend so long convincing everyone that you're a tough guy, you can't help but believe it yourself. So, when someone points out Auron of Tellmark in the tavern Zelos frequents and bets the warrior he couldn't beat him in a fight...' Auron sucked his teeth and shook his head. 'Well, I didn't actually have to put down my tankard to put him on his ass. Silly sod didn't even try to get me outside, just did it right at the bar, where everyone could see. I assume he was expecting impressed cheers from the patrons when he beat me, not the laughter he ended up getting when I dropped him like a sack of dung.' The spirit chuckled to himself. 'It wasn't even one of my best punches. But the bruise on his cheek... Deities, that man was delicate.'

'Please enlighten me as to the moral of this tale,' Nicolas said with a sigh, knowing it was coming whether he wanted it or not.

'Sometimes acting like a tough peacock just makes you a target.' Auron's smile dropped for a moment. 'Seriously though kid, if you want to show strength, relax. Show them that you're calm and collected around them. That'll unnerve them more than all the bluster in Etherius.'

Be calm and collected? Me? What sort of shit advice is that?

Not wishing to stay here arguing the toss, and very aware that ever stallholder was eyeing them suspiciously, he surrendered. 'I'll try.' Hopefully, that sounded sincere.

Either way, it was enough to get the rest of the group to move.

'It's just ahead,' Sergeant Tallith said as they came to a corner.

Shift suddenly came to a halt and turned around. 'In that case, you need to go back.'

Tallith frowned. 'I do?'

'We can't turn up at Maxas' door with a member of the watch,' the shapeshifter explained. 'It wouldn't set the right tone for our meeting.'

'Ah.' He was clearly disappointed. 'Of course. I'll go back to the main street and wait for you there.'

Nicolas felt bad as the sergeant turned to leave. 'We'll see you soon.'

That seemed to be enough to improve Tallith's mood.

When he was gone, the group rounded the corner. The street ahead ended in a formidable pair of wooden gates with an archway above them.

'I'll do the talking,' Shift said pointedly as they walked ahead of the group.

A sign above the wooden gates read *The Exotic Bazaar*. Flanking them was a pair of burly minotaurs.

Gangsters with minotaurs, again? Are they some kind of status symbol? Does the number of minotaurs you have show how important you are? Do you get them as a gift when you reach a certain level in the Guild? 'Well done on your promotion, Maxas. You've earned yourself a second minotaur.'

Mind you, it made sense. What better status symbol to keep the plebs in line than having a large, horned beast around to make an example of anyone who stepped out of line.

Unlike the last minotaur he'd met—Lucas—one of the pair smiled as they approached the door. 'Shift,' he boomed warmly. 'You sneaky little dog.' He put his hairy fists up.

Shift copied the gesture. 'But sometimes I'm a cat.'

Laughing, the pair began shadow boxing each other. After a few moments, the minotaur held his hands up, as if surrendering.

'Who knows what you'll be next.' He chuckled.

'Hopefully, I'll be let into the bazaar.' They winked. 'But pleasantries first. How's the kids, Boz?'

The minotaur let out a harsh laugh. 'Compared to busting heads and collecting debts, being a father is bloody hard work. What about you? Still stealing?'

'Whoa.' Shift stepped back as if struck, their face aghast. 'I don't steal things. Other people's valuables just *happen* to end up in my possession.'

'And I didn't gore that man. He just happened to have a horn-sized hole in him when I got there,' Boz replied with a sly grin, matching Shift's tone.

The pair laughed as if this was a private joke.

Nicolas really didn't wish to know the details.

'We need to see the boss,' Shift said, becoming more serious. 'Is he in?'

'Aye, he is,' Boz said. 'Just go on in. I'm sure he'll love to see you again.'

The large minotaur stepped toward the archway and pushed one of the heavy looking double gates open disturbingly easily. With a slight bow, he indicated for them to enter.

'Until we meet again,' Shift said, passing Boz and shooting him a sly wink.

Suddenly the minotaur's eyes widened, and he reached for his belt, breathing an audible sigh of relief when he jiggled the gold purse attached to it. 'Until then.' Boz smiled amiably.

As they crossed the threshold into The Exotic Bazaar, Shift turned and gave the minotaur another friendly wave. 'Be careful, guys,' they said quietly to Nicolas and the others from behind their false smile. 'Something's not right.'

'Why?' Auron asked, turning and eyeing the minotaurs suspiciously.

'Those two are Maxas' personal bodyguards,' Shift replied. 'You don't leave them on the door unless you're trying to lull someone into a false sense of security.'

Fantastic.

CHAPTER 6

Misreading something can lead to all sorts of awkward blunders. Well, things would've been awkward *without* the mistake. But at least he would've been a bit more prepared when he walked through the gates. He could picture the exact range of expressions on his face as he'd strode past the minotaurs. The initial confusion. The moment of understanding. The slack-jawed gasp. Then the quick throwing of his eyes to the floor as he turned bright red.

The sign above the gate hadn't read *The Exotic Bazaar*. The cursive writing and the lettering being partially obscured by a minotaur horn had caused him to mistake an *R* for a *X*.

'You are so cute,' Shift said, visibly suppressing a laugh. They shook their head, and their eyes widened. 'It's this village boy stuff. I can't get enough of it. Your naivety is like some sort of drug that makes me want to jump you.'

'You want to corrupt him, that's what it is.' Auron was half-smiling at the shapeshifter. 'Same thing I'm trying to do. I see the village boy and just want to make him a man...in a very different way to you, of course.'

'You should both stop,' Silva remarked curtly. 'I am using him as an example to follow.'

'Can you all just stop?' Nicolas asked in an urgent whisper. 'And can we please get through this place as quickly as possible?'

With a cough—and ignoring his companions sniggering—he forced his head up again and walked through the bazaar.

Eyes forward, Nicolas. Eyes always forward.

The plan sounded simple. The problem was that everything around him was trying to get his attention. The bazaar was made up of a long row of stalls in an open courtyard that almost created a single pathway through it. The stalls sold things he didn't want to describe. Some living. Some inanimate. All crude. At various intervals, men and women wearing so little they needn't have bothered gyrated on podiums to the nasally flute music that echoed throughout the place. Cloying incense filled the air, a mixture of various aromas that created something much worse than the sum of its parts and made the eyes of the uninitiated water on contact.

What I wouldn't give for Garaz's cloak right now.

That thought angered him. If Garaz was around, they wouldn't be here in the first place. It was another slight to add to the ever-growing list. Nicolas couldn't help but take perverse pleasure in the fact that if Maxas had helped Garaz leave the city, the orc would've had to come here too, and would have hated it more than he did. The orc was nothing if not a prude and would've covered himself in his cloak to keep the filth out.

He must've been desperate to do this. Why, though?

He still wanted some reason, a good and forgivable one, for the orc's betrayal. He had to believe Garaz hadn't just turned on them for a trinket. The reason behind Garaz's betrayal was like an itch he couldn't scratch, constantly nagging at him for attention but vanishing when he gave it.

'By the Deities...' Auron was decidedly more comfortable in the bazaar. Much too comfortable. The spirit moved from stall to stall as if he was shopping. He even started bouncing his shoulders to the music as he watched the dancers.

A flash of movement caught his attention then he really wished it hadn't and looked away again, wide-eyed.

'Good boy.' Shift smirked at his side. 'Don't give in to temptation and stand there with your tongue hanging out like the ghost.'

'Of course not,' he replied quickly. 'None of them are you.'

In one swift movement, Shift was standing in front of him. They faux bit their lip. 'Well, well, aren't you a smooth one, village boy.' They planted a kiss on his lips before taking his arm. 'Worry not, innocent soul. I'll lead you through this den of iniquity. You don't have to go looking at those terrible naked folk.'

'I think the touching gets you in more trouble than the looking,' Silva remarked in distaste.

'The *looking* would get him in a lot of trouble with me,' the shapeshifter answered quickly. 'But he's a good man.'

By the Deities, this bazaar will never end. I'm still dead, aren't I? This is Sha'then's idea of a good laugh.

Focusing again on their goal—and he really needed to focus, as they were in a gangster's lair—Nicolas and his companions continued through the bazaar. Various merchants tried to get his attention, but he focused on the music, and the destination.

Finally, the rows of stalls broke into an open area. At the end of the courtyard was a large, fenced-off area. Beyond the gate was a huge fine-looking open tent decorated with ornate coloured rugs and various silk throw cushions. Incense burners were positioned in a semi-circle around the tent. A single guard stood at the divider between the area and the bazaar. He was the kind of brutish brawler you'd expect to be working for a gangster. His squat nose looked like it had had more than a few encounters with fists in the past.

'Look at this,' Shift muttered. 'All nice and casual. No guards.'

'There should be more, I take it?' Silva asked quietly.

'Maxas likes to flaunt his status,' the shapeshifter replied. 'There should be men everywhere.'

Auron blew a raspberry. 'None of you should be worried about a trap set by some gangster. You're all too good for that.'

'I am not worried.' There was almost a growl behind Silva's words. 'I welcome it.'

I feel for the first person she gets to vent her frustration about Garaz on. Even if he is a gangster.

The group reached the guard, who held up a hand to make them halt.

Genially, Shift took a single step forward. 'We—'

'Shift?' Before the shapeshifter could finish their sentence, a figure nestled in a pile of cushions in the centre of the tent sat up. 'Is that you?'

Shift stepped to the side and held their arms out as they turned on the spot. 'The one and only.'

'Let them in, let them in.'

The guard stepped aside.

As they approached, Maxas dismissed his attendants with a wave of his hand.

If you sewed all the clothes the attendants were wearing together, you still wouldn't have enough of a garment to fully clothe an average male.

Maxas himself, who nestled back into his cushions, was a kascat wearing a thick blue gown. The fur on his cheeks had been tied into bows, and he wore a large signet ring on his finger. Obviously, life had been kind to Maxas, and he'd made the most of it. Nicolas doubted he could get up off those cushions without assistance. He was quite the fat cat.

'Welcome, welcome,' he greeted in a thickly accented voice. 'It has been an age, Shift. Make yourselves comfortable.' The kascat gestured to the scattered cushions.

Nicolas and Shift sat down, but Silva remained standing. The warrior glared at the servant who approached as if the man was about to pull a knife instead of serving the wine he was carrying. In the background, the flute music continued.

The servant put his tray down and opened the bottle of wine on it. Quickly, he poured three glasses, giving one to Nicolas and one to Shift.

He attempted to give one to Silva. She stared wide-eyed at the servant until he gave up and retreated with his tray.

'Please, enjoy my hospitality.' Maxas smiled. 'The wine is the very finest, and as you can see, we have plenty of food.'

The kascat told no lies. There were small tables of food all around. The lack of plates suggested Maxas liked to be fed by his attendants.

'Kid, do *not* drink that,' Auron cautioned. 'If it isn't laced with something, I'm a ghost.'

No comment.

'Thank you, Maxas,' Shift said, raising their cup in a salute. 'You always were such a gracious host.'

As they raised the cup to their lips, Nicolas almost reached out to stop them, even though he knew they'd heard Auron's warning. But he kept himself in check.

The slight dilation in Maxas' green eyes gave away the kascat's pleasure that they were about to drink. A second before the cup touched Shift's lips, they pulled it away, as if they'd thought of something.

'Deities.' Shift chuckled. 'Here's me about to start drinking and reminiscing about old times when we're actually here on urgent business.'

The kascat's mouth twitched, ever so slightly.

CHAPTER 7

'How tedious,' Maxas said with a tut. 'It must be very urgent for you to forgo the usual pleasantries, so I will indulge you. But first...' He held out his paw and presented his signet ring.

'So formal?' Shift asked with a raised eyebrow.

'One must keep up appearances in public.' Maxas gave a dismissive wave. 'You know how it is.'

Though Shift maintained a neutral expression, Nicolas knew them well enough by now to know they would openly scoff at kissing the ring on a normal day. This was anything but a normal day, though. Slowly, they got up, approached Maxas, and planted a small kiss on his ring. As they sat down again, Nicolas shivered at the outrage he sensed from them.

'Perfect,' Maxas said, clapping his hands together. 'Now we can talk business. Though it might be nice to introduce your companions first?'

This time Shift did scoff, loudly. 'Come on, Maxas. You know who they are.'

The kascat gangster seemed intent on letting the moment drag out slightly before he relented. 'I confess, I do.' He laughed, finally, wagging his finger at Shift. 'And it is a pleasure to meet you all. Young hero, Nicolas Percival Carnegie.'

Oh shit.

Nicolas was so used to people getting his name wrong—calling him the *other* name—that when they got it right, it concerned him. It meant they were paying very close attention. 'That'd be me, yes,' he answered after a moment, trying to sound as nonchalant as possible.

'And Silva Destrone. Beautiful and deadly.' Maxas' whiskers twitched as he made eye contact with the warrior. 'The glare is enough to chill me, even with my fur.' The kascat shook slightly and turned his attention back to Shift. 'So, what brings you to my humble abode?'

Like you didn't already know we were coming and why.

'Information, actually.' Shift smiled. 'We are missing someone, an orc companion of ours, and believe he's left the city. I don't suppose he came to you to find a way to slip out unnoticed?'

I wish I could unnotice that annoying flute music.

Maxas licked one of his sharp teeth. 'I am just a humble businessman who peddles in flesh and entertainments for discerning clients. Nothing more.'

'C'mon, Maxas,' Shift scoffed. 'This is *me* you're talking to.'

'But is it *you* I'm talking to, the Shift I knew so well?' Maxas asked coyly. 'You see, I have three problems with this. The first and foremost is your relationship with the city watch. I hear you are practically enlisted.'

Shift furrowed their brow. 'I aided the city watch in finding a murderer. That's the end of my relationship with them. Surely you know me better than that.'

The kascat shrugged. 'I do, yes. I suppose I can see the benefit to having that murderer caught. Riots aren't good for business. Plus, Lord Commander Greer needed taking down a peg or two. I feel I should reward young Nicolas for killing his wife for me.'

'No thanks necessary,' Nicolas replied coolly. He hadn't killed Greer's wife...technically. She'd been possessed by a demon. Even the Lord Commander understood that, to an extent. Though the group had kept their distance from him since, just in case.

'He's buying time,' Auron cautioned. 'And showing off. Smug bastard.'

'What's the second problem?' Shift urged.

Maxas smiled indulgently. 'If I *were* the type of person who could get people out of the city unseen, I would have...let's say, ethical issues with giving out client information.'

'Maybe the reminder that you owe me a pretty big favour would help you climb over that *issue*.' Shift smiled thinly.

'This friend of yours must be pretty important for you to call in *that* favour.' Maxas smiled knowingly. 'You've been sitting on that one for years now.'

Nicolas looked at Shift, who gave him a brief sideways glance. *Leave it,* seemed to be the unspoken answer to his unspoken question.

'Why do you need the orc so? Maybe because he had a certain item on his person?'

Though Shift and Silva kept their faces neutral, Nicolas knew he'd reacted by the flick of the kascat's eyes towards him. In that brief look, Nicolas got the impression he was being sized up for a coffin.

'And the third problem?' Shift pressed.

Maxas steepled his fingers thoughtfully. 'You and your companions were there when that greedy oaf Gorin Thundabrig murdered the High

Chair. Since then, there's been a power vacuum in the Guild. A lot of people are vying for control. Plus, you have this silly dispute between the Guilds. All of it is bad for business, yes, very bad for business.'

A year ago, the fact that the flute music had stopped would've been completely lost on Nicolas, but he wasn't that person anymore, and he noticed. In fact, all sound in the bazaar had died down. He shifted casually on his pillow, looking as if he were trying to get more comfortable, but in reality getting ready to get up quickly.

'We were there,' Shift replied. 'What about it?'

'Well,' Maxas smiled, 'this power vacuum presents an opportunity for me. If I were to capture those who took down Big Boss...well, let's just say my stock would increase exponentially.'

Shift laughed and shook their head sadly. 'There are goons behind us, aren't there?'

'Yup,' Auron confirmed. 'Bless them, they look so overconfident.'

Nicolas turned his head. Behind them were the two minotaurs and a handful of other muscle who worked for Maxas. All had clubs in hand. They'd positioned themselves directly between them and the exit. Casually, Nicolas rose from the cushions, as did Shift. Silva kept her arms folded as she regarded the group.

'Now, you can come quietly, or you can come covered in bruises.' The kascat chuckled.

Blowing a raspberry, Nicolas walked toward Boz. As he passed Silva, the warrior went to fall into step with him. With a hand on her shoulder, he stopped her.

'Let me,' he said with a wink. 'You can have your fun in a minute.'

When he continued onward, Boz lumbered forward to meet him. As they got closer to each other, the size difference between them became more apparent. Until the muscly minotaur towered over him.

'Problem, tiny?' Boz asked with a snort.

'Yup.' He smiled. 'I need your boss to give me some information. But apparently, I have to deal with you first.'

'*Deal with me*?' Boz roared with laughter. 'Human, you've gotten high off your own legends. I will crush you.'

Nicolas shook his head. 'You know you're not my first minotaur, right?'

Boz leaned in close, resting the large club he carried on his shoulder. 'I tell ya what. You can have the first punch.'

In the past, it was true, Nicolas hadn't been the most dutiful student when it came to learning to fight. He'd balked at the idea. But the universe kept putting him in fights, so he'd finally resolved to be a great student. Case in point, he'd really taken his lessons with Ban Dro seriously. Tensing his fingers into almost a spear tip, he drove them into the minotaur's throat. Boz reared back, hacking, and dropped his club.

Stepping to the side, Nicolas drew a knife from his boot and threw it into the side of the minotaur's knee. Boz roared as it stuck behind his kneecap and collapsed to a single knee. With a cry, Nicolas jumped, kicking Boz in the side of the head with both feet at once, dazing the minotaur, but not knocking him down. Landing on his back, Nicolas flipped to his feet—the fact that his new dwarven-made armour allowed him such agility was very impressive—before hauling Boz's heavy club from the floor, spinning in a full circle three times to gain speed, and striking the minotaur directly in the snout with it. Blood sprayed in the air as the minotaur fell backwards like a crashing tree. Boz hit the floor with a thud, throwing up a cloud of dirt. Nicolas couldn't help but chuckle as he stared at the unconscious minotaur. Briefly, he tensed to raise the club and finish the job, but he caught himself, letting it drop to the ground instead. Boz was done.

I really have changed.

'Damn, kid,' Auron whispered in awe.

After a moment of stunned silence, the second minotaur roared and charged.

Nicolas turned to a certain warrior and nodded. 'Your turn.'

Silva flashed past him. The second minotaur went from charging, to howling in pain as it clutched its broken leg, to lying on the floor with Silva atop it, beating it senseless.

I'd best get to Garaz before she does. I'm only going to punch him a few times.

Panting, fists bloody, Silva rose. Suddenly, the other assembled goons didn't appear so confident. Nicolas put his hand on the hilt of his sword.

'Come on then,' he said, beckoning them forward.

They didn't. Instead, they backed away slowly. Then quickly. Once he was sure they were going to stay gone, he turned back to Maxas, whose fur had managed to go whiter as he scurried back into his cushions, as if they'd somehow protect him.

'Tell us about the orc you helped leave the city,' Nicolas demanded, taking his hand from his sword and making a big show of curling his fingers into fists.

'Okay, okay,' the kascat said, breathing heavily and staring wide-eyed at Nicolas. 'There was an orc, yes. He needed a way out and was prepared to pay handsomely for it. I facilitated his exit.'

'Where did he go?' Silva asked.

'I...I don't know,' Maxas replied fearfully.

Shift shook their head slowly. 'So, you don't still have a seer scry the information from the minds of the people you *assist*, just in case you need to track them down later?'

The kascat's eyes actually managed to get wider. 'You know about that?'

Nicolas drew the *Dawn Blade* and placed the tip of it against Maxas' stomach. 'Where?' he shouted. It occurred to him that he was working out his anger about Garaz, just as Silva was.

'Home,' Maxas said, raising his hands in the air. 'He went home.'

CHAPTER 8

*H*ome. It wasn't much to go on, but it was all Maxas had. Apparently, the seer the gangster used had only got that one word because Garaz's mind had been 'too guarded.' That sounded plausible enough, given what Nicolas knew of his former companion.

Unsurprisingly, no one tried to stop them as they left the bazaar. Beside him, Shift examined their new signet ring.

'It's a bit gaudy for you,' he said as they put it on their finger.

'Well,' Shift said after a thoughtful pause, 'I put my lips on it, so it's mine. Just like you.'

Yes, I am.

'By the Deities,' Auron said, almost giddy. 'Did you see that?' The spirit jumped in front of the others, causing them to stop. 'So this one time, Nick Carnage walked into a bazaar. This once naïve village boy, who soiled himself in his first confrontation with a minotaur, absolutely kicked the shit out of one singlehanded. He barely paused for breath.' The spirit shook his head. 'It was beautiful. I've trained you well.'

'I did not *soil myself* when I faced Lucas,' Nicolas snapped, before calming. 'I just...cried and passed out.'

'And look at you now.' He could swear that Auron was shining more brightly than usual.

'It wasn't like you, though,' Silva remarked.

Nicolas gave the warrior a quizzical look.

'Not being in control. The anger. You nearly caved his head in.'

'You're one to talk,' he snapped.

'But that's just Silva,' Shift said with a hint of concern. 'You, though...you're angry.'

'Of course I'm angry.' It was difficult to keep his tone neutral. 'We've all been through so much with Garaz, and he just betrays us. Why? For some amulet I would've given him if he'd *asked*?'

'Would you, though?' Silva asked.

He thought about it for a moment and let out a frustrated grunt. 'No,' he admitted. 'I would've considered it, but I wouldn't actually have given it to him.'

'And he knew that,' the warrior said sympathetically. 'That's why he took it.'

Maybe if he actually told me why he needed it...

Shift didn't need to dramatically track their eyes down to his hands for him to realise that his fists were shaking, but they did anyway.

'Maybe I'm a bit angrier about it than I thought.'

'I don't blame you, kid. He clearly had a lot of secrets.' It was the first time he'd seen the outward effect of Garaz's betrayal on Auron—the telltale flash of a red vein in his aura. 'But don't worry, you'll have a chance to heal some wounds when we find Garaz.'

For a second, Nicolas was sure he heard Silva mutter, *'And create some,'* but he let it go.

'He'd better be damned forthcoming when we catch him,' Nicolas muttered sourly.

'So, we *are* going after him then?'

'Of course we are.' He was confused by Shift's question. Why wouldn't they go after Garaz?

'I'm...I just...I don't see why.' Shift folded their arms. 'He betrayed us and hurt you. Let him wander off in the snow. We're better off without him.'

'You don't want to know why he did it?'

Shift shrugged. 'Honestly, I don't care. If he wants to turn his back on us, I'm not about to chase him across Etherius in the middle of winter. So many people have attempted to double cross me in the past that, whatever their reason, it just gets tiresome.'

'We should pursue him,' Silva said, jaw set. 'He must be made to pay.'

Nicolas turned to the warrior. This time he wasn't letting it go. *'Pay?'*

'He has betrayed us and attacked you. There must be a reckoning for that.'

'I appreciate the thought, but we're not killing him,' Nicolas insisted.

Silva's brow darkened. 'Then you had best find him before I do.'

So, we have one 'I don't care' *and one* 'I'm gonna kill him.' *Fantastic.*

'Look,' he said evenly. 'It's not even all about Garaz. He took the amulet. It was entrusted to me and I need to get it back, no matter why he stole it.' He looked pointedly at Shift, ignoring their ensuing eyeroll. 'And when we find him, I want to talk to him, to give him a chance to explain before we resort to violence.'

However tempting it is. He knew from just looking at Silva that she was unconvinced. *When we find Garaz, I'm going to have to get between them.* A fun prospect.

'Are we agreed?' he asked leadingly.

Both Silva and Shift shrugged, which he took as an okay. It was likely to be the best he would get.

'So now we just have to figure out where he went.' Auron's tone suggested what he thought was the likelihood of them succeeding in *that* task.

'You two travelled alone for a while,' Nicolas said to the spirit. 'Did he never give you an indication of where home was?'

Auron screwed up his face as if wondering whether to answer. 'Not exactly. But Garaz is an orc, and they all come from The Wasteland.'

The Wasteland...or the northern wastes...or the orc wasteland. No matter your choice of name for the place, it conjured foreboding. But then it would. It was a land filled with numerous orcs bent on killing anything that even glanced in their general direction. As a rule, the place was never really talked about, save for such sentences as, *'Old Tobin died in a raid the other day. Bloody orcs from The Wasteland came down, killed as many people as they could find then pissed off back over the border with their loot.'*

Would I really go there to find Garaz?

His mind instantly answered, *Yes,* surprising him. Though he really hoped it didn't get to the point where he had to make good on that assertion. There was a lot of territory between here and the border to the Wastes. Chances were, they'd catch their errant companion long before then. Despite the two-day head start.

'We need to get moving and head him off before he gets there,' Auron said firmly. 'I don't ever want to go back to that place.'

'Back?' Shift asked with a frown. Auron closed his eyes and sighed. 'Once...' The eyes opened again as the spirit began to give information in his preferred way. 'So this one time, a crazy old baron got his hands on a treasure map. It was the location of a dragon's horde, but the dragon had been slain long ago. In theory, that meant the cave was unprotected, save for the fact that it was in the Wasteland. But like I said, this baron was crazy, so he decided he was going for it.' Auron chuckled dryly. 'I don't even know why. With the coin he threw around to hire the mercenary army to escort him, he didn't even need the treasure. I ended up joining the expedition because I was young and full of my own grandeur.' *As opposed to being old and full of it?* 'There were about a hundred heroes and sell swords, plus two hundred of the baron's household guard. We marched across the border like we were off on some fantastic adventure. We had pipers playing, we were carousing, we were idiots. Four miles later, we'd been butchered. I crawled back across the border, literally. It took me a month to learn to walk again.'

Seeing Auron so worried stoked a flame of fear in the pit of his stomach. Mentally, he tried to quash the fire, but a battle began inside him, neither side giving an inch. He wasn't used to seeing the brash hero so humbled. Auron was just so good at...everything.

Though, Nicolas had to admit, hearing about one of Auron's defeats made his legacy a little easier to live up to—the legacy that was now marked not only by the sword but the emblem on his armour. He was Auron's successor. Lucky him.

Besides, it doesn't matter how scared I am. I'm still going. My fear will just have to put up with it. He hadn't been a slave to it for a long time now.

'We'll get him long before then,' he said, knowing it was the worst kind of false confidence.

'He has a two-day head start,' Silva reminded him.

'And it's winter. Conditions are going to get pretty unpleasant the further north we go,' Shift added.

'Okay, guys.' Nicolas scoffed. 'Thanks for the dose of optimism. I'm going regardless. And alone if I have to.'

There was no further dissent.

Thank the Deities for that.

Focused, and in harmony, the group carried on. At the edge of the alleyway, Sergeant Tallith waited. He eyed them expectantly as they approached.

'How did it go?' the young sergeant asked earnestly.

'Garaz left the city and headed north,' Nicolas replied. 'And we're going after him, once we get some supplies.'

'I can hel—' Tallith stopped mid-sentence, pursing his lips thoughtfully before pointing at Shift's hand. 'Isn't that Maxas Thrall's signet ring?'

CHAPTER 9

Time was of the essence, obviously, but the speed of their preparations to leave had to be balanced by the fact that winter had come. It hadn't really hit around Babylon yet, but the further north they went, the harsher the conditions would be. And Nicolas had no intention of freezing to death beside a tree because they hadn't packed quite enough furs.

Thankfully, in that, Governor Morrow proved more than helpful. She ensured the group had enough coin and credit notes to purchase whatever supplies they needed for the pursuit—another token of gratitude for their help in saving the city. As it turned out, the shops and stallholders were similarly grateful, offering the group discounts on their purchases, since the city falling to chaos would've been very bad for business. Though there was, it turned out, a finite limit to their gratitude. Two percent off the price here and there didn't exactly excite Nicolas, but every little bit helped.

Due to his lack of experience travelling, Nicolas deferred to Silva and Auron for the preparations, and the spirit and warrior ensured they were ready to go the next morning. Nicolas had been loath to give Garaz more of a lead, but it made sense not to start a journey too late in the day. And it gave Nicolas and Shift a chance to make full use of the only bed they were likely to have for a while.

As Nicolas strode towards the marketplace that sat before the mighty city gates, his breath clouded in front of him. There was a bite to the morning air, giving Nicolas an insight into what was to come. According to the locals, the snow hit Babylon later in winter, but the kingdom of Ivilar—the most direct route between Babylon and The Wasteland—was most likely already beset.

His one comfort was that it should also keep any bandits or monsters in their caves and lairs, instead of trying to kill him. Though he had no doubt that if there was trouble out there, it would cross his path.

And the Maestro seems to have no end of minions.

His gaze turned back toward the city. It irked him that his quest to track down his people had to be put on hold. Since Professor Shaw's death, there'd been no sign of anyone affiliated to the Maestro. Governor Morrow had told him the search would continue, and that they would find a way to let him know if anything turned up.

Might as well use my time productively, instead of sitting here waiting out winter with my thumb up my ass.

Though he had to admit, a break would've been nice. It would've given him time to really train with Ban Dro. He'd used his evening to get in a last lesson before hitting the road again. His mind drifted back to the conversation he'd had with his teacher.

'You're leaving now?' The Master had spoken levelly, but the disappointment was blatant. 'You have only begun to scratch the surface of your potential and learn the real art of combat.'

'I know,' Nicolas had replied. 'But I have to do this. I can't turn my back on my duty.'

His Master had sighed. 'I understand. How soon until you leave?'

'My companions are getting the supplies now. So, in the morning.'

Dro had given him a half-smile. 'Then we have time for you to learn a little more. A couple of things you can practise on the road. Just remember, Nicolas, never let your training lapse. Any skill can stagnate if not properly nurtured.'

'I doubt there'll be any chance of that. We're bound to be attacked at least four times on the road.' Nicolas had laughed before becoming more serious. 'But I will keep training.'

He wanted more time to learn, but he still had Auron and Silva.

And I kicked a minotaur's ass.

Ahead, Auron and Silva were waiting for him and Shift. He was down to three true friends in the whole world. He didn't even have Potter anymore. Had his friend from Hablock somehow survived the attack on his home? Had the Maestro's minions taken him too? Whatever the answer, his list of enemies far outweighed his friends.

'Morning,' Shift said jovially to Auron and Silva as the pair reached them. They still weren't convinced going after Garaz was worth the effort, but they weren't about to just stay in the city and leave the others to it.

Nicolas found himself staring at the city gates that loomed ahead of him ominously. What lay beyond them? What would they encounter this time?

'You ready for this, kid?' Auron asked, as Silva studied the list in her hand.

'Have I ever been ready for any of this?' he shrugged.

The spirit smiled warmly at him. 'You walked into this city a scruffy kid in a torn leather jacket with a bit of training under his belt. Look at you now. You're leaving much better than you entered.'

Nicolas tapped his chest plate with his knuckles. 'At least I'm starting to look the part.'

The armour had been a very welcome gift from the dwarven people for his part in removing the stain Gorin Thundabrig had cast on their people's collective honour. He ran his hand over the rising sun carved into the chest plate. Auron had insisted that the sigil be put on it. It was a passing of the torch. He was the *Dawnblade* now.

Dawnblade the second? Dawnblade two? Dawnblade junior?

'It looks good on you.' It was strange when Shift was being sincere. 'If you lost the daft facial hair, trimmed the mop on your head, and looked a little less like you were going to cry when the city gates opened, you would almost look dashing.'

That's better.

'Write a list, and I'll address the improvements when I get a chance,' he replied, shaking his head.

Shift patted themselves down. 'I'm out of parchment. I think Silva took it all to make lists for the road.'

Speaking of...

'Are we ready?'

'The horses are loaded with as many supplies as they can carry,' the warrior confirmed. 'It won't be enough to get us all the way, so we will have to make supply stops. I've marked some likely places on the map.' Silva was already wearing several furs and a thick jacket and trousers over her armour.

'It makes a change to see you properly clothed,' Shift remarked.

Silva's armour didn't usually leave that much to the imagination.

Auron snorted with laughter at the warrior's cold glare.

'Hopefully, the chattering of your teeth will give us a break from your jesting on the road,' Silva told the shapeshifter cooly after a moment.

Nicolas found himself craning his neck to look at the parchment in her hand and ensure that everything had a tick next to it.

'We have everything we need,' the warrior said as they caught his look.

'Just checking,' he said sheepishly.

'Because you're nervous,' Shift said quietly at his side. 'I get that you're eager to go. I know you want to find Garaz and get answers.'

'I want to get the amulet back,' he corrected.

'No,' Shift corrected again. 'What you really want is answers. But you're also angry at his turning on us and interrupting what we should be doing.'

'Of course I am.'

'By the Deities.' Auron gasped. 'The kid admits his emotions instead of bottling them up and letting them explode at a later date. If I could still shed a tear…'

'You're all hilarious.' Nicolas scoffed. 'I'm learning. All the time. And my next lesson is what it's like to trudge through the snow.'

'True.' Shift kissed him briefly on the cheek. 'But at least you've got me to keep you warm.'

When they smacked him on the ass, Nicolas flushed and looked around to make sure no one had seen. That only encouraged Shift to do it again, and harder. The sound of the smack, and his little jump on impact, definitely got the attention of a few nearby citizens.

'Don't worry. I know how to keep things hot on a cold night.' They winked, enjoying his discomfort immensely.

'Not when you are sleeping a few feet from me,' Silva snapped.

Shift stared at Silva, biting their lip slightly and grabbed Nicolas's butt, giving it a firm squeeze as they kept eye contact with the warrior, raising their eyebrows playfully.

Nicolas flushed again.

At least the journey won't be boring.

'I think we'd best set off,' he said quickly.

'In a minute, kid. I think someone wants a word with you.'

Nicolas followed Auron's pointing finger and frowned.

CHAPTER 10

Nervously—caused by whatever random intuition humans possess that tells them they're about to have a conversation they don't like—Nicolas walked towards Sergeant Tallith and the group he was standing with. Every one of them had their eyes firmly on him as he approached, increasing his desire to walk in the opposite direction with every single step. There was an almost tangible excitement coming from the group.

'Hello,' Tallith said with an awkward cough as he stepped forward. 'Ready for the off then?'

Nicolas looked Tallith up and down. 'And so are you, it seems.'

The young sergeant was dressed in furs, and a sizeable pack sat on the floor where he'd been standing. Tallith saw where he was looking and briefly turned to regard the pack himself.

'Yes. Well, there's something I want to ask you.' Sergeant Tallith looked like a child about to ask for sweets in a shop.

Oh no.

'I was hoping to come with you.'

Nicolas bought some time with a little nodding as he tried to choose from the long list of reasons he'd come up with why Tallith could *not* go with them. His mind kept going back to *Silva will go nuts*. Whilst true, he needed something that sounded better.

Coming to a decision, he opened his mouth to share it, only to find himself cut off.

'I...need this. Please.' Tallith's voice actually cracked. 'Do you know why I'm a sergeant in the city watch?' He didn't wait for an answer. 'Because I'm good at organising. I carry out orders and do clerical work. I'm not...a man. When those men came to rescue Professor Shaw, I was useless. I watched good men die and was helpless to save them. Then I got kidnapped and used as bait to get your companion killed. I need...*would like* a chance to really prove myself. An adventure. I would like you to show me how to be...better.'

Oh, for Deities' sake. When did I become the great example to follow?

He stared into Tallith's eyes. Somehow, *'But you're needed here. The watch needs good people, and I can't deprive them'* didn't sound like such a good reason to make him stay anymore. Besides, Nicolas was ninety percent sure the sergeant would follow them regardless.

Best to keep him where I can see him.

Nicolas cursed himself. Tallith wasn't a child. They were at least the same age. Giving the sergeant a warm smile, he held out his hand. 'As you've packed already, it'd be rude to say no.'

For a moment, he was sure Tallith was going to shake his arm right out of its socket but then the enthusiastic sergeant caught himself.

'Thank you,' he said, composing himself. There was a gust of excited whispering from the people behind Tallith, who noticed it too. 'Can I introduce you?' he said, with a gesture to the group.

'Okay...' *Oh no.*

The terrible realisation of who these people were dawned on him the second Tallith motioned them to come over, and they swept toward him in a storm of excitement.

Oh no. Oh please, Deities, no...

Grinning faces stared at him as Nicolas wished the ground would swallow him. It was a mixture, to be sure. Male human twins with sandy hair, a stout dwarven woman with dark pigtails, a studious looking serian with glasses, and a young male fairy whose body twinkled in the light. Each of them held a piece of parchment in their hands.

'Nicolas Percival Carnegie.' Sergeant Tallith beamed with pride. 'This is the Dawnblade Speakers Society.'

I preferred going to the Underworld.

'Hello...' His voice initially came out as a wheeze. 'Hello there. Nice to meet you all.'

That did the trick. From the aura they gave off, he was a saint who'd just personally blessed each of them.

'Umm...nice morning, isn't it?'

Expectant glances were exchanged, and Nicolas inwardly sighed as he understood exactly where this was going.

'Do you have any questions for me?'

'Are these...' Auron pointed at the group as he appeared at Nicolas's side. The spirit's confused expression became a wide grin. 'Oh Deities. Your first time meeting a fan club. This is a special moment, kid. Cherish it.'

Bugger off, ghost.

'Where did the name *Nick Carnage* originate?' the dwarf asked.

'Um...I think Auron first said it. Possibly.' No, that wasn't right. 'Oh, no, actually, it was a friend of mine, Potter, from Hablock.'

'How's your quest to find them going?' one of the twins said quickly. 'Was it scary facing down Koth?'

'What is Sha'then like in person?' the fairy asked. 'He looks pretty dreamy in his statues.'

How do they know this stuff?

From there, it devolved into overlapping questions that never actually gave him time to answer any of them. Finally, Nicolas held up his hands to silence them.

'Thank you all for coming out,' he said. 'But I have a quest that cannot wait. So would you like me to sign those?'

He didn't even need to ask for a quill. One appeared in front of his nose, as if by magic. And he got to work signing parchments and exchanging pleasantries with...the fans.

'What's going on?' Silva called.

'His fan club's turned out. They want autographs,' Auron oh-so-help-fully answered.

'We do not have time for him to stand around basking in adulation,' Silva shouted back.

'Tallith's coming with us,' Nicolas told the warrior as he turned towards her. Perversely, he enjoyed watching Silva's face drop.

Quickly, he finished the other signatures, said a couple of polite plat-itudes, and returned to the others, Sergeant Tallith following him duti-fully.

'So, you're joining us then.' Shift was a little standoffish. 'Are you trust-worthy? We've had trouble with new additions to our group before. And old ones.'

Putting aside Garaz's betrayal, Shift was referring to Billy Bobknobs. Who'd turned out to be more than just a regular knob when he revealed himself as an evil faun.

'I will earn your trust,' Tallith said earnestly. 'I'll do whatever it takes.'

'And Lord Commander Greer is fine with this?' Silva asked, clearly hoping to find a loophole to get rid of Tallith.

'He...hasn't gotten out much lately.' *No surprise there after the death of his wife.* 'But the governor said it was okay.'

Silva's eyes narrowed. 'Very well.' Nicolas doubted it was well at all, but the warrior would have to put up with it. 'As long as you can hold your own. Winter conditions will be harsh, and you must be ready for them.

'Worried about the cold, are ye?'

Behind them was a stall with what looked to be various potions and charms strewn messily across it. Everything looked old and a little ill kept, the handwriting on the labels so poor they were illegible. Standing on the other side of the stall, a bearded man was grinning at them inanely, showcasing his single yellow tooth. His face was lined and worn, but he had a mischievous glint in his eye reminiscent of T'goth, when the Deity had been trapped in the form of a senile old man.

'We're having a private conversation,' Silva replied testily.

'Apologies, apologies,' the old man said, raising his hands. 'I was ad-justin' me stock an' overheard. But ye'll be thankful I did. Snaggletooth Joe's the name, an' potions an' charms are the game. Can ye guess why I'm called *'snaggletooth'?*'

After a moment of silence, Nicolas realised it was a serious question. 'Because of the tooth,' he said tentatively.

Joe jumped on the spot, pointing at Nicolas and touching his nose. 'We got a smart one here, don't we,' He grinned. 'Well, old Joe has somethin' that might come in handy, if ye'd care te walk yerselves over here an' have a lookie.'

Part of Nicolas wanted to give Joe the old, *'Thanks but we're in a rush,'* but for some reason, he couldn't bring himself to do it. Instead, he walked over to the old trader and inspected his stall. Yup, up close, it all looked crap too. There were some 'genuine choosing sticks' that made him want to flip the table over. But there was something endearing about Joe. Now he was closer, he finally noticed the little bell on the end of Joe's hat, which must've once been a pointed and proud wizard's hat, but now sagged sadly atop his head, with wispy, straw-coloured hair sticking out from beneath it.

'Interested, are ye, young'un?' Joe asked in a playful whisper.

Nicolas tried to play it nonchalant, lest he leave this stall with an empty purse. 'I'm listening.'

Joe bent down and pulled a small box from beneath the stall. Opening it, he presented Nicolas with four necklaces, each boasting a metallic fire emblem with yellow and orange stones set into it. Leaning forward, the trader put his free hand beside his mouth and dropped his voice to a whisper. 'They aren't mighty powerful, but they'll take the bite off the cold, sure as sure. And this time o' year, every little helps, especially on the open road.' Joe dangled the necklaces in front of his face and studied them, rubbing his chin. 'Seein' as yer new customers, I'll say one gold piece each. And that's a bargain anywheres.'

If it helps with the cold, and it's only a single coin...

'Nick.' Shift laughed incredulously as Nicolas rummaged in his coin purse. 'You can't be serious.'

'This time of year, every little helps,' he replied, echoing Joe's senti-ment.

Handing over the coins, he took the offered charms. Carefully, he placed one over his head and around his neck. It took a second or two, but suddenly the bite in the air vanished. Maybe it was his imagination, but either way, he considered it money well spent. He handed them out to the others, who put them on. Judging by the hums of surprise, they all felt the effects just like he had.

'There we go, there we go.' Joe clapped happily. 'Bless all yer souls.' The trader's face dropped for a moment. 'That's what I can do,' he exclaimed. 'A blessin' for yer trip, te aid ye on the road. No charge for this, young'un, because I like ye an' wish ye all well on the road, sure as sure.'

Nicolas opened his mouth to politely decline, but Joe had already thrown the handful of powder he'd produced onto the small brazier at the front of the stall. There was a *poof,* and Nicolas's face was engulfed by sweet-smelling smoke. His open mouth took a big gulp of it as the rest charged into his nostrils, despite his hands flailing to wave it away. As the smoke cleared, he doubled over, coughing and hacking.

'Young'un can't handle his blessin's.' Joe chuckled from behind the stall.

Shift slapped him on the back to help exorcise the last of the smoke, and he finally stood back up. 'Um, thank you,' he said with a thin smile, his eyes still watery.

'Think nothin' o' it.' Joe grinned. 'Be seein' ye.'

I bloody hope not. I don't fancy another cloud of smoke to the face anytime soon.

'If you have quite finished playing with that crazy old coot, we need to be on our way,' Silva said testily, one hand holding the reins of their three horses.

Hopefully, Tallith had one nearby, so they didn't have to dally longer whilst he found one.

Auron put his fingers to his mouth and whistled. His horse Mare appeared right in front of him, as if she'd been there all along. Patting his spectral steed, he jumped into the saddle.

'Right then, folks,' he said, raising his chin and staring toward the city gate. 'It's adventure time.'

CHAPTER 11

For the first leg of their journey, the going was good. Several farmers had seen Garaz at a distance, an orc in a red cloak being a rather unusual sight in this area, so they knew they were going in the right general direction at least.

Even at the crossing into Ivilar, the border guards had mentioned some hunters talking of an orc slipping into the kingdom. They'd conducted a search but found nothing. The soldiers had been on edge when they arrived, having heard enough tales from their comrades who guarded the northern border—the one directly beside The Wasteland—to know that an orc in the area could be a very nasty business indeed.

But this orc didn't stay around to cause trouble. He was moving quickly. A lot faster than they were. As far as Nicolas and the others could tell, Garaz was on foot but had extended his lead on them by half a day.

And it was a cold half a day. Despite the furs and Joe's amulets, the ever-dropping temperature had begun to make itself known. So much so that Nicolas was sure his nose would stay red forever.

The dramatic change to their fortunes came a day after crossing the border, when the snow hit. At first, it had been light and quite delightful. The group enjoyed the little flakes of white dancing down from the sky. It made even the plain fields picturesque. But it got heavier the further they travelled. Much heavier.

Suddenly, every mile seemed like five as they trudged through it, their horses' hooves making *crump* sounds with every step. To start with, it was quaint, but it soon became a constant reminder of the white nightmare they were trapped in.

The cold became oppressive. So much so that Nicolas took to shaking his amulet at random intervals, just to check it was still working. He was none the wiser afterwards. The conditions impeded their progress and eroded the group's camaraderie.

With a minor growl, Nicolas pulled the flaps of his fur cap tightly over his ears. They were so cold they stung. And the jaunty whistling beside him might as well have been a piercing banshee's wail. One he could take no more.

'Can you at least pretend to be cold?' His cracking lips hurt with each word.

Frowning, Auron stopped whistling and glanced at him. '*Brrr,*' the spirit said with a fake shiver.

I'm not sure what's worse, the sarcasm or the fact that it actually made me feel a little better.

It wasn't Auron's fault. The guy was dead; so was his horse. So, they got to just glide through the snow without suffering any of the effects of it. Thinking on it, the only time he'd been this cold was when Auron had possessed him.

That was a memory he didn't want to focus on. Instead, his mind drifted to where he would've been right now, if the universe hadn't started messing with him. Suddenly, he was home, there was a lovely, roaring fire in the fireplace, and his mother was making stew to go with the warm bread his father had just baked. He was lying on a blanket in front of the fire, his arms around Shift, and everything was perfect. Closing his eyes, he could practically feel the warmth of the fire on his face. It lasted for a second, then the cold came back. There was no level of delusion or fantasy that could keep it at bay for long. His weary sigh came out as a blast of steam, as if he were now part dragon.

Being part dragon would mean I'd be warm.

'I thought you'd be loving this trip. It was your idea.'

Snapped out of his fantasy, he turned and looked at Shift, who was just a nose and a pair of eyes emerging from the fur cloak wrapped around their head.

'This again?' he asked, with an edge of irritability. 'We're going after Garaz because it's the right thing to do.'

The longer they'd travelled, the more vocal Shift had become about not pursuing their former companion. Nicolas understood. Life in the Thieves Guild must've been tricky, never knowing who to trust. Shift was used to just letting go of people who'd betrayed them.

And I can't.

Though their attitude was probably better than Silva's, who was driven by the need to make Garaz pay.

'Don't bicker, children.' Auron's tone was that of a patient father. 'You're all struggling with the cold. Don't let it ruin your budding relationship.'

My lips being too numb to kiss them is doing that all by itself.

'Listen to him,' Silva said from the front of the group. 'If not, he may tell another story.'

Instantly, the spirit's back was up. 'What's that now?'

'You heard,' the warrior said, half turning to look at him.

'There was a time when you liked my stories.' The spirit suddenly clicked his fingers in the air. The sharp *snap* hit Nicolas's sore ears and made him wince. 'Ah yes, I remember now. Back before you killed me.'

Silva sagged in her saddle. This was followed by some very angry muttering.

Still, this was becoming a familiar pattern. During the day, they would all snipe at each other, but in the evenings, they came together around the campfire, and order was restored. The cold was fraying their tempers, but nothing could come between them again.

Except, I thought that about Garaz.

'It's still so strange hearing you talk to someone who isn't there.'

And then there was Tallith. His unrelenting enthusiasm was sometimes annoying, sometimes disturbing. He fussed over Nicolas, trying to help him as much as possible whenever they stopped to make camp. But the real problem was, Tallith was treating this whole thing the way Nicolas probably should've been: an exciting adventure, exploring new lands.

By the Deities. Thinking about it, I must come across pretty whiny sometimes.

Sitting up straighter, he resolved to do a little better. He reminded himself of the beauty around him. *Ooh, that's a nice snow-covered branch. Don't the fields look almost virginal. Aww, the snowflakes are so pretty when they dance down like...*

Bugger me. It's cold.

'We've seen stranger things,' Shift said to the sergeant.

The wave of enthusiasm from Tallith was like a bucket of water hitting him.

'Oh, don't I know it,' Tallith began eagerly. 'I heard Nicolas once rode a demon bear and charged it right into an army of zombies with a mighty battle cry.'

One day, I'm going to find whoever's spreading these stories and punch them in the throat.

Again, he checked himself. That wasn't him talking, that was his annoyance at the conditions, and Garaz, making him say stupid stuff. He wasn't at all comfortable with people knowing his business—and he was damned curious how they knew—but violence wasn't the answer. Probably.

'I did do that,' he said, indulging the sergeant's enthusiasm. 'But it wasn't exactly heroic or anything. I was clinging on for dear life. I nearly fell off about three times.'

'Who wouldn't?' Somehow, Tallith appeared to have decided he was being humble, and it'd only increased the adulation. Nicolas had just done the equivalent of pouring oil on a campfire.

'Stop selling yourself short,' Auron chided. 'You rode a demon bear. You rode a cow dragon. You rode—'

'Auron of Tellmark,' Shift snapped. 'If you looking at me has something to do with the end of that sentence, I suggest you rethink it. I can't hurt you, but I have no doubt I can make your afterlife very uncomfortable.'

The spirit made a big show of closing his mouth, though his smirk suggested he was unrepentant.

Nicolas couldn't help but smirk himself. Somehow, their camaraderie made things a little warmer.

But will it be gone soon? We've lost Garaz. Who's next?

'Stop it,' Shift said, side-eying him. Their gaze narrowed as he rolled his eyes. 'And you can stop that too. Just because Garaz turned out to be a disgusting, backstabbing, cowardly traitor doesn't mean the rest of us are going anywhere.'

Wow. Don't sugar your words, do you?

'There's a village ahead,' Silva called from the front.

Thank the Deities.

The light was starting to dim, promising that night would be coming soon. There was a gentle spattering of snow, but that could become heavy at any time, and it would be nice not to spend the night sheltered in a cave with Nicolas lamenting the group's newfound lack of fire magic. Another thing to be annoyed at a certain orc about.

Spurred on, as only the promise of a hot meal and a fireplace could in such conditions, the group passed the marker at the edge of the village. It read *Small Pond.*

Sounds delightful.

CHAPTER 12

Apparently, the person who'd named the village wasn't over encumbered by imagination. The scattered homes were all built around a small pond, which had frozen over for the winter. There were bright white furrows in the ice, suggesting that someone had been skating on it recently. But beyond that, the village was very quiet.

I don't like quiet villages. That's when we get into trouble.

Nervously, he glanced around as they rode through it, peering at each wooden building to try to discern some kind of ambush or trap. There was nothing obvious. In fact, the only sign of life was a longhouse on the far side of the pond with smoke coming out of its chimney.

Hopefully, it doubles as a tavern.

When he glanced at Shift, the shapeshifter was fully focused on the building. He knew how much they enjoyed a good bed. He could practically hear them picturing it.

This must be what it's like for everyone else when they see into my mind.

At the hitching post outside the longhouse, the group dismounted. Snow crunched beneath his feet, giving instantly under his weight so he sank in it a little. Nicolas was surprised by the rumble from his stomach as he tied his horse to the post. Only when he focused did he realise he could smell cooking food. He'd become so used to his nose being either numb or blocked, that he hadn't noticed it was working again.

Stepping up on the wooden porch, he stomped his feet a couple of times to remove the excess snow from his boots. Traipsing snow through someone's home or place of business wasn't a good way to ingratiate yourself when asking for shelter.

And some of that food.

Beside him, he saw the eagerness in Shift's eyes. Even Silva's had a hint of keenness in them. Tallith was watching Nicolas like he was mentally taking notes on how to behave or something.

I'd best set a good example then, I suppose.

Coughing a couple of times, readying himself to make a polite introduction, he knocked on the door.

There was no answer.

Frowning, he knocked again.

Nothing.

Leaning back, he double-checked the nearest window. There was definitely light sneaking out from the gaps in the curtains.

'Kid, do you want me to just poke my head in and see who's about?' Auron asked, smirking again.

'No,' he replied quickly. 'I'm quite capable of getting someone's attention.'

He knocked again.

Silence.

This is getting annoying quickly.

'It's not locked,' Shift said, pointing at the door.

'You can tell that at a glance?' Sergeant Tallith asked.

'Master thief.' They turned their attention back to Nicolas. 'Let's just go in.'

Nicolas couldn't help the sudden –and a bit silly– aghast sound he made. 'We can't do that,' he cried.

'Why not?'

'It's...it's rude.'

Shift sighed heavily. 'You're right.' Their eyes flicked to the left. 'Maybe he can let us in?'

'Who?'

Nicolas only realised he'd been conned when he'd finished turning around and heard the door handle click behind him. By the time he'd turned back, Shift, Silva, and Auron had entered the longhouse.

Dammit.

Sergeant Tallith offered him an awkward shrug then the pair followed the others.

Whatever Nicolas had expected when he entered, it wasn't pitchforks being wielded threateningly in his direction. Instantly, he raised his hands.

Did we stray off course and end up in Sarus?

What looked like the entire population of the village was barricaded behind some overturned tables, which the men of the village – armed with their farming implements – were treating like the battlements of a castle. Behind them, stood a red-faced, middle-aged fellow with hair that was long at the back but completely missing on top. As his head and shoulders were above the other men, Nicolas guessed he must have been standing on a stool...or he was part giant.

'*Out*,' he bellowed, pointing toward the door, just in case they'd forgotten where it was.

'Hospitable place,' Auron remarked ironically.

Holding up his hands slowly, in an attempt to de-escalate whatever this situation was, he took his hat off, making no sudden movements. He tried not to make it too obvious that he was checking that Silva's sword was in its sheath, knowing what she was like. Having a drawn sword might undermine the impression he was trying to give: that they were harmless. The warrior stood still, but he knew she was ready if things got worse.

'I'm really sorry we just barged in.' Nicolas glanced nervously at Shift. When one of the least diplomatic of the group tried their hand at diplomacy it had the potential to go horribly wrong. 'But it's getting pretty rough out there, and we're just travellers looking for shelter for the night. We're just visitors.'

Instead of calming the tension in the room, their words had the opposite effect. The armed villagers were instantly riled, as the others cowered behind their protectors.

'You'll find no shelter here,' the man on the stool howled. 'Not anywhere in these parts. Travellers ain't welcome.'

Nicolas kept a pleasant smile on his face, whilst enjoying the mental image of the man slipping off his stool.

'Look,' Shift began, 'we're harmless, weary, and hungry. If it's money you're worried about, we have plenty of—'

'Your coin ain't good here,' the man bellowed. 'And you ain't welcome. Now get out.'

'We can't go back out there.' Nicolas's tone reflected his desperation. 'We'll freeze.'

'You said it yourself, you're visitors,' a woman cried from the back of the room, pointing an accusing finger at them. 'We ain't taking the risk you're confederates of The Visitor.'

The *oh* from Sergeant Tallith made him curious, but right now, he had more pressing matters to attend to. 'I don't know who this Visitor is, but I can assure you, we are not confederates of his...hers...its.'

'That's exactly what confederates of The Visitor *would* say.'

Well, she's bloody well got me there, hasn't she?

'We need a place to rest.' Silva was making it more of a demand than a plea.

'The only rest you'll find here is an eternal one,' a man shouted, waving his pitchfork just in case no one had noticed it yet. 'If you want shelter, piss off to the manor up the road, and good luck to you there.'

'Yeah, piss off to the manor,' another shouted. 'If you dare.'

Silva looked at him and tilted her head slightly.

'No,' he whispered. Yes, the villagers were being paranoid dicks, but that didn't entitle them to a beating from Silva.

'Get out.'

At the roar from the man on the stool, the men of the village left the protection of the tables and edged towards them. The slight shaking in their hands, nervous expressions, and sweat on their temples told him they didn't want to fight, but Nicolas wasn't about to test that theory.

'The manor it is.' He sighed, backing out of the room.

Fumbling behind him, he found the handle and opened the door. One by one, he and his companions slipped back out into the night.

CHAPTER 13

T he very short time they'd been inside the longhouse had seen a very big change in the weather. The snow was coming down hard now. Urgently, Nicolas secured his hat as they went to the horses.

'Um, about The Visitor—'

'Not now,' Nicolas said, untying his mount. 'When we get to this manor and are sat around a fire, you can tell us all about it. Right now, we need to focus on not freezing.'

'I don't know, kid,' Auron said, staring back at the longhouse. 'That *if you dare* didn't sound too promising.'

'If it's a choice between the unknown and death by pitchforks...'

'Yeah, and stay gone.'

The shout from the window caused Nicolas to stop just as he was about to mount his horse. With a low growl, he stomped back toward the door to the longhouse. He grabbed the handle, opened the door as wide as it would go then returned to his horse.

'You know that was petty, right?' Shift asked from beneath their fur cloak.

'Yup.'

'And you know I loved it, right?'

'Yup.'

Wanting to waste no more time, he mounted and spurred his horse into motion.

'I'm guessing *up the road* means north of here,' Auron said. 'I'll scout ahead. You guys travel north, stick to the main trail and I'll find you when I've found the manor.'

The spirit galloped away, completely unbothered by the snow on the floor, the snow falling through him, or the general cold. There were times Nicolas almost envied Auron.

As it turned out, North was the right direction. The group weren't long out of the village, on what passed for the main road, when Auron returned. At first, the spirit was a blurry light in the dark, but soon he took form and pulled up in front of Nicolas and the others.

'Not far ahead, there's a turn off, and it takes us to this manor.' There was a hint of worry in the spirit's voice. 'It looks creepier than a gathering of necromancers. I entered very briefly but didn't see any sign of life.'

'It'll do,' Nicolas replied quickly. 'Lead us there, please.'

Though it was close by, the conditions made it a harsh trek. They were all hunched over in their saddles, as if having their bodies closer to their mounts would generate that essential extra bit of warmth to keep them alive. Their dogged determination soon bore fruit, and the manor came into view.

Auron wasn't kidding.

It was a large house set off the main road. Each window was a dark portal, and the leering gargoyles on the roof were framed by the snow, making them even more menacing. Nicolas saw three floors, but there might've been more where the roof began. He was no expert on architecture, but this house had probably been the height of fashion before weathering took its toll. With no one to care for it, plants had crept up the walls, only to die in the cold and leave their brown, withered branches attached to the walls like fingers rising from the ground, trying to grab the manor and drag it back into the earth.

It's shelter for the night. It's shelter for the night. It's...

Nicolas soon realised that he could repeat the mantra as many times as he wanted, that wasn't going to give the walls a coat of paint and make the gargoyles smile.

As they moved into the gardens, the dilapidation became even more apparent. Several of the windows were smashed, and the bushes in the garden hadn't been tended in a good long while. The place did not look inviting.

But the village hall did, so what do I know?

At the grand double doors, the group dismounted. Silva handed her reins to Nicolas, drew her sword and approached the door, just as Auron vanished through it. A few moments passed then Silva slipped inside too. Shift, Nicolas, and Tallith watched the doors warily until Silva reappeared, opening them both so they could lead the horses inside.

What greeted them was a vast and dusty gallery absolutely caked in cobwebs. Not that Nicolas was bothered about that. His focus was on the rows of statues lining either side of the walkway. They were seriously unnerving.

The problem was, they were just folk. These were no deities or heroes of old crafted into dramatic poses. Just regular people, standing exactly how regular people might.

Nicolas and Shift tied the horses to a nearby banister then carefully walked through the statues. Nicolas's mind decided now would be a good time to play tricks on him, giving him the impression their eyes were following him or that he'd just seen a glimpse of movement. Just as he was about to pass the last one, he came to a halt, finally realising what else was off about them.

There's no cobwebs on any of them.

'Reception room is this way,' Auron called from a doorway ahead. 'The windows are good, and it has a fireplace. Looks like some old wood too.'

His concentration being broken so suddenly made Nicolas start slightly.

'Don't worry.' Shift grinned. 'He's a friendly ghost.'

Auron wasn't so friendly toward Shift when he heard the G word, giving them a very unfriendly glare.

'This way,' Nicolas said to Tallith, who couldn't hear the spirit.

The reception room must've been grand once. A well-appointed room for the leisure of lords and ladies. Now it was worn around every edge.

'I wonder who lived here?' he asked as he looked up at the grand portraits of very serious people adorning the walls.

'No one for a long time, by the look of it,' Shift said, drawing a swirling pattern in the dust on a desk.

'How does the fireplace look?' Nicolas asked, rubbing his arms feverishly to implore the feeling to return.

'Serviceable,' Silva replied, already putting wood into it and trying to light it.

If it had been Nicolas, they might've been here all night waiting for it to light, but Silva had much better survival skills. Soon enough, the fire was roaring, and the lamps around the room had been lit. It wasn't perfect, but after the conditions they'd travelled in to get here, it felt that way.

Shift stood in the centre of the room and circled, arms outstretched. 'Isn't it nice to be somewhere people aren't brandishing farm implements at us?'

'Be hard to do worse than that.' Auron chuckled.

'Stupid suicidal villagers,' Silva muttered as she finished lighting the last lamp.

'Now all we need is a hearty meal,' Shift said.

Nicolas's stomach growled in agreement. Looking around, he wondered where the food was...then he wondered why everyone was looking at him. 'What?'

'Did you bring the food in?' Shift asked.

'Was I supp— Never mind.' With a sheepish grin, he trotted back out into the hall, slowing considerably as he warily passed the statues again.

Don't come to life. Do not do it. Do you hear me? Stay.

Another glint of movement caught his eye.

Stop being paranoid.

After grabbing their rations from the horses, he hurried back into the reception room, striding in, holding the bag aloft triumphantly. 'Got them.'

He stopped abruptly as he saw the others staring at him. He opened his mouth to ask what was going on, when Silva's hand slowly slid to her sword.

Oh shit.

Now his attention had been brought to it, he could sense the presence behind him. Judging by the others' reactions, whatever it was wasn't nice. Controlling his breathing, he prepared his muscles for what he was about to do. When he was sure he was happy with how he wanted this to go, he made his move.

Dropping the bag, he stepped forward and turned on the spot, drawing the *Dawn Blade.*

He took one look at what was behind him, screamed, and started stabbing.

CHAPTER 14

After the fourth stab, the hideous creature fell to the floor with a gurgle, the *Dawn Blade* still stuck in its gut. Nicolas jumped back and let out the panicked breaths that had been patiently waiting for him to finish.

'What...in the Underworld...was that?' he gasped.

'A ghoul,' Auron said, approaching the prone creature and leaning over to study it. 'Nasty old things, ghouls. Undead creatures.'

Another one to cross off the list of undead things I've come across...oh Deities, there's actually enough for a list.

The spirit let out a chuckle. 'Nice work, kid. Multiple stabs to the stomach. Effective. But you lose points for letting go of the sword.'

Somehow, I'll live with that.

Auron cried out and jumped back as the ghoul suddenly sat up. With the general appearance of someone who's been mildly inconvenienced, it looked down at the sword sticking out of its torn-up stomach.

'Well, gosh.'

Laboriously, the ghoul got to its feet. Its skin was a slimy, decayed green. Though its limbs appeared almost skeletal, it had a fat pot belly. Where a nose should've been was a snout, and the hair he had left was long, thin, and wispy. Yellow eyes inspected the *Dawn Blade* as the creature shook its head sadly. Turning towards them as Auron tried to recover his dignity after screaming – something Shift would surely be mentioning later – the ghoul sighed wearily.

'I feel we've gotten off on quite the wrong foot.' The ghoul's sheepish smile was at odds with its fiercely fanged mouth. 'Perhaps we should start over.'

Nicolas looked from the sword to the ghoul's face several times then gestured toward it with the knife he'd drawn from his belt when it'd risen. 'How are you not dead?' he cried.

With a deep breath, the ghoul steepled its fingers together in front of its chest. 'I will happy explain all of...this. But first, would you mind popping your sword out of my belly? There's a good chap.'

I... What?

Nicolas found himself sheathing his knife and approaching the ghoul. Though it looked terrible indeed, he didn't get a sense of danger from it. Trusting his fledgling hero instincts, he took the hilt of his sword, and with a couple of tugs—which made the situation more awkward—it came free. Yellow blood spilled out onto the carpet. The ghoul appeared unbothered by the loss of its vital bodily fluid.

'Much appreciated.' The ghoul grinned, bowing slightly.

'Sorry for stabbing you,' Nicolas said awkwardly as he cleaned and sheathed the blade.

'Completely my fault.' The ghoul laughed jovially. 'If I didn't want to get stabbed, I shouldn't sneak up on people in the dark.'

'Did he just apologise to the ghoul?' Auron asked, pinching the bridge of his nose and sighing.

'What's going on?' Shift said, their brow furrowed in confusion. 'How is it alive? Maybe you should've cut the head off. Ghouls are like zombies, right?'

'I don't know.' Auron sighed again. 'I just kill them. I don't do their genealogy.'

'Cutting my head off wouldn't have worked any better, just so you know,' the ghoul answered helpfully. 'And to answer your question, technically ghouls are a step or two up from zombies. We—they—both consume human flesh to live. But ghouls tend to be on the living side of the line between life and death. Zombies are on the other side.'

'Oh, thanks.' Nicolas turned to Auron. 'There you go then.'

Am I really having a polite chat with a ghoul?

'Might I enquire,' the ghoul asked after another polite cough, 'are you talking to someone I cannot see?'

'Oh yes, there's a ghost with us.' Nicolas kicked himself as soon as he said it. Yes, he'd made a mistake, but he didn't feel that justified the expletive Auron threw at him for it.

The creature clapped its hands together in a foppish way. 'Oh my, how fascinating. I would like to hear all about that. But first I feel like I should introduce myself.'

'Aren't you going to take care of that wound first?' Shift asked.

The ghoul looked down in surprise. It must've forgotten the large hole in its torso. 'Oh Deities, no.' It chuckled. 'That stuff takes care of itself.' With a broad smile, the ghoul bowed low. 'Reginald Galric the Third, at your service.' When he rose, he extended his abnormally large hand.

'Do not take that,' Silva cautioned, sword pointed at the ghoul and unlikely to be sheathed any time soon.

Ignoring the advice, Nicolas shook the hand then returned the bow. 'Nicolas Percival Carnegie. Nice to meet you.'

'Fabulous to meet you too.' Reginald beamed. 'Now I feel we've cleared the air a little, please continue making your food whilst I get to know the rest of you lovely people.'

'Do I have to put my sword away?' Silva asked, in an open-legged combat stance that didn't look comfortable.

'Yes,' Nicolas confirmed.

'Every damn time.' The warrior huffed as she made a big show of how irksome she found returning her sword to its sheath.

'I assure you I'm quite nice once you get to know me,' Reginald said with a wave.

'That's Silva,' Nicolas said. 'We also have Shift, there. That's Tallith and the g...spirit is Auron.'

Reginald pursed his lips thoughtfully. 'Isn't there a legendary hero called Auron?'

'*Wasn't,*' Shift corrected.

After a second, Reginald caught on. 'Oh, I see. Sorry.'

Auron took no offence. He was too busy peacocking with his *someone has heard of me* grin on his face. Nicolas could swear his aura was a bit brighter.

'I guess that line of work is quite dangerous,' Reginald pondered.

'Only if you answer the call of nature with killers around.' Auron glared openly at Silva, before looking back at Reginald curiously. 'A talking ghoul. I bet there's a good story there.'

The ghoul was about to speak again when something caught his eye. His face contorted in horror before he bounded over to the seats and began dusting the cushions with his long fingers. 'I am so sorry about the state of this place. It's been a while since I've entertained, and the upkeep of the house has gone downhill in that time. I mean, I am sure you can guess why I do not receive guests anymore.' Reginald gestured to his form.

Anymore?

The ghoul plonked himself onto a sofa like a sack of potatoes and gazed at them all expectantly. 'Please, make yourselves at home.'

Nicolas looked at each of his companions. Shift and Tallith shrugged at him. Auron looked just as expectant as Reginald, and Silva appeared at a loss. The warrior walked over to Nicolas, grabbed the food, and moved to the fireplace to prepare something for them to eat, making sure to keep one eye on the ghoul. Nicolas went and sat on the sofa across from

Reginald, which groaned under his weight. Shift joined him. Tallith just sort of made himself comfortable on the rug.

The ghoul leaned forward in his seat, steepling his fingers again. 'As you can imagine, it's also been a while since I've been to court. I must know everything that's going on in Etherius. Is Lady Ezmay still as promiscuous as usual? Did High Mage Balfour ever complete the book he's been threatening to write in forever? What news? What news?'

'Sorry, Reginald,' Nicolas replied, trying not to gawk at the way the wound he'd inflicted was slowly closing before his very eyes. 'But you give the impression you weren't always…a ghoul.'

With a laboured sigh, Reginald sat back on the sofa. 'Two years ago, I was a human, a Lord of some note, mind you. I suppose it's quite an interesting tale, if you'd care to hear it?'

'Yes, I *knew* he had a good story,' Auron cried. He pointed a finger at Nicolas. 'None of that overly polite *I don't want to pry* crap from you, kid. I want to hear that story.'

'If you wouldn't mind?' Nicolas replied to the ghoul.

'Well, let me preface this by saying that when I was a human, I was, and excuse my profanity, a bit of a dick.' Reginald shook his head sadly. 'A lot of one, actually. I was the embodiment of noble entitlement. Very privileged, very in love with my station, and very in love at looking down at those beneath me, sadly. All that changed when The Visitor came.'

Visitor? Didn't we nearly get stabbed with pitchforks for being allies of a Visitor?

'I remember it vividly,' Reginald said, closing his eyes to steel himself. 'It was a late winter night. There was a knock at the door. The butler opened it then came to me, telling me there was a man who needed to come in out of the snow. I told him to bugger off, obviously. Well, I told the butler to tell him. But the butler came back, saying he was insisting, so I grabbed a stick and went out to thrash the laggard. I got to the door, cursing and cussing and then…those bright red eyes. I was entranced, and I passed out. When I woke up, I was like this.' The ghoul looked sorrowfully at his long-clawed hand. 'In the second I caught those eyes I heard him say it. *Inhospitable.'* Sadness creased Reginald's features. He used his hand to slick back what hair he had left.

'I'm so sorry,' Shift said with genuine empathy. 'Is that what The Visitor does then? Transforms people?'

'He's a local legend,' Tallith said, paling. 'I always thought it was a scary story, told to stop people wandering around in winter.'

'I wish.' Reginald chuckled dryly. 'He's plagued these parts for years, appearing in winter, knocking on doors then cursing people he deems inhospitable, those who turn him away. I didn't even think when I stormed to the door, cane in hand...' The ghoul's head lowered. 'Suffice to say, I've learnt some humility since then.'

'You may wish to teach it to those down the road,' Silva grumbled from beside the fireplace.

'I tried.' Reginald sighed. 'I reached out to the villagers for help. I ended up getting stabbed by pitchforks and left in the snow to die.'

Sounds about right.

'They probably thought I was The Visitor coming for them. I can hardly blame them, given my appearance.'

Tallith drew Nicolas's attention by clicking his fingers in the air. 'Oh yes, there's that rhyme, isn't there?'

'You knew this was out there, it had its own song, and you didn't mention it?' Nicolas asked, wide eyed.

'I... Sorry.'

'Ah yes,' Reginald scoffed. 'How does it go? *The snow will fall. He's coming to call. The Visitor knocks. Undo the locks. Welcome him in. Or you'll pay for your sin'.*' Reginald singing it in a childlike voice made it all the more disturbing. 'Like the young man there, I never believed it. Childish nonsense and all that. It's a bit different when the monster's at your door.'

'All the creepiest monsters have their own rhyme,' Auron said, rolling his pupilless eyes.

'It was a monster?' Silva was suddenly more interested.

Reginald nodded slowly. 'I only caught a glimpse. I saw green skin and a dark, tattered cloak. Maybe red. But that could be because of the eyes. Those damned glowing eyes.' He cast a haunted look toward the door of the room. 'Those were the last things my human eyes saw.'

That description was a little too familiar for comfort. In his mind, he took the traits Reginald had described and put them together.

Surely not...

'No, it can't be,' Auron said with a chuckle in defiance of his worried expression.

'Green skin...red cloak...red eyes...' Shift went through the list slowly, staring into the distance.

Not so long ago, Nicolas would've laughed off the idea. But it wasn't *not so long ago*. It was now. And for the life of him, he couldn't find a compelling reason it *couldn't* be Garaz. His attention went to each of his companions in turn, hoping one of them had a very solid, logical reason, backed up by plentiful evidence that this *Visitor* couldn't possibly be their errant companion.

'Have I said something amiss?' Reginald asked, reading the room accurately.

The squeezing of his hand drew his attention to Shift. Judging by the hurt in their eyes, they hadn't written Garaz off as easily as they'd claimed. Silva had turned slightly away from them, as if they didn't know her well enough to sense her pain and anger.

'It can't be him,' Auron repeated. The words had no conviction behind them.

'So, how can this curse be broken?'

Nicolas could've kissed Tallith for having the wherewithal to change the subject, even if he might've just been genuinely curious.

Reginald let out a long, sad breath. 'Alas, there is no breaking it, my boy. I have never heard of anyone breaking The Visitor's curse.'

'The tales say that every year he's getting worse, cursing more people,' Tallith replied sadly.

'I must accept that this is my life now, trapped in this hideous form.' Reginald regarded his hand. 'I would do anything to take it back or have The Visitor return to see that I've learned my lesson. But I fear I'm feeding myself too much false hope. I must accept my reality. Some days are better than others.'

It was very hard for Nicolas to imagine Reginald as a bad person, try as he might. Though to be honest, it was hard to imagine Reginald as a human.

Poor man.

'This will not do,' Reginald said finally with a deep exhalation. 'We must not dwell on the bad. I have company for the first time in a long time. Please, tell me everything.'

CHAPTER 15

Really, the group should've slept in preparation for the next leg of their journey, but Reginald had been alone for so long and was so keen to talk that they indulged him. For his part, the ghoul was an excellent listener, enthralled as the group told the tales of their adventures. It was by the time they reached the story of their trip with Captain Roberto Ramirez that Nicolas had realised he was acting out his deeds...in a very similar manner to Auron. Instantly, he wanted to sit down and simply recount events, but he knew how much this meant to their host, so he continued to duel with the imaginary pirates in front of him.

Every so often, Reginald would chime in with a reaction or question. Once, he even joked that Etherius seemingly going downhill made him glad to be a recluse. Seeing something that appeared as horrific-looking as the ghoul acting so nice was just odd. It was clear Reginald had truly learnt his lesson. It was just a shame that he'd had to be taught it in such a terrible way.

As Nicolas finished recounting their latest adventure, ending with him entering a room and stabbing a ghoul, Reginald's shoulders sagged. That would be the end of their tales.

Except I know who has a lot more. He just needs a mouthpiece.

Flicking his gaze to Auron, he raised his eyebrows. With a wide grin, the spirit prepared himself.

As the hours passed, Nicolas's ability to play out the tales waned, and he found himself sitting on a sofa, Shift at his side.

'...and that's when he jumped off the balcony, right onto its back,' Nicolas said, repeating Auron's words as he struggled to keep his eyes open. He really wanted to sleep, but the spirit's enthusiasm suggested he wasn't going to stop any time soon, and somehow Nicolas couldn't bring himself to cut his companion off when he was in his element, nor deny Reginald. Who knew when the ghoul would get another visi...guest?

'Amazing.' Reginald gasped, wide-eyed. 'How did you dispatch it when—'

Everyone jumped at the cry of spooked horses. There was an urgent clopping of hooves and panicked whinnying from beyond the door. Something was spooking their mounts. Suddenly, everyone was wide awake.

'Oh,' Reginald said quietly. 'Midnight already.'

'What do you mean?' Silva asked, sword half-drawn.

The ghoul rose from his seat as if his body weighed three times more than it did and walked to the centre of the room. 'Apologies, my friends. In all the excitement, I forgot to tell you about this. Something is about to happen. I...well, you'll see.'

What's going on?

Nicolas jumped from his seat and drew the *Dawn Blade* as grey figures shambled into the room, their feet grating on the wooden floor.

'Please sheath your blades.' Reginald's smile was heavy. 'They will not hurt you unless provoked.' The ghoul's face became serious, his eyes pleading. 'Whatever happens, do not interfere. I will be fine.'

About to ponder what in the Underworld that meant, Nicolas found his concentration broken as he recognised the figures. They were the statues from the hall. Each one moved as if it were a man but was clearly still made of stone. It reminded him vaguely of the golems he'd faced outside Xedora's hut. But these were much more expressive...and clearly exceptionally pissed off.

'I'm so sorry,' Reginald said as the first of them reached him.

The snarling statue took a ridiculously big swing and cracked the ghoul right in the jaw. The snapped sound as stone connected with flesh and broke bone made Nicolas wince. As Reginald fell to the floor, he caught a glimpse of the ghoul's jaw hanging limply from his chin. Instantly, the rest of the statues fell on him, shouting oaths and curses as they pummelled him with boots and fists of rock. The ghoul vanished under the furious assault. But even that appeared to be not enough to sate the statues' desires for violence, as some began to grab nearby fire pokers.

Nicolas stepped forward and found Shift holding him back. 'He said not to get involved.'

'What?' he cried. 'We can't just stand by and let this happen. We need to do something.'

'You will bastarding not,' one of the statues roared, pointing an accusing finger at him. 'If you do, you'll get some of what this asshole is having.' The statue crouched next to Reginald. 'And you know how much you deserve it, don't you?'

The ghoul's shaking body let out a murmur of agreement, and the statues instantly resumed their beating. The fury of it all was striking. This wasn't a simple beating. They hated Reginald, to their very core.

Nicolas kept catching himself wanting to charge in and break it up, but he remembered Reginald's request and honoured it.

As quickly as it had begun, the assault finished. Looking at their victim with utter disdain, the statues began to leave the room.

'Until tomorrow night, asshole,' the last one said as he vanished through the open door.

On the floor, Reginald's body was covered in bloody wounds from the attack. Several of his limbs were at very incorrect angles, and yellow blood pooled all around him. And yet he continued to breathe.

'No one could live through such an assault.' Silva gasped.

'No one could've been stabbed in the stomach that many times and survive,' Auron said thoughtfully.

As the warrior ran to the doorway to check that the statues intended to stay gone, Nicolas and the others hurried over to Reginald. He could still hear the stomping of the statues' feet receding into the distance as he gently turned the ghoul over. It took all his will not to visibly wince at the mess they'd made of his face. But he didn't want to upset Reginald by reacting. He'd been through enough already.

'Reginald?' Shift said nervously. 'Reginald?'

The eye that wasn't a mashed pulp opened wearily. There was a snap as the ghoul's arm twitched violently and somehow repaired itself. Reaching up, Reginald put his jaw back into place with a crack.

'I'll be okay.' The ghoul's voice was weak. 'Thank you for your concern.'

As Nicolas watched, the indents in Reginald's body smoothed out. Limbs moved back into their proper places, and cuts and bruises started to vanish. Already, the ghoul's second eye was reappearing.

'How do you do that?' he asked.

Is it some power the undead have? Maybe I can channel it as I'm a bit...dead...ish?

'That,' Reginald began with a thin smile, 'is the second part of the curse. The Visitor decided it wasn't enough to just change me. My servants were guilty by association, so he turned them all to living stone. By day, they're frozen in place, never ageing but completely aware. Between midnight and dawn, they come to life. It's become quite the routine. They wake up, beat me senseless then go play cards in the servants' quarters.'

'Why don't they just go to their homes?' Nicolas asked.

'Some tried. They always end up back on the pedestals in the morning.' Following the ghoul's gesture, Nicolas helped Reginald to his feet. 'The Visitor knew what they'd do, exacting vengeance upon me whenever they can. That's why part of the curse is ensuring I cannot die. I can heal any wound to ensure my suffering is drawn out. I found that out when I first saw my new form and threw myself from the roof of the manor.' Reginald caught Nicolas's look of horror. 'As I said earlier, there are good days and bad days.'

'Haven't you tried talking to your servants and reaching some kind of accord?' Tallith asked, glancing toward the door.

'No,' the ghoul answered firmly. 'I deserve it. I treated them all abominably in life, and now they're cursed to live as statues, never to see their families again.'

'By the Deities, that's sadistic,' Nicolas said.

'It's my life now.' Reginald took a step toward the sofa, but wavered. Nicolas and Tallith caught him before he fell. 'Would you mind?'

The pair helped him cross the room and sat him down gently.

'I apologise,' Reginald said sadly. 'I am afraid this has put quite the dampener on our evening.'

Just a little, yes.

CHAPTER 16

Considering there were violent walking statues in the house, Nicolas and the others slept pretty darned well, perhaps from the exhaustion of everything that had come before. Despite Reginald's assurances that they were safe, the group barricaded the door, and Auron went to keep an eye on the former servants.

As soon as Nicolas woke, he opened one eye to check the door. The barricade was still in place, and Auron was hanging around. Light was peeking between the curtains, and Reginald was up by the fireplace. Unless his nose deceived him, their host was preparing breakfast.

Raising his head slightly, he saw that he was right, the ghoul was cooking something. Judging by the fact Auron wasn't screaming at them to wake up, it wasn't a stew they were going to be thrown into. It was still difficult to match the ghoul with the person he'd said he was.

Why doesn't The Visitor come back to see if people have learnt their lessons?

And what about the statues? Poor men who just happened to work for the wrong man. Would he be so vengeful if it happened to him?

'Did you sleep well?' Silva asked. The warrior was sat against the wall to his right. Judging by her bleary eyes, she'd just woken too.

'Yes, I think so.'

'You did,' Shift mumbled beside him. 'You draped your arm over me, and it was basically a dead weight all night. I was half tempted to turn into a giant hedgehog to get you to back off.'

'Why didn't you?'

Their eyes still closed, Shift half smiled. 'Because the other half of me liked it.'

Shift lazily swatted him away as he planted a kiss on their temple before rising. Stretching his arms high, he then pushed his elbows behind him as far as they would go. It was darned satisfying.

'Any problems in the night?' he asked Auron.

'No,' the spirit replied. 'I kept an eye on the statues, but like Reg said, they just played cards. They're quite a funny bunch, really. Damn shame what happened to them. They're all back out on the pedestals now.'

A damn shame indeed.

Nicolas turned to find his armour being presented to him. It looked suspiciously like it'd just been polished.

'Ready for the day?' Tallith asked. 'I suppose we'll be getting going soon? New deeds and all that?'

Somehow, the sergeant was managing to become a little more endearing each day. 'Not quite. I'd like to have some breakfast before I'm back in the armour again.'

Putting his chest plate carefully back on the floor, Tallith shook his head. 'Of course. Sorry.'

'Cut it out.'

Tallith was instantly confused. 'Sir?'

'The *sir* business, for starters,' he said patiently. 'I'm not your superior. And you don't have to fuss around me. I don't need a squire.' Instantly, Tallith looked crestfallen. 'Because you're your own man,' he added quickly. 'I don't expect you to go running around after me. We're all equals here.'

Tallith's crestfallen expression disappeared quickly, replaced by a warm smile. 'Of course. Sorry again. It's just...it's you.'

'Well, I'm just me.' He shrugged. 'You just be you.'

'If that's what passes for wisdom in the group now, we are truly lost without—' Silva caught herself, and her face hardened slightly.

'Breakfast is ready,' Reginald said, waving them over with enthusiasm. 'Now, we are a bit poorly provisioned here, but I've made the best of what I've got. If I were to pop down to the local shop, it would cause quite the uproar.' It was nice to see the ghoul in good humour about his form. 'But I do maintain a small vegetable patch, to keep myself busy mainly.'

'Do you not eat?' Shift asked, deciding to grace the group with their presence as they sat up and stretched.

'I...do,' Reginald was blatantly unsure whether he should be answering the question or not. 'But ghouls consume flesh. Unfortunately, my body rejects carrots and the like quite violently.' The ghoul held his hands up as soon as he realised that his proclamation had caused all his guests to stop where they were. 'Not human flesh. Goodness, no. I use rats as a substitute. I breed them out back. Well away from the vegetables, never fear. They are...a source of food.'

I really hope he isn't having breakfast with us.

Happy he wasn't about to be eaten, Nicolas walked over and took the bowl Reginald offered him. It was hot and smelled delicious. The taste matched what the scent promised. Soon, Nicolas was gobbling it down as quickly as he was able—it still being pretty hot.

'Nick.'

Nicolas looked up from his bowl. He was about to ask what Shift wanted, but then he realised that everyone was looking at him strangely. 'What's going on?'

'Enjoying your food, kid?'

'I...am,' he said nervously. 'Why?'

'It was a rhetorical question. We can tell,' Silva interrupted bluntly.

'*Tell?*'

'Nick, you're making the kind of noises you normally reserve for when you and I are alone.' Shift raised their eyebrows as if he should instantly understand what they meant.

He didn't. 'When we're alone? I don't make noises when we're alone. We—'

Oh.

His face must've given away his epiphany. 'Yes,' Silva remarked cooly. 'Um...sorry.'

'Heh.' A mischievous grin crossed Auron's ethereal lips. 'Delicious breakfast. *Yippee.*'

Funny ghost.

'Think nothing of it.' Reginald laughed. 'I take it as quite the compliment to my cooking. I do not get to do it often.'

Nicolas finished his food a lot slower after that.

Once breakfast was done, it was time to leave. Garaz wasn't going to chase himself down. Or was he? Who knew anymore? Nicolas's eagerness to get back on the road dwindled quickly when he entered the hallway and realised he'd have to walk through the statues to get to their horses.

They all look...stiff.

Deities, Nicolas, that's a poor choice of words.

'They are fine,' Reginald said sadly. 'They are aware but cannot move during the day.'

Warily, he followed the pathway they made toward the big stairway and his horse. As he reached the end of the row of statues, he turned back. 'I'm sorry this happened to all of you. If I can ever find a way to break this curse, I will.'

'Usually, killing the curser will do it,' Auron told him.

We just have to find him first. And hopefully it's not who I worry it is.

After gathering their horses, the group led them toward the double doors of the manor.

'Thank you all for visiting,' Reginald said with feeling. 'It was lovely to have some company, even briefly.'

'And thank you for your hospitality,' Nicolas said, shaking the ghoul's outstretched hand. 'I meant what I said. If I can find a way to lift your curse, I will.'

'Being unable to go out gives one a lot of time to think.' The ghoul smiled thinly. 'I was not a nice person and was most deserving of this. It's just a shame that my servants had to suffer for my arrogance. Though I must admit I wish they would give me a night off every now and then.'

Judging by the way the statues were last night, Nicolas highly doubted it, but he hoped it anyway. Reginald really did seem a decent sort...now.

Would I be any more forgiving if I was cursed for all eternity because of him?

CHAPTER 17

As eager as Nicolas had been to continue their quest, he hadn't been looking forward to being out in the cold again. But today seemed better. It wasn't snowing, and his nose was just tingly and not outright numb. The heavy snow of the previous night had covered everything in a layer of bright white, making Etherius look positively glowing. And the crunching of hooves in the snow was almost soothing after a night in decent shelter and a hearty meal.

Reginald had stayed at the door until they were out of sight, and maybe after. Nicolas had made sure to wave just before they reached the main road again. It was returned with enthusiasm.

I hope we get to visit him again one day.

'Are any of us going to say it?' Silva asked suddenly, about half a mile down the road.

'What?' Nicolas didn't know why he asked. He knew what she was talking about.

'This *Visitor*,' Silva answered. 'It sounds like someone we may know well. Or thought we did.'

'It can't be though.' Auron scoffed. 'We've known Garaz for an age. We would've noticed him disappearing during the winter.'

'We haven't actually been with him during a winter yet,' Shift reminded him stiffly.

The spirit furrowed his brow in thought. 'Well, blow me, we haven't, have we? I suppose time seems longer when you're in mortal peril a lot.'

That's true enough. I could swear I first left Hablock a couple of years ago.

'I know I'm the biggest naysayer in all of this,' Shift said firmly, 'but we really don't know him at *all*. And that's the way he kept it. None of us can presume what he did and didn't do before we met him. Besides, Silva and I saw his brother. Shagraz was very much your typical orc. How can Garaz be so different to his own brother?'

'I know I'm new and don't really know Garaz,' Tallith began. 'And the description does sound like your companion. But it's best not to make assumptions, or you'll end up looking for evidence to prove you're right, instead of proving *what's* right.'

'Very well,' Silva said after a moment. 'But if it is him, he deserves to be put to the sword.'

What else has The Visitor done to people who were inhospitable?

Nicolas breathed out heavily. 'Let's put aside the issue of whether it is or isn't Garaz and focus on The Visitor instead.'

'His behaviour suggests he's punishing people for an injustice committed upon him,' Sergeant Tallith said thoughtfully. 'Most likely he was driven out of somewhere or shunned. Now he's taking it out on the world. Whatever it was, it must've been pretty traumatic.'

'I can see why you're in the city watch.' Nicolas smiled. 'You're a good investigator.'

Tallith was practically glowing. 'Shame I wasn't as on the ball with the murders in the city,' the sergeant said, his smile dropping. 'But I doubt anyone who didn't have experience with demons could've guessed that.'

'It was a terrible way to gain some experience.' Shift said with sympathy.

Meeting a demon was the worst kind of way to broaden your horizons. Nicolas knew that firsthand. The first demon he'd met was Koth, and he'd ended up with an arrow in the chest and his soul in the Underworld. At the merest thought of the demon, his scar itched beneath his chest plate. He was well aware it was in his mind.

Where is Koth now? Where are my people?

Dreamily, he gazed into the distance, as if he could suddenly acquire some magical sight that would show him exactly where the people of Hablock were. This amazing power never manifested. The horizon was still the horizon. Every day they delayed, his people could be getting further away. He'd made his peace with that when he knew they would be stuck in Babylon for the winter, but now they were out on the road, resentment for Garaz grew. The orc could be leading them further from his people.

We planned to wait out the winter, but when we are forced to travel, it's because of him.

His grip tightened around the reins.

Garaz's apology and explanation better be pretty damned good.
****

The fields are large squares of pristine white, practically glowing in the...urgh.

Nicolas was getting bored with metaphors about how lovely winter made everything look. There were only so many ways you could say *'the snow makes it look nice'* before you wanted to put your head in said snow and scream. The only thing he wanted to see—the red blob on the horizon of a certain orc's cloak—was the one thing that never seemed to appear.

'There's a hamlet ahead.' Silva hadn't really needed to call it out. Even Nicolas could make out the blocky, unnatural shapes on the horizon.

That are dusted white by the snow so they look like...white...topped...cakes?

'Taking your bets on whether or not they're friendly,' Shift announced to the group. 'I'm putting two coins on unfriendly.'

'I'm not taking that bet,' Nicolas said quickly.

'I'll take it,' Tallith said eagerly. 'I'm sure they'll be welcoming.'

'Two coins says they are all dead.'

'*Silva*,' Nicolas cried out in shock.

'I am just getting involved with the group,' the warrior replied.

'I know, but...' He rolled his eyes. 'You know, we meet plenty of friendly people in villages.'

Other than Tallith, everyone stopped and looked at him.

'Are you referring to the village back down the road?' Shift asked. 'Or maybe the one that nearly lynched us all for trying to kick a chicken? Or possibly the one where you ended up being a wanted assassin? Or—'

'Okay, thank you,' he said testily.

Maybe The Visitor has a point. There are a lot of inhospitable folk in Etherius.

'At least there's only a handful of dwellings, kid,' Auron interjected. 'If they do cause trouble, there won't be enough of them to be any real problem. We'll just get Silva to glare at them until they wet themselves.'

'That'll work.' Shift nodded.

The hamlet itself was built around a small hill. Atop it sat what appeared to be a lumberyard, surrounded by trees.

Odd not to have cut them down first.

The closer they got to the settlement, the closer Nicolas's hand got to his sword. There was a wrongness about the place. There was no wood being cut, no children playing, and most importantly, no smoke from the chimneys.

'Your hero instincts are getting better,' Auron said, gesturing to his hand. 'Something's definitely awry here.'

'Glad to hear it,' he said quietly. 'I was worried I'm just getting paranoid.'

'A bit of paranoia is healthy,' Shift said, studying the dwellings ahead. 'Especially with the amount of times we get attacked.'

'Trouble?' Tallith asked, suddenly picking up on the conversation.

'Maybe.' Silva brought her horse to a halt, and the others stopped alongside her, eyeing the small collection of shacks warily.

'Wait here,' Auron said after a few moments of expectant silence. 'I'll go and have a look around, see what evil lurks therein.'

The spirit rode ahead of them, not disturbing even a single snowflake. It felt wrong letting Auron ride ahead and scout every time, but the spirit couldn't die. Well, that wasn't quite true. When the demon possessing Beba Greer had attacked them, it had hurt Auron. Nicolas could've sworn the spirit's aura was still a bit dimmer than it had been, as if, like any normal wound, it needed to recover.

The spirit pulled Mare up alongside several of the buildings and popped his head in, literally.

'It's deserted,' Auron shouted back after the fifth building. 'No sign of a fight. They're just gone.'

That was probably more worrying than if there were bodies. Carefully, Nicolas and the others advanced into the hamlet.

'People don't just vanish,' Shift said warily, echoing Nicolas's own concerns.

Dismounting, the group spread out, checking the homes. There were, indeed, no signs of foul play. Everything was neatly in its place. It just lacked people.

'Over here,' Silva called, waving the others over.

The warrior was crouching when Nicolas and the rest reached her. 'There are very faint tracks in the snow, leading up the slope,' she explained, pointing to a place in the snow that looked like every other place in the snow around them. Still, Nicolas trusted her judgement.

Quickly, they moved up the slope, finding themselves slipping between the trees, weapons drawn, as they approached the mill. At a glance, it appeared as deserted as the rest of the dwellings.

'The tracks are gone,' Silva said, frowning as she looked around her feet. 'They've just vanished.'

'So, the people came up here and just disappeared?' Tallith said, scratching his chin as he looked around. 'That doesn't make any se—*aaaarrrrrgggggh.*'

Everyone was in a fighting stance before Tallith had even hit the ground. Eyes wide with fear, the sergeant scurried back, his feet kicking long furrows in the snow.

'What is it?' Nicolas asked quietly, just in case whatever had spooked Tallith got riled by loud noises.

'The...the tree...' Tallith stammered. 'It...looked at me.'

To anyone else that would've seemed absurd, but Nicolas and his companions had talked to a tree once. Carefully, he stalked forwards, towards the tree Tallith was pointing to. Slowly, he scanned the rough bark, looking for any sign of— He jumped back slightly as eyes stared back at him.

All it took was one glance into the bulging, pleading pupils to realise what'd happened here. Turning his attention to the next tree, and the one after that, he saw that they all had eyes—fearful, desperate ones.

'By the Deities,' he whispered, his sword arm falling limp.

Once Shift realised, they held their hand to their mouth and gasped. Auron looked dumbstruck.

Now he was looking for it, Nicolas could see that some of the lower branches from each tree were bent like arms and legs might be. Sheathing his sword, he approached the nearest tree.

'My name is Nicolas Percival Carnegie. Can you talk?'

The tree said nothing, but its eyes said everything. The horror of what this was gripped Nicolas with fingers colder than the snow he stood on.

'Can you blink?'

The tree could.

'Was this *The Visitor*?' he asked.

The tree blinked emphatically.

'How many days ago?'

The tree blinked two times.

Dammit, that'd be roughly the time Garaz passed here.

Removing his glove, Nicolas put his hand on the cold, coarse bark. 'I'm so sorry this happened to you. I promise I'll do everything in my power to undo this.'

The tree's eyes gripped his own for a long moment...before they closed. Nicolas could swear he saw a tear. He really didn't know what else to say—or do, for that matter.

'Auron,' he asked desperately. 'What can we...?'

There were red veins on the spirit's back. Quickly, he jogged over to Auron. The spirit was glaring at a tree that hadn't once been a person. Parts of it were blackened.

'Scorch marks,' Nicolas said, touching the affected area, which crumbled to dust.

'Fire magic.'

Auron's words made the ground drop from under him. It couldn't be. It really couldn't.

But the evidence says otherwise.

CHAPTER 18

Ironically, the only constant about the weather was that it changed. Their travel was hindered by light snow, heavy snow, medium snow, light snow and then heavy snow again. It was exhausting. But no matter how heavy the snow, Nicolas saw exactly the same thing ahead of him: those eyes. The pleading ones surrounded by flesh made of bark. They haunted him. Another group of people he couldn't help.

Nicolas had hated the idea of leaving the villagers, but the best—only—way to help them was to find someone who knew magic who could undo the curse. According to Auron, wizards didn't hang around small villages. Apparently, having magic generally caused a bit of snobbery, so they'd need to find a good-sized town to get help breaking the curses. Though Sergeant Tallith had never heard of The Visitor's curses being broken before.

Without any nearby settlements, the group had made camp beneath some overhanging rocks just off the main trail. Nicolas had no idea if the snow was light, heavy or non-existent now. He was too busy staring into the fire, picturing the eyes amongst the dancing flames.

Why couldn't I have done more?

And it wasn't just the cursed people he meant, but those much closer to home. Some of the dancing flames seemed to almost change form, until he could see his parents clearly where the eyes had just been. How was he supposed to save others, when he couldn't save those closest to him? He'd tried to help them, but had been brushed aside – well, thrown to the floor by the arrow in his chest.

At least I can remember their faces. I do get hit in the head a lot.

Another face appeared alongside his parents. Potter. Behind the roguish smile was the mind busy planning how best to make a name for himself in Etherius. Those dreams would be shattered now, as he lay shackled in whatever pit Koth had thrown him and the other people of Hablock into. All their faces flashed past him, faster and faster until he couldn't pick out single people anymore.

The Maestro certainly got his revenge on me. I may have lived, but I lost so much.

The images in the fire slowed, changing again into a single face. Nicolas's jaw clenched at the familiar genial smile staring back at him.

And even those few things I have left are turning sour. Why did you do it?

Frowning, he watched as the orc's smile contorted, first into a snarl then a soundless roar. He was unable to tear his eyes away as the fanged mouth grew bigger, as if it were jumping out of the fire to consume him.

'Ow.' Nicolas rubbed the spot on his temple where Shift had flicked him.

'Well,' the shapeshifter replied, 'you needed to come back.'

'Did I have to?' he asked with a strained half-smile. 'It was warmer where I was.'

Even though the pair were wrapped tightly together under the same blanket, Shift managed to elbow him in the ribs. 'It's warm enough here, Nick.'

He couldn't dispute that. It was fair to say that a lot of bad stuff had happened since the Oracle had chosen him to deliver a message, but some good things had come out of the mess too. So far, the best thing was Shift.

I'm sure I'd get teased for admitting that aloud, though.

Shift squinted at him in distaste. 'Quit giving me doe eyes. Sitting in the cold under a rock is no place to get romantic.' They lowered their voice to a whisper. 'Besides, the others are watching.'

See?

Nicolas had to catch the *eep* before it escaped his lips as—contrary to what they'd just said—Shift grabbed him in a very personal place under the blanket. He could tell they were highly amused by the way he'd jumped. Across from him, Silva raised a quizzical eyebrow.

'Anyway,' Shift continued, resuming their usual tone. 'You were staring into the fire dwelling on all the bad stuff that has happened. That isn't good for anyone. You, doubly so.'

The plan when he opened his mouth was to deny it. 'You're right,' he admitted instead. 'I was thinking about the tree-folk. The people from Hablock. And Garaz. I still can't make sense of it.'

'It's not him, you know.' All eyes—except Sergeant Tallith's—turned to Auron. 'Garaz isn't The Visitor. Can't be.'

'Because?' Silva's scepticism was blatant.

Auron frowned in confusion, as if he'd just been asked the stupidest question ever to be asked in the history of Etherius. 'My hero instincts,' the spirit scoffed finally. 'I've spent years dealing with thieves, villains, dark lords, monsters, and general scoundrels. I couldn't travel with someone for so long and not at least have an inkling that there was something off about them.'

'And you'd like to account for me being stuffed into a cupboard...how?' Nicolas asked.

'That, I don't know,' the spirit admitted. 'But I know Garaz isn't bad. He must've had his reasons. I just wish he'd shared them with us before smacking you with his staff.'

You and me both.

Shift shook their head and laughed. 'You're just going to deny the evidence then? Monstrous visage. Big cloak. Green skin. Red eyes. Does magic. Are you waiting for a signed confession too?'

'I'm sure that description could fit numerous people in Etherius.' Nicolas had no idea what side of the argument he was on anymore. Tallith looked equally confused as he sat quietly watching them. It was probably hard to keep up when he couldn't hear one half of the conversation.

'It isn't him,' Auron asserted stubbornly. 'You can be reassured by the fact that I said so.'

'So, you've never been wrong before?' Shift asked leadingly.

Nicolas really hoped he wasn't this time. Because the only way to break the curses might be to kill The Visitor. And if it *was* Garaz...

'You don't have faith in my hero instincts?' The spirit was practically aghast as he stared at Shift.

'You have been wrong about people before.' Silva spoke quietly, yet somehow it carried across their camp like a battle horn being blown.

'Hey,' Auron snapped, veins of red in his aura as he pointed an accusing finger at the warrior. 'I chose to believe in you, and them, despite what you think.' The finger lowered, and Auron's face softened. 'It took me a while to warm to the idea. But your hearts were all in the right place.'

Silva stared into the fire just like Nicolas had. Who was she seeing in the flames?

'A lot of good it did us.' The bitterness in her voice was old, and well-rooted.

Auron stormed over to the warrior, putting himself between her and whatever apparitions were in the fire. 'They died doing what was right,' he whispered fiercely. 'Don't you *dare* sully that.'

When the warrior looked up at Auron, Nicolas could swear there were tears in her eyes. But it was hard to tell with the ethereal form between them.

'You are right,' she whispered. The breaking of her voice confirmed Nicolas's theory. 'I am sorry.'

'One day we're going to need to hear the full story of what happened between them,' Shift whispered in his ear.

Do we want to hear it?

'No, you bloody won't,' Auron growled, clearly overhearing Shift. Jaw set in a scowl, he vanished into the woods, his light slowly dimming the further away he got until the night swallowed him completely.

'I gather he's gone?' Tallith asked cautiously, as he followed their gazes in the direction Auron had left.

'He'll be back in a bit,' Nicolas said. He then turned to Silva. 'Are you—?'

The warrior's eyes locked on his, making it extremely clear that questions about her wellbeing would be very unwelcome. Instead, he offered her a sympathetic smile. She closed her eyes then looked away.

'Can I ask...' Tallith began hesitantly. 'How do you do it?'

'Do what?' Nicolas replied, after he realised he was the one being addressed.

'How do you do *this*?' Tallith asked, bolder now that Nicolas had engaged with him. 'Legend says you were just a village boy?'

Legend? Oh, for Deities' sake.

Part of him wanted to tell Tallith to sod off and mind his own business. 'I don't know,' he replied instead. 'I just...put one foot in front of the other and keep going.'

In his mind, it sounded shit. But Tallith seemed to take it like words of wisdom spoken by a divine prophet. 'Can you tell me one of your tales? Maybe the one about going to the Underworld?'

'Can you tell me how you heard about that?'

The sergeant stared at him blankly, before shrugging. But there was still that expectant look in his eyes.

'Fine,' Nicolas relented. 'So, I was killed by the demon Koth, kind of, and sent to the Underworld. There I met Sha'then, who'd been deposed by Avus Arex and was fighting a war to take back his kingdom. Auron and I joined him, got into the necromancer's lair, killed him, then we were sent back to Etherius as a reward.' Unsure what else to say on the matter, he simply punctuated his story with, 'The end.'

'What in the Underworld was that?'

Nicolas nearly jumped right out of the blanket as Auron suddenly appeared beside him.

Does the word tale *summon him instantly?*

'Deities, kid,' the spirit cried, arms wide. 'How have you been around me so long and *not* learned how to tell a story properly? Where's the theatrics, the dramatic hand movements, the pitch changes to match the mood of the event? That wasn't telling a story, that was listing a chain of events in a very boring way.' Auron shook his head and tutted. 'You showed a bit of promise when you were telling stories to Reg, so I know you've got it in you. Also. you didn't even mention riding the giant demon bear.'

'You can't leave out the giant demon bear. Only you would do that and not shout it from the rooftops,' Shift admonished in a very unhelpful way. The smirk they gave him suggested that whatever came next was going to be equally unhelpful. 'Auron, educate him, please.'

'Oh, I intend to,' the spirit replied firmly. 'Get up.'

'It's cold.'

'*It's cold*,' Auron said, mimicking his words in the tone of a pouty child. 'The fire is going, and it hasn't snowed for an hour. Get up. It's time to show you how to spin an epic tale.'

Nicolas grimaced as Shift pulled the shared blanket off him, so he got up grudgingly. Neither Tallith nor Silva rose to his defence. Instead, both appeared curious about what would happen next.

First Garaz, now they're all betraying me.

Auron circled him, looking him up and down. It was highly awkward.

'Right, first off: posture,' the spirit declared. 'Stand up straighter, chest out. It's all about the confidence. And with your chest out you can project more. No mumbled whispering malarkey.'

The others looked at him appraisingly.

Centre of attention. Yay.

'Do I really need to learn this?' he asked.

Auron stared at him. 'One day, you'll be recounting your deeds to people. A lot of those deeds will include me. I won't have you slouched over mumbling the epic tale of my afterlife. Besides, you've done a lot of good. Have a bit more pride in yourself.'

'At least you're learning from the master,' Shift teased.

He glared at his companion...though he couldn't really call Shift that anymore. They were now his...what? *Girlfriend? Beloved? Sweetheart?* He couldn't imagine Shift would take well to being referred to as any of those things. Either way, they were being annoying.

Deciding that the best thing to do was just go with it and get this over with as quickly as possible, Nicolas adjusted himself per his companion's request. Only Standing up straighter appeared to present more of his body to the cold.

'Better.' Auron sounded begrudging. 'Now, enunciation. Your voice comes from your lungs, not your throat.'

Nicolas allowed his posture to drop. 'What?'

'When you speak, drive the words out of your lungs. If you get the correct speaking voice, you'll have your audience rapt with your first syllables.'

'Are you jesting with me?'

Auron pointed an accusing finger at him. 'Behave, and do as I do.' The spirit turned so he was facing the same way as Nicolas. 'Repeat my words and my gestures. And if you don't, we'll keep doing this until you get it right.'

Please, Deities, no.

'Repeat after me...' Auron began to speak, utilising his full flare for storytelling, and Nicolas kept in step. 'So, this one time,' dramatic pause, 'my eternal soul was banished to the Underworld by a foul demonic creature.' He looked off into the middle distance. 'I thought my lot was to be tortured for all eternity, my body abused and broken until my mind could take it no more. But no, fate had worse in store for me than that.' Auron glared back at him. Evidently his voice wasn't matching the spirit's standards, so Nicolas put a little more gusto into it. 'But it turned out I was instead thrust into a war, not between men, but between the forces of the undead. The nefarious necromancer, Avus Arex, had overthrown Sha'then and planned to take over the living world. Though his undead forces were legion, we used stealth and deception and a giant demonic bear to break into the throne room for the final epic confrontation.' Nicolas chided himself; he was starting to get into this. 'There, my powerful enemy faced me down, no less than the fate of the entire afterlife at stake. He had magic, but not enough to deter me. Our battle was furious, but at last I stood tall, impaling my 'mortal' enemy on a giant skeletal tusk. And thus, the Underworld, and Etherius, were saved.'

Tallith clapped enthusiastically. Shift soon joined in, adding a couple of *whoops*. Even Silva managed an impressed nod.

Nicolas was exhausted. That whole process was a lot of exertion.

'And *that* is how you tell a story,' Auron said with a proud nod. 'We can flesh out the details later.'

'Much obliged,' Nicolas said with a bow, before reaching down and grabbing his sword.

'Where are you going?' Shift asked.

'To...um... Let's just say that all that theatrical gyrating awoke my bladder.'

Silva's lip curled in distaste. 'That is an awful way to put it.'

'You need a sword to go for a piss?' Shift asked.

'Do you know how many times I've been attacked answering the call of nature?' he replied. 'Enough times to know to carry a sword when I do.'

'The kid has a point,' Auron agreed. 'Answering the call of nature can be deadly.' The spirit made no attempt at all to be subtle about the glare he cast at Silva.

CHAPTER 19

Several days passed with no sign of Garaz—or anyone else, for that matter. Knowing the orc would be taking the shortest possible route home, a straight line, Nicolas and the others had no choice but to follow his course. This had meant leaving the main roads behind as they made their way through the kingdom of Ivilar. There were only smatterings of civilisation, like the odd farm, but at least there was no one threatening them with pitchforks. For now.

'So,' Shift said casually as they rode alongside Nicolas, 'do you think we'll get married in winter? Or do you fancy more of a summer wedding?'

Not only did Nicolas spit out the water he was in the middle of drinking, but he did so with such a jolt that he nearly slipped off his horse. Gripping the reins, he fought to right himself as he coughed aggressively. Finally, he regained a semblance of stability.

'Are you messing with me?' he asked carefully, studying the shapeshifter through narrowed eyes.

Shift's jaw set in an indignant scowl. 'You think our future together is a source of fun to me?'

'No,' he replied, knowing he had to tread very carefully here. 'But you like teasing people, doubly so when you're bored. And trudging across an endless white landscape is pretty boring. *And* you know I'm an easy target.'

Shift looked away, shaking their head. 'I was just thinking...' They held a hand up. 'It doesn't matter, actually.'

'No, no,' Nicolas replied quickly, fidgeting in the saddle. 'I just. Well, I always thought autumn would be best. Maybe in a forest somewhere. The brown and orange leaves would create a nice ambiance with the rising sun as we make our vows.' He clicked his fingers in a moment of inspiration, his voice becoming dreamier. 'We could arrange the fallen leaves into a path...with an arch at the end we could stand under, looking into each other's eyes as we pledge to spend our lives together.' In his mind, he could picture it perfectly.

'Wow,' Shift said with a guffaw. 'I knew you wanted to marry me. Deities, you've planned this to the last detail, haven't you? Did you come up with that in Babylon, or the moment you first saw me trapped in that wagon?' They let out a faux gasp. 'Is *that* the only reason you came to rescue me? So that you could get into my breeches and seduce me into marrying you? For shame, Nick.'

Nicolas ran his tongue across his teeth. He'd been had again. 'Ha bloody ha.'

'Don't be embarrassed,' Shift continued with a wide grin. 'I'm sure one day I shall bear you many children and greet you at the door of our cottage with a kiss and a freshly prepared meal when you return from your noble adventuring.'

'Up until about five minutes ago, I wouldn't have dreamed of leaving you with the kids whilst I buggered off adventuring,' Nicolas retorted. 'But *now*? Now I look forward to having you clean my armour when I return from all my daring battles with evil—'

'Quiet.'

At Silva's command, everyone went silent. The warrior tilted her head slightly, listening. Auron was doing a similar thing, frowning at the nearby treeline, which rose above them on either side of the sunken trail they were currently following.

Extending his senses, Nicolas caught some sounds. Snow crunching at a frantic pace. Branches being forced aside quickly. Panicked panting. Listening intently, he quickly picked out the direction the sound was coming from. Staring at the tree line, he put his hand on his sword.

With a puff of snow, a woman burst from the undergrowth, clutching her shoulders as if she were scared. In the moment before she slipped down the embankment, Nicolas caught red, tear-filled eyes.

The village woman slid down the slope and onto the trail. She didn't even acknowledge them before darting across it and trying desperately to scrabble up the other side. The snow betrayed her, and she slid back to the ground. She let out choked sobs.

Nicolas frowned down at her. 'Are you—?'

'There you are, sweetness.'

The speaker was definitely a man of ill repute. His beard was scraggly and his eyes wild, fixed on the woman. His hands opened and closed as if anticipating grabbing his prey. On his hip was an axe that appeared to be well-used. His leather armour was simple and covered with a fur cloak, but the double-horned helmet on his head was fancier. He licked his lips in the most disgusting manner before he slid down the slope himself.

The woman crawled away from him, eyes wide.

'There we go, lovely,' the man said in a gruff voice, rubbing his hands together. 'Got's you now. Time to see about that kiss I promised you were going to give me.' There was a leering manner to the man that made Nicolas's stomach clench in revulsion.

'Hey,' Nicolas shouted. 'We're right here.'

Incredulously, and acting as if he'd only just noticed them, the man half-turned toward them. His pudgy cheek sported a tattoo of the horned helmet he wore.

'So I see,' he said dismissively, before turning back to the woman again. 'Now, lovely, pucker up.'

Not while I'm here, you son of a bitch.

Nicolas jumped off his horse, landing heavily. 'Oi.' His voice echoed down the trail.

The man slowly turned back towards him, half surprised, half annoyed at the interruption.

'You will not be getting a kiss. You are going to leave her alone.'

The man let out a belly laugh. 'Oh, am I now?'

Nicolas covered the distance between them until they were stood face to face. 'Yup.'

The man leant toward him slightly as Nicolas slipped off his glove. 'Are you soft in the head, boy?' he spat, unleashing pungent breath to assault Nicolas's nostrils. 'Do you know who I am? I'm Bril Callow, second in the Horned Horde.' He pointed at his tattoo and his horned helmet to emphasise his point.

'And they are?' Nicolas asked with a frown as he closed his fingers into a fist.

'You *are* soft in the head,' Bril bellowed. 'Everyone knows the Horned Horde. We're the deadliest group of marauders hereabouts. Now, if you think I'm gonna let a runt like you ruin my fun then—'

Nicolas's fist cracked across Bril's jaw. The man toppled backwards and crashed to the ground...as much as you can crash in snow. Groaning, Bril tried to raise his head. Nicolas kicked him in the face then shook his hand and casually replaced his glove. This time, the marauder stayed down.

'You ever heard of that lot?' he asked Auron.

The spirit shook his head. 'Nope. Must be new. Seem to fancy themselves though.'

He gazed down at the unconscious thug in disgust. 'You'll have to show me how to dramatically retell this later. I just had the honour of knocking out the second in the Horned Horde, don't you know.'

'Amazing.' The way Tallith was gawking, it was more like the fist of one of the Deities Themselves had descended through the clouds and smacked Bril to the ground, and not Nicolas, who was really starting to become annoyingly accustomed to punching people.

Ignoring the undue adulation, Nicolas approached the woman slowly. Fear was still clear in her eyes, as was confusion. Slowly, she backed away from him, pressing herself into the embankment as best she could. Crouching, Nicolas held up his hands and gave his most reassuring smile.

'It's okay,' he said softly. 'You're safe now.'

He could see her mind working as she looked from him to Bril. Carefully, as if Nicolas might stab her at any second, she rose. Nicolas rose with her, keeping the smile steady. Then she threw herself at him. He was sure he made an awkward noise as the woman wrapped her arms around him tightly, sobbing into his furs. After a moment of uncertainty, he put his arms around her and held her.

Finally, the woman released him, stepping back and brushing herself off. The way she was gazing at him was eerily reminiscent of Sergeant Tallith's.

How did Auron ever get used to this?

'Thank you,' she said finally, her voice still a little frantic. 'Thank you so much. You saved me from that animal.'

Behind Nicolas, Bril groaned again. It stopped when someone punched him. By the time he heard the third punch, he correctly guessed it was Silva ensuring he stayed down.

'Think nothing of it,' he replied finally. 'Can we escort you home?'

The woman's eyes widened and her face paled. 'Home?' She began to lose control of her breathing again. Quickly, she grabbed Nicolas's collar. 'My home. It's where they are. Please. You have to help them.'

'Your village?' he asked.

'Yes, yes. The Horned Horde have settled in with us for the winter. They've been... They've done... Please...' She was so desperate for help she couldn't even string a sentence together.

'Okay, okay,' he soothed, taking her hands. 'We're going to help. Lead us to your village, and we'll do the rest.' Nicolas turned back to his companions. 'Looks like we have a detour, but...' He caught the way Auron was smiling at him. 'What?'

'Nothing, kid,' the spirit said. Though a certain amount of paternal pride was clear.

Nicolas struggled with the concept. As much as he liked it, it made him feel guilty. His parents were no longer around to be proud of him.

'Are you sure about this?' Shift said with mock fear. 'I'm not sure we're ready to face the Horned Horde. They're the deadliest group of marauders hereabouts...allegedly.'

'Absolutely sure,' he replied firmly. 'Silva?'

The warrior looked up from binding Bril. 'You are seriously asking if I am interested in fighting bandits?'

Not really, no.

'You know I'm with you,' Tallith said eagerly.

Here we go then. Another story for the legend. And the end of the story of the Horned Horde.

CHAPTER 20

Copying his companions, Nicolas edged forwards, raising his head just enough to peer over the ridgeline whilst doing his best to remain concealed. Though doing so felt strange when Auron was blatantly standing up straight, hands on his hips.

Hopefully, they don't have a necromancer with them, or we might as well have lit a beacon announcing our arrival.

He studied the village. Snow-covered homes clustered around a longhouse at the centre. Nicolas could've mistaken it for Small Pond, if it had a pond. Amongst the buildings, people moved. Luckily, it was easy to tell who was who, so there wouldn't be any accidental injuring of villagers. The bandits all wore those daft horned helmets as they strutted here and there, whilst the people who lived there shuffled around, their eyes downcast. Whenever a villager happened to catch the eye of one of their new overlords, or the bandit fancied a laugh, they would get shouted at, pushed, or have something thrown at them.

That's all about to come to an end.

'There are more of them in the hall,' the woman, Diedra, explained. 'Their leader, Granith One Horn, has turned the place into his court.'

Auron tutted loudly. 'These people and their stupid names.'

'How many are normally in there with him?' Silva asked.

'A handful.' Diedra shrugged. 'They don't like us looking at them, so we don't really count.'

'Coupled with the ten or so we can see, it's hardly a *horde*,' Shift remarked.

'It's enough,' Nicolas noted. Snow wasn't exactly ideal conditions for fighting in, and they were outnumbered. But the villagers weren't going to save themselves.

'Oh, and they have a wizard.'

Of course they do.

At least his companions were as displeased by Dierdra's revelation as he was.

'What kind of wizard?' Tallith asked.

The woman shrugged. 'I don't know. We've never seen him do any magic. But he wears a robe, and the others all seem wary of him, so I just assumed.'

'Could be just a visible deterrent,' Auron remarked. 'It wouldn't be the first time a bandit group pretended to have access to magic.'

And we don't. Thank you, Garaz, you giant prick.

'We can't take the chance it's just a guy playing dress-up,' Nicolas said thoughtfully. 'We need to do this as quietly as we can. I think we should wait until nightfall.'

'I agree.' Silva nodded. 'With their superior numbers and potential magic, it is best to use the element of surprise. If we go now, even these fools will see us coming.'

Though it made sense, Nicolas did hate his own idea. It meant more hours of the poor villagers being bullied. Part of him wanted to charge in, sword swinging. But the villagers could be hurt, which was contrary to their objective.

That's the Nick Carnage way, not the Nicolas way.

Inwardly, he cursed himself for using that name.

'Watch where you're going, old man!'

The bellowing voice drew his attention. Though they were a distance away, the way the bandit was stood, furiously rubbing his breeches, said *old man* had just spilled something on him. The rest of the village had become a horrified tableau around the scene, as if they were all frozen in place.

In front of the bandit, the old man stood proudly. Nicolas had an inkling the spillage hadn't been an accident.

The thug cocked his head, as if listening. 'You old fool,' the bandit raged, his voice carrying easily. 'Who do you think you are?'

Standing upright and defiant, the old man wagged his finger in the bandit's face, apparently telling him at great length who he thought he was, and most likely, who he thought the person he was talking to was. Whatever he said, the bandit didn't care for it, knocking the old man to the floor with a vicious backhand.

'Oh, is that so?' the horned warrior roared. 'Lads, we need to make an example of this one.'

The old man was hauled from the floor by two of the bandit's brethren.

'We go now,' Nicolas said firmly, drawing his sword.

'We will be in the open.' Silva wasn't arguing.

'Then we go carefully,' Shift replied, knives in hand.

Crawling over the lip of the ridge, Nicolas watched the old man get dragged to his feet. Defiance still radiated from him. Other members of the Horned Horde began to herd the villagers, striking anyone who moved too slowly for their liking. That actually worked in their favour, as the bandits were arranging the people in such a way that the majority of them had their backs to Nicolas and the others.

Moving quickly but carefully, the group crossed the gap between the ridge and the village. The Horned Horde was making such a din as they raised their axes and cheered that it easily concealed the sound of their steps in the snow. Auron had bounded on ahead of them. Soon, they reached the edge of the village.

Using the nearest building for cover, Nicolas peered out. With all the people standing around it was difficult to see clearly, but he caught a glimpse of the old man knelt on the ground, his head placed on a log. The bandits stood with their backs to him, and the villagers who were facing him were too transfixed by what was about to happen to notice the newcomers.

One of the Horned Horde – the one the man had offended, judging by the stain on his breeches – licked his thumb and ran it along the edge of the blade of the large axe that he held.

Auron was stood right beside the axe man. He caught Nicolas's eye and nodded.

'Okay,' he said quietly to the others. 'We still have the element of surprise. Let's sneak up on them and take out as many as we can before they realise what's going on. Auron is ready to help the old man.'

'There was a time I would be explaining this to you.' Silva smiling was odd.

'I've grown a bit since then,' he said with a half-smile. 'Let's go.'

Steeling himself, Nicolas emerged from behind the home. Carefully, he stalked forwards, willing the bandits in front of him to keep facing the other direction. They were actually right in the would-be executioner's line of sight, but he was so busy leering at his intended victim, he'd probably have missed a centaur stampede.

The bandits beat their fists on their chests rhythmically.

Using the background noise, Nicolas and the others sped up.

A sudden crash drew his attention.

What?

Turning, he saw Tallith, face frozen in horror as he looked at the barrels he'd just knocked over.

Bugger.

Nicolas could tell there were numerous eyes on him. Slowly, he turned back around. Ahead of him, a line of horn-helmeted bandits stared at him with confused expressions. The executioner had already raised his axe overhead, his urge to kill thwarted by the sudden interruption.

'*Auron, now,*' Nicolas cried.

'*Finger poke of doom.*'

The bandit cried out as an ethereal finger jabbed him in the eye. His hands opened to clasp his ruined eye, and the axe fell. Auron caught it and launched it, and one of the bandits facing Nicolas jerked forwards as the axe embedded into his back. He crashed to the ground, and his companions looked back to try to see who'd thrown it.

Using the distraction, Nicolas uttered a battle cry and charged.

The nearest marauder was still swinging back to face him as Nicolas introduced his abdomen to the *Dawn Blade*. Before the bandit had even hit the ground, he'd stabbed another in the gut.

The moment of surprise Auron had bought them didn't last very long. Soon the men of the Horned Horde – minus the five Nicolas, Shift and Silva had accounted for – got their wits about them and attacked.

Nicolas deflected an incoming axe using his vambrace, the dwarf-made armour thankfully living up to its crafter's boasting. With two quick swings, he cut the attacker in the back of the leg then across the ribs. Swinging the blade, he parried an incoming axe and sliced his would-be killer from shoulder to hip. Nicolas tried not to gag as blood splattered his armour and cheek.

A worried cry caught his attention. Behind him, Tallith was wavering under the ferocious assault of one of the horde. That man struck down on Tallith's sword again and again, forcing him to a single knee under the onslaught. Flicking a knife from his belt, Nicolas launched it. The problem was, as he held the *Dawn Blade*, he'd used his left—weaker—hand to throw the knife. Instead of embedding in the marauder's neck as planned, the hilt struck him on the temple. But it gave Tallith an opening to finish the bandit. And judging by the look on the sergeant's face, it was as if Nicolas had planned it exactly that way.

And then it was done. The snow had been grotesquely decorated with splashes of red. Silva hadn't been fussy when it came to chopping off limbs, and there were squelchy bits hanging from wounds that he'd rather not look at.

'You were right,' he grinned to Shift. 'They definitely stretched the definition of the term *horde*.'

The shapeshifter stared at him aghast as Nicolas winced at his own stupidity. They were both aware that fate didn't like you saying things like that.

And, lo, as if on cue, the door to the longhouse opened and out poured another, larger group of warriors.

'Idiot,' Shift said with a shake of their head.

Nicolas lined up with the others and prepared to meet the charge. Though standing and waiting whilst armed men ran at him was very contrary to his survival instincts.

'A fireball would be handy right now,' Shift commented as the bandits closed, their breath fogging in front of them.

An army of knights would be handy right now.

'Our blades alone will be enough,' Silva said, giving off her usual aura of relishing combat.

Instead of barrelling into them, axes swinging, the Horned Horde's charge came to an abrupt halt as snowballs hit them in the face. At his side, Auron launched the snowballs, laughing like an excited child. Soon, the villagers joined in, shouting something that sounded a bit like *wololo*. It must've been some kind of local battle cry or chant. Either way, the marauders flailed under the onslaught.

Nicolas and his companions charged.

The warrior he ran toward readied himself, a small axe in each hand. His smile said he relished furious hand-to-hand combat, but he didn't get his wish. A snowball hit him in the face with a *whumph*, and Nicolas ran him through.

Using his agility and superior footwork, Nicolas ducked and dived and swept through the warriors, sword swinging. Silva and Shift engaged in an equally deadly dance, until the sum total of the horde was a load of bodies lying in the snow.

Several of the bandits had survived, though they would possibly soon wish they hadn't. The villagers inched towards their groaning bodies until they became bold enough to set about their captors with fists, feet, and anything that happened to be lying within arm's reach. Tracking his blade around, Nicolas checked to make sure no more were going to suddenly appear.

The only thing that did appear were their spirits. Confused, ethereal figures shimmered into existence over the bodies of the men they'd once inhabited. Closing his eyes, Nicolas shook his head. He didn't want to see ghosts every time he killed someone. Killing them was bad enough.

When he opened his eyes, though, they were gone.

Hopefully, that means I get a choice.

'May the Deities bless you,' the old man cried, as he approached Nicolas with several others who weren't currently beating horned bandits to death. 'You delivered us from the grip of evil. We are eternally grateful, noble heroes.'

Sheepishly, Nicolas waved away their blessings. They'd been passing, and it had been the right thing to do, nothing more. He didn't need commending for that. 'Please, think nothing of it.'

Not wanting to look into the villagers' adoring eyes, he found his gaze wandering until it lingered on the open door of the village hall.

We aren't quite done doing the right thing.

'I take it the leader's in there?' he asked, pointing with the *Dawn Blade*.

The old man spat fiercely on the ground, as did several others. 'He's in there, all right,' he barked. 'Nasty piece of work, but no match for you lot, I'm sure.'

'Shall we?' Silva asked, already striding towards the building.

Apparently so. Nicolas jogged quickly to catch up with her, the villagers cheering in their wake.

CHAPTER 21

The group stopped short of the open door to the longhouse. There was no clear line of sight to whatever or whoever was inside. Nicolas caught the vague shapes of tables and chairs, but not much beyond that.

'Shall we call him out here to fight?' Nicolas asked.

'It's probably warmer in there,' Shift remarked.

'Not with the door open.'

Shift winked at him. 'There's only one way to be sure.'

Shame it's open. I could kick it in and...for Deities' sake. I'm turning into Auron.

Shaking his head, he walked into the village hall.

There was nothing fancy about the place. It was basically a big room with some tables and chairs in it. On one side there was a large fireplace housing a roaring fire, above which sat the skulls of some animals likely hunted by the villagers.

I might knock those off later.

The tables were littered with the debris of festivities. Half-eaten food and drink was everywhere. A lot of it over the floor. The Horned Horde had nothing in the table manners department.

Were they all drunk? Maybe that's why it was so easy...

Beside the fireplace, a man lounged in a chair. He appeared to be nude. At his side stood a robed man with scraggly hair and wild eyes, who played with his own fingers nervously. A glint of metal caught Nicolas's eye. Behind the pair, in the corner of the room, stood a giant suit of armour. It was broad and tall, too big for any man. The ribs of the armour were open, as if someone could slip between them and stand in it. Atop the helmet was a single, long horn.

In the chair, the man idly regarded the trespassers as he chewed loudly on a leg of meat. Nicolas winced as the man stood up, but thankfully he was wearing a loincloth. Tossing the meat into the fireplace, he stood with his hands on his hips. The wizard cowered behind his master's chair.

'Granith One-Horn?' Nicolas enquired.

'Tis I,' the man replied in a deep voice, a piece of half-chewed meat falling from his mouth. 'So, what've we got 'ere then? Some 'eroes?' He tilted his head to look past them. 'You took care of my boys then?'

'Yup,' Shift said breezily. 'No more horde for you.'

Granith laughed heartily. 'I can always find more muscle. That's never been a problem.'

The wizard tittered as if this were some kind of private joke.

'Well, it's winter, so finding some will take a while, and we are here now,' Nicolas replied. 'Therefore, I'm assuming you're going to yield?'

Come on. Just once, can one of them yield?

'You demand it, not ask for it politely.' Auron tutted in his ear.

More booming laughter, more spilled, half-chewed food. 'You assume wrong, hero.'

Must people keep calling me that?

'Four on two.' Shift smiled sarcastically. 'That's all I'm saying.'

Granith looked at the shy wizard and guffawed. 'Four on one,' he bellowed. 'I'm going to kill you all myself. Old Shazard here is just to make sure I'm at my peak when I do.'

'What's he talking about?' Nicolas whispered.

Granith walked to the armour and slipped between the plates so he was stood in it.

What in Etherius was he thinking? The man would have to eat a lot more to fit in that armour, and he barely kept the food he *did* eat in his mouth.

Auron's white eyes widened. 'Oh no.'

Half covered by the chair, the wizard worked his hands in circles until yellow energy gathered around them. With a shrill cry, he launched it at Granith. The pulse struck him in the chest then seemed to extend through his body like a wave. Granith's laughter became deeper as his body expanded. He went from barely reaching the bottom of the helmet to the armour fitting perfectly around his now juggernaut-sized form.

Oh shit. Shitty shit.

With a roar, Granith punched the floor, his huge fist crashing through the wood with a loud crack.

'The wizard's a boon granter.' Auron sighed.

'A *what?*' Silva asked.

'They're very rare,' he explained. 'Basically, they learn magic to empower others. Bit of a daft discipline. Why learn magic just to make others stronger? They're generally a weird lot. A bit voyeuristic.'

It certainly didn't look daft from where Nicolas was standing.

All those logs Silva had me lifting, and this asshole gets magic muscles. Not fair.

With a snarl, Granith lifted the chair he'd been sitting on singlehanded and smashed it on the floor, shattering it into numerous pieces.

Show off.

'Any suggestions?' Shift asked.

'Yeah, piss him off,' Auron replied.

'Any *serious* suggestions?' Nicolas cried.

'*Piss him off,*' the spirit hissed. 'Stop him thinking about what he's doing, just keep him angry and reacting. That's your advantage. Short temper is a general side effect of being a giant, muscled asshole. Keep him unbalanced, and strike at the opportune moment.'

Nicolas rubbed his hand over his face. This wasn't getting any more sensible, but Auron seemed so damned sure. With a sigh, he lowered his sword and, keeping his face neutral, began to address the bandit leader. 'I'm sorry, but I can't fight you today.'

'What?' Granith grunted, already on the back foot. 'Are you serious? Why not?'

Here we go then.

'Look, you called me a hero, and that's not really true, in my opinion, anyway, but I'm working on it. Maybe one day, I'll have this amazing legacy that will be told, or sung, from town to town. And I don't really want part of that legacy to be my battle with a man dressed as a unicorn.'

A sudden guffaw caught Nicolas's attention. What surprised him was that it was Silva who'd laughed.

'I am *not* dressed as a unicorn,' Granith boomed, spittle flying from between his teeth. Thankfully, no meat though. 'My armour is modelled on the mighty rhino.'

'Not well,' Nicolas fired back.

'You know, I think you're right.' Shift sighed. 'There really is no glory in fighting a unicorn enthusiast.'

Granith was seething so hard Nicolas could hear his ragged breathing from the other side of the hall. 'I am a *rhinoceros.* A glorious and fearsome rhino who stomps everything in his path.'

'The important thing is that *you* believe that.' Nicolas smiled. 'Because I'm not sure anyone else is convinced.' Thoughtfully, Nicolas pursed his lips. 'Do you have your own unicorn name? Do your unicorn dress-up friends call you Dream Cuddles or something?'

That did it.

With a roar, Granith dipped his head and charged. Suddenly, pissing him off didn't seem like a sound strategy at all. Apparently, he could move very fast for his size—most likely another boon of the wizard's spell.

Concentrate.

He'd been staring at the incoming horn for too long. At the last second, he jumped aside. But Granith wasn't so easily dodged. The bandit leader flicked his head to the side, and pain flared in Nicolas's left arm. Now he was closer, he could see the horn was actually a long blade, and it had his blood on it.

Booming laughter echoed around the hall as the giant bandit leader slowed to a stop. 'First blood to me.'

Nervously, he checked his arm. The cut wasn't too deep, but it was bleeding. His instinct was to tend to it right away, but somehow he didn't think Granith was the sort to give an opponent the opportunity to take a break from their fight to dress his wound.

'Don't get distracted kid,' Auron chided.

He looked at his arm again. *No fear of that.*

Especially now they'd lost the advantage. Granith was no longer enraged and liable to make a mistake.

Well done, Nicolas.

Reaching behind him, the bandit leader produced a large, two-handed axe. This time, Nicolas dodged the swinging blade in plenty of time, and the floor that'd been beneath his feet was turned to kindling.

Swinging again, Granith spun his body in a complete arc, the weapon sailing in a perfect circle to take a chunk out of the wall. The single worst part was when he saw the axe blade slow to a crawl as it bore down on Shift, his heart clenching in his chest as ice cold fear ran through his veins instead of blood for a single, terrible moment. But he needed not fear. Shift threw themselves aside before any decapitations occurred.

'Kid,' Auron shouted from the door. 'When I said *piss him off*, that didn't mean do it once and stop. Think, kid.'

The spirit had a point, but he doubted the unicorn jibe would work again. With a sigh, he realised he'd have to go for more low-hanging fruit. Literally.

'So, that horn, it's pretty big,' he shouted as he tossed himself aside to avoid the axe blade again.

'So?' Granith snarled, heaving the large weapon at Silva.

'Well, I just wondered if there's a reason.' Nicolas pointedly looked down.

'What?' Granith grunted.

'Maybe it's something fancy to show the maidens, so they aren't...disappointed later.'

The bandit leader's lips worked wordlessly as he tried to understand what Nicolas was alluding to. Then it hit him, and his face reddened with rage. Granith charged again. But this time, Nicolas didn't freeze. Instead, he rolled to the side in plenty of time as Granith's horn embedded itself in the wall.

'*Dammit,*' the bandit leader roared as he pulled to try to extract his now-stuck horn.

Nicolas wanted to press his attack, but Granith's armour was really thick. His only real weakness was his head, but...

As an idea hit him, Nicolas charged forward at speed. Timing it perfectly, he leapt from the floor and kicked the bandit leader in the side of the helmet with both feet and his full bodyweight behind it. Really, the strap should've kept the helmet on Granith's head, but luck favoured Nicolas, and the bandit leader staggered back, dazed as his helmet remained pinned in the wall. He clasped his throat, gagging where the helmet strap had caught taught across his neck. He'd even dropped his axe. Flipping to his feet, Nicolas stabbed him right in the chest. Coughing up a glob of blood, Granith cried out in pain.

Then a wave of yellow energy engulfed him. The wound knitted itself back together, and Granith became revitalised. The giant fist caught Nicolas before he could react. Next thing he knew, he was on the floor staring up at the ceiling, which shook as if there were an earthquake.

Bloody wizard.

His face was numb. That was bad. That meant a lot of pain later. There was the taste of blood in his mouth and wetness on his chin and cheeks. But there was no time to concern himself with that; a giant boot was descending towards his face at speed.

The thump when it hit the floor where Nicolas's head had been made his heart skip a beat, even as he rolled himself away. If only he'd rolled far enough. Again, the speed of the giant was surprising. The boot struck him in the ribs with an audible crack.

Nicolas gagged as a hand wrapped around his throat and lifted him into the air.

'Not so funny now, asshole.' Granith sneered.

Nicolas had no idea what the bandit leader planned to do to him. Everything was happening too fast for him to even consider the terrible options. Before the final blow could be delivered, though, Shift appeared on Granith's back, driving their knives down into either side of his neck. The bandit leader's eyes widened in shock and pain as he coughed up blood, his hand opening, dropping Nicolas to the ground with a teeth-jarring *thud*.

Hitting the floor hard, Nicolas heard a faint yelp on the other side of the room. He guessed Silva had silenced the wizard before he could cast some kind of stupid resurrection spell.

Though everything was a bit blurry, Shift's familiar form stood over him, looking down at him wide-eyed and sucking their teeth.

'Dat bad?' He groaned weakly.

'You won't be able to kiss me for a while,' they said with a sympathetic smile. 'So, I'll settle for a passionate embrace as thanks for me saving you again.'

'Dod worry.' He chuckled. The chuckling stopped as he realised how he was talking. 'Jusd geb be ub den Garaz cad ged all of dis...'

Oh crap. No instant healing magic.

Taking a deep breath, he gently touched his nose, instantly regretting it as white light flashed before his eyes. It looked like the days of easy recovery were over for them. It was like the floor had vanished beneath his feet. He'd been beaten, injured, even whipped once, but Garaz had always been there to heal the worst of it, and now he was...gone. Not that he could use healing magic now anyway. It had a bad effect on him since his return from the dead.

'That doesn't look pleasant,' Auron commented as he hovered over him. 'Are you okay?'

With his voice the way it was, he simply replied with a thumbs-up.

'I've seen worse,' the spirit said as he rubbed his chin. 'Silva should be able to pop that back into place.

'*Whad?*'

Before he could react, a hand reached across his face and grabbed his nose. The scream he gave, loud and passionate, was still not enough to drown out the sound of the *crunch*.

CHAPTER 22

E merging from the building, Nicolas was quite surprised to see the assembled villagers awaiting him. A sea—well, pond—of faces stared at him expectantly. After a few moments of awkwardness, he finally realised what they were waiting for.

'Gradith is dead,' he said. 'You are free.'

Stupid nose.

A resounding cheer rose from men, women, and children alike. This was followed by lots of mutual hugging and the occasional impulsive dance. Then they began to move towards him, as if responding to some unspoken invitation.

'Enjoy your moment, kid,' Auron counselled.

He tried to force a smile as the people closed around him like a spiked wall. He had nowhere to go as the throng surrounded him. The numerous thanks overlapped into a wave of noise, from which he could make out no single sentence. He thought he caught several people blessing him. The noise was almost oppressive, making him want to back away. So much so, that when the old man raised his hand to shush the crowd, Nicolas could've kissed him on the mouth.

Appearing well for a man who'd just had his head on a chopping block, the old man gave a rough approximation of a courtly bow. One he nearly didn't come back up from. 'On behalf of our village,' he declared, holding his back, 'I want to thank you and your noble companions for coming to our aid. If it weren't for you, that scum would've been here all winter, pillaging our stocks and ravaging our women.'

Strangely, several of the younger women in the village looked like they wanted to ravage him.

I'm not Auron, so they'll have to live with their disappointment.

'Thik dothig ob it,' he replied finally. 'We were bassig, and you deeded helb.'

'Just passing, in winter?' one man cried. 'No, no. You're a blessing from the Deities themselves.'

'You certainly are to our village,' the old man said with a nod of agreement. 'But please, young sir, what is your name?'

'Nicolas Carnegie.' Knowing his voice was not behaving, he said his name slowly and with purpose. Normally, he'd introduce himself using his full name, but his voice still sounded weird, and who knew what it would do to *Percival.*

The old man clapped his hands once. 'A name that will go down in the annals of our history. It is a pleasure to know you, Nick—'

'Nicolas Carnegie,' he cut in quickly, lest the old man use the moniker that had somehow dogged him across all Etherius. Which he knew was coming, because it always did.

'Oh apologies.' The old man chuckled. *I was right then.* 'Nicolas Carnegie. These old ears, don't you know. But pray tell, are you and your companions knights? Or heroes from the Hall?'

'This is the new *Dawnblade.*'

Thank you so much, Silva.

There was a moment of confused silence. 'Forgive me,' one villager said. 'But we thought Auron of Tellmark was...well...older.'

Beside him, the spirit raised an eyebrow. 'Many times, I've been told I can pass for twenty-one,' he scoffed.

What blind hags enchanted him to believe that bullshit?

'As I said, this is the new one.' *Silva's being helpful today.* 'Auron of Tellmark passed his mantle on to Nicolas, who took up his sword to forge his own legend.'

Nicolas smiled at Silva, hoping his eyes were telling her to shut up.

'And he already has many great deeds to his name.' And Silva began listing them, to the villagers' delight.

Nicolas wished he could retract his head into his armour like a turtle until it was all over.

'By the Deities,' the old man gasped, as stunned as his fellow villagers, as Silva finished her brief recounting. 'We will speak of the day you came to our village for generations.'

Please don't. 'I would be odoured to be pard ob your billage's history.' It seemed like the thing to say.

'It's good to have brave young men like you out there,' the old man continued, playing to the crowd now. 'Too many undesirables about nowadays. We even saw an orc pass three nights hence.'

'Ad orc?' The old man looked uncertain as to the reaction he'd provoked. 'Whad cad you tell be aboud de orc?'

'Ah,' he replied. 'Tracking the fiend, are you?'

'Sobethig like dat.'

'Good, good.' He nodded, before leaning in and lowering his voice. 'Can't have creatures like that roaming around. Mr Helstrum knows all about it. He knows what they're up to.' The old man tapped the side of his nose.

'Ideed.' Nicolas fought back the disgusted reaction at that name before it showed. 'Where did you see hib?'

The old man gestured to one of the women, who seemed almost delighted to be chosen to speak. 'Saw him in one of the fields yonder,' she said brightly. 'Heading north. Big guy in a red cloak. I saw him through the bushes when I were out picking berries. Made sure I kept my distance, of course. It could've been The Visitor for all I know. Matches the tales.'

Closing his eyes, Nicolas allowed the relief at that news to sink in. They were heading in the right direction. But they'd lost some time and needed to make it up.

But first.

'Cad you direcd be to your healer blease?' he asked, gesturing to his wounded arm and nose.

The instant he drew the villagers' attention to it, some of them sucked their teeth. It must've been that bad. 'Ain't got one.'

'You...dod hab a healer?' he said slowly, with a sigh. 'I deed do ged dis stitched ub.' He turned to his companions. 'Botion?'

'We do not have anything that will take care of...all that,' Tallith said diplomatically. 'The ones we have will do for minor cuts and bruises, but...'

I need more than a little pick-me-up.

He guessed that his skull might be fractured. His ribs too. Everything seemed brighter than it should be, and a little hazy. But they couldn't waste time whilst he recuperated.

'We have a seamstress?' the old man ventured.

Ah. 'I'b dod sure...'

'It is fine,' Silva interrupted, stepping to his side. 'I have stitched up many of my own wounds in the past. I just need a needle and thread.'

The warrior raised a confused eyebrow at the horrified expression Nicolas gave her. As much as he appreciated the idea, Silva was known to be a little heavy handed. And impatient. He certainly did not want her going at his arm with anything sharp.

'De seabstress will be fide.' Smiling made his nose hurt. 'I'b sure she'll do a gread job.'

Judging by the long stare he got before Silva handed him the potion from her bag, she was a bit offended. He'd have to make it up to her later. He'd put it down to a concussion or something.

'Dank you.' Taking the bottle the warrior had given him, he unstopped it and drank the potion inside.

With a deep breath, he waited for a reaction. He didn't expect to fly into the air and suddenly grow mighty muscles like Granith, but something would've been nice. After a few moments, the blurred edges in his vision sharpened slightly. That was something, at least.

'Before we get you stitched up, I just wanted to ask,' the old man interrupted behind them. 'Just now...it sounded like you might be leaving urgently, and...well. We were hoping to throw a celebration in your honour.'

'We...hab do go. We hab do ged after dad orc. Tibe is ob de essence.'

'I understand.' Despite his words, their intended host was clearly upset they couldn't stay. 'At least let us give you some supplies for the road.'

Nicolas smiled. 'Thad's very kind ob you.'

'Now, let's see about that arm.' The old man took him gently by the shoulder and began to lead him toward one of the houses. Waving, he gestured for a young maiden to follow them. She was obviously the seamstress.

'Just make sure you give that orc one for us, won't you.? Filthy green cur,' one of the villagers cried with enthusiasm.

Nicolas's smile tightened. These people had obviously been at the Helstrum pamphlets too often, but he didn't care to make an argument of it now. They had to go.

'Nicolas Carnegie,' the old man repeated to himself. 'People will hear about you.'

'If this keeps up, we'll need an extra horse to carry your reputation around.' Shift smirked, following along. Maybe they didn't trust the maiden. The seamstress was certainly making doe eyes at him.

'Fuddy,' he replied dryly.

'What's the matter?'

For a moment, he didn't want to say, but the words spilled out anyway. 'Eber sidce I lebd hobe, all I seeb do meed are badits, cribidals and billains. Is Etherius jusd a terrible blace?'

'I've seen a lot of bad in my life, kid,' Auron answered. Apparently, everyone was following him to get his arm stitched up. 'Unfortunately, the life you've found yourself in attracts it, or you go running towards it. It doesn't mean the whole world is bad. It's just the bad is more prominent for people like you and me.'

He wasn't convinced. All he'd seen of the world was death, murder, and war. Everywhere he went he saw the *bad*, as Auron put it, and ended up having to fight it. Could Etherius be saved, if every tavern, every village they visited was infested by it?

And is Garaz part of the problem?

'Here we go,' the old man said with a smile as he gestured to the door of the hut he'd led them too. 'In you go. Young Erin here will have you stitched up in no time.'

Glancing at the seamstress, she gave Nicolas a sheepish look suggesting that she may not be able to live up to the old man's optimism. But he couldn't just walk around with his arm bleeding, so whatever help he could get would be appreciated. Getting it stitched up would give it a chance to heal properly, though it was bound to leave a scar.

What's one more?

CHAPTER 23

For the fourth time, he pulled up his sleeve and checked his arm. The seamstress had clearly been nervous, but she'd done a nice job. The stitching was very neat. Staring at it, he imagined how the cut would look once it was healed. Initially, he had written it off as just another scar. Now though...*it would be another scar.* One to add to the growing collection. Harpy talons, a whip and an arrow had already left their permanent marks on his body. In truth, there were probably a couple more if he cared to check. Though this one was small by comparison, it was another reminder of a near miss that could have easily been the end of him.

How many near misses do I have left before someone or something finally kills me? Or I just become a giant walking scar?

'Stop playing with it,' Shift admonished. 'You'll end up opening the wound, then Silva will have to re-sew it.'

Knowing his companion was right, he let his sleeve drop. He should be elated. They'd survived another battle, and rescued a whole village. The people of said village would certainly be celebrating.

Once they finally disperse.

The uncomfortable sensation of being watched made the hairs on the back of his neck rise. Though they were far down the road from the village, its inhabitants were still assembled at the edge of it, watching them intently, as if to try and sear this memory into their minds forever. Somehow, Nicolas doubted they'd ever forget the day the Horned Horde came to visit.

Speaking of...Don't they have to get to work removing all those corpses from their village?

Thinking of those behind him reminded Nicolas of the last time he'd left a village with such a fanfare. Hablock. When he'd first left to deliver the message that had blighted his life. Back then, he had a home and a family. Now, he had no home, a very new family and a different quest every other week. Despite himself, he glanced back, and the crowd cheered. Even muted by distance, he could still clearly hear the passion in their hurrahs.

'Why do you get all the adulation?' Silva asked. 'We all take part in your adventures.'

'It's because the kid is...was...so unsuitable for it. People like an under-dog,' Auron answered.

'What he means is that Nicolas is nice and you're scary.' Shift made the remark sound casual, but they were clearly watching the warrior's reaction in their peripheral vision.

Silva made a big show of staring at Shift until they looked away.

'Can I just say that I'm so sorry for what happened back there,' Tallith said suddenly. He spoke quickly, as if worried nervousness might close his mouth at any second. 'I just slipped and hit the barrels and then...I can't believe I gave you all away.'

'Doh harb dud.' Nicolas smiled reassuringly. 'You cad hardly be held accoundable bor sdow fallig. Besides, I'b had edough accideds like dat byself.'

'Like the time you bumped into the gangster in a gaming hall who could recognise you, and you didn't realise,' Silva said.

'Or the time you dropped a large case and gave us away on a pirate ship.' Shift smirked.

'Or the time you fell from your horse during a fight,' Auron added.

'Yes, danks everywud,' Nicolas replied testily 'I ab still idjured, you dow, so you cad go easy on be, ib you like?' He touched his nose tenderly; it rewarded him with a throb.

If only I had a remedy to just make it go away.

But that wasn't going to happen. It might take weeks for his nose to heal. Then there were all the other potential internal injuries. In his mind, Nicolas tried to focus on his body. But instead of finding any real sources of pain, it conjured a hundred fake ailments, all crying for his attention, telling him he'd be dead soon if he didn't act.

And then there's my voice. I might have to become a bit of a brooding warrior type for a while. Saying little. People will think I'm enigmatic, but really, I just sound like an idiot when I talk.

'How is the arm?' Shift asked.

'Sore.'

Shift, despite their earlier warning, gestured for Nicolas to show them. Carefully, he rolled his sleeve up. Cold prickled against his skin. It was hardly new. Even with the furs and armour, the cold had a way of slipping in and chilling.

Shift took his arm gently and examined the stitching. 'It *is* good work. Though I'm sure that was more to do with the woman wanting to impress you than any actual skill.' Shift stared at the stitches like they offended them. Then something caught their attention. They squeezed his arm. 'This is getting bigger. All those logs Silva has you lifting are doing the trick.'

'I hobe it doesd't wasde away. I wod't be liftig buch wid dis arb bor a while.'

'I might be able te help with that.'

At the group's cries of surprise, the horses startled and reared. Quickly, Nicolas stroked and soothed his mount before he was thrown off.

'Wod are you doig here?' he cried, as he realised who'd spoken.

At the crossroads, Snaggletooth Joe smiled from the seat of his wagon, which was pulled by one of the mangiest looking donkeys Nicolas had ever seen. It looked like it was one loud cough away from death. And how it pulled the large wagon, which appeared to be Joe's home, was anyone's guess.

'Well, young'un,' Joe said with a single-toothed grin after slapping his knee, 'I'm a travellin' trader. Clue's in the word *travellin'*.'

'In winter?' Silva scoffed, sword at the ready. The accusatory tone was poorly masked, if she was bothering at all. 'I go where the business is.' Joe shrugged. 'What a nice coincidence te meet ye folk hereabouts. I loves a good coincidence. Usually means I'll make some coin. Speaking o'...' A bony finger pointed at Nicolas's nose. 'Ye need some help with that, sonny?'

'No, no,' Silva shouted. 'First you tell us how you are here. No sane trader travels in winter.'

Joe's mouth fell open then closed and opened again several times. 'Well, missy, people need supplies in winter too. Can't leave me customers hangin' just cause o' a bit o' snow. Not a good business model at all, missy.'

'*Missy*?' Silva hissed.

'Yes, bud—'

Joe jumped down from his wagon. 'Hush now, folks,' he said with a dismissive wave of his hand. 'We can stands here in the cold jabberin' away all day. Or I could get the young fella something te fix that broken hooter o' his, lest his companion there don't come near him again.'

Nicolas looked at Shift questioningly. They shrugged apologetically. 'It really isn't pretty.'

'Fix by dose,' he cried as he looked back at Joe.

Joe shuffled to the back of his wagon as Nicolas dismounted and followed. It was almost a small shack on wheels, very ramshackle, with various items hanging from hooks all over the outside.

'Sure I gots just the thing.' Joe stopped suddenly and turned to face him, studying his face. 'Sum leeches may do that hooter the world o' good,' he said, thoughtfully looking towards his wagon.

'Doh leeches, dank you,' Nicolas replied quickly.

'Fair enuf young 'un,' the trader shrugged. 'In that case, I'm gonna brew you up summit to take care o' that nicely.

'Ub, waid,' Nicolas called quickly.

Joe scratched his chin idly as he waited for Nicolas to continue.

'I struggle wid healig bagic. I kind ob...died once. Add I'b still a bit...dead.'

'Pish,' Joe said, waving a hand in the air. 'Already know that. I'll whip up just the thing...providin' you 'ave the coin, of course?' The trader rubbed his fingers together pointedly.

Nicolas gestured for Shift to join them. Walking over, the shapeshifter took a pouch from their belt. Opening the string, they reached inside. Before they could, Joe snatched it out of their hands.

'Hey,' Shift snapped.

The trader bounced the purse in his hand a couple of times, one eye closed. 'This oughta about cover it,' he declared. 'It's a very special recipe.'

'You don't steal from me, you little—'

'Do ye want him healed or not?'

That doused Shift's ire nicely. 'Fine,' they said through gritted teeth.

With no more preamble, Joe ascended the steps and disappeared into the wagon. The moment he did, Shift took a piece of junk from the side of his wagon and pocketed it.

'What?' they asked at his look. 'Thieves code. If someone steals from you, you steal from them right away. It restores the balance.'

'What an odd fellow,' Auron remarked as the group sat there, listening to the sound of fervent rummaging within.

'How does he dow dad?' Nicolas huffed, shaking his head. 'How do beoble dow stuff aboud be?'

All he got in response were shrugs.

After a few minutes and a lot of *where is its,* Joe finally emerged triumphantly, holding up a small green vial. Descending from his wagon, he shuffled over to Nicolas, unstopped the vial and handed it to him. 'This oughta clear that up.' The trader beamed. 'One o' my own homemade remedies. Good for what ails ye, especially if yer a little on the dead side.'

'I ab dod...' Nicolas controlled his temper. 'Neber bind.'

Raising the bottle, he held it up to the light. There was definitely liquid in there. Did he trust it? Kind of. He had to admit, Joe's amulets had actually taken off the worst bite of the cold. None of the group had been sure about them until they'd taken them off. They went back on again pretty quickly. And Joe was wearing four of them.

It appeared Joe was honest in regards to his products. But he hadn't had to drink the amulets, and he really wished he hadn't smelled what was in the bottle. It certainly didn't smell like something someone ought to put in their mouth, and that was *with* his nose not working at peak efficiency.

I suppose if it is some kind of poison, at least Silva will kill him moments after I'm dead.

Closing his eyes, he put the bottle to his lips and downed the liquid. Seconds later, his tongue emerged from his mouth as the taste of the foul concoction caused his face to spasm in a way that drew chuckles from Auron and Shift. It tasted a really odd combination of sweet and sour.

After a couple of *acks* and a cough, Nicolas wiped the residue of the potion from his mouth. Only then did he notice the tingling around his nose. *Something* was happening. Hopefully it was good. Around him, all his companion's eyes became wide as the sensation grew then stopped abruptly.

'Handsome again.' Shift half-smiled. 'Now I don't have to go to the trouble of finding someone else to keep me warm at night.' They winked playfully at his outraged expression.

Instead of responding, Nicolas tentatively touched his nose—first a little prod then grasping it. Everything appeared to be where it should, and no pain.

'It worked.' He closed his eyes and tilted his head back.

Thank the Deities.

Rolling up his sleeve, he checked his arm. The wound was healed, but the stitches were still there. Getting those out later was going to be fun.

'Told ye.' Joe grinned.

'Thank you,' Nicolas said with feeling.

'Ye already thanked me.' Joe jiggled his cloak, and coins clinked together within.

Without another word, the trader returned to his wagon. With a grunt, he hefted himself into the seat and took the reins, urging the donkey to action. It pulled the creaking wagon with surprising ease.

'Be seein' ye.' Joe waved. A few moments later, he'd disappeared around the corner of the trail.

Nicolas took another moment to massage his nose and relish in the fact that he could talk normally again. 'That potion is fantastic, an absolute marvel. No mispronunciation. I could sing if I wanted to. *La, la, la, la-la.'*

'Before you join the Guild of Bards,' Silva said dryly, 'we may want to stop Joe and stock up on some of those potions. The road ahead is long, and I doubt this is the only time we'll need them with...' She trailed off before saying, *'with our healer gone.'*

'That's a good point,' Shift said. 'I'll fetch him back.'

They ran to the edge of the crossroads then looked down the left-hand road blankly. 'He's gone.'

'What do you mean?' Nicolas asked, approaching Shift. They were right. Joe had vanished. Ahead of him stretched a long, straight road, with no sign of a rickety old house wagon.

'How can that be?' Tallith asked.

As Nicolas nervously checked again for evidence of side trails ahead and saw none, he began to feel more than a little uncomfortable. 'It can't,' he said quietly.

CHAPTER 24

Enthusiasm at knowing they were on Garaz's trail, even though the orc had a significant lead, was quickly eroded by the travelling conditions. The familiar pattern continued. Travel, travel, travel, rush to find warm shelter for the night. Villages were generally unwelcoming due to the widespread paranoia regarding The Visitor. Which was ridiculously ironic, considering The Visitor only punished those who were inhospitable.

Farms were often happier to take them in. Small families were more open to sharing their supplies for some extra coin and the opportunity to talk to some new people. So, when they spotted a farm ahead as the sun began to get low in the sky, there was a collective sigh of relief. At least they had potential shelter at the end of day...who knew? They were all so zombified by the relentless, gruelling travel that they'd lost track of time.

After making their way to the gate, Nicolas and Shift dismounted and approached the door of the main dwelling, set in the centre of several barns and outbuildings. Though the dwelling was small and squat with a thatched roof, light in the windows promised a fire, which would be welcome, as the sun was already beginning to set. Knocking three times, Nicolas stepped back, just in case a pitchfork came stabbing outwards when the door opened.

'Who goes there?' The voice was obviously deepened to sound intimidating.

'Just some weary travellers looking for somewhere to rest for the night,' Nicolas replied. 'If you would be so kind?'

'Does this look like an inn?' the voice asked curtly.

'No, it does not,' he answered honestly. Well, he hoped it wasn't. Inns were just fancy taverns, and they'd had enough trouble with taverns in the past. 'We can pay our way though, sir. All we ask is a roof over our head.'

'*Sir?*' Shift whispered, scrunching up their face. 'You're so polite.'

'A little politeness makes a difference.'

His companion remained unconvinced. Tallith appeared more impressed at his attempt to get things off on the right foot.

The click of a lock signalled the door opening, but it didn't open far. *'Sir*, he says.' The man chuckled. 'Nice to meet a young man with a bit of respect these days.'

Smiling a self-satisfied grin, Nicolas turned to Shift, raised his eyebrows and nodded to the door. The shapeshifter copied his expression, but in a mocking fashion.

'We are a respectful group, and we won't be a burden,' he said to the crack in the door.

'You warriors?' It was a rhetorical question. They could hardly pass for travelling bards.

'Adventurers, sir.' *I said that without thought.*

The door opened a little more. 'Don't none of you look too dangerous. Save yon woman on the horse.'

'We keep her around to scare the trolls away,' Shift answered quickly.

The door opened further. 'Bloody pesky, those trolls.'

'Indeed.' Nicolas shook his head at Shift, remembering a time when they'd been the pesky troll.

And now I sleep with them.

The man stepped out to greet them. He was on the older side of middle-aged, with a lined face and short, messy greying hair. His skin spoke of long days working outdoors.

'Nicolas Percival Carnegie.' Nicolas smiled, offering his hand.

'Wyan Bru.' Even the skin of the man's hand was rough from years of physical labour. 'Best hitch the horses up in the barn then come on in. Try not to track the snow in with you. It's a bugger to get back out again.'

'Thank you.' Nicolas took note of the crossbow resting by Wyan's side. 'Not a flake shall enter your house.'

They hitched the horses quickly and ensured they were fed then the group proceeded into the house. Everyone was careful about stomping the snow from their feet before they entered. Save Auron, naturally.

'I count a snowflake or two.' Wyan chuckled, nodding to the floor. 'But I'll not hold that against you.' He gestured to the hearth. 'Fires going so get yourselves warmed up. But food is a bit sparse for dinner parties.'

'We have our own provisions,' Silva replied, looking around the room. 'The fire and a place to sleep will be sufficient.' Nicolas looked at the warrior until she caught herself. 'Thank you.'

Wyan nodded thankfully. 'Well, what hospitality we can provide is yours to share.' Turning, the farmer gestured to the woman and two young children in the corner. They were warier of the newcomers than

Wyan. Both children pressed themselves into their mother's apron. 'That's my wife, Galla. And yon little ones are Zel and Lin.'

Nicolas rummaged in his coin purse and put a handful on the table. 'I believe this should cover our stay.'

Wyan whistled. 'That'll cover you a couple of nights and breakfast in bed, I reckon. You sure?'

'Of course,' Nicolas said firmly. 'It's the least we can do for your kindness.'

Wyan lit a pipe and put it to his mouth as he went and sat in the rocker by the fire. He was making a big show of being at ease for his family. 'Well, it's nice to have some sword hands around for a night or two,' he said between puffs of smoke. 'You've got bandits, those bloody horned fellas, and the thrice-damned Visitor knocking around. A night without worry would be nice.'

'Don't worry, you're safe whilst we're here,' Nicolas said with a wink to one of the children.

She reacted as if Nicolas had given her the middle finger.

'Husband...' Galla began, her tone suggesting some unpleasant words to come.

'Hush, wife,' Wyan said cooly. 'These are good folk, I reckon.'

'Look, ma'am,' Nicolas said genially, 'if you aren't comfortable with us being here, we can leave. We don't want to cause unease.'

Shift's gaze suggested they weren't too impressed that he'd volunteered them to leave. Taking a couple of steps forward, they crouched in front of the children.

'Do you want to see a trick?' they whispered conspiratorially.

Childhood curiosity overcame their fear. After a few moments, both the boy and girl nodded shyly.

'Name a race,' Shift said. 'Anyone.'

'...Kascat,' the boy, Zel, said quietly.

'Kascat?' Shift nodded approvingly. 'That's a good choice. So...' Their nose began to twitch. 'Ah...ah...ah...' Shift's head went back a notch with every *ah*. '*Achoo.*'

Their head snapped forward with the fake sneeze. As it did it, Shift's face turned into a purple-haired kascat. Both children shrieked in fear, as did Galla. Then they all looked at Shift in wonder. Shaking their head, Shift returned to their preferred form.

'Oh, sorry about that.' The shapeshifter grinned. 'Must be the dust. What race were you saying again?'

'Troll.'

'Serian...no, no, centaur.'

Shift glanced around the room. 'Might be a little tight in here for a centaur. But I will sssssee what I can do about the ssssssserian.' Their face morphed again, skin becoming scales as their nose extended.

Stepping forward in wonder, Zel and Lin reached out and stroked Shift's cheek. At the touch of the scales, they shrieked then giggled.

'That's quite the trick,' Wyan said, pointing with his pipe. 'You a wizard?'

'Shapeshifter,' Shift answered, their face returning to their usual look, before they winked at the children. 'Much more fun.'

'You're welcome enough,' Galla said after smoothing her apron with a suppressed smile. 'But we have children here, so you can sleep in the barn.'

Wyan cast a sharp look at his wife, which was returned with interest. Finally, the farmer broke the gaze. 'It'd just make us all a little more at ease.'

'Of course,' Nicolas agreed. 'We just appreciate somewhere to stay.'
****

An hour later, everyone sat around the dinner table enjoying some hot food. Though they hadn't much to share, Wyan and his family had been happy to cook up some of the group's own provisions. Eating their rations hot for a change completely transformed the taste. Nicolas wasn't aware of the pleasurable noises he was making again until Shift jabbed him in the ribs and suggested that maybe him and his bowl of food needed to be by themselves.

'Don't worry about it.' Wyan chuckled. 'You've got the hearty appetite of those who've travelled a long way.'

'You have experience?' Silva asked, picking up on Wyan's tone.

'Tried it once.' The farmer chuckled. 'Back when I was young and full of fire. Thought I could make a name for myself and get accepted by the Guild. Dreams are all well and good when you actually have some skill to back it up. Fell on my ass during the trials and realised it wasn't for me.'

Nicolas was about to respond when he noted a tugging on his sleeve. The young boy next to him was looking up at him with a question on his lips. 'Mister, are you a hero?' The young man's eyes went to his sword, which sat by the door of the house. Wearing weaponry at the dinner table wasn't at all polite.

'Not really.' Nicolas smiled warmly. 'I'm just—'

The sound of a drink being spat out made his head turn. '*Not really?*' Sergeant Tallith scoffed, once he'd finished coughing. 'Do you know, this man actually went to the *Underworld*?' Nicolas closed his eyes and sighed at the gasp from their hosts. 'A demon banished his soul down there, and he had to fight a necromancer to be able to return to his body.'

Nicolas shuffled awkwardly on his chair. 'It wasn't quite like that.'

'I think the sergeant should tell us what happened. I'm sure our hosts would love to hear about some of your adventures.'

Nicolas hoped his eyes properly conveyed his current thought. *Dammit, Shift.*

'Personally, I think the kid should tell his own story, seeing as I've trained him in the art now.' Auron huffed.

It's not an art I care to practise.

The boy looked to his father. 'Can we hear the tale? Please?'

Wyan lit up another pipe. This was his fourth now. Nicolas suspected the man had a problem. 'I reckon so.'

If they're going to hear it, it might as well be from me, I suppose.

As he began to recount the story of his trip to the Underworld, he found the children hanging on his every word, which caused him to utilise every one of Auron's storytelling tricks. Soon enough, he was bouncing around the room, clashing imaginary blades with fictitious foes. The children—and Tallith—were rapt as he told the tale, cheering and clapping. Every so often, he caught Auron's look of pride and wasn't sure whether he wanted to punch or hug the spirit. Neither would work out well.

'Well, stone me,' Wyan said as the story finished and Nicolas sat heavily back in his chair. 'You're the *Nick Carnage* I heard someone yapping about at market last month. I'm sorry, I didn't realise.'

Nicolas held up a hand. 'Don't worry. It's not actually my name.'

'Still, if I knew a hero like you was at our table, I wouldn't have had you eating your own food.'

'We're just happy to have a roof over our heads,' Shift interjected.

I'd be happier to know who's sharing my stories.

CHAPTER 25

'*Kid, kid, kid.*'

Auron knew how weary they all were, so the spirit shouting in his face told him it was urgent, and he snapped awake. Sitting up quickly, he almost ended up inside Auron's aura, but the spirit jumped back quickly and the pair just avoided each other.

'What's wrong?' he asked.

'I think there's trouble,' the spirit said quickly. 'I was strolling past the house, and I heard knocking then raised voices.'

'Shit.' Nicolas grabbed the *Dawn Blade* and unsheathed it. 'Shift.'

'I'm up.' Surprise caught him as he saw the shapeshifter already rising and drawing their knives.

The barn door was rattling slightly, suggesting unpleasant conditions outside. Silva was already by the door waiting for them. Nicolas tried to listen for anything beyond the rickety wood doors, but all he could hear was the wind. And the rattling.

'There's a snowstorm out there,' Silva told him. 'We will need to go single file or we could get lost.'

It must be bad. The barn isn't that far from the house.

'What's going on?' Tallith asked, still half-asleep.

'Trouble,' Silva snapped. 'Get up.'

The sergeant snapped to attention with parade-ground precision. Soon they were all assembled at the door.

'I'll lead, you follow,' Auron said firmly. 'Just keep an eye on my aura.'

Nicolas put his hand on Silva's shoulder, just as Shift did to him. When they were ready, the warrior pulled the bar back. The minute it was clear, the doors tried to fling open, able to hold out no longer against the assault from the elements. Snow blasted into the barn, as did biting wind. Silva held on to the door, obviously straining.

'This way,' Auron shouted over the wind.

Though their task was urgent, they couldn't move fast. The wind pelted them, trying to force them backwards with every step. Snow slapped them in their faces, getting under the arms they raised to try to cover themselves from the worst of it. It was pitch black, save for the flurries of white. In between the gusts of wind, Nicolas thought he heard a cry.

Trudging on, Nicolas could just about make out Auron's hazy aura ahead of them. He clung fiercely to Silva's shoulder. Soon, there was another light: the light from the farmhouse. Except it wasn't complete. It framed a large, hunched silhouette.

'Inhospitable.'

The voice was everywhere and nowhere. It could've come from the house or it could've been whispered in his ear. It was followed by a flash of red, and a scream.

'Go,' he shouted. 'Go.'

With a grunt, Silva moved faster. The light ahead of them grew as the shadowy figure blocking it moved, then it vanished. No. There was a little light left, marking out the edges of the farmhouse door. Straining his eyes to try and focus on the light as the biting cold made them water, he allowed his grip on Silva to falter for a moment. An errant gust of wind caught him, and he staggered backwards, tripping over something and falling. Scrabbling to his feet, Nicolas could no longer see his companions.

'Nick?'

The voice came from the darkness. He could still make out the house and Auron, barely. But he was also aware someone was close by. Getting to his feet, he slowly turned on the spot, sword at the ready.

'Who's there?' he shouted into the night.

A flash of movement caught his attention. Swinging round, he caught the flap of a cloak before it vanished into the night.

What colour was that? Brown? Red?

'Garaz?' he bellowed into the storm. *'Garaz?'*

There hadn't been enough time to tell. He wanted to march off in pursuit, but he wasn't clear which way to go.

'Nick.'

Using his forearm as a shield again, he turned back toward the sound of his companions, and the house.

'Kid, what are you doing?' Auron cried as he appeared at his side.

'Someone went in that direction,' he shouted, pointing with his sword. 'Go after them.'

'Right.' Face set with determination, the spirit ran into the storm, whilst Nicolas turned back to the house. The door was open again, creating a bright beacon to guide him.

Fixing on the light from the doorway, Nicolas charged toward it, forcing one leg in front of the other until he burst through the door. His first worry was the snow they'd all trudged in. Then he saw his companions' faces.

No. Please, Deities, no.

'Where are they?' he asked.

'Over there, I think,' Shift said, indicating the darkest corner of the room.

'Hello,' he called gently. 'Wyan? Galla?'

The large shadow in the centre of the room moved. He heard sobbing. Taking a lantern from the wall, he approached it slowly.

'It's me, Nicolas,' he said, keeping his hands in clear view. 'Are you okay?'

It became deathly quiet. As the lantern chased the shadows away, he saw the family, huddled together in the corner, clinging to each other fiercely. Fear at what he was about to see gnawed at him. He wanted to stop so he wouldn't know for sure. But he couldn't.

None of them reacted to the sudden light over them.

'It's okay,' he said softly. 'It's Nicolas.'

Please don't be grotesque monsters. Please don't be grotesque monsters.

There was no response.

Placing the lantern on the floor, he removed his glove. Reaching out carefully, he gently touched Wyan's shoulder. The skin twitched under his touch, and with a muffled cry, a fist swung at him. Nicolas caught it.

'It's me. It's Nicolas. I'm...'

He looked at Wyan, and his words faded away. His arms dropped to his side. Inside him, his heart clenched.

He needs you.

Shaking himself out of it, Nicolas moved closer, hugging the farmer tightly. After a moment's struggle, it was returned. Wyan let out muffled sobs.

'It's Nicolas,' he repeated. 'You're safe.'

No, they're not.

The damage had been done. A figure began to stumble past him, but he grabbed Lin and hugged her too. The child fought against his grip at first but soon realised there was no danger. He looked at the child, and a tear ran down his cheek. Behind him, weapons clattered to the floor. Both Wyan and Lin let out cries and scurried back into the corner. Shift stood rooted to the spot, dumbfounded. Their knives lay on the floor at their feet.

'No.' The shapeshifter's voice was hoarse and pleading.

Beside Shift, Tallith took a step back, hand to his mouth.

'I lost him,' Auron snarled, entering the house. 'What's going on? Are they...? Oh no.'

'He took in their faces.' Nicolas's fists clenched until the knuckles turned white. Right then, he wanted to punch a hole in the world itself for allowing such evil to exist.

None of them had a face. There were bumps where noses, mouths, eyes, and ears should've been, but it was like it was all covered by a layer of extra skin. They could clearly hear and make noises. But that was all.

'They'll die,' Tallith cried suddenly. 'They can't breathe.'

'They'll live,' Nicolas countered, his voice a low growl. 'The Visitor likes the people he punishes to live. So they'll live. Like this.'

Standing, he stalked the room, clenching and unclenching his hands, impotent to do anything to help this terrible situation. The family were destined to live like this, maybe forever.

'What sort of monster would do this?' Silva asked, equally shaken.

Nicolas pictured the cloak in the storm. Stomping to the door, he stared out into the night. 'I'm going to find you,' he screamed into the dark. 'I'm going to hunt you down, and when I do. You're dead. You hear me. Dead. *Deaddddddddddd*.'

Shift took him by the arm, bringing him back inside and closing the door. 'We'll get him,' they said quietly. 'Even if it is Garaz, he'll be punished for this. But right now, we need to help this family.'

The red rage receded, and necessity took over. 'Of course,' he said quickly. 'Let's get some blankets and make them comfortable. Silva, get that fire roaring again. In the morning, we'll get them to the nearest village. Hopefully, someone there can help them...or take care of them until we can break the curse.'

Every time I think I've seen all the evils of this world, something happens to surprise me anew.

The group went about their tasks in silence. What words were there for something like this?

Mumbling caught his attention. Wyan was trying to say something.

'Meh my. Meh my. Meh my.' Over and over again, he repeated it.

Nicolas had no clue what he was saying. He opened his mouth to ask the others.

'He's saying *red eyes*,' Silva said before he'd even uttered a word. 'Red eyes.'

CHAPTER 26

Leaving with all urgency the next morning, the group reached the nearest village quickly. Initially, the villagers had been keen to drive them off. One look at Nicolas's face—or, more likely, Silva's—convinced them to be a bit more welcoming. Bringing Wyan and his family forward, the people rallied round to take care of them, once the horror of what had been done to them passed. The village had no healer, but they would do their best to look after the family.

Nicolas was going to do *his* best to track down The Visitor and kill him. Auron had mentioned before that it was the most likely way to lift the curses, and after what he—or it—had done to that poor family, Nicolas no longer had any qualms about doing it. It was just finding the bugger. The storm had wiped away all trace. But whatever it was seemed to be moving in the same general direction as them. Nicolas just hoped that was a terrible coincidence.

The group travelled in silence for a good long while, each haunted by the harrowing experience. Even Auron kept his stories to himself.

What is Etherius coming to?

That was a silly question. He was well aware. He'd seen the Helstrum pamphlets, the chaos, the death. The world was turning into a giant ball of shit.

Not while I've got breath left in my body.

'I think we need to discuss what happens next,' Shift said, looking out over the fields instead of at the others. 'Are we going to acknowledge how much of a coincidence it is that we and Garaz and The Visitor are all travelling in the same direction?'

'What did you see?' Silva asked.

'A bit of a cloak,' Nicolas answered quickly.

'And that was all?'

'Yes.'

'No, it wasn't,' Auron said. 'You saw more than you think.'

Nicolas scrunched up his face in confusion. 'I did?'

'Of course you did,' the spirit said. 'That's why you're going to close your eyes.'

'Whilst riding a horse?'

'I won't let you fall off,' Shift said.

'You're the one most likely to let me fall off.'

Shift opened their mouth to argue then just shrugged.

'Here you go,' Tallith said, beaming, clearly thrilled that he could be helpful as he took the reins. 'I've got it.'

'Can't we just stop...?'

'Just close your eyes, kid,' Auron insisted. Nicolas did as bidden and listened to the spirit's calm voice. 'It's nighttime again. You're in the storm. It's cold.' *Obviously*. 'There's snow flying everywhere. It smelled earthy and woodsy.'

Despite his initial scepticism, Nicolas found himself drifting back to the night. All around him, the snow hung frozen in mid-air, like he was in a painting.

'What do you see?'

Studying the scene, he picked out the flash of cloak he'd caught sight of. 'I see The Visitor's cloak. It's brownish. Maybe red.'

'But what else? Really think, kid.'

'I don't see... Hang on...' Squinting, he craned his neck forward. There was something in the darkness. Moving his head from side to side didn't really help much. He could see fangs and... 'Green skin.'

Opening his eyes, he sank in his saddle slightly. He hadn't seen enough to be completely positive. But he was getting surer by the day.

'If it isn't Garaz, it's the most Garaz-looking thing possible.' It was like Shift had plucked the thought from his head.

'Red eyes,' Silva snarled quietly.

'You all believe it then?' he asked after a loaded pause.

'I believe we have been fooled and betrayed,' Silva snapped suddenly. 'The orc played us all then turned on us. Now there is some monstrosity out here that looks just like him committing atrocities.'

'We've seen plenty of unfathomable things,' Nicolas replied. 'All we really have to go on is some kind of cloaked monster. That's vague at best. We know Garaz.'

'Do we?' Shift scoffed. 'I mean, really know him? Or do we know what he wanted us to know? Why are you clinging on to the stupid hope that there's a reasonable explanation for all this?'

'All the evidence points to Garaz being the—'

'Quiet.' Nicolas pointed an accusing finger at Tallith, who looked at it as if it were a nocked bow. 'You don't know him, so you don't get to speak.'

'Only because you know he was about to talk sense,' Shift said cooly.

Nicolas sighed heavily. They were right. His efforts to deny it were getting weaker by the second. All the evidence pointed to their former companion, but he just couldn't bring himself to believe it. Was that due to hope or delusion?

'Sorry,' he said to the sergeant.

'Don't worry, I understand,' Tallith replied with a nod.

'What about you?' Nicolas asked, turning to his left. 'You've been quiet this whole time?'

'Because I'm thinking, kid.' Auron chuckled. 'I don't think it's him.'

'How?' Shift scoffed.

'These curses,' Auron replied. 'Granted, we haven't known Garaz that long, and yes, he keeps a lot to himself. But these curses. How many near-death situations have we been in? There's no way he would've hidden that ability until he decided to ponce around the countryside using it on random folk.'

Hope kindled in Nicolas. That was actually a compelling argument. It wasn't like someone just forgot they could curse people when in peril.

'You make a good point,' Silva relented. 'But we must agree on one thing. If we catch up to Garaz and he is The Visitor, he dies.'

'After we've given him a chance to surrender,' Nicolas said firmly. 'In all our near-death experiences, how often has Garaz been the one to save us?'

'That only gets him so far,' Shift interjected. 'If he's The Visitor, he gets one chance to undo what he's done. Beyond that, we can't take any chances.'

'If it comes to that, yes.' It hurt him to think it, let alone say it. But innocent people were getting hurt. He just prayed it wasn't Garaz.

'Do you remember that vampire child?' Auron said.

Nicolas remembered vividly. The little girl who'd been one of the heads of the five vampire families. Sweet and innocent on the outside, blood-thirsty monster on the inside.

'So, this one time, I had to hunt down a pair of those, a brother and sister who'd been turned and were making travellers down the Ale Trail disappear. They were playing the whole 'lost children' routine. They'd ask for help looking for their parents, isolate the well-meaning travellers, then drink them dry.'

'I've done that myself before. Works like a charm every time.' Shift didn't exactly look proud to admit that. 'But I didn't kill them...just stole their coin,' they added hastily.

'Exactly,' the spirit said. 'So, I corner them pretty easily. But it was the first time I'd ever fought that type of vampire. Instantly, they start pleading, *'We're only children. Please don't hurt us. We just want to go home to our parents.'* Nearly bloody worked too. The human mind is conditioned to sympathise and be merciful when it comes to children. I couldn't help it. Luckily, my reflexes were well-honed, even then. Still, I earned myself a nasty scar to remind me to never let that happen again.'

'And your point?' It was easy to see; Auron was being pretty heavy-handed with this lesson.

The spirit looked into his eyes sadly. 'If – and I still don't think it is – The Visitor turns out to be Garaz and there's no other choice, don't hesitate.'

'I've already said I'll do it,' Nicolas practically snarled. 'If he is The Visitor and won't come quietly, I'll kill him.' He hated each and every word coming from his mouth.

'I don't think you will,' Auron said firmly, before turning and winking at him. 'Chances are you'll drop your sword before you get the opportunity.'

Nicolas needed the laugh, despite it being at his expense.

****

As the group settled down for the night, Nicolas took off his glove and gently applied snow to his knuckles. Once they'd eaten, he'd taken the opportunity to get some time alone and train. Unfortunately, that training had turned into *I'm going to punch a tree really hard until the anger goes away.* He had succeeded, after a fashion. For a little while, at least, he'd been distracted by the pain in his hand.

Beside him, Shift regarded his hand and gave him a sympathetic smile. Lying back on the blankets, they gestured for him to join them. Lying beside Shift, he fidgeted for a few moments to get comfortable.

'We're going on a holiday,' Shift said suddenly.

'What?' he asked, turning toward them.

'Just keep looking up. At the break in the branches. Focus on it.'

Unsure where this was going, he lay back regardless. They'd found a nice patch of forest to camp in when nothing better had presented itself. In the canopy directly above him was an almost round hole where he could see the starlit sky clearly. How long had it taken scholars staring at the sky to come up with constellations? It seemed too complicated for Nicolas. The best he'd ever done was a cloud that had been vaguely shaped like a bottom.

'Right now,' Shift said softly. 'You and I are on a beach.'

'Oh, for Deities' sake,' he whispered with a laugh. 'Are we stranded on an island again?'

Not a bad prospect, if I'm honest. If there are no zombie ships lying around.

'Shut up.' The command came with an elbow to the ribs. 'We're on a beach, taking a much-needed rest and just...being together.'

'That sounds nice.' He knew his voice was dreamy.

'At the edge of the beach is the little lodge we're staying in.'

'How many children do we have running around?'

Another elbow to the ribs. 'Shut up and stop ruining it.' He looked across briefly and saw them smirking. 'So, it's just you and me. Really listen. Can you hear the waves? They're swishing in and out. *Swish. Swish. Swish.*'

Listening hard enough, he deluded himself that he could. 'Yes.' He could almost pretend he felt warm right now, though that warmth was coming from inside him.

'And right now, we're on a blanket on that beach, just listening to the waves and being together.'

'And what else happens when we're alone on a beach together?' he asked leadingly.

Shift rolled over and put their arm around him. 'Oh, I'm sure your imagination can handle that.' They smiled.

'The rest of us are still here,' Silva called from across the campfire.

'You can also shut up,' Shift barked back. 'You're ruining the moment too.'

'Just be careful how far you let that *moment* go.' Auron chuckled. 'The rest of us are watching.'

Shift closed their eyes and grimaced. 'And now we're back in a snowy forest surrounded by assholes.'

Nicolas smiled, leaned forward and kissed them. 'One day we'll be on that beach.'

Shift cocked an eyebrow at him. 'Of course we will. I'm not the one of us who needs reminding to be optimistic.' With a huff, Shift rose.

'Where are you going?' Nicolas asked.

'To answer the call of nature, if you must know. Apparently all that listening to waves had an effect on my bladder.'

'Don't forget your knives.'

Shift looked at their weapons and laughed. 'I think I can handle peeing without needing weapons. Not all of us are as paranoid as you.'

'Actually, doing your business outdoors can be very bad for your health,' Auron remarked grimly, casting a glare at Silva.

'Oh yeah, sorry,' Shift replied awkwardly before walking into the forest, leaving their knives behind.

'Must you?' the warrior asked.

Auron tilted his head slightly, looking at Silva as if she'd asked him something absurd. 'Yes.'

'At least he has other uses than just biting at you,' Nicolas said, trying to lighten the mood. 'He can scout. And throw things.'

'I'm going to be much more useful soon.' The spirit smiled indulgently.

'What do you mean?' Silva asked.

There was a twinkle in Auron's ethereal white eyes. 'I've figured it out. This Visitor must be a demon of some sort. That makes the most sense. And that means I can fight it. So, when we do find it, I'm going to need you all to step back so I can do my thing.' The spirit's voice became firm. 'And when I do, you'd best pay close attention. After I'm done, I'll need you to recount the story to the next bard we meet. In great detail.'

'I'll even cheer you on.' Nicolas had no wish to try to fight a demon again. Although...that wasn't strictly true. There was one demon he planned on fighting. Koth. He owed the creature a sword in the gut, or five.

Auron rubbed his hands together gleefully. 'I'm thinking of giving it the old *'Auron's not as good as he thinks'* routine.'

After a moment of silence, Nicolas realised the spirit was dying for someone to ask. 'And what's that then?'

'Glad you asked.' Auron grinned. 'So, I'm sure I don't need to tell you that there's a certain *legacy* surrounding me. Legendary hero and all that.'

'You may have mentioned it.' Silva sighed.

Auron cast her a disapproving glance but continued anyway. 'Well, as with any legend, there are always people who refuse to believe it. More often than not, it's the people who think they can take me in a fight.' The spirit took a deep breath, which was nonsense because he didn't breathe. 'So this one time, this guy was hired to kill me. Big guy. Forget the name, but he had muscles on his muscles. Anyway, he finds me, because I made sure he could, and gives me the whole *'you can't be him'* crap. *'But you're small.'* All that. I let his overconfidence work against him. The odd uncertain glance, a fake shaking of my sword arm, and he comes in axe swinging. Two seconds later, he had no forearms.'

'And that's what you plan to do to this demon?' Nicolas asked.

'I reckon so, kid.' Auron half-smiled. 'It's a demon, so it'll think it's all powerful. I'll just reel him in and finish him.'

'Are you going to use the *finger poke of doom*?' Nicolas asked, referencing Auron's alleged *special move* he'd learnt after dying.

'I just might,' the spirit said thoughtfully. 'Maybe I'll also—'

A fierce rustling in the bushes cut off their conversation. The group were up with swords in hand in an instant.

Shift burst through the foliage, eyes wide with panic. 'Wolves!'

CHAPTER 27

A mere second after Shift charged out of the undergrowth, they threw themselves to the ground and into a roll. Creating a trail in the snow, they came up fluidly, grabbing their knives as they rose. Nicolas scrabbled to his feet as a giant snarling shape flew through the air where they'd just been standing, jaw snapping the air where Shift's head had been.

Descending in an arc, the animal landed on all fours, skidding slightly in the snow. Growling, its feral eyes darted left and right, realising it was surrounded. Saliva dribbled from its mouth as its furred body heaved with big breaths. It looked like a right nasty bastard. But a smart one too. It knew it was out in the open and outnumbered. Nicolas took a tentative swipe at it with the *Dawn Blade*.

'Get,' he shouted. 'Go on.'

The wolf stalked back a couple of steps, growl never letting up. Then it snapped forward with its powerful jaws. Standing his ground, Nicolas turned the sword to the flat side and slapped the creature across the side of the head with it. The wolf yelped and vanished back into the bushes, snow falling to the ground as the branches where it rested were suddenly disturbed.

'There we go,' Nicolas said, keeping his sword ready. 'It's gone.' He half-turned to Shift. 'Are you okay?'

'No,' they answered quickly. 'None of us are. You need to listen.'

'To what?'

'I didn't say *wolf*,' his companion said, watching their surroundings carefully. 'I said *wolves*.'

As if on cue, the calm night air filled with numerous growls from unseen predators.

Bugger.

'They're surrounding us,' Silva said, glancing from side to side as the group formed a defensive circle around the campfire.

Bushes rustled, drawing their attention this way and that. The growling seemed to be focusing on the northern side of their camp. At the nearby tree, the horses began to panic, whinnying and crying as they yanked on their reins to try to get free.

Dammit. They're too vulnerable.

He took a step forward.

'Stay in the circle, kid,' Auron shouted.

'But...the horses...'

'Let me deal with them,' the spirit said, running toward their mounts. 'They're trying to goad you into breaking formation so they can pick you off.'

'That was a big wolf.' Nicolas tried to ignore the shaking in his voice as his eyes searched the dark forest around them. 'Are they normally that big?'

As his eyes tracked across the foliage, he stopped for a moment and blinked.

What...?

For a second, he thought he'd seen a pair of red dots in the black. But there was nothing.

'No,' Shift answered between pants. 'Nor that angry. Something has them riled up.'

'Should we run?' Tallith asked, his eyes wide.

'No,' Silva said firmly. 'If we run, they'll pick us off one at a time. If we're in the circle, we're strong.'

Several wolves emerged from the forest as one. The snarling beasts made a big show of passing them and heading straight for the horses, which Auron was currently untying. The animals bounded toward their prey, bloodlust in their eyes. Auron glanced back, tutted and worked faster.

'Our mounts!' There was a moment of confusion at Tallith's cry. Then Nicolas realised the sergeant hadn't heard Auron saying he'd untie them.

'No, wait,' he cried, reaching out and trying to grab Tallith.

But it was too late. He broke formation and ran for the horses, a very unpleasant curse word from Silva right on his heels.

Nicolas had to give the wolves some credit. They'd planned it brilliantly. The moment the defensive circle was broken, the others attacked. But it still didn't make them easy prey. Seeing three of the beasts bearing down on him, Nicolas stabbed the *Dawn Blade* into the campfire and flicked a flaming log in their direction. The wolves yelped and jumped aside as the log fell amongst them. By that time, Silva had already killed one of them. Another was reeling from a nasty gash on its nose, the price for biting at Shift.

'We can't stay here,' Nicolas cried, swinging the *Dawn Blade* left and right to discourage attacks. 'It's too open.'

'No,' Silva shouted. 'Reform the circle with the three of us. By the fire we're strong.'

A cry caught their attention. Auron had succeeded in freeing the horses, who had promptly bolted, but Tallith had been knocked to the ground by a wolf. He was using his forearm to keep its snapping jaws at bay. And he was losing.

'Dammit.' Breaking into a run, Silva charged the creature, stabbing it in the side. Instantly, its body fell limp.

'No.' Nicolas watched in horror as time slowed.

Silva was still drawing her sword from the wolf as another leapt at her. Turning, the warrior saw the attacker, let go of her blade, and drew a knife from her belt. The wolf crashed into her, knocking her to the ground. There was a sickening crack, and a yelp of pain.

Running forward together, Shift and Nicolas used their weapons to keep the other wolves at a distance.

'Silva? *Silva?*' Nicolas cried as they reached the warrior.

With a grunt, the wolf atop her rose then dropped to the floor beside Silva, dead. But the warrior hadn't come out unscathed. A bone protruded from her leg via a bloody wound. Nicolas tried not to gag.

'I'm okay,' the warrior replied through gritted teeth. 'Just get me up.'

Taking a few dissuading swipes at their attackers, Nicolas watched Shift's back as they hauled Silva to her feet. The warrior gasped in pain as she put weight on her broken leg.

'You can't stay here,' Auron called, throwing a stone that caught a wolf directly between the eyes. 'You need a more defensible position.'

'If we run, we'll be picked off,' Nicolas shouted back over the massed snarling.

'You have a chance,' Auron replied quickly. 'Some of the pack have run after the horses, there's an opening. And I have an idea.'

Tallith ran over and took Silva's other arm around his neck. 'I'm sorry.'

'Quiet,' Nicolas snapped, delivering a boot to the head of a wolf trying to bite him. 'We're leaving.'

Desperately, they made for the gap in the attackers' line. Nicolas walked backwards, swinging his sword left and right as the other wolves slowly stalked toward them. Shift and Tallith took Silva, but there would be no fast escape for them.

Reaching the tree line, Nicolas entered the forest, a line of wolves following him. The tree beside him suddenly shuddered violently, and thick snow fell from the top-most branches, hitting the ground with a *whumph*. The wolves cried out in surprise and jumped back as it landed between them and their intended kills.

I don't know how Auron did that, but bless him.

Moving as quickly as they could through the dark, snowy forest, the group had no idea where they were going. And with Silva slowing them down, the seconds Auron had bought them would run out quickly. They had to walk a fine line between moving swiftly and moving carefully. A trip or slip now would cost them dearly. Howling suggested the pursuers weren't about to take a break. In fact, they seemed to be calling back the others.

'Up ahead,' Shift shouted, pointing.

It took a minute to spot the outcrop with a cave in its side. 'We don't know what's in there,' he cried, his breathing laboured from the flight.

'We don't have a choice,' Silva said firmly, her voice thick with pain.

Reaching the entrance, Shift laid Silva against the rock. The warrior still had her sword in hand and was determined to fight. The group formed a rough semi-circle around the opening. They had a defensible position but were still outnumbered, Silva had a broken leg, and Tallith was proving himself a bit of a waste of space.

This time, the wolves weren't concerned about being seen. That was worrying. That meant they weren't scared of Nicolas and his group. Numerous growling creatures stalked forwards, ready to attack.

'Any advice?' he asked Auron.

'Don't die,' was the spirit's grim reply. It hadn't really needed saying.

As much as he didn't like the idea of killing animals—they weren't necessarily evil, but just acting on instinct—if it was a choice between stabbing a wolf and getting eaten by one, he didn't have to think twice. Somehow, he doubted the pack would let up unless it took mass casualties.

A crunch in the snow behind him alerted Nicolas that they weren't alone. Half turning, he saw a furred form flash past him. Despite the surprise, he didn't strike at it. Within a moment, he realised why. It was a man in a bearskin cloak. He screamed aggressively, waving the flaming logs he carried high, before launching them at the pack. The wolves scattered.

'That won't keep them at bay for long.' Though the man had just been screaming, his voice was prim and proper. 'They'll be back, but I believe I've bought us a few minutes.'

Actually, it was only thirty seconds.

CHAPTER 28

The bear-skin figure's shoulders sagged as the wolves stalked back into the open. 'Oh darn. I rather thought it would see them off for longer than that.'

'Look at them,' Shift said, eyes narrowed. 'They're reluctant.'

The shapeshifter was right. Nicolas recognised the forced, nervous steps the beasts took toward them. He'd done that exact walk himself. Many times. Just on two legs instead of four.

Shift's understanding of animals came in very useful sometimes. 'They aren't being brave. They're being rallied.'

Parting, the wolves made an opening for something much bigger. Almost like they were forming an honour guard, they bowed their snouts low. Nicolas had thought the other wolves were big, but the one that emerged from the wood was huge. There was a large, muscular form beneath its grey fur. Its eyes were fully feral, and set on them. Fangs the length of fingers were bared. This was a pure killing machine.

It doesn't look natural.

'You thinking the same thing as me, kid?' Auron asked, somehow reading his mind. 'That thing doesn't look right, at all.'

'The alpha,' the fur-covered man said. 'Oh dear. He seems quite the beast.'

Quite the understatement.

Now their leader was here, the other wolves were getting braver. Soon, the whole pack would rush them as one. Nicolas could tell. And when they did, several of the wolves would die. But so would all of them.

'Would there be a handy back door?' he asked the fur-covered man.

The only answer he got was the shake of a head.

Turning its head from side to side, the alpha wolf snapped at several of the pack, almost like it was talking to them. Nicolas couldn't speak wolf, but he gathered it could be loosely translated as *'kill them now'*. As its beastly eyes turned back to its prey, the wolf hesitated. Another thing Nicolas knew well...an expression of confusion.

'Shit.'

Nearly jumping right out of his armour, he pressed himself to the cave wall but stayed his sword. His instincts told him the giant wolf beside him was a friend. More than that...

No.

'Stop,' he called, his voice pleading. But Shift was already moving.

Padding towards the alpha, Shift snarled a challenge. Raising themselves up as high as they could, they tried to intimidate the alpha, but he was having none of it. One of the braver members of the pack stepped forward, only to fall back with a yelp when his leader snapped at him. Apparently, this was between the alpha and Shift.

As Nicolas moved, the furred man grabbed him. 'No,' he said with urgency. 'This may be the only way. But if you involve yourself, the whole pack will attack both of you.'

'But...I can't...' He looked to the others for support. 'We can't just let Shift do that. Have you seen the size of that thing?'

'Trust them,' Silva said, busily creating a splint for her leg whilst keeping half an eye on what was going on outside. 'They would not try this if they didn't think they could win.'

'She's right, kid.' Auron didn't look any happier about it than he did, though.

'Well, it doesn't help,' he hissed. But he stood down. He couldn't deny the logic. Yet he kept himself ready to go if the battle looked to be going the wrong way.

His heart fell from his chest as he watched the two opponents, the wolf and the shapeshifter, circle each other. Then they leapt.

Within moments, it was hard to make out detail in the melee as both wolves clawed and bit at each other. Splashes of blood lined the snow as they fought intensely. When he saw blood on the alpha's snout, it took both Tallith and the fur-cloaked man to hold him back.

'Let go of me,' he cried. 'I need to—'

A pained yelp froze the words in his throat. Shift was staggering, clearly favouring one of their front legs. The alpha barrelled into their side, knocking them to the ground. Sensing victory, the beast gave up all semblance of caution and went straight for the kill. That's when Shift struck. Slipping under the alpha, they gripped its throat in their jaws and ripped it out with a wet tearing sound. With a gargle, the alpha fell to the floor dead. Shift rose on shaky legs.

The rest of the pack milled around uncertainly. It was almost like they'd woken from a trance. The animals stopped snarling, shaking their heads and looking at each other in confusion, seeming more like normal wolves now, rather than the ferocious monsters they had just been. Shift bared their fangs and snarled. Each member of the pack tucked their tails between their legs and fled. Only when they'd all vanished did Shift finally collapse.

'No.' Throwing both men holding him aside, Nicolas ran to Shift.

They were back in their preferred form, but they were a mess. Deep red gashes covered their body. Nicolas's hands hovered above them, not knowing what to do, his mind too panicked to think.

'They aren't breathing,' he cried, tears streaking his cheeks. 'I don't think they're breathing.'

Desperately looking around, as if a bottle of healing potion would just be lying in the snow beside him, Nicolas caught sight of two red dots in the dark. Then he made out a vague outline between the trees.

You.

'Help us,' he shouted. 'Garaz. Help us.'

Slowly, the figure turned away and vanished into the night. He heard a single word whispered on the night air.

'Weak.'

'You bastard,' Nicolas screamed after him. 'They're dead. And you could've helped.'

Part of Nicolas wanted to run him down and drag him back, but instead he turned his attention to Shift.

'What do I do?' he called to Auron.

'Calm down,' the spirit snapped. 'They are breathing. Get a cloak over them and get them into the warm before they freeze to death.'

'What...' His mind took a moment to process the information. *They're alive.* Taking off his cloak, he wrapped Shift in it. Tenderly, he lifted them and carried them toward the cave, trying not to notice the way their head flopped as he moved.

They're alive. They're alive, and they're staying that way.

'This way, young man.'

Following the fur-cloaked man, they went deeper into the cave. After a couple of turns, he was surprised to find a very well-appointed camp, with a small tent set up. One with a roaring fire. As he laid Shift beside it, the man rifled through one of his packs.

Gently, he brushed Shift's cheek and moved his head close to theirs. He praised every Deity when he felt their breath on his cheek.

'You'll be okay.' He had no idea how he intended to keep that promise, but right there and then he would've punched a dragon in the face if it somehow made them well. But there was no dragon, and he was no healer.

What can I do? How can I make this go away?

Please just keep breathing.

'Ah-ha,' the fur-cloaked man exclaimed. 'I knew I had some left.'

Rising, the man studied the pot he'd pulled from his bag. Even with the light of the fire, he couldn't clearly make the man out, save that the bear head wasn't attached to the rest of the cloak. With a shudder, he remembered the last person he'd met with a penchant for bears.

When he shuffled toward them, Nicolas rose and barred his way. 'Before I let you do whatever you're going to do, I need to know who you are.'

'Is this the time?' Tallith asked nervously.

'Yes,' he said firmly. 'We've travelled with people before who haven't been true. The faun Fo, Garaz…I need to be sure of who this is before I let him minister to Shift. I'm taking no chances.'

'A fair and sensible precaution, young man.' The bear head nodded at him. 'I am quite happy to prove that I am not one of those vile blighters.' Quickly, he removed his hat, revealing a genial-looking, middle-aged man with slicked back grey hair and a pencil moustache that pointed upwards. There were no horns on his head, nor signs that he was a vampire or anything untoward. Nicolas sheathed the sword he hadn't even realised he'd drawn.

'Sorry,' he said with a tight smile. 'I had to be sure.'

The man held up a hand. 'Think nothing of it. I completely understand, young man. There are not many travelling at this time of year who do not have some nefarious purpose. So, allow me to soothe your nerves with an introduction.' The man bowed low. 'Dieter Von Ostric. Writer, explorer, and generally curious fellow, at your service.'

'Oh,' Auron exclaimed, snapping his fingers. 'He wrote that travel book about Etherius.'

'You wrote a travel book?' Nicolas asked.

Dieter grinned broadly. 'You have heard of me then? I would say *The Traveller's Guide to Etherius* is my most popular work. But I have also written on philosophy, religion, legends…anything that takes my fancy, really.' The writer put a hand beside his mouth and lowered his voice. 'Plus, it pays to diversify one's income.' Taking Nicolas by the arm, he gently guided him aside. 'But right now, I must look after this brave shapeshifter of yours.'

Dieter approached Shift. As he removed the blanket covering them, Nicolas placed some bits of cloth over their most intimate areas. Worry disorientated him for a moment as he saw the claw and bite marks decorating their body.

'Quite the mess,' Dieter muttered with a frown as he opened the pot. 'I have no healing potions to hand, but this salve should prevent the wounds from becoming infected and offer some mild relief. It should stem further blood loss too.'

What about the blood already lost? How long will this temporary fix hold for?

Shift moaned as the salve was applied to their wounds. Though their groaning pained Nicolas, at least it was a sign they were still alive. All he wanted to do was take them in his arms, but given their weakened state, he thought it best not to.

'Will that really help?' he asked Dieter.

'Trust me young man,' the writer smiled as he continued. 'This is not my first time tending to bite or claw wounds. Though usually I'm ministering to myself.' He caught Nicolas's look. 'Occupational hazard of being an explorer,' he explained with a shrug.

'Shift is strong,' Silva said. 'They will recover.'

Absentmindedly, Nicolas turned and looked at the warrior. 'Oh Deities, your leg.'

Silva had tied a strong-looking splint around her leg. Crouching by the warrior, he looked at her broken bone. Nicolas couldn't stop himself sucking his teeth as he looked at the bloody wound.

'Don't worry.' Silva laughed, a little grunt of pain escaping between the chuckles. 'I'm also strong.'

'What can I do?' he asked. 'Is there anything at our camp I can get?'

Frantically, he tried to remember what they had brought with them. It was hard to focus his racing mind.

'No,' the warrior said firmly. 'You cannot risk it. Those wolves and that thing in the woods are still out there. We need both you and Tallith here to defend us.' Silva stared down at her protruding bone. 'I am going to need you to reset the bone.' She allowed herself a small smile. 'It seems you shall have vengeance for your nose.'

'I have to what?'

'I'm going to be very clear,' Silva said slowly. 'I am going to need you to reset the bone. Now, this injury is very painful, so I cannot have you taking three or four tries to do this. I need you to grip my leg firmly and push the bone back into place.'

Nicolas's hands hovered over Silva's leg. 'I'm sorry...I have to what?'

Silva removed a knife from her belt. 'Just do it.' She went to put the handle in her mouth but stopped just short. 'And understand that I won't be happy with you after.'

I was hardly grateful when you snapped my nose into place.

Nicolas squinted slightly as Auron leant in close. 'You going to help?'

'Kid, I'm not generally a petty man, but she did kill me,' the spirit said solemnly. 'What I'm going to do is enjoy this.'

Silva told Auron exactly what she thought of that before putting the handle of the knife into her mouth and biting down on it.

Hovering over the leg again, Nicolas took a few deeps breaths. Silva's gaze got fiercer the longer he dallied. Finally, he gripped the leg and pushed on the bone firmly. Silva's body spasmed as the handle of the knife muffled her wide-eyed scream of pain. After what looked to be a moment of intense agony, Silva's body slumped, the knife falling from her mouth with teeth marks in the handle as she breathed heavily.

'Are you okay?' Nicolas asked, hands hovering again.

Silva slapped him across the face, hard, knocking him to the floor. Going to rub his tender cheek, his hand stopped short, freezing as he saw Silva's furious eyes boring into him. After a moment when Nicolas genuinely feared for his life, the warrior closed her eyes and shook her head. When they opened again, they were softer.

'Sorry,' the warrior said with regret. 'I'm used to reciprocating when someone causes me pain.'

Nicolas finally rubbed his cheek as Tallith tore some cloth from his shirt and dressed Silva's leg. Nicolas looked from the warrior to Shift. Right now, their group was in very bad shape.

CHAPTER 29

Though staring at the salved wounds—the ones not currently covered by a blanket, anyway—wouldn't make it work any faster, he couldn't take his eyes off them. If he looked away, even for a second, Shift might die. There was no sense nor logic behind his assertion, but that didn't make it feel any less real. At least their breathing had evened out.

Weak. He said they were weak. Idiot. Shift is one of the strongest people I know.

'Here you go, young man,' Dieter said, pressing a steaming bowl into his hand. 'The soup will warm you.'

'I'm not—'

'Ah, ah,' the writer interrupted. 'It isn't necessarily about you being hungry. You've just been through a very bad experience. You need your strength. Now, eat up.'

He had to admit, it did smell nice. The steam from the chicken broth teased his nose. There appeared to be vegetables in it too. 'Thank you.' With a smile, Dieter turned away. 'Hold on.'

The writer looked at him expectantly.

'You've been around.'

'Gosh, I should say so.' Dieter chuckled. 'Around, and around again. One does not write a bestselling travel book by sitting at home and making things up.'

'Is...' He knew what he was about to ask was silly. But right now, he needed reassurance. About anything. 'Is Etherius a bad place?'

'That is a very odd question,' Deiter said after a thoughtful pause. 'What makes you ask?'

'Ever since I've been doing...this,' he gestured to his armour, 'all I meet are bad people doing terrible things, or scared folk giving into their anger and hatred. It's hard to believe the rest of the world is any different than what I've seen so far.'

The writer hummed as he considered this. 'Etherius itself is not an inherently bad place,' he began finally. 'It's just a place. It's the people in it that are more of a conundrum. And that comes down to choices.'

I can't remember the last time I felt like I had a choice.

'Every day, people make choices about who they want to be. Sometimes it's as simple as *'I want to do that, so I will.'* And sometimes their choices are shaped by outside influences, like the rallying cries of others. But it's all choice. You took up a mantle.' Dieter tapped the rising sun on his chest plate. 'And when you did—because it was your choice—you set yourself on a path of standing up to those who make bad choices. Seeking them out, or having them seek you out, became inevitable. And it will continue to be that way until you stop.'

Nicolas couldn't help but chuckle. Though he'd never thought about it like that, he supposed he had made a choice. At any point, he could've said no and stopped. No one had wrestled him to the ground and made him put on the armour. Though it could be argued that the choosing stick had forced him here, at any point he could've run in the opposite direction.

'Once you don armour and stand up for what is right, you are destined to live a life seeing the worst kind of people.'

Destiny was a dirty word to him. Dangerously near the term *chosen one*. Which Nicolas was sure he was not, save for having chosen himself, after a fashion. But Dieter's logic made sense. He was on a quest to vanquish evil, therefore he'd see evil.

Nicolas found no comfort in that answer, but at least it was an answer. 'Do you write about the bad parts more than the good?'

Dieter chuckled. 'What do you think would sell more books?'

Now it was Nicolas's turn to chuckle. 'I suppose you have to fund your expeditions somehow.'

'Exactly,' Dieter said, slapping him on the shoulder. 'Now, if I may ask a question of you? When you drew my attention to your armour, I could not help but notice the crest. It is very reminiscent of the sigil of the *Dawnblade*, Auron of Tellmark.'

'That's because I'm the new one, apparently.' He sighed wearily. 'The new *Dawnblade*, that is.' He extended his hand. 'Nicolas Percival Carnegie.'

Instead of taking the hand, Dieter started wagging his finger excitedly. 'Goodness me, I've heard of you, I think.'

He thinks?

Dieter ran back to his pack and rummaged again. Soon enough, he produced some papers, which he flicked through. 'Ah yes, here it is, here it is,' he muttered as he returned to Nicolas. 'I have heard a fair few tales about you. Some so unbelievable I initially wrote you off as some sort of folktale, or maybe an adventure story someone had mistaken for a biography. Happens more than you think.' The writer chuckled, probably at some memory that what he'd just said had evoked. 'But I took account of them anyway. I had planned to look into it further once my current expedition was finished.'

'I'm sure whatever you heard was true,' Nicolas remarked sourly. 'Apparently, everyone knows all the details of my life, down to any particularly difficult bowel movements I've had.'

Dieter looked up from his notes. 'Well, I don't have *that* in here, I assure you. Though I do have conflicting accounts of your name. Some tell me the name you introduce yourself by, whilst others call you *Nick Carnage*. Is this some sort of adventurer moniker you gave yourself?'

'No,' he replied definitively. 'That name is a mistake that destiny's saddled me with for all eternity, apparently.'

After producing a pencil from his jacket, Dieter scribbled on the paper. 'Excellent, excellent. *Destiny*, you say.' *Sigh.* 'I do like to give my readers the most accurate information possible. It's an artistic integrity thing, you understand. Also, professional pride.'

'I'd be the same.'

The explorer bit his lip thoughtfully before he spoke again. 'I don't suppose you'd take a moment to corroborate some of these facts, would you? There are a few tales that stretch credulity somewhat.'

If stories about me have to circulate then I guess they should at least be true. And it would be good to focus my mind on something other than worry.

As it turned out, Dieter had quite the list of questions. His notetaking was nothing if not thorough. Though in his clear excitement, he rattled them off almost too quickly to keep up with, and Nicolas had to ask him to repeat a couple of the questions, whilst he thought of proper answers for the ones he'd heard.

'Vampires, yes. No, I did not frequent the brothel the secret tunnel came out in.' Squinting, he tried to recollect the next question. 'Yes, to the dwarf gangster. But I didn't kill him. A Deity fed him to a chicken. Yes, I rode both a demon bear and a cow-dragon. I think it was about four taverns that I actually entered and got into fights in on the Ale Trail.' *Or was it three?* 'I did die and go to the Underworld. And finally, no, I did not moon Captain Kilgore to distract him so Captain Ramirez could run him through.'

Perhaps the details of my tales are a bit less thorough than I thought.

'Excellent, excellent,' Dieter said, scribbling away furiously.

'Any questions about the demonic killer in Babylon?'

The writer looked up from his notes in excitement. 'I have not heard of that one. A firsthand account would be fantastic. But first, can I ask about the seduction of the Gorgon Queen?'

'I beg your pardon.'

Parchment was shuffled until Dieter found what he was looking for. 'Yes, here it is. I was told you journeyed into a cave to face the Queen of the Gorgons. Knowing that she could turn you to stone with a glare, you strolled into her lair blindfolded.' His finger traced the words as he read. 'Unable to fight her effectively without being able to see, you opted to instead seduce her. You charmed the beast until she could no longer resist you then you lay together. Once she was asleep and her eyes were shut, you put a pillow over her head and decapitated her.'

'I... What...? I most certainly did not. What is a gorgon, anyway?' he spluttered.

'It's a half-snake, half-woman creature with snakes for hair,' Auron informed him helpfully from behind his stifled laugh.

'*Snake creature*?' Nicolas cried, nearly spilling the contents of his bowl into his lap.

'I beg your pardon?' Deitier asked, clearly confused by his exclamation.

'We have a spirit travelling with us. Auron of Tellmark. You'll have to quickly get used to us talking to him.' He offhandedly gestured in Auron's direction, before moving on to something he deemed much more important. 'And for your information, no, I did *not* lie with a snake woman thing.' Putting his soup down, he grabbed the papers from Dieter. Feverishly, he read the supposed accounts of his deeds. 'What else does it say here? I neutered a famous kascat bandit...what *is* all this?'

'Apparently, your legend's grown enough that people are embellishing it,' Auron said sympathetically. 'Happens to the best of us.' The spirit stopped for a moment. 'Oh, I think the kascat bandit might be one of my stories.'

For Deities' sake.

His hand with the papers fell to his side as he rubbed the bridge of his nose. With all he had to worry about in his life, now people were saying he lay with snake monsters and grabbed cat's balls. 'Okay,' he said after a deep breath. 'After my soup, you and I are going to sit down and sort the shit from the truth.'

'Fantastic.' Dieter beamed. 'And probably for the best.'

The thought of how hard Shift would be laughing at all this caught him unawares, making him ache inside. Glancing over, he saw they hadn't moved, but they were still breathing. And hopefully recovering.

Tearing himself away from Shift, he looked back at Dieter. 'Before we begin, I need to know something.'

The explorer gestured for him to continue.

'What are you doing out here, in a cave, mid-winter, by yourself?'

Dieter wagged his finger excitedly again. 'An excellent question, young man. Currently, I am writing a work on the legends of Etherius, trying to prove or disprove them. The one I am working on at the moment is that of The Visitor.'

'You're hunting him?' Silva asked.

'Goodness, no.' Dieter laughed. '*Investigating* him. And as he is only known to come out in winter, here I am.'

Tallith screwed his face up. 'But, alone?'

'Well,' the explorer shrugged, 'curiosity is my addiction, I'm afraid. And one that sometimes necessitates travelling alone. I did attempt to secure the services of some local guides, but apparently, I am, and I quote, *'a stark raving lunatic for going looking for The Visitor.'*

Nicolas wasn't sure he entirely disagreed.

'How do you defend yourself?' Tallith asked, looking around. 'I don't see a sword.'

'Oh dear, no.' Dieter laughed. 'Ghastly killing tools. No, I am blessed by being a fast runner due to years of practise. Plus, I have my trusty walking stick.' The explorer held up a five-foot-long knotted cane. 'And of course, looking a bit like a bear at a distance keeps some of the nastier folk away. But if it comes down to it, I do have the odd trick or two up my sleeve.'

'I bet he has some fascinating stories,' Auron said, staring at Dieter like a thirsty man might stare at a pool of water in a desert.

'Have you learnt much about The Visitor?' Silva asked.

'Not as much as I'd have liked.' The explorer shrugged. 'I was hoping for at least a sighting by now. Though I believe I have a rough hypothesis that he must do some form of reverse hibernation in the summer months. Maybe this speaks to his ethology, if he isn't human, or some specific mental trait. Either way, I'm sure he keeps to a certain area.'

'He has a specific territory?' Sergeant Tallith asked.

'Indeed, my boy.' Dieter nodded. 'His movements in it are random at best, but I have a rough idea. He operates primarily in the central areas of Ivilar, though he has been known to stray further on occasion. I believe we are at the edge of his territory.'

And yet it's the bit he's currently active in. Lucky us.

Despite the slight uncertainty that would always be there, Nicolas was relatively sure it wasn't Garaz. Especially if Dieter's *'reverse hibernation'* theory was accurate.

Still, Garaz, The Visitor...it was all secondary now. All he cared about was getting Shift the help they needed.

CHAPTER 30

Sleep wasn't even an option that night. With the wolves still out there, and Shift on the cusp of death, he wouldn't even try. Besides, if he didn't watch Shift like a hawk, they might die. If he even blinked for too long, they might die. There was no medical basis for this assertion, yet he couldn't shoo it away. But Shift was strong. They clung stubbornly on to life. As the hours went on, they showed no signs of getting either better or worse, they just continued living. For now, that was enough.

Why can't their wounds just vanish?

How could the universe allow Shift to die, when they'd acted so selflessly to protect the others? Sighing with the knowledge that he was being silly for thinking that watching Shift would affect the outcome of their life and death struggle, he rolled over onto his back. The cave's ceiling was low. The light from the fire marked many of the dips in it, small islands in a sea of shadow.

'Did you choose me?' he asked quietly. 'Did you influence that stick? If you did, then why me? Because you knew I wouldn't run, despite myself?'

No answer came. Only increased frustration.

'Nothing to say? You're very chatty when you have a message you need delivering, but when someone actually asks you something, it's silence.' His voice became more of growl with every word. 'Everything I've done, seen, and had done to me because of that stick, and you can't just come down and help Shift? T'goth, I saved you once, and you said you owed me. You said you'd send me home, and instead, I ended up on an island, which led to me getting whipped by pirates, amongst other things. So, I think one favour is still due.' He gestured toward Shift. 'Come on then. Get to it. Get your ass down here and perform a miracle.'

Still nothing.

'*Now.*' Nicolas shook his head angrily. 'I'll stop doing it, you know. I'll just pack up and go home. Adventuring done. Off to the nearest village to live in peace.'

Dammit.

Grunting with annoyance, he raised his middle finger to the ceiling. He was going nowhere. He knew it, and the Deities certainly did. He was in too deep now. Even without needing to seek vengeance for his parents and save his people, he'd seen too much evil to turn a blind eye to it ever again. There were too many corrupt or inept officials to simply trust them with the fate of Etherius.

Though I'm not sure it's in any better hands with me.

'Bemoaning your lot, kid?' Auron asked at his side. 'Because I don't think giving the Deities the middle finger will improve it any.'

'Probably not,' he replied with a dry chuckle. Giving Auron a sad smile, his eyes caught the sigil on the spirit's ethereal armour. It was the same one he now wore. How had he managed to become the new *Dawnblade*? 'Do you think I was chosen? Like, not by the stick landing on me. But *chosen* chosen.'

With a smile, Auron looked him up and down. 'Kid, if the Deities did choose you then objectively, they made a strange bloody choice.'

'Charming.'

'Grow up.' The spirit tutted. 'You know exactly what you were like when we first met. You've grown into it, but honestly, when we set off for the necromancer's fort, I thought you'd be dead within a day or two.'

'And you still dragged me along?'

Auron shook his head. 'I didn't drag you anywhere. Remember what Dieter said. You made a choice. Reluctant or not. What I did was use the only available resource I had and hoped for the best. And we haven't done too badly so far.'

'Tell Shift that.'

Auron crouched beside him. 'They aren't dead yet. I could tell you a thousand tales of how I was closer to death than this. But what I will say is that fate can flip quickly and dramatically when it wants to. You, of all people, should know how life and death can change. And Shift is strong and stubborn.'

A ragged breath from Shift got his attention. Nicolas sat up expectantly. Was this the last one? No, there was another. Then another.

Why didn't I dance with them on Ramirez's ship? What if I never get another chance?

'Snap out of it, kid.' The spirit clicked his fingers in front of Nicolas's face. 'It's time to go.'

'Go?'

'The sun's up, hence me not being on watch anymore.'

Though going back to their camp at night was too risky, they'd decided that at sun-up, Nicolas would venture back to the camp to get what supplies he could, especially any healing potions. Hopefully, he could find the horses too. But he highly doubted he'd be that lucky. They wouldn't have stopped running for a good long time.

According to Dieter, there was a settlement about a mile from here. Getting there wouldn't be easy with Shift comatose and Silva crippled, making it essential to find what they could before setting off.

Rising made him realise how stiff and tired his body was. But that could go hang. He would happily ignore it. This was more important. Briefly, he checked his sword, to ensure it could be drawn easily when needed. Sun-up didn't always chase away the bad things.

'Guard them with your life,' he said to Tallith, as the sergeant stood.

'Of course.' Tallith nodded, his face solemn with the responsibility he'd just been given.

Nicolas glanced back. He wanted to stroke Shift's hair and plant a kiss on their forehead before he left, but he resisted the urge, lest it somehow set in motion the chain of events that finished them off. 'I'll be back soon.'

'Are you sure you don't want me to come with you?' Dieter asked.

'No,' he replied quickly. 'It may still be dangerous out there. I'll move faster if I don't need to worry about protecting someone.'

'What about me?'

Nicolas looked at Silva. The warrior lay by a rock, splinted leg outstretched. 'You could limp to the gates of the Underworld and still face down a horde of the undead.' He smiled. 'But I'd rather you wait here and kill anything that enters this cave that isn't me.'

The warrior was clearly incensed at being left behind but didn't argue.

Wasting no more time, Nicolas and Auron left the cave. Outside, the body of the alpha wolf lay in the snow, waiting for decomposition to set in. Nicolas kicked it as he walked by.

Entering the forest, he drew his sword and readied himself for anything. Though their flight had been panicked, and it had been dark, Auron knew the way back to their camp. Balancing speed and the need to be careful, the pair wove through the trees. Nicolas kept his senses sharp, but there was no sign of trouble. Part of him was sad about that; he was in the mood to stab something deserving.

A sound caused Nicolas's ears to prick up. Auron looked at him sharply; he'd heard the same thing. There was a shuffling sound, possibly rummaging. Someone, or something, was ahead. Readying his blade, Nicolas stalked forward. The spirit moved ahead of him and disappeared through the bushes.

'Huh.' Auron said. 'Kid, come out.'

Moving silently, Nicolas broke through the foliage to the remains of their camp then stopped abruptly.

Nicolas gasped in surprise. 'What in the Underworld are *you* doing here?'

'Ah, 'tis ye, young'un,' Snaggletooth Joe grinned welcomingly, looking up from the pack he was rifling through. 'I wondered who this mess belonged te. Now I knows.'

'No, wait a minute,' Nicolas shook his head. 'How are you *here*?'

Joe shrugged. 'Travellin' trader.'

'Travelling through the middle of a forest?' he asked incredulously.

'Shortest distance between two points is a straight line.'

Nicolas opened his mouth to press the issue, when Joe suddenly shuffled up to him. The trader got uncomfortably close as he looked Nicolas up and down.

'Somethin' bad happened. I can see it in yer eyes, an' by lookin' at yer mess o' a camp.' Joe's gaze narrowed. 'Mayhap ye need some help?'

'A couple of my companions are injured,' he said, talking quickly. 'I need you to come with me and help them.' He grabbed Joe by the sleeve and started to pull him towards the treeline.

'O' course, o' course,' Joe said, raising his hands with a grin. 'I'll be with ye. Just lemme get my wagon, and we'll get yer people all patched up for a nice reasonable price.'

Nicolas had to bite his lip. Being reminded that Joe would want payment was unnecessary and unwelcome. But the trader was the best chance he had of saving Shift, and snapping at him might not be helpful.

'Thank you,' he said instead.

Joe wandered back towards his wagon, continuing to talk as he did. 'Oh, and by the by. I've come into possession o' four new horses. I can't help but notice yers have buggered off. But I'd happily let ye have these at a discount. Can't have ye wanderin' around in the snow barefoot now.'

If he looked a little less crusty, I'd kiss him on the mouth right now.

'That's a blessing.' He sighed as Joe mounted his wagon and spurred the donkey into life. Instantly, he saw the horses trailing behind it.

'Kid, you are dumb as a stone sometimes.' Auron sighed. 'Where do you think he found those horses?'

'He prob—' Nicolas shook his head. 'That tricky old bastard. Well, I'm not paying for them.'

'Good luck with that,' the spirit muttered. 'But let's get Shift and Silva healed first, thanks to Etherius's most convenient trader.'

Waving Snaggletooth Joe over to him, Nicolas pointed out the more passable trail to the cave. It wasn't as quick, but it was quick enough for the wagon. As he led the way, his hope increased with every step. A dark cloud in the back of his mind rumbled, wondering if it might already be too late.

That sort of thinking can bugger right off. Shift is going to be fine.

CHAPTER 31

As Shift opened their eyes after a few weary blinks, Nicolas's sigh of relief drove every drop of air from his lungs. Groaning, Shift raised their head and studied their surroundings with narrowed eyes. Finally, they lifted the blanket and peeked beneath it. Their eyes widened, and they sucked their teeth fiercely.

'That looks nasty,' they remarked, their voice croaky. 'Feels it too. Seems I'm not a natural wolf fighter.'

'You won.'

'Really doesn't feel like it right now.'

'Would you like me to bring you the carcass of the dead alpha as proof?' Silva asked.

'By the Deities, no,' Shift's voice suddenly had more life in it. 'I'll take your word for it.'

'This un's strong,' Snaggletooth Joe remarked at Nicolas's side. 'I reckon their ability te change makes 'em heal faster. That potion shouldn't have had 'em up an' about just yet.'

Strong...not weak.

Nicolas had to admit, whatever Joe had given Shift had really done the trick. Even if the trader's statement about Shift's ability helping them heal had a lot to do with it.

'I'm hardly *up and abo*— What are you doing here?' Shift double took as they realised who they were taking to.

'Travellin' trader.' Joe shrugged.

'You should've stayed with us,' Nicolas said as he passed them a cup of water. 'You could've been killed.' His attempt to keep his anger from his voice failed miserably.

Shift took a sip from the cup, their eyes closing as they drank, as if it were the sweetest thing they'd ever tasted. The second sip they spat in his face.

'You're welcome, you ingrate.'

Wiping his face, he couldn't help but smile. They were certainly getting better.

'Well, yes, thank you, obviously,' he tried to recover. 'But it was silly, and crazy, and...what were you thinking?'

'Very smooth, kid,' Auron remarked behind him.

Suddenly, Shift let out a choked cough. They winced, their eyes narrowing as if concentrating hard on breathing. Panic gripped Nicolas. Shift gestured for him to come closer.

'What is it?' he asked urgently. 'What can I do to help?'

'I...I...' They appeared to be struggling to speak. The room seemed to shrink. All Nicolas could do was watch, desperate to help, but having no idea what to do. Then Shift's face became neutral, like nothing had ever been wrong. 'If you ever tell me off after I've nearly died defending you again, I'm going to break your face. Clear?'

Yup. That's a fast recovery.

'Clear.'

The shapeshifter kissed him, and he returned it passionately. 'Right,' they said as the pair's lips parted. 'Now that's out of the way, I'd like some clothes, please.'

'You aren't going anywhere yet,' Nicolas said firmly.

Shift's eyes narrowed then they tilted their head to look past him. 'I'm going to talk to the sensible people in the room. Now, I'm not planning on going anywhere. But I would prefer not to lie here naked under a blanket with you all looking at me. I tore my clothes up turning into a wolf. Where are my spare sets?'

'Kid, I'm pretty sure you didn't pick any up when we went to the camp,' Auron whispered in his ear.

'I was too worried to think about it.'

'Go and get them,' Shift said cooly. 'Now.' Something caught the shapeshifter's eye. 'How's your leg?'

'Fine,' Silva answered quickly.

That wasn't entirely accurate. Joe had given the warrior a potion to knit the bone back together, but it would still be hard to use for the foreseeable future. The trader had told her to take it easy. Silva hadn't cared for that idea, but she'd relented enough to use a single crutch fashioned from a branch.

'I had best go get their things,' Nicolas said to break the tension in the air. 'Tallith, I'll need you to come with me.'

'Of course,' the sergeant said eagerly.

'And I'll lie here and get acquainted with this interesting looking fellow,' Shift said, waving at Dieter.

'Dieter Von Ostric, at your service,' the writer said with a low bow.

'Courteous and famous.' The shapeshifter nodded. 'That should keep me entertained until you're back.'

'And safe,' Nicolas said quickly. 'Keep them safe too.'

'I am quite capable of doing that.' Silva was clearly incensed at him asking Dieter to protect Shift. 'One aching leg does not make me an invalid,' the warrior continued. 'I would be equally as deadly with no legs.'

'I know,' Nicolas said, holding his hands up in surrender. 'I was asking Dieter to be sure he would. It goes without saying that you'll protect Shift.'

The warrior didn't seem at all placated, so Nicolas hurried from the cave with Tallith in tow. Moving with purpose through the snowy forest, it soon became clear that Tallith had something to say. Nicolas knew exactly what it was. He could've prompted the conversation, but he was too busy enjoying the fact that Shift was alive. Tallith would speak up sooner or later.

Any second now, in fact.

It was like a pressure building at his side. A giant bubble waiting to pop.

'I am so sorry.'

There it is.

'No apology necessary,' he replied quickly.

'There certainly is,' the sergeant insisted. 'This is the second time I've messed up and put you all in danger. First the horned bandits, now I caused Silva to get her leg broken.'

'You're lucky *she* hasn't come to that conclusion.' Nicolas smirked. 'Or you would be sorry.' An aura of guilt struck him, and he stopped and turned to Tallith. 'Look, you've nothing to be sorry for. It happens. Learn from it, and do better next time.'

'Like you did?'

'I... Yes. Like I did. Apologising is nice, but it doesn't take it back.'

He continued on his way, knowing the longer the pair took, the greater Shift's ire when they did return. At his side, Tallith's eyes were downcast. He'd heard Nicolas's words, but he wasn't quite ready to accept them yet.

'How are you finding this?' he asked. 'The adventuring lark.'

'A lot tougher than I imagined,' Tallith admitted. 'I... There's a certain romanticism to the stories. The truth of it is a lot worse.'

'Long stretches of boring travelling then a few minutes of intense fear and danger?'

Tallith laughed. 'I think that sums it up nicely.'

Nicolas stopped again. He thought about what Dieter had said regarding choices. Though Nicolas had made the choice to keep going, it never felt like he really had any say in the matter. It would be a shame to put someone else in the same position.

'Look,' he began as he gathered his thoughts. 'This isn't for everyone. And if it isn't for you, you don't have to keep going.'

The look of sheer despair on Tallith's face made him feel like the biggest ass in all Etherius.

'You don't want me around anymore?'

'That isn't what I said,' he replied firmly. 'I'm simply saying that if you do want to go back, you can leave with Joe whilst we go on. No one will think less of you.'

'*I'll* think less of me,' Tallith answered without hesitation. 'I started this, and I want to finish it. I came to learn, and I will.'

For a reason he couldn't verbalise, Nicolas smiled. 'Very well then. Just stay clear of Silva for a little while. She may not be angry at you now, but that could change.'

'I'll keep my head down.' He nodded.

Nicolas went to carry on but stopped suddenly. 'And...you really need to change the way you talk to me.'

Tallith raised a confused eyebrow. 'I've stopped calling you sir.'

'I know that. But your tone. You talk to me like you're talking to your superior. We're the same age.'

A look crossed Tallith's face.

'No,' Nicolas said, holding up a finger. 'I can hear you thinking about how humble and gracious I am. Enough of that.'

'I'll try, but I can't guarantee anything.' Tallith shrugged. 'You're a legend.'

'A dead legend if we don't hurry up.'

Taking Tallith by the arm, he guided him in the direction they were supposed to be walking.

CHAPTER 32

By the time they returned with supplies, Tallith's choice had been taken away from him anyway. Snaggletooth Joe had vanished. Literally. Auron explained that he'd been there one minute then gone the next. The spirit appeared quite unnerved. No one could understand how the old donkey moved so fast. Nor the ass pulling his wagon.

'How does he just vanish?' Tallith asked, peering at the treeline.

With all that had and was still happening, a disappearing one-toothed trader wasn't high on Nicolas's list of things to worry about.

'He's a strange man.' Nicolas shrugged as he checked his saddlebag. 'Etherius is full of them.'

'And this one is quite a bit richer.' Silva wasn't pleased about the amount they'd been charged for the potions and horses. The group treasury was running low. But it was a small price to pay. Shift was alive, and they had their horses back.

Though the price had been high, Joe had offered them a half price discount on the horses when Silva realised they were theirs anyway and pinned the trader to the wall. Nicolas couldn't resist smiling when Auron told him.

'Handy, though,' Shift said from atop their horse. They were pale and weak but trying their best to sit proudly and upright. It had taken a couple of attempts before they'd grudgingly asked for help to get up into the saddle. Nicolas had offered Silva the same assistance, but he'd been told where to insert that.

Putting a foot in the stirrup, Nicolas took a moment to acknowledge the lingering ache between his eyes. Shift had flicked him pretty damn hard when he'd suggested they find a nearby village where they could stay and recuperate. His ears were still ringing with their curses.

Still, they could've kicked me in the balls.

Despite half their party being 'walking wounded', it looked to be a decent day. The sun was bright, making the snow-covered ground almost glow. There was only a minor chill in the air, and Joe's amulet nullified that.

Mounting, Nicolas looked back at the others. Though he wouldn't admit it aloud, they were going to be moving much slower now, and there'd already been so many delays. How far away was Garaz now? Would they ever catch him? Trying was starting to seem like a fool's errand, but he couldn't let it go. None of them could. But a certain unspoken fatalism hung over the group. Their chances of catching up to the orc were slim, and if he made it to The Wasteland, he'd be gone forever.

Would we even dare follow him in there?

Whilst he still hoped that Garaz might be a shining example of orcishness, his people had their reputation for a bloody good reason.

A polite cough got Nicolas's attention, and he blinked himself out of his daydreaming.

Dieter stood at the mouth of the cave, hands clasped behind his back. 'Excuse me, young man,' the writer said formally. 'I would like to petition you to let me accompany you on your journey.'

'Why?' Nicolas hoped the question didn't sound rude, but it needed asking.

'Excellent question.' Dieter smiled. 'First, for the chance to travel in your company. I think it may be a fascinating journey. Maybe I could write a book about you.'

Just what I want. A bloody novel—or novels—written about my life.

'Second, I've heard about your quest, and I believe you may end up venturing into orc territory. This is a region I've been eager to explore but always lacked the proper travel companions.'

By which, you mean people mad enough to go in there.

'I hate to disappoint you, but we have no plans to go walking into The Wasteland.'

Nicolas winced. For a moment, he could picture the universe turn a giant flaming eye in his direction, taking what he had foolishly said aloud as a challenge to be met. Now it was almost certain that they would be visiting the land of the orcs.

'It'll be dangerous,' he continued, shooing the image away. 'And what about your research into The Visitor?'

Dieter shifted on the spot uncomfortably. 'Well, that is the third thing, you see. With your reputation with the nastier side of Etherius, chances are you will stumble across The Visitor at some point in the near future. Or he will find you.'

Oh, come on. This is beyond a joke now.

'So, we are bait?' Silva asked coolly.

'Not at all,' Dieter protested. 'I am just playing the odds that you will cross paths with him.' The writer smiled thoughtfully. 'Let me ask you all this. You have seen what The Visitor has done to people. Do you really have no plans to hunt him down?'

The group exchanged a few glances. None of them denied it. Even Silva knew an indefensible position when she saw one.

'He'll be handy to have about,' Auron said. 'Plenty of local knowledge.'

Nicolas looked at his other companions. Judging by the shrugs he received, they didn't mind either way. At least Dieter was personable. And it might be nice to travel in sophisticated company for a change.

'Fine,' Nicolas relented. 'But we find Garaz first. Then we hunt this Visitor down.'

'Excellent.' Dieter beamed. 'Whilst we find your companion, I can work on your book.'

'What are you going to call it?' Shift asked. '*Tales of a Sword Dropper? The Reluctant Village Boy Who's Often a Bit Clumsy?*'

Funny.

'No, no,' the writer said, shaking his head. 'A tale like this should have a more adventurous title. Something with more punch. Maybe...' Dieter scratched his chin thoughtfully. '*Chronicles of...*'

'Can you go and get your horse, please? We need to leave,' Nicolas interrupted.

'Yes, of course.' Dieter smiled. 'I have already packed everything up.'

'Strong. She livessss.'

Nicolas had his sword drawn by the time he looked up to the source of the voice. On the embankment above the cave stood a large, hunched figure in a dirty brown cloak. Judging by the bumps and lumps in the cloak, this person was oddly malformed. A chain dangled from beneath the hood which covered its face. Attached to it was a wooden mask carved in the likeness of a laughing trickster, with two bright red jewels for eyes.

'She passssed the test.'

Though they were in danger right now, relief gripped him. This was clearly The Visitor, and it wasn't Garaz. But whatever this creature was, it was obviously deadly and not afraid of them. The fact that it was confronting them during the day, when it was supposed to hunt at night, was unnerving. That meant whatever it wanted was urgent, so chances were it wouldn't give up easily.

'It will take more than a broken leg to fell me,' Silva roared from her saddle. 'But feel free to come down here and test that theory.'

The figure grabbed at the hood of its cloak as if enraged, pulling it tightly around its head. *'Why doessss no one undersssstand me?'*

Nicolas couldn't help but notice The Visitor's hands. One was human looking, the other covered in green scales and ending in thick claws. *'Not her. I didn't mean her. I wasn't talking to her. I meant her, the other her. Why does nobody listen. Why?'*

As it sank in who The Visitor was referring to, his mouth dried.

'Herrrrrr,' The Visitor snarled, pointing a claw at Shift. *'Herrrrrrr.'*

'I'm not a *her,*' Shift snapped back defiantly. 'And certainly not a *herrrr-rrr.*'

Maybe doing bad impressions of him isn't the way to go right now.

'Rrrraaaagggghhhh.' The Visitor clawed at the hood of his cloak again. *'Doesn't matter. Doesn't matter. Shapeshifter. Strong shapeshifter. Cure. Special. Is special. That'sssss why I need you.'* The hands reached in Shift's direction, clasping.

Nicolas brought his horse between Shift and The Visitor. 'No,' he said firmly.

Whatever was beneath that cloak was big, so it would take a lot of stabbing. But he was up to the task. Even without taking Shift into account, it would save a lot of people.

'They are what I've been missssssssssing.'

He was starting to get the impression that sanity and The Visitor had parted company many years ago and not even kept in touch.

'Missing?' he asked.

'The secret to the undoing.' Nicolas wasn't sure if The Visitor was talking to him or himself. *'I can finally undo it. After so long. So long. So many inhospitable people. No more. Welcome me now. Yessssss. Welcome.'*

'The only undoing will be yours if you come down here,' Silva bellowed. 'But I invite you to. We have curses to undo, and I hear killing you is the way to do it.'

The Visitor stopped suddenly, craning its neck toward the warrior, as if seeing her for the first time.

'Sssssilva?' There was a harsh chuckle. *'Ssssilva. Is Silva. After so long.'*

Everyone looked at the warrior, who seemed momentarily disarmed. 'I am Silva,' she said cautiously.

The laughter began again, a sharp, hissing sound. *'It'ssssss niccce to see you. You haven't changed much. You are harsher, I think, not like when last we met. I have changed. Sssso much. Not for long.'*

'You know him?' Nicolas asked.

Silva's mouth was open, but all she could do was shake her head and shrug.

'I changed. Changed soooo very much. Can you still see me in here?' Holding the hood, The Visitor pulled it back.

Nicolas gasped. Half the face was human, that of a scholarly man. But at the nose, the skin and form changed. Green scales covered part of his head and large fangs deformed a mouth too small for them. Atop one side of his head was a thick horn. One eye was human, one was yellow and bulging. *'Changed. Big changes. Terrible changes.'*

'Avin?' Auron's voice was choked.

There was a thump in the snow. Silva had dropped her sword. Looking up in horror, she shook her head slowly. 'No,' she whispered. 'Avin...'

The Visitor glanced around thoughtfully. *'Avin? Yes, once Avin.'* He nodded. *'But not for a long time now. Not a long time. Avin no more. Just...this now. Visitor. Visiting. Checking. Who's hospitable? So many aren't. They must learn. People have to learn. Be welcoming.'*

Silva held her hand to her mouth for a moment, clearly shocked. 'Avin, whatever you're doing here, please let us talk about this.'

'No,' The Visitor, Avin, snapped. *'No talking. Too many words. Harsh words. Hateful words. Nasty glares go with them. Won't matter soon. No. Won't matter. Not once I have shapeshifter. Can undo it. Undo it all.'* The creature's longing smile was disconcerting. *'Maybe Avin again.'*

'The Underworld you will *have shapeshifter,*' Nicolas declared firmly. He was sure there was some kind of tragic backstory here, but any potential sympathy went out the window when it talked about abducting Shift.

'What have I told you about protecting me?' Shift asked him curtly.

'That you don't like it, and that you are capable of defending yourself, which you are,' he answered quickly. 'But you're still recovering, and that looks pretty formidable. So...tough.'

Shift's eyes widened then they smiled. 'Fair point.'

'Kid.' Auron's voice was filled with concern. 'Whatever happens next, try not to hurt him too much. Only if you really have to.'

How do I use my sword gently?

'Avin,' Silva persisted, her voice pleading. 'Please remember who you are. This isn't you. You wanted to help people, and now you are hurting them. You—'

'Deserved,' Avin shrieked. *'Deserved. A thousand times deserved. I tried to help them once, and it cost me. My face. My mind. Terrible price. Now they shun me. Inhospitable. They must pay. It's the only way they learn.'*

Except they aren't learning, are they? This guy has a song about not turning him away, yet we've still been chased away from several places.

'You are not a monster.' Silva's voice was choked with tears. 'Do not throw away everything the others fought for. Died for. I am begging you.'

'What do you know of it? You weren't even there,' The Visitor hissed. *'After that day...am I not a monster?'* He ran a claw down the scaled side of his face. *'I look like one. I am treated like one. Therefore, I am one.'*

'You silly boy,' Auron whispered in shock.

'Av—'

'No.' Avin pointed a claw at Silva. *'No more talk. Words. Poison words. Sweet words. Came for the shapeshifter. Give them to me. Or I'll show you what a monster can do.'*

They had reached the point of no return. This was going to get ugly, regardless of anyone's hope that it wouldn't. As Nicolas readied himself, his eyes were drawn to the mask dangling from Avin's neck. Somehow, he knew there was magic in it. Not in the way that Garaz could sometimes sense strong magic. It was those instincts of his again. They told him, very firmly, not to let the creature put the mask on.

Mask or not, he's not taking Shift.

Dismounting, Nicolas took several steps forward, getting into his fighting stance. His companions did the same. Silva didn't take her eyes off Avin as she picked up her sword from the ground. The horses dispersed, sensing that danger was near.

Readying himself for a fight, he stared up at The Visitor. 'You can take the shapeshifter over our dead bodies.'

Why in the Underworld did I say that? Am I inviting death now?

The Visitor smiled. *'Your proposal is acceptable.'*

Nicolas, you idiot.

Wafting his cloak open, The Visitor revealed his body, which shared his face's disfigurement. The way one side of Avin's body was disproportionate to the other almost reminded him of Koth. Rising to his full height, The Visitor leant back. For a second, it looked like he was chewing something...sucking something, maybe?

'Fascinating,' Dieter, who'd been writing all this down, muttered in awe.

Really not the time.

'Shit,' Auron cried, his pupilless eyes wide. 'Kid. He can breathe fire.'

Shit.

Nicolas threw himself aside, grabbing Shift as he did. Halfway through the motion, he realised it was probably silly. It was unlikely The Visitor would launch a stream of fire at someone stood directly in front of the person he wanted to kidnap. Still, Avin clearly wasn't sane, so best not to take any chances.

Nicolas was right. The Visitor didn't unleash his fire at them. Instead, gouts of flame poured from his mouth, striking the snow all around them. Within an instant, the air was filled with mist. Visibility vanished. He could make out shadows and hear people calling out in confusion.

'Are you okay?' he asked, clinging to Shift.

'Just about,' the shapeshifter replied, scanning the grey around them. 'I'm trying to change, but I'm still too weak. The one bloody thing I can do...'

Nicolas's head snapped this way and that as he saw flashes of light in the mist. More fire.

'This way,' he whispered.

Carefully, he led Shift towards what he hoped was the treeline. The floor was mushy and wet, making walking treacherous. Every step required his focus. Then The Visitor hit him.

The green hand appeared through the mist, swiping him across the jaw. Staggering back, he lost his footing and fell to the ground. Instantly, he tried to scrabble up, but a large, scaled foot stomped down on his chest. Even through his armour, he felt the impact, taking a single sharp, gasping breath. The same foot then kicked him. Losing his grip on his sword, Nicolas slid across the mush that had not long before been snow.

Not wasting a second, Nicolas drew the knife from his boot and got to his feet. Then he heard the flapping. A great wafting sound. The mist began to clear, driven away by gusts of wind from The Visitor's giant wings.

For Deities' sake. He's half human and half dragon, yet he has two *wings? Just our bloody luck.*

'Yes. Yes.' Avin rose into the air, Shift slumped over his shoulder.

'Noooooo.' Nicolas flicked the knife in his hand, ready to throw it. But Shift was there. He couldn't risk hitting them.

Turning, The Visitor flew away.

Screaming, Nicolas tried to pursue him, but there was little traction on the ground, so for all his movement, he didn't get very far. Finally, he came to a halt.

'Here.' Tallith handed him his sword, not that it'd do him any good now. With a cry, he used it to bat the nearest piece of remaining snow aside.

'We'll get him, kid,' Auron said, watching The Visitor become a speck on the horizon.

'Deities right, we will,' he growled, turning around. 'Dieter, I need to see all your research on The Visitor and his territory.' His eyes flicked to Auron and Silva. 'Then we're going to have a talk about exactly what in the Underworld that is.'

CHAPTER 33

Nicolas stared at the map laid out on the cave floor so intently that he wasn't sure he was actually picking out any details. Closing his eyes, he fought to calm himself. He wouldn't help Shift by panicking. At least Dieter's research had been thorough. The map had numerous Xs drawn on it, indicating sites The Visitor had been seen or attacked someone.

'I have the dates of each one written down in my notes,' the writer explained. 'The Visitor has been active for three years now. He appears in winter, visits and curses a smattering of remote villages or manors then disappears again until next winter. He never strikes a major population centre.'

'So, where does he go when he isn't cursing innocent people?' Nicolas asked, frowning. There were so many options on the map, and he couldn't fathom how to even begin narrowing them down.

'Interesting question,' Dieter said, nodding. 'I am assuming he is some form of half-dragon hybrid?'

'Yes.' Silva's voice was hoarse, and she kept her gaze on the floor. Seeing the warrior so stricken was jarring. But Nicolas had more pressing concerns.

'Interesting. Dragons do hibernate,' the writer continued. 'Sometimes, they can remain dormant for centuries, especially if they have a sufficiently large treasure horde. That is the exact reason dragons are not seen today. Not since The Hording.'

'The what?' Tallith asked.

'About a century ago, the dragons went crazy,' Dieter explained. 'There was a month of widespread chaos where the creatures flew everywhere, grabbing every treasure trove they could. Apparently, it was quite the frenzy. When it was done, the dragons took their loot, returned to their lairs, and have not been seen since.'

'Can we focus on now?' Nicolas instantly regretted snapping. But they didn't have time for this.

'Apologies, young man.' Dieter smiled, appearing not to be offended. 'I sometimes get carried away. I was just thinking maybe that would give us an answer as to why The Visitor only comes out in winter.'

'It's about limited travel.'

Nicolas gestured for Tallith to elaborate, which he did with an awkward smile.

'Due to his ability to fly, and breathe fire, he isn't restricted when travelling in winter. Everyone else is. His victims are almost trapped in their homes and villages. Easy pickings. And he's unlikely to be seen by other travellers on the road.'

'And he can't be pursued,' Silva said sadly.

'Exactly.' The sergeant nodded.

Quite ironic, seeing as hunting someone down is the whole reason we're out in this ourselves.

'It's also to do with his mental state.' Tallith was in his element now. 'Winter has long nights. I bet each attack happens at night, because he doesn't like to be seen by people. I can't say I blame him for that, with the way he looks and all. For him to come at us in the day...he must've really wanted Shift.'

Sighing, Nicolas turned to Auron and Silva. 'The way he looks,' he repeated. 'Care to explain that?' The pair exchanged a loaded, and pained, look. 'Come on, out with it. Someone doesn't get to be a half-dragon, half-human creature without a tragic backstory. So, let's hear it.'

Oh, maybe it isn't tragic...but kinky. Do I want to hear it?

No. I need to.

'It'll have to be you,' Auron told the warrior. 'Half the people in here can't hear me.'

At least we avoid, 'So this one time...'

Silva didn't look grateful for her task, but she didn't shirk her duty either. 'Avin Hipmuck is...was...is...a wizard,' she began. 'His chosen school was shapeshifting. He had perfected a way to change himself into a dragon.'

'It wasn't as exciting as it sounds,' Auron chimed in. 'It was a small dragon, and it took him about half an hour to do it.'

'I would argue then that he hadn't perfected it,' Nicolas commented dryly. When Deiter gave him a quizzical look, he nodded toward Auron. Their new companion still hadn't got used to them talking to the spirit yet.

'Avin was an idealist. He saw a skill he had that could help others, and he wanted to use it.' Whatever fond memory that conjured up made Silva smile. 'He left home to pursue a place in the Guild of Heroes. He petitioned to join at the same time myself and several others did. We all passed the trials and became New Bloods. When they saw us together, the heads of the guild had the idea that in these troubled times, maybe teams of heroes, rather than solo adventurers, would do more good.' The warrior's face hardened. 'We were supposed to be the future. Each of us was full of our own dreams and beliefs that we could take on the world. They thought that too. So, they sent us to the most prestigious Hall of Champions in Yarringsburg, to have a real legend train us.'

Nicolas glanced at Auron, guessing who that legend was.

The spirit's face was unreadable. The red in his aura wasn't.

'It went wrong.' It was a statement, not a question. Nicolas wasn't even sure he needed to say it aloud.

'Do you recall Vargas Quell?' Silva snarled.

Instantly, he recalled the smug warrior who had boastfully claimed to be Auron's nemesis. 'Yes.'

'It turned out he was heading a secret campaign to bleed the guild to death.' Silva closed her eyes. 'When he heard about us, and who was training us, he assembled his own group of warriors.'

'All dead now.' From Auron's tone, it was clear he was the one who'd made that so.

'Vargas used a group of villagers to lure them into an ambush,' Silva continued. 'They all fell saving the very people who had sold them out.'

'The innocent people who didn't have a choice,' Auron corrected bitterly.

Suddenly, Nicolas picked up on something Silva had said. '*Them*? Where were you when they were ambushed?'

The pointed looked between Silva and Auron explained everything. Suddenly, Nicolas knew exactly why the warrior had killed Auron.

'I was in his bed,' Silva admitted.

'Don't say it like that,' Auron snapped. 'You make it sound like I seduced you. You're the one who came to *my* chambers and stripped off.'

And that right there is all I ever want to know about that.

'It doesn't matter. I should have been there.' Silva closed her eyes. 'But I was not, and my friends died. That day I became the person you met on that bridge. There...was more to it. But that event was the tipping point.' When she looked up at Nicolas, her eyes burned with regret. 'But you gave me a second chance.'

Walking forward, he put a reassuring hand on her shoulder. 'I don't regret it.' Pursing his lips, he thought for a moment. 'So, Avin should be dead then?'

'No,' the warrior replied. 'Before my friends were slaughtered, there was another ambush. Quell and his minions attacked us in the woods. We were still training and had yet to form a cohesive team, so it was not going well. Avin saw we were in peril and rushed his change. The spell backfired, leaving him...as you saw.'

'Not quite,' Auron added thoughtfully. 'That mask is new.'

'I have never seen it before,' Silva replied.

'Did this Avin fellow have the ability to curse people before his accident?' Dieter asked, finally looking up from his furious notetaking.

The warrior shook her head. 'The focus of his magic was shape changing. The only other discipline he mentioned was healing, in which he had some minor skill.' Silva frowned. 'He was not the type to be interested in curse magic.'

A healer becomes a monster. A lot of that around.

'Then I'd wager the mask has the power to curse folk.' The writer used his pencil as a pointing stick. 'There are many strange, powerful, and deadly artifacts appearing in Etherius of late. No one knows where they come from, or even who makes them. But they are there, being misused.'

'Why not just burn people, if he can breathe fire?' Nicolas asked.

'Someone like that would be overwhelmed with shame and rage,' Tallith interjected. 'I imagine he's been shunned by society, so he needs venge— No.' The sergeant looked like an epiphany had struck him. 'It isn't about vengeance. He could just kill them. He's trying to teach people a lesson. He's trying to show them what happens if they become freakish, like him.'

That made a terrible sense. Nicolas had his own tragic backstory. Parents killed, sent to the Underworld...but he hadn't let it turn him into a villain. It probably helped that he wasn't horribly disfigured. Nicolas couldn't help but feel sorry for Avin. But he couldn't just ignore what The Visitor had been doing to people, or that he had Shift. Avin had turned his accident into fuel for a figurative fire that was burning everyone he came into contact with.

Then another thought occurred to him. Magic artifacts. Dieter was right, he had seen a lot of those around lately. A focusing crystal, this mask, the healing amulet, a set of pipes.

The pipes. The faun.

He was going off topic now, but the question needed to be asked. Nicolas looked at their newest companion. 'Dieter, when I checked you weren't a faun you made a remark. It sounded as if you'd met one before. Have you?'

'Terrible little buggers,' Dieter said, tutting and shaking his head. 'I've seen many of them around lately. Always stirring up some kind of trouble, or there is trouble already and a faun just *happens* to be nearby. It isn't easy to make these connections, but I travel, and I observe, and

I noticed. Usually, there's magic involved. They are strangely powerful, considering traditional fauns are quiet folk who keep to themselves.'

'Did they ever have magical artifacts?' Silva asked, evidently picking up on the reason for his question.

'Hmm.' Dieter thought for a moment. 'Once or twice, yes. Not the type of thing I've seen before, truth be told. But powerful.'

'Any idea where they got them from?' Nicolas asked.

'No, sorry,' the writer said after a moment.

So far he'd faced two fauns, and neither experience had been pleasant. And both had been servants of the Maestro. Was it a coincidence that Avin was using a powerful magical artifact too? Maybe finding the origin of these items would lead them to The Visitor, and in turn the Maestro and his people?

No. We can't waste time with a side quest that may take us further from Shift.

Who knew how long Avin would keep Shift alive? Right now, every second was precious. They needed to focus on the map. It had to have the answer.

'You know,' Tallith began slowly, as he crouched down and traced the X's on the map with his finger, 'There is a roughly circular pattern to these attacks. If you look at where we are now, and the direction we know The Visitor went, it actually goes right to the centre of this circle.'

Nicolas frowned, his eyes flicking from X to X.

He's right.

Hope caused him to smile. Tallith had narrowed down a search area. It would take them away from Garaz. They'd never catch the orc now. But saving Shift was far more important.

Though knowing Shift, they've already saved themselves.

Using his finger, Tallith gently traced lines across the map to a central point. 'Here,' he said giddily. 'I'm sure he'll be in this area. Eligorn Forest.'

'Eligorn?'

'It's one of the enchanted forests of Etherius,' Auron explained. 'If memory serves, there's a small cave network this side of it. If I was a half-dragon monster, I'd make my lair there.'

'Based on?'

The spirit shrugged. 'Dragons love caves.'

That answer pretty much equated to Auron's usual answer of *'hero instincts,'* which, in turn, were usually spot on.

It wasn't definite by any means. But it would have to do.

'Then it's time to go rescue Shift.'

CHAPTER 34

Nicolas's statement would've been daring and heroic if The Visitor's lair had been just around the corner. Instead, it had proven to be two days of hard travel. Though the weather at least gave them a pass to move relatively unhindered, travelling through the snow was still frustratingly slow. Nicolas had spent much of the first day worrying that Shift was already dead. But in the end, he reasoned that if that were the case, somehow, he'd know. He had no logical basis for this assertion, but he asserted it, nonetheless. So, the second day was spent moving forward with grim determination.

Finally, they caught sight of Eligorn Forest ahead. The canopy was dusted with white, making it look like a large collection of snowballs assembled next to each other. Even from this distance, he could feel the purity radiating from Eligorn. Despite their reason for being here, it was comforting. This would be his second visit to an enchanted forest, and he knew them to be magical places, full of life.

And a good place for villains to hide.

The last enchanted forest they'd visited, Edmoor, had been the hideout for the Big Boss and his numerous goons. It still rankled him that evil could exist in such pure places. And here it was, happening again. But he couldn't let himself get distracted.

Dieter wasn't going to make that easy. 'Do you see the tower over yonder?'

It was hard to miss. In the distance, maybe at the centre of the forest, the tower rose high into the sky. It was bright and white, almost as if it was made from snow itself. Though it was hard to pick out detail at this distance, everything looked smooth and elegant. It was like a giant work of art, rather than a building.

'That is Isaline, the last tower of the elves,' Dieter explained. 'A living piece of history.' The writer's voice was dreamy, to the point that Nicolas wasn't sure if Dieter was just talking to himself. 'Oh, how I would like to explore it. It is bigger than even the Heaven Towers in Invictra. A true testament to the elves' craft, and their desire to be closer to their gods, or maybe the notion that they saw themselves as gods. History from that time is a little sketchy.'

'I'm sure it's fascinating,' Nicolas replied absentmindedly, his eye caught by the rising hills to the east of the forest and the caves that peppered them.

'Since the elves left nearly a thousand years ago, the tower has stood a tall, proud monument to the race that was.' Dieter tilted his head, as if to see it better. 'Many cities in Ivilar have elven architecture, but they've weathered over the years and been added to. Not this. This is the same as it always was.'

'Does anyone live there now?' Tallith asked.

'Deities, no.' Dieter gasped then caught himself. 'Well, nobody believes so. They say the place is protected by old and powerful magics. Anyone who has tried to explore it has not returned. After a while, people got the message and stopped trying. Maybe one day, when I am old and have nothing left to lose...'

'Are we sure The Visitor isn't camped inside it then?' Nicolas looked to Tallith for the answer. Though the sergeant lacked a little in the soldiering department, his insights had proven pretty invaluable. Assuming they were right, of course.

Tallith scrunched up his face as he studied the tower. 'I don't think so,' he said finally. 'The tower looks too pure. Avin's rage derives from the way he looks, the melding of man and dragon. He wouldn't be able to stand living in such a place. Dwelling in the dark would fit much better with how he sees himself.'

Nicolas tilted a questioning eyebrow at Auron.

'Sounds good to me,' the spirit said. 'He's handy to have around.'

'You are talented at this,' Silva noted as she flexed her leg. Snaggletooth Joe's magic had done its business, but the leg still bothered her, especially with the cold. But the warrior wouldn't let it get in the way when called to action.

'Thank you.' Nicolas smirked as Tallith's cheeks reddened. 'The mind, and people's motivations, have always fascinated me. Which is quite effective in my line of work.'

'Care to use the skill to pinpoint the exact cave?' It was likely a silly question. But time was of the essence, especially now. Shift had been in The Visitor's clutches far too long already.

They're alive. I know it.

'I don't think I can. Sorry,' Tallith answered. 'Each looks as likely as the last. But chances are they're all connected.'

'They are,' Auron confirmed. 'We don't have time for a story, so I'll just say that I slew everything that was in there.'

A plan that was still sound.

Except for Shift, of course.

'Then we search them all,' Nicolas said with a deep breath, hoping that whatever power let him know Shift was still alive was also letting Shift know they were coming to rescue them.

After a short ride, the group dismounted and hitched their horses to trees at the bottom of the sloping path leading up to the start of the cave network. After checking that his sword could be drawn quickly, Nicolas looked down at the mushy snow around his feet.

'We're at the right place,' he said, turning his gaze up to the caves.

'And he's been on the move recently,' Auron said, crouching to study the ground. 'There's signs of tracks, going both in and out.'

Nicolas's urge was to charge in, sword drawn, but that was his inner Silva talking. They needed to do this right. If they alerted The Visitor that they were near, he could spirit Shift somewhere else...or worse. At least there was a path, so they wouldn't need to climb.

But it's still a lot of caves.

'Perhaps we'll be lucky, and The Visitor won't be home,' Tallith ventured.

'That'd be welcome.' It'd certainly make their task of saving Shift easier if he wasn't here. 'And if he is, this is one visit he won't care for.' Nicolas frowned as he caught Auron's bemused expression. 'What?'

'You...using an amusing hero line before entering a villain's lair.' Auron shook his head. 'I'm just kind of proud.'

Shaking his head, Nicolas led the way, moving slowly to ensure he kept his footing and that no errant crunches of snow underfoot gave him away. Halfway up the first slope, he glanced back.

'You coming?'

Silva appeared to snap out of a trance. She'd been staring blankly at the caves, and when she caught his eye, for a moment, he was sure she was going to say no, but she shook herself and followed wordlessly. He understood her hesitance. He would be the same facing a former friend turned enemy. Something he may need to face first hand if they ever caught Garaz. If it came to it, he would try his best to leave Silva out of the fight, for her own sake. Part of him wanted to ask her to stay with the horses, but who knew what else was in there? He needed every sword he could get.

As they progressed up the path the trek became more treacherous. Each step may have been the one where they slipped and tumbled back down the slope. Or worse, fell off the side completely. Nicolas remembered the first time he'd gone to save Shift from a cave—that one a vampire's lair. Then he'd assumed—incorrectly—that they were a damsel in distress. This time, though, they did need his help.

'I reckon this one's a good bet,' Auron said at the third cave mouth they approached. 'The snow's melted here too. It's practically a welcome mat.'

At Nicolas's nod, the spirit vanished inside to scout the immediate area whilst they stood guard.

Silva sidled up to him. 'Nicolas, if we—'

'We'll take him alive if we can,' he answered quickly, seeing on Silva's face how difficult it was to speak. She and Avin had obviously been—

Oh.

Sudden understanding hit him. It wasn't just that Avin was her friend. It was that Avin's story almost exactly mirrored her own. He'd been part of that band, something bad had happened to him, and he'd turned to the dark side. Nicolas cursed himself for not thinking of it sooner.

'You aren't like that anymore,' he said softly. 'If we can do the same for Avin, we certainly will.'

There was gratitude in Silva's eyes. 'But I will not hesitate to do what must be done...if it comes to it.'

That was handy, because somehow Nicolas didn't think Avin would stand down. And he was guilty of some heinous crimes. Wincing, Nicolas realised that Silva was too, but he didn't want to think about that. He couldn't. Besides, she was turning out to be a truer companion than a certain orc, who was likely now well beyond their ability to ever find.

'Entrance is clear.' Nicolas caught himself in a slight flinch as the spirit reappeared by his side. 'No sign of traps or guards.' Auron leant in and lowered his voice. 'So, no need to flinch.'

Ha bloody ha.

'Another adventure, another underground lair,' he muttered.

'Kid,' Auron said quietly at his side, 'before you go in—'

'I don't want to have to hurt Avin,' Nicolas interrupted, having just had the same conversation with Silva. 'I understand his pain. But he's hurting people, and he has Shift. Meaning that if I have to, then I have to. I get you feel obligated or responsible, but I can't let that get in the way of what needs to be done.'

Auron raised a brow. 'So this one time, I was hunting a troll that had been harrying travellers in a mountain pass. I tracked it back to its cave, assuming there was only one. Instead, I found four, and as it turned out, they weren't average trolls. The cave had been used by smugglers transporting Screel, a potent narcotic, before the trolls took the cave and used its previous occupants for afternoon tea.' The spirit shuddered slightly. 'After the dealers were eaten, the creatures went at the Screel stash. It made them crazed and things got messy quickly.' Auron then looked at him sternly. 'So don't jump to conclusions. I was going to say, 'Take Avin down quickly. Don't give him a chance to use his fire breath or curse magic'.'

'Oh, sorry.'

'I appreciate the thought, though, kid.' Auron looked toward the cave. 'But you have to do what you have to do.'

And right now, that's rescue Shift.

Briefly, he caught his reflection in the *Dawn Blade*. The look of determination on his face surprised him, as did the facial hair. Once this was over, a good shave was in order.

Steeling himself, Nicolas entered the cave.

CHAPTER 35

By now, traversing dark underground tunnels was barely an inconvenience. His eyes adjusted to the dim light quickly. Auron's aura helped. Once upon a time, he would've still been stumbling around half blind. Now, it was practically a lantern. His footing was sure with every step, even on stones slick with the moisture that had dripped from the stalactites. And more importantly, he was silent. Thankfully, Tallith was moving relatively quietly, and Dieter could've been a ghost himself for all the sound the writer made. He'd wanted to ask him to stay outside but doubted he would've complied. Besides, if The Visitor *was* out, coming home and finding Dieter lounging around at the door to his lair might not go down too well.

Though Avin didn't seem the type to have minions, it never hurt to be careful. Though Auron took the lead, Nicolas was the first mortal an enemy would come across. This was as it should be. Moving with purpose, he followed the spirit down a path that sloped up and down as it wound through the earth. Nicolas was slightly surprised that it was a single path, with no side passages or crossroads to confuse them. That was something of a boon in the tense silence.

'Up ahead.'

Nicolas was glad Auron was calling back quietly, it was a good precaution. Avin hadn't seemed to notice the spirit during their last encounter, but that didn't necessarily mean that he hadn't, or that he wouldn't have people around him who could.

Edging forwards, there was light up ahead, an unnatural light. Were they close? Anticipation gripped him as Auron stalked ahead carefully. Nicolas readied his body for action as the spirit peered into the room. Nicolas's heart froze for a second as Auron's head stopped abruptly.

What's caught his attention? Is it Shift?

'Here,' Auron called back, disappearing into the room.

Urgently, Nicolas moved forwards, forgetting himself and nearly slipping on a wet patch on the floor.

Reaching the mouth of the cavern, Nicolas came to a halt as he tried to take in what he was seeing. There was so much in the room that for a moment it was hard to pick out any one thing. It appeared to be some kind of laboratory. Numerous tables were covered in vials filled with colourful liquids. Some were bubbling due to small fires lit beneath them. Old books lay open on benches or discarded on the floor. There appeared to be some kind of ritualistic table, covered in runes. But his eyes soon fixed on what he'd come for.

'Shift.'

Heedless, he ran to the centre of the room, sheathing his sword as he tugged at the chains holding his...whatever they were now... to the giant table they lay on. After several fierce tugs, he instead turned his attention to the person themselves, brushing their hair aside and looking for some sign of life. When their chest rose with a breath, it was like a bag of rocks had fallen off his shoulders.

They were strangely better than the last time he'd seen them. Shift's skin was less pale. They almost looked stronger. Again, he turned his attention to the chains. There appeared to be locks on them inscribed with glowing runes, most likely designed to somehow block their ability to change shape. Beside the larger table was a smaller one with numerous implements on it.

What was he doing to you?

Angrily, he kicked the table over. It crashed, and the implements clattered to the ground around it. Silva and Auron both turned and glared at him from the side passages they were checking. He didn't care. Let Avin come.

'By the Deities, you don't like to let me sleep.' In an instant, his anger was forgotten. Blearily, Shift's eyes opened. When they found him, Nicolas was greeted with a weary smile. 'I really hate this adventure.'

'I'm not too fond of it either,' he said, kissing their forehead.

'Pfft,' Shift scoffed. 'I bet your inner hero is loving this. You're finally getting a chance to save me properly.'

'Actually,' he corrected quickly, studying the chains again, 'I would be quite happy for you to save yourself. And I'd be quite happy with you lording it over me.' Grabbing the lock, he gave it another tug. 'Are you good at teaching lock-picking?'

'Not when my hands are tied.'

'You are well, though?' Silva asked as she came to the table with Dieter, after bidding Tallith to keep watch. 'He didn't hurt you?'

'Actually, quite the opposite,' Shift replied. 'He's been helping me heal. He rambled a lot, but he wanted me fully recovered. He said *strong* a lot.'

'That makes no sense.' The warrior frowned.

'Actually, it does.' Shift scowled. 'He was studying my ability. He wants to replicate it so he could change back to human form.'

Auron approached and flicked the lock on the chains. 'Suppressing your ability so he can study it. Avin was never the sharpest sword in the rack.'

'And his conclusion?' Dieter asked, examining a jar that had been left on the table.

'That's the part that makes me extra pleased to see you.' Shift grinned. 'He'd come to the conclusion that draining all my blood and drinking it would allow him to have my gift. I would be dead, of course. But as long as he's fine.'

'He will not be fine for long,' Silva growled.

Shift smirked. 'That's a sweet way of displaying affection.'

The warrior gave a passable smile. 'Nicolas does that enough for everyone.'

'Where is Avin?' Auron asked. 'Seems odd that he's not here doing it already.'

'He was about to, but he was called away. His minions were going to get me ready for when he gets back.' Shift's head moved sharply as they looked at each of their companions, noting their confused expressions. 'You did kill his minions, right?'

'Um...'

Shift rested their head back on the table. 'Oh, for Deities' sake. They're probably behind you.'

'Thou shalt *not* take our master's property.'

Oh, you poor, stupid bastards.

Drawing his sword, Nicolas slowly turned around. He should've been cursing his lack of awareness that let someone sneak up on him, but right now, he just felt sorry for whoever it was.

Six whoevers.

In a very neat line were six figures in brown robes. Their hands were hidden inside the sleeves, which met in front of their bodies, and their hoods were pulled down over their heads.

Silva stood beside Nicolas. There was a fight coming. And Shift was still tied up.

'Do not fear,' Dieter said, noting the worried glance he cast back at the table. 'I am quite the dab hand at picking locks. One cannot explore places without knowing how to circumvent the odd lock. You concentrate on fighting these fellows, and I will free your companion.'

'There's a magic key around my neck,' Shift told the writer. 'Just slip it off and use it.'

Happy Shift would be free soon, Nicolas turned his attention back to the robed men. 'And you are?'

'We are his acolytes,' one of the figures replied.

With flicks of their heads, all the hoods were thrown back. They were human, so that was a decent start, but they were all very…generic looking. Each had close-cropped hair and the same harsh expression. It was genuinely impossible to tell if any of them were male or female. Maybe they were siblings? Honestly, Nicolas was disinclined to spend too much thought on it.

'That's very nice,' he said. 'I don't feel the need to introduce myself because we're about to leave. Only I notice you're blocking the exit. You're going to want to move.'

Auron tutted towards the group. 'When he isn't formally introducing himself to people, you know the kid is serious.' Not that any of them heard him.

'Thou shalt not take his captive.' One of the robed folk pointed an accusing finger. 'The shapeshifter is his.'

'Interesting,' Auron said as the spirit walked up and down the line. 'Normally, people like this would say *my master's*, not *his*.'

'There is no one here capable of stopping us,' Silva growled.

It was slightly worrying that the warrior was using her full—and quite formidable—power to intimidate people, and the acolytes weren't reacting. Nicolas studied them. At first glance, they didn't appear to be much. Slight, and a little gaunt. But that didn't mean anything. Who knew what they had up their sleeves?

'Foolish wench.' *Ah, so that acolyte's chosen to die first then.* 'He has taught us the magic of the change. We have the ability to become mighty and smite you down. Behold our gifts.'

Oh, so literally up their sleeves then.

The baggy sleeves parted, and each acolyte held a rune-etched medallion in his or her hand. With a grunt, they thrust them forwards and said the name of a creature.

Ogre. Troll. Chimera. Minotaur. Basilisk. Werewolf.

Tingling brought Nicolas's attention to his arm. The hairs on it were rising. There was magic in the air.

'Oh, I remember this,' Auron said, clicking his fingers. 'This is what Avin did. They're going to wave those medallions around a bit, say some magic words then change form.' Stepping away from the acolytes, Auron put his hands on his hips. 'I suggest you kick the shit out of them before that happens.'

Nicolas and Silva accepted the invitation with enthusiasm.

Two of the acolytes cried out as Nicolas sheathed his sword then ran between them, his arms outstretched to either side, knocking them to the floor. Reaching out, he grabbed the arm of the third and pulled it taut whilst striking the back of the elbow hard. The snap that followed was accompanied by a cry of pain. Slipping under the now-broken arm, he sent the acolyte reeling with a thunderous uppercut.

Seeing one of the two he'd knocked down reaching for their medallion, Nicolas stomped down on the acolyte's hand. Another crack, another cry of pain. A kick to the side of the head silenced the minion.

The other was up, but clearly disorientated, considering the way they couldn't hold their medallion straight. Nicolas slapped it out of their hand and punched them hard in the face, dropping them back to the ground.

'You...you bastard. I'll kill you.'

Nicolas raised his eyebrows. If someone had just broken *his* arm, he doubted he'd be stupid enough to threaten to kill the person who'd done it. He rewarded the acolyte for getting his attention by striding over, grabbing his head, and introducing it to the nearest table a good three times, before letting the limp body slide to the ground.

'Well, that was nice and... *Silva!*'

CHAPTER 36

The warrior looked at him in confusion. 'What?'

He found himself flapping his hand in the warrior's direction. 'That seems a bit...gratuitous.'

Frowning, Silva looked at her work and shook her head. 'I don't see the problem. You sheathed your sword, so I knew you'd think it unsporting to kill them as all they had were their medallions. So, I simply disarmed them.' Casually, she discarded the severed arm she was holding.

'You...cut all their arms off.'

The warrior shrugged. 'They can't pick up their medallions again.'

'It is strangely efficient,' Auron remarked.

'You aren't helping,' Nicolas cried. 'You killed them.'

Silva kicked one of the acolytes, and he moaned softly. 'He is still alive.'

Am I the only one seeing this?

'Yes,' he said with forced patience. 'But not for long. Look at the blood all over the floor. They're all going to die anyway.'

'If they are too weak to survive, maybe they don't deserve to live.'

Nicolas's jaw worked up and down. 'I... I...'

'You.'

He turned his attention to the person yelling at him. Somehow, the three acolytes he'd beaten up were back on their feet and had knives in their hands. He severely doubted they were in any shape to use them, but this was getting silly now.

'You will die. We will kill you. Then fornicate with the creature you came here to save.'

Leaning a bit closer to the robed trio, Nicolas put his hand to his ear. 'What's that now?'

'You heard,' another cried. 'We shall play with the shapeshifter before we send its soul to the Underworld after you.'

Its?

'I think I see your point,' Nicolas said a few moments later, wiping his bloodied sword on the edge of the robe of one of the three people he'd just killed. 'They weren't giving up without a fight.'

'That was all a bit sad,' Shift remarked as they hopped off the table. 'But you gave them a chance.'

Sheathing the *Dawn Blade*, he walked over to Shift and held them tightly, an embrace which was returned.

'I'm going to say this quietly, so not everyone hears,' the shapeshifter whispered in his ear. 'But thank you for coming to save me.'

'Wellllll,' he replied, 'I can't tease myself now, can I?'

Shift broke the hug and kissed him on the lips. 'You'd be bad at it if you tried.' They smiled as they finally pulled back. 'Now, you'd better have brought some clothes.'

Clothing was definitely needed. Shift was only wearing a couple of scraps that bordered the line between *dressed* and *naked.* But it gave him a chance to see that whatever Avin had done to heal them had worked. The scars from the wolf fight had practically vanished. Quickly, he gestured to Dieter, who he'd given Shift's spare clothes to before the group entered the cave.

The writer rummaged in his knapsack and produced them then everyone turned around politely to let the shapeshifter get dressed. Allowing him to address an annoyance.

'You call that keeping watch?' he said quietly but fiercely to Tallith. 'You let six people sneak up on us. What were you watching? Your feet?'

'I'm sorry,' the sergeant said, face reddening. 'I was looking to see if Shift was okay, and I...I...didn't do my job.'

'No, you didn't,' he said bluntly. 'So do better next time.'

It was hard to be too angry with the sergeant. Months ago, he would've done exactly the same thing himself. But the problem needed to be noted, so it didn't happen again. Deities knew he'd been called out many a time when he'd made a mistake.

And I'm better for it.

'I will,' Tallith said firmly. 'I swear.'

'I know you will,' he said with a nod, before turning back to Shift. 'Where's Avin?'

The shapeshifter, now fully dressed, nodded to a right-hand tunnel. 'I think he went down that one.'

He must be quite far away, not to hear all the commotion we made.

'I'm going to go and finish this then,' he said, drawing the *Dawn Blade*.

'*We*,' Shift corrected. His companion took a step away from the table and stumbled. Quickly, they leant back, catching themselves before falling completely. 'I guess after spending two days lying on a table I need to learn to walk again.'

'Dieter, can you and Tallith help Shift outside please?'

'*Help me outside?*' Nicolas ducked as a jar flew past his head. 'I'm not being walked out of here like some infirm old woman. Now, I'm not silly enough to go and get into a fight, but I am quite capable of going outside by myself.' The shapeshifter stood up straight and proud. They took a single—very tentative—step forward. Pursing their lips, they looked down at their wobbling legs. 'Now, if these two gentlemen happen to be going outside at the same time as me, that is fine.'

'As coincidence would have it, we are.' Dieter smiled with a slight bow. 'And I would be quite honoured to have some company on the way.'

'These cave networks do become quite boring.' Shift nodded, playing along.

As Shift left, with Dieter and Tallith happening to be following along, Nicolas turned to Auron and Silva. 'You don't need to be part of this. I understand if you want to go outside too.'

'I am not leaving you to face him alone,' Silva snapped quickly.

'No, kid,' Auron said firmly. 'We need to be part of this.'

The tunnel Shift had indicated turned out to be a downward slope, and quite a long one. Soon enough, they heard the whisper of voices ahead. As they stalked carefully forwards, the voices became louder, until they reached the opening to another cave. This one was small, a single chamber. And most of it was dominated by Avin.

'*But I am so close. So close. I can be me again.*' The Visitor was standing near the back of the room, facing the wall as he hunched over something.

'I understand your desire to be whole again, Avin, but whilst you aren't, you can't forget the good work you need to do.'

That voice? It...

Nicolas had only heard it briefly, once. But it had been enough to make him sure. Avin was talking to the Maestro.

I knew it. Of course he's behind this. Of course. If I get a splinter in my toe, I'll eventually find out the Maestro was the one who planted the damn tree it came from.

'*I know I must educate them,*' Avin continued. '*I know I must. They all need to learn. But I need to be whole.*'

'I fear you are giving yourself false hope, my friend.' The Maestro's voice was smooth and alluring. It made Nicolas sick. 'The shapeshifter cannot help you. I told you I would cure you, once the work is done. All you are doing is courting disappointment. Let the acolytes bring Shift to me. Then you won't be distracted from your real goal.'

'*No.*' Avin's scaled hand punched the wall. '*No. You say the same every year. The work must be done. You gave me the mask so I could teach them, make them understand what it is like to be shunned. To punish their rudeness. But it is enough. Enough now.*'

A tense silence followed.

'I am the one who says when it is enough,' the Maestro said coldly. 'I gave you a purpose, Avin. Acolytes. A home. I can take all those things away.'

Nicolas was suddenly glad he'd killed the robed fools. Having minions of the Maestro running around with the power to change form would not be good for Etherius at all.

In theory, right now, he was in a good position. Avin had his back to Nicolas. It was the perfect time to strike. But he couldn't ignore the niggling voice telling him that Avin himself wasn't bad. What had happened to him, and his likely treatment after, had turned him into a monster. And now he knew that the Maestro was manipulating him too.

But then, Avus Arex had a way to justify what he did. A tragedy in his life that set him down a dark path...

'Kid, do it now. You aren't going to get a better chance.' It was clearly hard for Auron to say, but he knew what was right. And deep down, so did Nicolas.

Carefully, blade at the ready, he stalked into the room.

'*I am not your puppet. I am not your slave. I...*' The Visitor was so lost in his ranting, Nicolas could've marched through the room shouting his name, and he doubted Avin would've noticed.

Closing in on Avin, guilt welled up in him. Avin wasn't evil, just misguided. But he was clearly under the Maestro's thrall, and he'd hurt so many people. His mind went back to the cow-dragon. A poor melding of two creatures that had wanted to be put out of its misery.

'You silly creature.' The Maestro sighed. 'Why must you force my hand like this?'

Nicolas froze as his eyes caught movement. Something dropped from the ceiling onto Avin's back. Nicolas frowned at the little tentacled creature then winced as its landing made The Visitor spin around.

'You,' Avin cried in fury. '*You've come to take my shapeshifter. Thief.*'

Beyond The Visitor, he caught sight of a viewing globe, similar to the one the faun Fo had used but larger. And the globe caught sight of him.

'*You,*' the Maestro, a hazy shadow in the globe, cried. 'Avin, kill him. Kill him now.'

'*Thief.*'

Avin reared back then unleashed his fire breath. Nicolas rolled aside, dodging the stream of white-hot fire. Avin's fury caused his aim to be poor. The fire struck above the entrance to the cave. Instantly, the heat in the room became oppressive.

Urk.

Nicolas was hauled from the ground. Reacting, rather than thinking, he grabbed a stone from the floor and swung it. It cracked The Visitor across the jaw, causing it to sit at an odd angle.

Using the sword would've been smarter.

Before he could, Avin launched him across the room. Crashing against the wall just beside the tunnel entrance, his whole body shook from the impact, though the armour saved him from the worst of it. Above him, he heard a deep creaking as the top of the entrance that had been struck by Avin's breath became unstable.

'Kid, get out of there.'

Following Auron's voice, he rose and slipped back into the tunnel. Just as he did, the entrance to the cavern collapsed. Nicolas covered himself as stones fell and dust was thrown up. The noise was almost ear-splitting.

Beyond the collapsing rocks he caught a brief glimpse of a pair of bright red eyes.

'Thief.'

A wave of energy passed through Nicolas, and his whole body began to tingle.

CHAPTER 37

For some strange reason, everything smelled. Literally everything. He could smell the sulphurous odour of the rocks that had just collapsed; there was a tangy odour, which he quickly identified as Silva's sweat; he could even smell the dead acolytes' blood as if he were lying in it.

That's bloody weird.

Actually, it was overwhelming. All the scents came at him at once, each screaming for attention. Opening his eyes, he shook his head.

'Nicolas?'

Silva was stood over him, mouth open and eyes wide. It took him a minute to realise what else was odd about her. It was the perspective. She appeared to tower over him. Making to move, he bumped something. Quickly, he turned around and sniffed it. It was distinctive.

Metal. It's metal.

'Kid?' Auron appeared just as dumbfounded as Silva. 'Um...kid?'

'Woof.'

...what did I just say?

'Woof.'

...

'Woof, woof.'

Oh no. No, no, no. You are f—

'Shift sent me back to help. What's happened?' Tallith skidded to a halt beside Silva. Frowning, the sergeant followed the warrior's gaze to him. His mouth began to open and close, but no words came out for a good few moments. 'Is that...?'

'He's been turned into a dog,' Silva clarified helpfully. Then the warrior sprang to action. 'Quickly, grab his clothes and armour. I'll grab him.'

Dog? I'm a dog? He turned me into a dog?

He yelped in surprise as Silva scooped him up and tucked him under her arm. He yelped again when he caught sight of his feet...paws.

'It'll be okay,' Auron assured him. 'Just be a good...' The spirit coughed awkwardly. '...kid.'

Nicolas growled at him. It was cut short as Silva sprinted down the tunnel, Tallith on her heels with his clothes and armour. The warrior made good time out of the tunnel and back down the slope to the others. Shift and Dieter were already waiting on their horses.

'Where's Nick?' Shift shouted, gaze switching between Silva and the cave mouth. 'And why do you have a...' The shapeshifter sighed heavily. 'He got himself turned into a dog. Didn't he?'

As the warrior reached them, Shift hopped down from their horse. Silva put him down, and he found himself bouncing on the spot, tongue hanging out. Crouching, the shapeshifter tentatively rubbed his head.

Oh wow, oh wow. That means I'm a good boy. Yes, I am.

Hopping up, he licked Shift's face.

'Get off, you furry fool,' the shapeshifter cried, pulling him off her. 'You're covering me in slobber.'

'Woof. Woof—woof.'

'Yes,' Shift said, rising. 'Whatever you said.' They turned their attention to Auron. 'How do we break this? We need to kill Avin?'

'I don't think that's wise,' the spirit said. 'He's trapped under a load of rubble, but he's mad. He'll burn his way out then come after us. You're still recovering, Tallith is untested, so all we've got is Silva. We need to get out of here.'

'But...'

'We cannot face him right now,' Silva said, backing up Auron. 'Especially out here. He will be able to fly over us and burn us from the air.'

'Dammit,' Shift hissed. 'I don't like it when people are right, and it's something I don't want to do. But we can't just leave him like...that.'

Why does everything suddenly smell so bad? Deities, Silva is sweaty. Oh, Tallith had some meat in his knapsack. I think the horse just farted.

'I do not think he got the whole curse,' Dieter said thoughtfully. 'There must have been more to it than that.'

'Reasoning?' Silva asked.

'When does The Visitor only change someone into a dog?'

'True,' the warrior agreed. 'It happened during a cave in, so maybe the falling rocks blocked part of the magic? Or the line of sight was interrupted?'

'I'm not sure if I get a vote,' Tallith began, 'but I think we need to regroup.'

Rabbit! Rabbit! Little bastard rabbit! Over there! 'Woof, woof, woof, woof.'

'Nicolas, here,' Silva commanded, pointing at the ground by her feet.

Whimpering slightly, he trudged back to the warrior.

'We need to go,' Shift confirmed. Picking him up, the shapeshifter held him at arm's length, regarding his new form with unease. 'We will fix this. I promise.'

I don't need a promise. I need a time frame.

'Woof.'

Putting him down again, Shift mounted their horse, whilst Nicolas fought the nearly overwhelming urge to lick his own balls.

Everything that's happened in my life...and now I'm a dog. Fan-bloody-tastic.

'How do we stop The Visitor tracking us?' Tallith asked, eyeing the cave nervously. 'When he's free, he'll just follow us.'

'Fear not, young man,' Dieter exclaimed. 'I can help with that.' The writer played with a roll of cloth on the back of his saddle, and it suddenly unfurled. Dieter laid it on the ground, but it was still attached to his saddle by two ropes. 'This isn't the first time I've had to make a swift exit and cover my tracks,' he explained. 'I've had to flee monsters, cannibal tribes...the occasional tavern owner who didn't care for a review I wrote... My line of work can be quite dangerous.'

'Excellent,' Silva said, turning her horse toward the road. 'Auron will scout ahead, I will lead, and Dieter will bring up the rear.'

With that, the group kicked their steeds into action and began their flight, followed by the dragging noise of Dieter's blanket as it removed the traces of their passage. And Nicolas, who ran after the others. Part of him had to admit that being faster because he was on four legs was quite nice. He easily kept up with the horses as the group tried to put as much distance between themselves and the cave as they could.

****

It was a hard ride. Progressing up the main road a way—and continuing generally north—the group finally left the trail and kept to the forests, ensuring they stayed under the thickest canopy where possible. Only once did they see a sign of Avin, a large flapping shadow that passed overhead, circling a few times before leaving again. Even then, the group waited in place a while, tensely watching the sky in case he doubled back.

The need for shelter became apparent as the sun got low in the sky. In that, fortune favoured them, as they soon stumbled on an abandoned farmhouse.

It appeared to have been deserted for a while and was a bit of a wreck, but it had four walls and a roof, and was confirmed to be empty after Auron had scouted it. Nicolas found himself whimpering slightly. It reminded him a little too much of the farmhouse from which he'd dropped down into in the Underworld. But shelter was shelter.

'This place has seen better days.' Dieter chuckled as he picked up the shaft of a broken farm tool and examined it. 'And a fair while ago, I'd wager.' He discarded the stick casually with a shrug, throwing it across the courtyard.

Mine. My stick. Get my stick.

'Woof, woof, woof.'

'Now look what you've done,' Silva commented dryly.

Nicolas didn't care; he'd gotten his stick. He carried it proudly in his jaws then dropped it at Dieter's feet, watching the writer expectantly. The fact that he knew his tail was wagging was slightly embarrassing, but...

Throw it again. Throw it. Throwwwwwwwww it.

'Woof.'

'Aw,' Dieter said, crouching. 'He makes quite the adorable dog.' The writer scratched Nicolas behind the ear.

Get off, I'm a hum— Aaaaaaaaah, that's amazing. Oh Deities.

'Stop petting my man,' Shift snapped.

'This is ridiculous.' Silva sighed. 'We need to make this place secure then figure out a way to change him back.'

I know how to make this place secure.

'What's he...? Oh.' Tallith quickly looked away. 'He's, um, marking his territory.'

Nice and secure.

'This sort of shit never happened in my day.' Auron sighed. 'I swear my adventures were more serious than this.'

'We will change you back,' Shift told Nicolas firmly. 'Don't worry. And when we do, we've got your clothes.' They removed his shirt from their pack. 'See? Here's your shirt. You remember your shirt, right?'

Nicolas was sure Shift was still talking, but his entire focus became the sleeve dangling from the garment they were holding.

Gonna get it. 'Woof.'

'What in the...? Nick...let go!' Shift snapped. They tried to pull the sleeve out of his mouth. 'Nick, no.'

Ooooh, a game. My sleeve, mine. My sleeve. Give it. 'Grrrrrrr.'

'Will you let go?' Shift tugged on the shirt. 'Nick. You furry little idiot.'

Nicolas rolled back in the snow as the sleeve tore. But he'd gotten a piece of it. He began to run around in circles, tail wagging furiously as he displayed his trophy.

I am the sleeve-getting champion.

None of the others appeared proud of him. In fact, they were all looking at him sadly. Stopping in his tracks, he tried to understand why. Which wasn't an easy thing to do.

I'm human.

The revelation itself was that he'd forgotten—or was forgetting. Lowering his head, he began to remember every human thing he'd ever done. He thought about the basic things, like washing his hands—having hands—eating dinner with cutlery, chopping wood, anything that would anchor him to who he was.

'Come on,' Silva said to him softly. 'Let us go inside, get this place secure, and set up camp.'

Thankful for some kind of purpose, though he didn't know how much practical help he'd be, he followed the warrior into the farmhouse, sniffing everything he passed curiously. With each step, he made a conscious effort not to wag his tail.

I am not a dog.

CHAPTER 38

Within the hour, they had a serviceable camp in one of the less mould-infested rooms and were all eating a hot meal. Even Nicolas. It wasn't exactly dignified, eating out of one of his upturned shoulder pauldrons, but they were lacking in bowls, and he drew the line at eating off the floor like a...well...

'How do we help him?' Silva asked after swallowing her last mouthful. 'You said that killing Avin would break the curse.'

'I did,' Auron confirmed. 'But I think we can simply smash that mask of his. I'm thinking it's the source of his power.'

'But where did he get it?' Shift asked. 'The Magical Cursing Artifacts Store?'

The Maestro gave it to him.

'Woof.'

Bugger. Bugger. Bugger.

'I am guessing you are referring to Avin's mask?' Dieter asked thoughtfully. 'I assume your undead companion believes it the cause of these curses?'

'Yes.'

'I think that, as a group, mayhap we aren't in a fit state to face Avin in the hope of snapping that mask.' Dieter produced a map from his bag. Unfurling it on the floor, the explorer studied it intently. 'I do believe the best course of action would be to find a city with a Magic Guild Gathering Hall. I doubt a regular Healer's Temple will be able to help our poor young fellow.'

'There's a city not too far from here,' Silva said, pointing to a spot on the map. 'But we need to assume Avin would expect us to go to it.'

Is there any point even thinking about going after Garaz anymore?

'We will be able to change him back, right?' Shift tried to ask the question quietly, but Nicolas's hearing was really good now.

'I really hope so,' Auron replied. 'There is anti-curse magic, but it depends how strong the item that cursed him was.'

'So, he may be a dog forever?' Silva asked, glancing at him sadly.

Nicolas whimpered. His companions turned to him, giving him sympathetic glances which only served to reinforce his plight.

'It'll be okay,' Shift said softly, smoothing him gently, if a little uncomfortably. 'We will find a way to break the curse.'

Slowly, Nicolas rolled over and put his paws in the air.

'Oh Deities,' Silva sighed, 'I believe he wants his belly rubbed.'

Belly rubs, belly rubs, belly rubs.

'Then one of you will have to do it,' Shift replied. 'If I start doing that, it'll be all I think about every time I look at him when he turns back.'

A hand touched Nicolas. Looking up, he saw Silva squirming as if she were putting her hand in manure.

'Never mention this again,' she said threateningly.

He couldn't even be bothered to bark a response, those rubs were sooooo good.

'We're going to the city then?' Tallith asked.

'After a good night's sleep,' Silva said.

'You all need to rest, so I'll keep watch,' Auron said. 'Fingers crossed, we manage to stay out of trouble for one night at least.'

****

Nicolas's nose twitched until he finally sat up. Something was amiss. Tilting his head, he used his newly enhanced senses. It was there. On the air. A strange smell. A lot of strange smells. Having only been a dog for a short while, it was difficult at first to discern what it was. There was sweat, definitely. Furs. Something metallic.

We aren't alone.

Urgently, he clambered up to Shift, who he'd been curled up beside, and butted them with his snout.

'Whas... Bugger off...stupid dog...' the shapeshifter slurred, slapping him away before turning over.

Dog? Shift called me a dog.

Growling slightly as he realised the smell was getting closer, he ran over to Silva. Twice, he nudged her with his head, but she didn't move.

Oh, for Deities' sake. Fine then.

Silva's eye shot open, giving him a murderous glare. 'Why, in the name of the Deities, are you licking my face?' she snarled.

Nicolas pointed his head in the direction of the smell and growled. The warrior got his meaning. Within an instant, the other eye was open and she was on her feet. Securing her sword to her belt, she kicked Shift's foot.

'Dammit, Silva,' Shift snapped. 'You're as bad as the... Nicolas.'

'We have company.'

'Dammit.' Shift quickly got to their feet. Dieter and Tallith soon followed.

'Hey, we've got—' Auron stopped abruptly as he appeared through the wall. 'You're awake.'

'Nicolas alerted us,' Silva said, drawing her blade.

'Good boy.' The spirit smirked at him before getting back to business. 'Apparently, we didn't completely eliminate the Horned Horde. We just thinned them out. The rest appear to want to make us pay for it.'

Dammit, I knew there'd be more of them.

'Then the Horned Horde die for good,' Shift said, staring toward the window.

'The *Horned Horde*?' Dieter remarked, grabbing his walking stick. 'Those are very unpleasant fellows indeed.'

'We killed a lot of them,' Tallith said. 'You should've seen Nicolas. He was amazing. He defeated their leader too.'

'Used to be a time that bandits had the good sense to piss off after their leader died.' Auron sighed. 'Where have the standards gone?'

'We will go around the side of the house,' Silva said, ignoring Auron's moaning. 'We will let some of them enter then strike the others from the rear. I take it there's more than a couple?'

'About ten,' Auron answered.

Nicolas's nose twitched again at a strange and sudden new smell. Turning, he almost jumped out of his fur at the large wolf standing beside him.

'Can you understand me?' Shift said in their wolf form.

'I can now, yes,' he said with a tail wag. 'Thank the Deities. I was getting tired of saying *woof* to everyone.'

'How do you feel about mauling some bad guys?' Shift asked, tilting their head.

'Very enthusiastic,' he growled.

'Good.' Shift went to pad away then stopped. 'By the way, as I'm now a wolf...don't get any ideas.'

'What?' he asked in confusion. 'What do you mean? Ideas about... Ew. That's disgusting,' he said as their meaning suddenly dawned on him.

Even though Shift was a wolf, he could tell they were chuckling.

CHAPTER 39

The plan worked like poetry in motion. Which was a nice novelty, for them. It also helped that the Horned Horde had the strategic acumen of a sack of rocks. Their, for want of a better word, tactics, seemed solely based on kicking the door of the farmhouse in and piling through it shouting loudly. The group let about half of them into the house before making their move.

Nicolas and Shift sprinted ahead of the others, growling angrily. The marauders were too busy with their own shouting to register the new noise until the pair were upon them. In almost comical slow motion, one of the horde turned towards Nicolas. His eyes widened, and his mouth contorted as if he was either going to scream or swear, when Nicolas leapt at him, knocking him to the ground.

Now, Nicolas only really had a single option. Without a sword, he had one weapon at his disposal, which he wasn't keen to use. But the warrior had an axe, so Nicolas didn't really overthink it before biting the man's throat out. Judging by the screams beside him, Shift was doing the same.

Then Silva and Tallith piled into the fray. The warrior had killed three men whilst the sergeant was busy fencing with one. Jumping from his own felled opponent, Nicolas bit the man in the back of the leg, allowing Tallith to deliver the killing blow.

Even Dieter was giving a good account of himself. The writer was using his stick to crack men across their jaws, staggering them so someone with a more pointed weapon could finish the job.

Giving in to his animal instincts, Nicolas bounded from one opponent to another, biting and scratching at legs and arms. Part of him wished he was this graceful as a human. Another part knew he'd be throwing up for a week with all the blood he was accidentally digesting.

We're in a battle. Best not think about it.

The barbarians already inside the house tried to force their way back out, to get into the fight. Waiting, and establishing a defence inside the house would've made more sense. But apparently the horned hats were given out based on brawn rather than brains.

Putting her sword to his throat, Silva dispatched the last man to exit the house. With a gurgle and a splash of blood, the man collapsed to the floor with his comrades.

'Is that all of them?' Tallith asked as he clustered around the door of the farmhouse with the others.

Nicolas's nose twitched.

No.

A deep thud shook the entire structure. A long creaking sound followed. Nicolas's hero instincts—or maybe canine instincts—realised what was about to happen. Whimpering, he ran out of the way just in time. The others looked up just as the snow on the roof slid from it, collapsing onto them all. Silva was knocked to the ground, arms held high as she tried to shield herself.

The door of the house was now obscured by a large pile of snow. And somewhere under it were all his friends. Urgently, Nicolas sprinted to it and began to dig.

'Dammit, kid,' Auron said, emerging from the mound. 'Even I was wincing when that fell, and I can't die.'

Working his forepaws as fast as he could, Nicolas dug and dug through the snow. He only stopped digging when the side wall of the house burst open.

Wow. He's big.

The warrior was thickly muscled. Did all those muscles produce heat? He wasn't dressed at all appropriately for winter and didn't seem to notice.

'I am Vrax Two-Axe,' the man declared, holding his dual axes high in the air. 'Third man in the Horned Horde. Now last man. I shall avenge my fallen brothers this day.'

'Who in the Underworld is he talking to?' Auron asked with a raised eyebrow. 'Does he think they can hear him under all that snow?'

'Prepare to suffer death at the blades of my mighty axes.'

Oh. He actually does.

As Vrax lumbered forward, Nicolas clambered around the snow pile, putting himself between it and the warrior. He growled fiercely. Head lowered and ready to attack.

'Ha, ha, ha,' Vrax boomed once the surprise wore off. 'Puny dog, you are no match for me. Step aside, mutt. I like dogs, but I will not hesitate to gut you if you stand in the way of my vengeance.'

Nicolas's answer was to growl louder. He had a few ideas for witty retorts, but they'd all come out as *woof*, so he didn't bother.

'Very well, silly dog.'

The warrior charged forwards, swinging one of his blades. Tensing his back legs, Nicolas thrust forward, grabbing the arm on the downward swing and sinking his teeth into it. Following his leap, he dragged Vrax back a couple of steps, unbalancing him.

With a roar, the marauder swung at him with the other blade. Not wanting to present a dangling target, Nicolas let go and dropped to the ground. Barking, he threw himself at Vrax's knee joint, ramming it. The warrior collapsed to a single knee. Jumping up, Nicolas grabbed the back of the man's fur cloak—which was about all he wore—and pulled him to the ground.

Grunting, Vrax turned and tried to scrabble to his feet. He'd made it to all fours when Nicolas attacked, scratching at his face. Nicolas had expected Vrax to protect his face from the onslaught, but the warrior reached out instead and grabbed his body with both hands. Rising to his rather formidable height, Vrax held him overhead then launched him into the nearest wall, which vibrated with the impact.

Whimpering, Nicolas fell to the ground. That had hurt him, badly. One of his legs was numb and it hurt when he breathed. Maybe due to some broken ribs?

Yelping, Nicolas just managed to jump aside and dodge the spinning axe that had been flung at him. Luckily, it had gone slightly wide anyway, thanks to the blood in Vrax's eyes from his scratched-up face. The weapon embedded itself in the wall with a *thunk*.

'Damn you, dog,' Vrax bellowed as he charged.

Nicolas readied himself as the warrior closed on him. Briefly, he glanced at Auron, who was watching the whole thing. That was a shame, because he doubted he was going to live down what he was about to do now.

Still...needs must.

Leaping up at the last moment, he clamped his jaws around Vrax's groin. The warrior screamed in pain as he was knocked to the floor. Nicolas tried not to focus on what was in his mouth as he thrust his head from side to side, tearing at it. Vrax kicked and thrashed in agony.

Only when he was completely certain that the warrior was exhausted did he let go. Padding up Vrax's chest, he ripped his throat out.

But there was no time to celebrate his victory. A noise behind him caught his attention. The mound of snow bulged, before bursting apart as Shift clawed their way out. Silva followed soon after.

Snarling, the warrior glared around her. 'Where is the man who dropped a pile of snow on me?'

'Dead. The kid got him,' Auron said, voice tinged with awe. 'Now get the others out.'

'Even as a dog, you are mighty.' Silva gave him an impressed nod before getting to work.

Soon Tallith and Dieter were free, and Shift was back to their preferred form, and clothed.

'Nice work,' Shift told him as they looked over Vrax's body. 'I see your tactic was to pretty much destroy his groin.'

Here we go...

'It worked a treat.' They smiled. 'You aren't the only one to have used that.'

'If it works, it works,' Auron agreed.

Tallith was staring down at the marauder's body, wide-eyed. 'He defeated a mighty opponent, single-handed, as a dog. Is there no end to his talents?'

Nicolas snarled at his tail, which was threatening to wag again.

His ears suddenly pricked up as he heard a *whumph* nearby. It was accompanied by a musky, burnt smell tinged with magic. There was also a multitude of different herbal smells that made his nose tingle, the smell of a donkey, and for some reason, the scent of old cabbages. Nicolas stared at the corner of the farmhouse, knowing something was coming, but also that it wasn't dangerous.

'Sorry I'm late,' Snaggletooth Joe said as he ambled around the corner. 'Got held up doin'—' The old man stopped and stared at Nicolas, frowning. 'When did ye lot get a dog? An' where's the boy?'

CHAPTER 40

S ilva pushed passed the bewildered trader as she walked to the corner of the farmhouse. The warrior frowned at whatever she saw around it.

'His wagon is here,' she told the others, before putting a sword to Joe's throat. 'How do you keep appearing?'

'A good trader always knows when his customers need him.' Joe grinned, gently trying to push the blade away from his neck. It did not budge. 'An' I think yer in need again?'

'That depends,' Shift began warily. 'Are you any good at undoing curses?'

Pursing his lips thoughtfully for a moment, Joe's eyes flicked to Nicolas. 'Ah. The young'un got himself turned into a mutt, did he?'

I'm not a mutt. I'm a do...human. I'm a bloody human.

'He might have,' Silva answered coldly.

'Then I *might have* a way te change him back.' The trader flicked his gaze to the sword, and Silva finally lowered it.

Giving the warrior a theatrically thankful grin, he ambled over to Nicolas and crouched in front of him. Before Nicolas could even bark, the trader scooped him up, holding him under his front legs. With one eye closed, Snaggletooth Joe studied him.

'Ah yes, Joe sees well,' the trader mused. With one quick motion, he pulled a hair from Nicolas's fur and put it in his mouth. 'Yes. Powerful curse, this one. Nasty stuff. But not undoable. Don't think te boy got the worst o' it, don't ye know.' Joe nodded thoughtfully as let Nicolas go.

'You can help him?' Shift's eyes narrowed when Joe answered with a broad grin. 'How much?'

Clapping his hands and rubbing them together, Joe rose. He then held out his palm.

'Start puttin' coins in me hand, an' I'll tell ye when te stop.'

Taking a coin pouch from their saddlebag, Shift slowly dropped coins into Joe's palm, one by one. It got to the point where Nicolas thought Joe's arm might give under the weight.

'That'll do nicely,' the trader said finally, quickly pocketing the coin. 'Now if ye excuse me, I'll go rummage somethin' up.'

'Shall I follow him?' Silva asked as the trader hobbled back to his wagon.

'He won't run off with the money,' Auron said with a half-smile. 'We're proving to be too good as customers for that. Well, you lot are, anyway.'

He's certainly making his fortune off of us. And he always seems to turn up just when we need him.

Nicolas had an inkling about that, but he was going to save it for when he was human again.

Around ten minutes later, Snaggletooth Joe returned, bowl in hand. Medicine wasn't traditionally known for smelling nice, but it was a lot worse when your sense of smell was improved ten thousandfold.

'Here you go.' Joe grinned, placing the bowl, and the thick pink concoction in it, in front of Nicolas. 'This oughta undo that nasty curse. Lap it all up. There's a good boy.'

Piss off.

Tentatively, he approached the bowl. It looked as nasty as it smelt. But he didn't want to be a dog anymore, so he stuck his snout in it and gobbled it down. Around halfway through the bowl, he was sure he was going to throw it all back up again, but he persevered.

Finally, the bowl was empty. Nicolas felt uncomfortably on show as the others gathered around. Watching him expectantly.

'If this doesn't work, I'll be having our money back,' Shift warned after a few moments.

'Patience,' Joe said with a dismissive wave of his hand. 'Have patience. Old Joe's curse cure-all is good stuff. Potent stuff. But ye can't rush it.'

I wish I could. I've spent far too long as a dog already.

Everyone started as Nicolas's stomach gurgled loudly.

'By the way, this ain't gonna be comfortable for ye.'

Now you say that?

The gurgling became worse. Nicolas nearly threw up again as his insides moved around. He could literally feel his organs rearranging as his body began to stretch. He was getting bigger, but it also felt like he was getting smaller at the same time, as his arms lengthened, but his snout squashed back into his face. Every inch of his skin tickled as fur receded into it. The sensation of the tail withdrawing into his body was just so very wrong.

How can someone be squashed and stretched at the same time?

With one last gasp, he crumbled to the ground. His eyes shot wide as his naked body touched snow.

'Why did we do this outside?' he cried, jumping up. 'Wait…I didn't say woof.'

He looked down at his freezing body. Then realised it was *his* body. Throwing his hands in the air, he danced around.

'I'm not a dog anymore. I'm not a dog.' Bouncing over, he hugged Joe tightly, barely even registering how uncomfortable the trader was with it or that the others were blatantly averting their eyes, save for Shift. 'Thank the Deities. And thank you, you beautiful little man.'

Kissing Joe on the forehead was a mistake, and he winced at the sudden taste of cabbage, but he was too excited to be upset about it.

'Kid, for Deities' sake, put a hand over it,' Auron cried.

Oh no.

Nicolas covered his personal area. 'Um, can I have some clothes, please?'

Shift already had them in hand. Offering them to him, the shapeshifter quickly pulled them out of reach just as he was going to grab them. Three times they did this, earning a glare each time. Finally, with a wide smirk, the shapeshifter threw him his clothes. 'Now you know what I have to go through every time I change and my clothes aren't ready for me.'

Nicolas was pulling on his breeches so fast that he tied the end of the leg up and had to hop a couple of times to prevent himself from falling back into the snow. 'Lesson learned,' he groaned.

'Good boy.' Shift smiled.

He kept the unimpressed glare from when he put his shirt over his head to when his head popped back out. Getting his arms in was another matter entirely. It was like he'd forgotten how to work his limbs properly. He wished he could forget what'd just happened to him.

'By the way, the training's paying off,' the shapeshifter added with a whistle. 'Your scrawny frame is finally getting some muscle to go with all those scars.'

Was it a slightly backhanded compliment? Yes. But it *was* a compliment, and his heart soared because he was just that easily flattered, especially by Shift, for whom compliments were rarer than a two-horned unicorn. They rolled their eyes at him puffing his chest out as he put his armour back on over his shirt. Then it was time to cover it all in plenty of furs and get warm again.

Fur. Deities, I had fur.

'That's better,' he sighed as the warm feeling came back.

'Not for me.' Shift winked. 'I was enjoying that.'

Nicolas's lip trembled as he fought to contain his beaming smile as a wave of giddiness passed over him. Suddenly, he was very warm. He did notice Silva shaking her head in the background.

'How come you don't travel around undoing The Visitor's curses, if I may enquire?' Dieter asked the trader as Joe admired his handiwork.

'Because I'm a travellin' trader, not a travellin' saint.' Joe scoffed. 'Plus, them anti-curse potions are hard te brew.' For a second, he pursed his lips. 'An' as I said, I don't think the boy got the whole dose o' the curse magic. It should've taken longer than that te work, if it would at all.'

'So, what do we do now?' Tallith asked Nicolas.

That was the big question. They had two options.

'We continue after Garaz,' he said finally. 'I doubt Avin will go back to his lair until he finds Shift. He wants them too badly. And hopefully, whilst he's hunting us, he won't have the time to curse innocent people. We find Garaz and get that amulet. I bet its healing properties can cure the people Avin has cursed. Once we've done that, we come back here and kick his ass.'

'I love your naïve optimism that we have a chance of catching Garaz,' Silva remarked. 'But it will never happen. He is too far ahead of us. And dodging Avin whilst we travel will slow us down.'

'Silva's right. He's gone,' Shift said. 'We need to concede defeat here.'

'Don't swear like that in front of me,' Auron scoffed. 'Defeat is for people who don't try hard enough.'

'We won't have a problem making up the lost time,' Nicolas said with a smile. 'Because Joe's going to help us.'

'I am?' the trader asked with a frown.

'Yes, you are.' Nicolas nodded. 'Because you can teleport.'

CHAPTER 41

J oe shifted uncomfortably on the spot. 'Now who's gone an' told ye that nonsense, boy?'

'It isn't nonsense,' Nicolas retorted quickly. 'You appear whenever we need you then vanish afterwards. I've seen that donkey of yours. It isn't that bloody quick. Therefore, you can teleport. The one thing I'm confused about is how you always know when we're in trouble?'

The old man stuck his chin defiantly in the air, a visual symbol of his refusal to answer.

With a growl, Silva took a couple of steps towards him.

'I tethered ye,' he answered quickly. Nicolas gestured for Joe to elaborate, and with a sigh, he did. 'When I spot a potentially lucrative customer, I do a magic tether. The little puff o' smoke at me stall, that was it. It means I'll always know where ye are, an' when yer in enough trouble te make me a nice pile o' coin.'

'Why, you little...'

Nicolas got between Silva and Snaggletooth Joe. 'I think, as I'm no longer a dog, we can let this go.'

The answer was a single grunt.

'Look, I just need te know when yer in peril so I can—'

'Sell us things?' Shift ventured, with raised eyebrows.

'Yeah, pretty much.' Why *wouldn't* Joe sound casual about it? He was a trader; that was what they did. 'It's me own magic, an' I'm pretty damned good at it. Helped me run a successful business.'

'Why do you travel in a wagon if you can teleport?' Nicolas asked.

'Where would I keep me stuff?'

Stupid question, I guess.

'So, if we were to give you some coin, you could teleport us out of here?' Shift asked coyly.

'No.'

Nicolas's eyes widened. 'What do you mean...no?'

Joe raised his palms in the air. 'I'm no charity, boy,' he said. 'Te transport all o' ye, an' yer horses an' gear? Well, let's just say that after me last couple o' jobs fer ye, ye can't afford it.'

'Or maybe you can't afford to say no.' The implication of Silva's words was clear.

'Lady, I can vanish before ye get te me,' Joe said, waving his finger in the air. 'Then I ain't comin' back when ye lot next get in a pickle.'

'Perhaps I can help.' Dieter strolled over to his horse and messed about in the saddle bag. Finally, he came back with something wrapped in a rag. Slowly, he unfurled it, displaying a jewelled item akin to an egg. 'This is an ancient Serian fertility charm. I found it in a ruined temple I visited just last year. I believe this may cover your expenses.'

Joe was practically drooling as he stared at the egg. 'That'll do it,' he mumbled in his hypnotic state.

'Dieter, you don't have to—'

'Nonsense, young man.' The writer smiled. 'I don't really have a use for it. It's just been weighing down my saddle bag for a year. Besides, I've heard about everything you've done for Etherius, and I am aware of all the trouble going on. If it's allowed to continue, Etherius will become a very dangerous place, indeed, and I am fond of travelling around it. Let's just call it a business investment.'

'Thank you,' Nicolas said, with a solemn nod.

'Think nothing of it.' Dieter wrapped the egg up and handed it to Joe. 'Besides, I expect to make its value back with the book I write about you.'

'For that, I'll give you a very detailed account of all my adventures.' Nicolas smiled. Then something occurred to him, and he addressed Silva, Auron, and Shift. 'By the way, when I snuck into the cave, Avin was talking to the Maestro. My guess is the Maestro gave him the lair, the acolytes, the curse mask, and the purpose to punish people.'

'Can he not take a day off and let someone else have an evil scheme?' Shift snorted.

'He does appear to have his finger in every evil pie,' Auron remarked, shaking his head. 'Etherius will be a much better place without him.'

I second that.

'Now, this covers the cost o' the trip.' The egg had vanished into Joe's robe. 'But we need te figure out the where. Unless I'm tethered te someone, I can only go where I've been before. So where am I droppin' ye?'

'Ask him if he's been to Tellmark before,' Auron said thoughtfully.

Nicolas posed the question, and the trader nodded.

The spirit grinned knowingly. 'My hometown is very near the border of orc territory, and if Garaz isn't deviating from his path, he should pass close to it. We may even be able to head him off, if we're lucky.'

With our luck? We won't be heading him off then.

'Can you take us to Tellmark?' he asked the trader.

Joe let out an even longer whistle. 'That's far, but I can do it. Ye'll need te give me time te prepare.'

That's fine. It gives me time to get used to not being a dog anymore.

'That's settled then,' Shift said, clapping their hands together and staring at the farmhouse. 'I'm going to sort us out some more money, for the next time Silva breaks her leg or you turn into a dog.'

'We spent a bit on you too, you know.' Silva was clearly affronted by having her weakness pointed out.

Nicolas asked the more important question. 'Where are you getting money from?'

Shift stopped looking at the house and glanced at him thoughtfully. Holding up a finger for him to wait, they turned their head. 'Dieter, how old would you say this house is?'

The explorer and writer took in his surroundings, playing with his moustache as he considered the question. 'I'd say early late third era.'

'That's what I thought.' Shift smiled before turning back to the others. 'Then I think we can refill our coffers.'

Before Nicolas could ask them to elaborate, Shift grabbed his arm and dragged him into the house and down what was left of the hallway. 'Houses of this era always had a secret basement in which people would hide their valuables.'

'Okay,' Nicolas said. 'But what's to say the valuables are even still there?'

'Because I'm optimistic, and you're pessimistic,' they replied instantly, stepping heavily at points on the floor with their boot. 'I had a nose around earlier whilst you were licking yourself. There are old clothes thrown everywhere upstairs. Whoever owned this place left in a hurry, so my bet is they didn't have time to clear out any stashes they had.'

On this, he decided to defer to the thief's experience.

Finally, there was a hollow bump beneath Shift's feet. Crouching, they moved a decaying piece of carpet aside and traced a square in the floor with their fingers until coming to a small hole. Shift pressed the magic key gifted to them by T'goth to the lock, and with a click, the floor raised slightly. Keeping eye contact with Nicolas, lest he miss their smug smile, Shift lifted the door open. Just as they were about to head down the stairs, the shapeshifter stopped, turned, and kissed him passionately.

'Welcome back, by the way,' they said before starting down the stairs.

The basement was old and dank, the age of the air making Nicolas's eyes water slightly.

They proceeded down the steps, cut their way through several thick cobwebs, and came to a storage room with pots lining one wall and a large, open-doored safe halfway across the other.

'See?' he said. 'It's empty. Someone got here first.'

When he didn't get a response, Nicolas looked round to see Shift studying the pots carefully. 'I said the safe's empty,' he repeated.

'Of course it is,' Shift said, turning so he could see their eyeroll. 'But only an idiot keeps all his money in the obvious safe. The well-to-do always had a second stash hidden, so any thief couldn't ruin them completely if they got this far.'

'So, you're suggesting one of those pots is full of coins?' he said sceptically.

Shift picked up a thick piece of wood. 'That's what I'm hoping.' They turned and looked at him askew then held the stick out and shook it slightly. 'Do you want me to throw this for you *before* I use it?'

'Very funny.'

Laughing to themselves, Shift turned and set about the pots, smashing them one after the other with powerful swings. When the fourth pot was smashed, a pile of coins spilled out onto the floor. Shift threw their club aside, grabbed Nicolas, and kissed him again. 'Now we can retire from this life of adventure.' They sighed before screwing their face up. 'Oh wait, no we can't. We still have an orc to find, a village to rescue, and a dark lord—or whatever the Maestro is—to vanquish.'

'At least we have some good company to share it all with.' Nicolas smiled before kissing them again.

'I hope you mean the adventure and not the money.'

CHAPTER 42

When Nicolas and Shift exited the house, Joe had moved his wagon to the front of the building. Their horses were gathered around it, as were the rest of their party. Joe himself was sat atop his wagon, eyes closed.

'Are we all ready to go?' Nicolas asked as they rejoined the party.

'Just about, I reckon,' the trader answered, bouncing the pouch he held in his hand. 'Just need a good hit o' this then off we go.'

'What's that?' Shift asked.

Snaggletooth Joe gave them a wide grin. 'The good stuff.' Opening the pouch, he tilted it down so they could see.

'*Stop,*' Nicolas cried, holding his hands wide. 'Don't move.'

'What's gotten into ye, young'un?' Joe asked with a frown.

What had gotten into him was that he instantly recognised the red powder in the pouch. The last time he'd seen it, a wizard had snorted it then tried to blast Nicolas to dust with lightning, before promptly exploding.

'That red powder's dangerous,' he said slowly. He wasn't the only one backing away. Silva and Shift were too.

'Naw.' Joe cackled. 'It's only a bit o' Boost.'

'*Boost?*' Nicolas asked warily.

'Oh,' Dieter said, clicking his fingers. 'I've heard of that.'

'Aye,' the trader said. 'It gives ye a nice little power-up. Really puts the fire in yer furnace, if ye know what I mean.'

'And it makes you explode,' Silva said, still backing away.

'Pfft,' Joe scoffed. 'Maybe one or two who overdo it. But Joe knows what he's doin'. Not my fault some idiots can't follow instructions.'

Well, this is a dilemma.

On the one hand, this was the only way to catch up to Garaz, and the most likely way to help those Avin had cursed. On the other, there was a good chance the air would soon be raining chunks of crispy Snaggletooth Joe...and him.

'It's a potent narcotic for the magically inclined,' Tallith interjected. 'We had a spate of users in Babylon until Lord Commander Greer threw them all out and burnt the dealers' warehouses down. But no one blew up.'

'Yeah, well, ol' Joe ain't some idiot junkie,' the trader spat. 'I know how te use it safely. An' it's good for business. Now, do ye lot want te go te Tellmark or not? Because the only way I'm sendin' all o' ye all that way is with this.'

Taking a deep breath, Nicolas weighed up the pros and cons of the situation. He had to believe that Joe had been using it to bounce around this whole time, implying he could regulate himself. Or maybe Oleg Hobrath had just had a bad batch of the stuff.

'Okay, we'll go,' he said finally. 'But what about Auron?'

'Who's Auron?' Joe asked, narrowing a single eye.

'A spirit we travel with.'

The trader ruffled his long, knotted beard. 'Well, the spell I'm doin' teleports everyone in me immediate area. If he stands close, it should work. If it don't, the ghost'll have te walk.'

'*Maybe* he shouldn't refer to me as a ghost,' Auron said slowly. 'I'm a spirit.'

'Or maybe he can hang around here an' haunt this half a house?' Joe grinned.

The stream of curses from Auron's mouth made Nicolas blush. 'I'm sure it'll be fine,' he said finally. T'goth had managed to teleport Auron, and though Joe was far from a Deity, the principles must be similar.

Or is he?

Nicolas looked at the trader suspiciously. He'd asked the Deities, T'goth specifically, for help. And it wouldn't be the first time T'goth had been in the guise of a crazy old man. Narrowing his eyes, he scrutinised Joe, comparing him to his memory of the Deity he'd met before, both in his true form, and that of the crazed old man. There was no obvious similarity.

No. It can't be him. If it were he'd introduce himself, surely.

'If not, I'll catch you guys up eventually,' Auron confirmed, still glaring darkly at Joe, bringing Nicolas back to the present.

'One thing,' Joe said seriously before he got started. 'It's a long way between here an' Tellmark. I think this spell will wipe me out for a while. Don't go relyin' on me te suddenly appear if ye break anything else.'

'You won't have the chance anyway.'

Joe stared at Silva quizzically.

Instead of explaining her comment to him, she explained it to Nicolas. 'We cannot have someone running around with the ability to track us. We have too many enemies. If one of them were to find out, they could make

Joe bring them to us or find a way to home in on the spell themselves. Either way, it's too dangerous.'

'I think the positives outweigh the negatives,' Shift said. 'Shake your leg and tell me otherwise.'

The warrior gave Nicolas a hard stare. 'You know I'm right.'

Bugger.

'Yes, she's right,' he confirmed. 'Shift, I'm going to need that coin we just found.'

The shapeshifter instantly put their hand on their purse. 'Why?'

'Because once we're no longer tethered to Joe, we have no support left,' he said. 'So we're going to need to stock up on whatever potent potions, cure-alls, and anti-magic charms he has.'

Shift's lip curled into a slight snarl. 'Fine. But he can have it after we get to Tellmark.' They cradled the coin purse fondly. 'I just want to hold it for a little longer.'

'Fine with me.' Joe giggled. 'Like I said, I'll be needin' a rest after this anyhow.' With that, Joe took a handful of powder from the bag and inhaled deeply. His old body shook slightly as his eyes widened. 'Wooo,' he said finally. 'That is the stuff. Got a lovely kick te it.' There was a flash of red veins between his wrinkles. His hands shook. 'Ye bugger,' Joe cried, stamping his foot several times. 'That's the good stuff right there.'

Maybe this isn't the best idea.

Before Nicolas could voice the mass of concerns that had suddenly appeared in his mind, Joe said some words he didn't recognise, and there was a blinding light.

Nicolas had only just gotten used to being back in his own body, so having it thrown through a swirling abyss was very unwelcome. A myriad of colours flashed past his eyes. His limbs writhed as if he no longer had any bones. Parts of his body ballooned then shrank again. He simultaneously felt like he was falling and swimming.

The horses appeared to be taking all of this in their stride. His companions weren't. Beside him was a flying blue flame he assumed was Auron. As for the others, they looked as if they were made of pools of liquid Their forms grew and shrank and bubbled. Shift, Silva and Tallith all had their teeth clenched in discomfort whilst Dieter...appeared to be asleep Well, it was obviously not the explorer's first time doing this.

Nicolas found himself praying for his soul, and also quite thankful he hadn't experienced this the first time, when T'goth had sent them to that thrice-damned island. Or he may have never suggested this in the first place.

With an audible *pop*, they left whatever vortex they'd been fired through and returned to reality.

Nicolas fell from the sky.

CHAPTER 43

The fact that it was a short fall was a blessing. Whereas the horses, Joe and his wagon, and Dieter all almost floated to the ground, landing on their feet, Nicolas and the others crashed to the snow. Nicolas rolled over and began hacking violently.

'Oooo eeeee,' Joe exclaimed, slapping his knee. 'That's the rush.'

Nicolas turned his shaking head and stared at the trader incredulously.

'Damned lay-folk. That's the only way te travel.'

'I...respectfully...disagree,' he managed finally. That had been worse than the demon bear and cow-dragon combined.

Holding his stomach, mainly to ensure his organs were all in the right places, Nicolas shakily got to his feet. The world was rocking slightly. He didn't care for it. They'd just been launched through a void. The least Etherius could do was stay still for a minute whilst he came back to his senses.

'Urgh, by the Deities,' Shift said with a cough as they wiped their mouth on their sleeve. 'I did not care for that.'

'Oh, I don't know,' Auron said with a nod. 'Good to air out the old spirit every now and then.' A snowball – more of a handful of snow than an actual ball – that Shift lazily flung flew directly through Auron's ethereal form. 'Hey.'

Allowing himself a chuckle, Nicolas turned.

How did he get there?

He was surely still disorientated, because somehow Auron had gotten to the other side of him. Nicolas squinted. For some reason, the spirit was darker. Almost more solid. And taller?

Why does he have that stupid grin on his face? And what's he holding that sword up for? Why is he flexing his bicep like that? Who's he trying to impress? Joe?

'Oh, for Deities' sake.' Silva groaned, looking in the same direction. 'It looks like we made it to Tellmark.'

Nicolas caught himself as he was about to ask why. The reason was obvious. What he was staring at was a giant statue.

'Like the statue, kid?' the spirit asked, looking at it with pride. 'I think it definitely captures the essence of *Auron of Tellmark*.'

He turned to look at his companion then turned away instantly. The spirit was standing very close to him, and his eyes were still a little light sensitive after the recent ordeal. 'We're in Tellmark then?'

Auron opened his arms wide. 'Hometown of the legendary hero. Where better to build a statue to me?'

Nicolas didn't want to respond. Nausea was punching him repeatedly in the torso, demanding attention that he didn't want to give it.

I really need this to go away now.

'Am I feeling sick because of the teleporting or because of *that*?' Shift groaned weakly.

'*Hey*,' Auron snapped. 'I'll have you know that was crafted by one of Ivilar's premier artists. A true master, crafting a true masterpiece. So, show some respect.'

'And I'm sure you were more than happy to pose for it,' Shift replied with a cough. 'I can't even fake respect at the moment. Right now, I just want to die.'

I know the feeling.

Nicolas started as someone shoved a pouch into his nose. Flailing, he swatted it away, but not before inhaling some of the sweet-smelling powder, which irritated his nostrils.

'Son of a— Hey, my nausea's gone.'

'Darn right.' Joe beamed as he shuffled over and grabbed Shift's head, repeating the process. 'Good for hangovers too.' The trader gave him a mischievous, one-toothed smile. 'I've tested it rigorously.' Despite the way he carried himself, Joe did look drained, his skin greyer and his face drawn. The trip must've really taken it out of him.

'Well, it worked.' Carefully, Nicolas took a couple of steps forward. There was still a little dizziness, but nothing he couldn't handle.

He laughed as Joe tried to grab Silva's head. The warrior jumped to her feet and raised her fist threateningly. Keeping it aloft and not taking her eyes off Joe for a second, she took the pouch, sniffed deeply, and handed it back. Only then was the fist lowered.

Murmuring caught his attention. A crowd had gathered at the entrance to the town. Quickly, he scanned it for pitchforks. None yet.

That can change quickly, though.

A stout, balding man with large but well-maintained sideburns pushed through the crowd. 'Where did you lot come from?' he demanded. 'Did you fall out of the sky?'

'If they try to run us off, I swear...' Nicolas placed himself tactically between the warrior and the villagers, before whatever the end of her sentence was going to be got them into trouble.

'Um, yes, we did sort of fall out of the sky, a little,' he said with a hopefully warm smile. 'I'm sorry to startle you.'

'Startle us?' the man cried. 'You're bloody right you startled us. Popping out of the sky without as much as a by your leave. The pigs are over there shitting kittens.' He helpfully pointed in the direction he meant.

I hope not. If they are, I'm not taking responsibility for it.

'Again, sorry. We're travellers, and we—'

'No, no,' the man said, waving his hands in the air. 'You can't just appear in the sky around nice, Deity-fearing folk like us. It's just... Well, it isn't done.'

Steeling himself, Nicolas approached the man, who he assumed to be the mayor, and held out his hand. 'I'm sorry we've gotten off on the wrong foot here. Or wing, I suppose.' His poor attempt at a joke was met with cold silence. 'I'm Nicolas Percival Carnegie.'

For a moment, the man regarded the hand as if it were a spear tip pointed at him. But, finally, he took it in a nice firm handshake. 'Bransius Cole, Mayor of the fine town of Tellmark, birthplace of legendary hero, Auron Shallbutt. Also known as the *Dawnblade*.'

'Ha,' Shift laughed behind him. 'Your name is Shallbutt? But what shall you butt, good sir?'

'Now you know why I refer to myself as Auron of Tellmark,' the spirit grumbled.

'I've heard of him,' Nicolas replied to the mayor.

'So I take it...this was magic?' the mayor asked, waving his hand towards the sky then at Nicolas's companions.

'Yes.' Nicolas nodded, looking back at the others, who were all putting on their best temple-visiting smiles. Except Silva. 'Apologies for the suddenness of our appearance. But our quest is urgent and time is short, so we had no opportunity to write ahead.' As he turned back to the mayor, Bransius wasn't looking at him. Well, he was, but not in the eye. His gaze was low.

What in the Underworld is he looking at? It better not be my—

'That sword,' the mayor whispered, pointing at his belt. His eyes rose to Nicolas's chest plate before they widened. 'Oh, my days, it's *you*!' Arms in the air, hands shaking like a child being presented with a large, wrapped gift, the mayor turned to the rest of the crowd. 'It's *him*. It's only bloody *him*.'

Murmuring spread through the crowd, gathering in pace and volume as the townsfolk grabbed each other and pointed at someone who utterly hated being the centre of attention.

Nicolas jolted forward as Bransius grabbed his hand in both of his and shook it again with vigorous enthusiasm. 'I'm so sorry,' he bellowed. 'I didn't recognise the name right away. I'd heard you were called *Nick Carnage* or something. *Nicolas Carnegie*, easy mistake to make, I suppose.' He beamed.

Aaaaarrrrrrgggggggghhhhhh. 'Think nothing of it.'

He heard a noise behind him.

Laugh it up, Shift.

'Ah.' The mayor clapped before opening his arms wide. 'And these must your squires, scribes, and other followers.'

'Squire?' Shift said quietly behind him.

'Don't be upset,' Auron said, his chest moving up and down rapidly with suppressed laughter. 'I think you'd have made an adequate squire.'

Nicolas didn't need to look to know the face they were pulling right now. 'You can shove that right up your... Actually, you *shall* shove it up your *butt*.'

The spirit was suddenly silent.

'They're actually my companions,' he corrected, trying not to chuckle himself. 'And we are all at your service.'

Bransius laughed aloud, pointing his chubby finger at Nicolas as he turned back to the crowd. 'Do you hear that? He's *at my service*. The new *Dawnblade* is *at my service*. What a day, what a day.'

Judging by the reactions of the townsfolk, it was a pretty big deal.

'Please allow me to introduce my companions.' Nicolas smiled, gesturing to each in turn. 'This is Shift, my amazing shapeshifting companion. That man there is explorer and writer Dieter Von Ostric. The gentleman in the armour is Sergeant Tallith of the Babylon City Watch, and the gentleman by the wagon is travelling trader Snaggletooth Joe. He's how we came to appear here so suddenly.'

'I'm aware of Joe,' Bransius muttered, stroking his chin with a furrowed brow.

Nicolas turned to find that Joe had disappeared into his wagon.

'And this is...is...Dalia,' he said finally, fumbling out a name. 'Warrior and...my tutor.'

There was the very slightest twitch of Silva's brow, but she seemed to understand the necessity. They'd probably be much less welcome if it was discovered that they'd brought the woman who'd killed their beloved town hero with them.

'Fantastic to meet you all,' Bransius boomed. *'Except Joe'* was the unspoken part of that sentence, but it was very clear. 'And fantastic of the new *Dawnblade* to bless Auron's birthplace with a visit. Tell me, have you come to pay homage to your lost mentor? It was a sad day, a sad day indeed when we heard the news.'

Many of the townsfolk's eyes were downcast now, and it was only then that Nicolas noticed the black armbands they all wore.

A certain spirit was loving every second of this.

'Actually, as I mentioned just now, we're here on a quest.'

That snapped the mayor out of his mourning. 'A *quest*, you say? Do you hear that? The *Dawnblade* is mid-quest, and his noble endeavour has brought him to our door. Oh, what a glorious day indeed.'

'It *is* so glorious, having you around.'

Nicolas ignored Shift. 'Unfortunately, we cannot stay. We need to—'

'Oh no, oh no,' Bransius said, wagging his finger. 'You can't travel now. A storm is on the way. You mark my words. Won't be fit out there for a dog.' Nicolas bit his lip at Shift's giggle. 'You and your entourage can bed down here until it passes. We have hospitality in droves for the venerable *Dawnblade.'* The mayor's brow furrowed again slightly. 'I suppose Joe can stay too.'

Slowly, Nicolas turned and looked directly at Shift. 'I'm sure my *entourage* would welcome that.'

Funnily enough, Shift wasn't so chatty anymore.

CHAPTER 44

Apparently, there *was* something worse than Auron's constant stories. And that was a long line of people waiting to tell him stories *about* Auron. One after the other, the people of Tellmark shared tales of events they'd never seen with their own eyes like they'd been stood in the room when it happened. It was made less bearable by a certain spirit sitting right beside him, correcting or embellishing in his ear.

Perhaps I didn't change back from a dog. Maybe I died during the transformation, and this is the Underworld again?

But he couldn't deny the love the people of this town had for Auron. Nor how quickly they could throw a party. It was almost like they had all the garlands, food, and musicians ready, just in case some visitor should happen by and need to be told all about the *Dawnblade*. Nicolas realised annoyingly slowly that they probably did this all the time. Of course Auron's birthplace would attract tourists, and naturally, the town would want to capitalise on that.

Winter would have naturally slowed the number of people visiting Tellmark, forcing the townsfolk to take a seasonal break. But now they had some new arrivals it was business as usual, showcasing the towns favourite son. And Nicolas being the new *Dawnblade* only poured oil on the flames of their enthusiasm. So much so, that the entire town was crowded into the hall for the occasion.

And the celebration was in full swing. The roaring of the fire was drowned out by the eager musicians, firing out jaunty tune after jaunty tune. As much as he hated being the centre of attention, Nicolas couldn't deny that the town could put on an amazing spread. The smell of beautifully cooked meat and bread melded with the ripe ale odour in the air. It somehow all mingled together nicely.

The happiness of the people was almost infectious. *Almost*. Him having to hear stories he'd already heard dulled it slightly. Yet he listened politely, nodding along with a smile. The only time he really got distracted was when several children ran past with toy figures carved in Auron's likeness.

His gaze flicked to Tallith, to try to discern if the sergeant had noticed them.

I don't want him getting any ideas and whittling a Nicolas figure.

The running children jumped as they passed a window and it banged slightly, a reminder of the storm outside. The mayor had been right. Nicolas hadn't poked his head out the door to check, but the occasional banging of the shutters told him conditions out there were not good at all. Which was one of the reasons they hadn't set off after Garaz already.

I just hope we've managed to overtake him.

Half-listening to the woman telling her tale as his mind drifted to his former companion, Nicolas took a swig of his drink. '...after he saved me,' she continued coyly, 'I asked if there was any way I could repay him. He had a suggestion, I tell you. Quite an inappropriate one, if you catch my drift.' Knowing Auron, it was hard not to. 'But as it turned out, he gave me one more blessing, when he put his seed in me.'

He spat out most of his drink then choked on what was left in his mouth. 'He what?'

The woman turned and gestured someone forwards. It was a young boy, maybe fourteen or fifteen. There was no doubt who his father was. The jawline, the hair, the twinkle in the eye.

'He blessed me with a strapping boy.' She beamed before becoming serious, leaning in and lowering her voice. 'Now, by rights, he should be Auron's successor, blood and all that. But I get what happens out in the wild. He didn't have time to come back and train his son up to take over the family business, so he left it to you. But you've a fair list of deeds to your own name now. I'd be honoured for you to take him as a squire. Teach him what his father taught you.'

The boy seemed less than enthused by the prospect. Nicolas suspected he was slouching that badly on purpose, to give the appearance that he wouldn't make a worthy squire. He even picked his nose to complete the look.

'Get your finger out of there,' his mother hissed, slapping his hand away. 'You don't want the new *Dawnblade* thinking you can't live up to your father's legacy.'

The look on the boy's face—as if he were chewing a frog—seemed to sum up his thoughts on that nicely.

Nicolas looked briefly at Auron. The spirit's mouth was hanging open, and it looked as if his aura had dimmed slightly. 'I'll give it due consideration,' Nicolas said finally, as he turned back to the woman.

The boy looked almost relieved. His mother was less than pleased with the response. 'I'll look forward to hearing the outcome of your *consideration*.' She sniffed before rising and leading her son away. As she did, the boy mouthed, *'Thank you'*.

I was a boy who didn't want to leave a village once. I'm not about to force anyone down my path.

'Any more of those?' he asked his companion.

'Probably all over Etherius,' the spirit replied with a sigh. 'I have...had a tendency not to look back once I left the bedroom in the morning...or snuck out in the night.'

'Charming.'

'It really wasn't.' Auron's frankness shocked him so much he nearly spat his drink out again. 'All that fornicating on the road...now I look back on it, it's kind of sad. Who knows how many little Aurons are out there who will never know me? Gift of hindsight, I suppose.' The spirit frowned at him; he must've been letting his pity show. 'Don't worry, kid. I've got you to pass my legacy on to.' Auron allowed a small smile to lift the corner of his mouth. 'Who knows, I did pass Hablock a time or two in the past. Maybe...'

'Don't you dare suggest what you're about to.'

The spirit put his hands up in mock defeat.

Still, Nicolas couldn't help but feel sorry for him. The closest Auron had ever come to a real relationship, that he knew of, was with the Princess of the Tidal Kingdom, Janessa, a love that was never meant to be. Plus, now that he knew the history between him and Silva, Nicolas saw how terrible the outcome of being a travelling womaniser could be.

But I've got something better than a thousand women on the road.

It was only when Shift raised an eyebrow questioningly that Nicolas realised he'd been staring at them dreamily. He shrugged and looked away. He wasn't about to admit how happy he was to have someone to be close to in what was turning out to be a very unpleasant world. Although if Dieter was to be believed Etherius was decent enough. He just had a bad habit of visiting the unpleasant places.

Shift suddenly plonked themselves down on the bench beside him. 'Are you okay?'

'Oh, um, yes.' He probably answered that a little too quickly.

'Okay.' Shift sounded less than convinced. 'Stop staring at me strangely and I'll believe you.'

'It's just,' he scrabbled for something to justify his oddness, 'parties. Being the centre of attention. It makes me uncomfortable.'

Shift rubbed his arm mockingly. 'Just put up with it for another hour or two and you'll get me all to yourself. All of my focus will be on you and...oh. Hang on. You don't like being the centre of attention, so perhaps I shouldn't...'

'I'll be fine,' he said with an eager grin.

Shift looked away and smirked. 'Somehow, I thought you might be.'

A young child approached their table. 'Excuse me, ma'am,' the girl said nervously to Silva. 'But are you a warrior?'

'Yes, I am, little one,' she replied. 'My name is S...Dalia.'

The girl nodded knowingly. 'Is that your sword?'

'It would be strange of me to wear someone else's.'

'I want a sword like that one day.' The girl drew an imaginary blade and brandished it in front of her, face attempting to be fierce but being cute instead. 'I will travel and slay monsters and discover lost dungeons and save handsome princes.'

Silva pursed her lips. 'Are you brave?'

The girl puffed her chest out proudly. 'Sooooo brave.'

The warrior stroked her chin thoughtfully then faux-lunged at the girl, making her hands into claws. '*Rrraaggghhh.*'

The child cried out, dropping her fake sword as she jumped back.

Silva picked up the blade, putting it back into its owner's hand before gently guiding the imagined sword back to its sheath. 'Maybe you will one day,' she said gently. 'But don't be in a rush to grow up. Enjoy being a child. When the time comes for you to choose your path, you'll know which one is right for you.'

'Motherly Silva, who knew?' Shift whispered.

Nicolas looked at his tankard longingly before putting it down on the table.

What's the point of trying to drink when everyone around you is making you spit it out again?

Frowning at the warrior, he wondered if Silva ever wanted children. Nicolas thought about it and cursed himself. He'd never asked if she already had any. He'd just assumed because...of the way she was. It wasn't likely, though.

Will I ever have children?

Nicolas shuddered. That meant thinking about a normal life. Lately, he didn't dare to dream of one. It seemed too far-fetched, and it would make him think of the one he'd had, once upon a time. Auron could have easily found someone to settle down with, but he never did. He just travelled and adventured until he died. Was that his lot now? In it until the bitter end?

In his mind he tried to summon up what his life could look like after all this was done, and he'd somehow miraculously survived. A hazy image began to form of a house, the one he'd live in. There were figures in front of it. But before it could become clear he dismissed it. He didn't want to give himself false hope of a future he may never attain.

No, right now, it was best to just drink and be merry. Because who knew what Etherius was going to throw at them tomorrow?

CHAPTER 45

There was a time when Nicolas had taken sleeping in a bed as the norm. Nowadays, it was a luxury. A warm room was quickly becoming one of those, too, but that night they had one. There'd been no need to wrap up tightly under a mound of blankets and furs. Which was good, because Shift had ensured he hadn't slept in any clothes. Not quite ready to face the day yet—if it was indeed the start of a new day—he turned over and put his arm around the shapeshifter lying beside him. For a second, they flinched as his breath tickled the back of their neck, but then they shimmied into him slightly, enjoying the embrace.

Smiling as Shift cuddled into him, he glanced toward the window. There was no sign of light yet, but it was coming. And with that, the search for Garaz would continue. Would today be the day they caught him?

At least he didn't turn out to be The Visitor.

But he still had so many questions, Garaz's strange change of eye colour amongst them. Searching his memories, he tried to find signs, things he'd missed that had given away the potential betrayal. Something he could use to beat himself up because if he'd noticed, he could've prevented this.

One single memory stood out from the rest. A dockside warehouse fight against Big Boss and his assorted goons. Nicolas and the dwarf wrestling on the ground with the power of a Deity at stake. For a moment, in the chaos, Garaz had held the staff, which contained the power of T'goth, in his hands. In his mind, Nicolas played the scene out in slow motion. Enemies had charged the orc, and Nicolas had asked Garaz to throw it to him. There had been a clear second where the orc had hesitated, as if he were torn about keeping the staff for himself.

He did *want to keep it.*

Was that his true purpose, to steal magical artifacts? What did the staff and the amulet have in common? He supposed T'goth's staff could be used to heal, and Garaz was a healer.

So, who does he need to heal so badly?

An elbow dug into his ribs. 'You're cuddled up next to me—naked, no less—and you're worrying,' Shift turned their head slightly, so they could see him in their peripheral vision. 'You have a strange sense of priorities.'

'I didn't know you were awake,' he answered quickly. 'I was just thinking about Garaz.'

'Wow,' the shapeshifter said as they turned over. 'That's worse. You have me here, in bed, and you're thinking about an orc? I have a good mind to be offended, Mr Carnegie.'

'But...I...well...'

'Calm down.' They said with a sleepy smile. 'It's too early for you to start flapping.'

He let out a sigh. 'But there's so much to flap about.'

'Do you want to see a magic trick?'

The strange question caught him completely off guard. For a second, he frowned before framing a response. 'Okay,' he said slowly.

Shift flexed their fingers in front of his face, before smoothing back their short auburn hair. 'I will make your troubles vanish. So much so, that you won't even remember what you were flapping about.'

'Then you would be a mighty sorcerer indeed,' he said, getting comfortable and wondering what was to come next.

After rubbing their hands together then working their fingers in circles, as if conjuring a spell, Shift lifted the bedsheet and directed his attention to everything below their neckline. *Alakazam,*' they said, playful biting their lip.

Nicolas looked down, blinked a few times, and smiled. 'That's quite the trick. I have no idea what we were talking about just now.'

****

Rubbing his face, Nicolas reached the bottom of the stairs and the ground floor of the house where they were staying and stretched his arms wide until his back was taut. It was damned satisfying. Not as satisfying as what had happened upstairs, but good.

There'd been a lot of petitions from the townsfolk about who got to put them up for the night. Apparently, having Nicolas drooling on their guest pillow was considered quite the honour. At one point, two very passionate gentlemen were on the cusp of getting into a fistfight over it. But the choice had been simple enough. Bransius was the only one with a home big enough to accommodate all of them. The disappointed sighs of those who weren't able to host them made Nicolas feel awkward. But he could only sleep in one bed a night.

All the others were sat around the table, already eating—aside from Joe, who wasn't welcome in the mayoral residence, or any other, and had slept out in his wagon. The trader had gone to sleep just after they'd arrived, telling them he wouldn't be awake for a good while as he slept off the effects of teleporting them over such a distance. Not knowing when he might wake again, the group had stocked up on potions just before his nap began and asked him to break that magical tether of his. Joe had assured them he would break it once he'd fully recovered, as his magic was still weak. Silva had informed him in graphic detail what would happen if he didn't.

'No guessing how your morning started.' Auron grinned at him. 'You're glowing more than I do, kid.'

'Mind your business,' Shift said sternly as they walked down the stairs.

Auron held his hands up. 'Just commenting. I don't really want to know.'

'Yippee,' Silva said quietly, cup to her lips, which now creased in a smile.

Nicolas glared at the warrior. It seemed that his errant cry the first time he and Shift had been intimate was doomed to dog him for all eternity.

Shift tilted her head in Silva's direction. Slowly, they sauntered over to the warrior and leaned over the table to grab a piece of bread that sat near her. 'He only said that because I *made* him say it,' Shift told the warrior.

Suddenly, Silva didn't appear to be enjoying herself as much.

'Look at these honoured guests in my home.' Bransius swept into the room with open arms, his dressing gown wafting open as he did. 'This is a day I won't soon forget.'

'Thank you for your hospitality,' Nicolas said, shaking the mayor's hand. 'You and your whole town.'

'Nonsense, young man,' the mayor said, sitting at the table and getting stuck into breakfast. 'Having you visit is a boon for us in these cold months. It'll give us some nice new stories when the tourists start coming back.' Bransius dropped his voice to a conspiratorial whisper. 'I have no doubt there'll be one or two babies named Nicolas in your honour here in the next few years. I'll have to put a cap on it, though. Can't have them doing it to every newborn boy.'

Oh, for Deities' sake. He suspected Bransius would get first use of the name, his wife being heavily pregnant with her third child.

'You could call the girls Nicola.' Thank goodness Bransius couldn't hear Auron. Nicolas didn't want the spirit giving him ideas.

'I'm just sorry we can't stay longer.' And he genuinely was.

'I understand.' The mayor smiled. 'Quests wait for no man, nor do they respect the creature comforts us humans require to live. I couldn't do what you do.' Bransius patted his belly. 'I love my fine dining too much.'

Sitting at the table, Nicolas began to eat but nearly spat out his food when he saw a certain pamphlet on the edge of the table. 'A fan of his work?' he asked, eyeing it with distaste.

Reaching over, the mayor picked up Tobias Helstrum's published hatred and turned it over in his hands. 'Ah, Mr Helstrum. Quite a divisive fellow.' It was hard to tell from his face whether the mayor liked the ideas in the book or not. 'There's some scary stuff in here. All that business about crossbreeding...non-humans trying to breed us out because they can't conquer us. Scary business.'

Utter bullshit.

Nicolas wanted to snatch the document from his hand, tear it up, and stamp on the shreds, but he couldn't exactly do that to his kind host.

'He's a bit of a local celebrity, in his way,' Bransius told them, putting the pamphlet back on the table. 'His estate is not too far from here.'

The only reason that information was handy was so Nicolas could avoid it like the plague.

'Don't you think Helstrum has a very *good and evil* view of other races?' There was almost visible tension in Shift's face as they struggled to remain diplomatic.

Bransius pursed his lips before responding. 'That's the big debate, isn't it?' he replied solemnly. 'There is undeniable trouble hereabouts, and it does seem to come from the non-humans. We have so many problems with the orcs...and then these fauns I hear a lot about. Now you have demonic killers running around Babylon. And have you heard about this *Visitor* fellow down south? They say he's some type of crossbreed.'

'We're familiar,' Nicolas said, eyeing the others.

'But then we hear tales of hope,' the mayor continued. 'Tales of people like you, out in the world, fighting these pests. Makes us realise it isn't all bad out there. I don't think you know the effect your tales have on people in these dark times. When we hear about you stopping wars, saving good folk. Well...it warms the heart on cold days, let me tell you.'

Nicolas was genuinely shocked. He'd been so busy being annoyed about his *legend* spreading that he hadn't even considered the positive impact it might be having on people. Did some of these isolated villages find comfort in the idea that someone was out there fighting the good fight?

'They have a good effect.'

He stared at Tallith, who gave him a knowing nod. Perhaps he'd misjudged his *fan club* too. Maybe they weren't loonies but people who needed hope in a time when a killer was stalking their city. It was as if responsibility suddenly manifested into a human form, put its hands on his shoulders, and whispered, '*You're mine now*' in his ear.

'Stories are powerful things, young man,' Dieter said, backing up the sergeant and the mayor. 'For both good and ill.'

'Aye, but I fear it will all come to a head soon, one way or the other.' All eyes turned to Bransius. 'I've heard rumblings.'

'About?' Nicolas asked.

'Well, I often call upon one of the local lords, who quite enjoys my company and has an ear at court. They're trying to call a King's Moot.'

From Dieter's gasp, it sounded important. Too important to feign that he knew what it was. 'A what now?'

'It's a gathering of the rulers of the Nine Kingdoms of Man,' the writer explained. 'They can be called to discuss matters that potentially affect them all. There hasn't been one for fifty years.'

'Some say it should already have happened,' Bransius said thoughtfully. 'Apparently, the High King was set on calling it when Merida was on the cusp of war. And when the killer stalked the streets of Babylon. But each time the crisis went away, and so did the urgency to call it.'

Because of me.

Silva, Shift, and Auron had all clearly come to the same conclusion. Was *this* part of whatever grand plan the Maestro was conceiving? But to what end? What would happen at this King's Moot?

No wonder he's so pissed with me.

He highly doubted anything good would come of this meeting if the Maestro was the one orchestrating it. Apparently, he'd managed to delay it several times without even knowing about it. Could he find a way to stop it completely? Would that even be possible?

I'll just have to keep doing what I'm doing and hope for the best.

Fate seemed to have him blunder into these things quickly enough. Right now, if he just concentrated on finding Garaz, he was sure the rest would end up falling into place.

Somehow.

CHAPTER 46

There'd been so much going on that Nicolas decided a morning run would be the best way to try to clear his mind, to focus. But no matter how quickly he ran, all the things demanding his attention snapped at his heels. Also, he probably should've left it a little longer after breakfast. The food sat heavily in his stomach as he bounced it around.

Reaching the crest of the hill, he allowed himself to slow to a stop. It wasn't a huge hill, but big enough that he could see Tellmark spread out below him. Smoke rose from chimneys as the black shapes of people went about their day.

Getting out of the town had taken quite a bit of effort, with well-wishers bombarding him. He was even asked to bless a newborn. Too awkward to say no, he'd mumbled a blessing, which had appeared satisfactory, given the pride on the faces of both the child's parents. Then there was the maid who'd made a valiant effort to hypnotise him with her cleavage. He wasn't interested.

All that had only made being alone more important. So, he stood and stared out at the fields and forests surrounding him—cast in a bright glow from the early morning sun—and a modicum of peace washed over him. For a few moments, he just breathed in the invigorating fresh air.

With a satisfied smile, he prepared himself to train. Between Auron, Silva, and Ban, he'd learned much about the art of fighting, but it only mattered if he kept up his practise. His muscles were already warm from the run, so he needn't worry about getting cold for a little while. Plus, it was good to train in the snow. Enemies came at you no matter the conditions, so he'd best be ready to fight in all of them.

Taking a shoulder-width stance, bending his knees slightly to drop his weight, Nicolas began to move, slowly and with purpose, making each muscle work as if it carried a great weight. Going over one of the forms Ban Dro had taught him, he circled his arms, pushing them in and out with intent. He wished he'd had more time to learn all the applications of what he'd been taught, but being backstabbed by an orc had cut his time short.

Breathing deeply and evenly, he let everything else go until it was just him, and nature, and the movement. Dreamily, he allowed his gaze to wander over the world around him.

Huh?

Nicolas stood up straight, frowning. Below him, in one of the fields, was a spot of colour. Narrowing his eyes, he tried to focus on it.

Red.

Nicolas snarled as he realised what he was looking at. *Who* he was looking at.

That son of a bitch.

Anger instantly revitalised and fuelled his muscles as Nicolas charged down the hill, keeping his eyes fixed on the trudging red shape. Half running, half sliding, Nicolas reached the bottom of the hill, and his target vanished, obscured by trees and the curving of the earth. But he knew where he was.

Driving himself onward, he jumped fences and dodged obstacles as he raced to catch Garaz. He had no idea what he'd do when he caught up to the orc; right now, he just needed to catch him.

I'm not going to lose him.

He hopped across a gorge and over one more fence, and Garaz was finally in sight again. Nicolas came to a halt for a second, breathing heavily as he stared at the orc, fury boiling inside him. With a growl, he charged through the field separating them.

Ahead of him, his former companion appeared not to notice his approach. When he reached the fence at the edge of the field, Garaz threw his staff over it then began to climb. He was so close now. Nicolas pumped his arms and legs faster and faster.

The orc sat atop the fence, one leg on either side of it.

'*Garaz.*' The roar echoed across all the fields. Maybe all of Etherius.

Frowning with confusion, the orc turned towards him. 'Nicolas?'

He launched himself into the air. It was probably the best jump he'd ever done. Tackling the orc across the mid-section, he knocked Garaz off the fence to come crashing down on the other side. Rolling with the fall, Nicolas scrambled to his feet, fists clenched. Slowly, the orc unfurled himself from his cloak and rose.

'Surprised?' he growled.

'Yes,' Garaz said, yellow eyes wide. 'How did you get here?' Seeing him so flustered was strangely satisfying.

'You seriously thought I'd let you attack me and lock me in cupboard and get away with it?'

'Please, you do not understand—'

'And for what?' Nicolas cried. 'To steal that?' He pointed to the object bundled in rags. He knew it was the amulet. It was almost as if he could sense its power.

Patting his cloak in surprise, the orc took a step towards the amulet.

Nicolas took a step forward too. 'Oh no,' he said. 'You aren't just picking it up and walking off. We need to talk.'

Garaz licked his lips and shook his head.

'What's the matter? Lost your tongue? You're the wise one who likes to explain things, so explain this.' Nicolas knew the next thing he was about to say was petty, but he was mad. 'And use small words. My brain is struggling to cope with being betrayed and locked in a cupboard. It can't handle fancy talk right now.'

'I am so sorry.' From the pain in the orc's eyes, he meant it.

'Then explain.'

The orc shook his head again. 'I cannot.'

'You won't.'

Garaz's mouth opened hesitantly. 'I…I… Are the others with you?'

'They're close.'

Sighing heavily, Garaz smoothed his orange hair, gaze firmly on the floor. 'I did not want this.'

'And I didn't want to be betrayed, knocked out, and stuffed in a bloody wardrobe. I also didn't want to be in a field in the middle of winter after Shift and Silva were nearly killed and I was turned into a dog.'

Garaz looked shocked. 'They nearly… *A dog?*'

'Oh yes,' he snarled. 'We've had quite the adventure tracking you down.'

The orc's face hardened. 'I never asked you to do that.'

'You think we'd just let you go?' he scoffed. 'You're lucky Silva isn't here. She wanted to kill you outright. I'm giving you a chance to explain. So…'

'I told you I cannot,' Garaz snapped.

'*Won't,*' Nicolas corrected again. For a long moment, he stared at the orc, waiting for something, anything. Soon, it became clear no explanation was going to come. 'You know what, fine. You want your secrets, keep them. But I'm taking that.' He pointed toward the amulet, just in case Garaz was having a slow day.

Garaz rose to his full height. 'I cannot allow that.'

Nicolas shrugged sarcastically. 'And I can't let you out of this field with it. I warn you: you won't catch me off guard this time.'

Garaz closed his eyes sadly, lowering his head. When they focused on Nicolas again, there was disconcerting resolution in them. 'Then we must both do what we must.'

What?

There was a time when shock and inexperience would've kept him rooted to the spot; fortunately, those days were long past. Rolling to the side, he dodged the fireball. Just. Back on his feet, he used a nearby tree as a shield as the second hit it in a flash of flame. He winced as three more struck the tree.

Then there was silence. When he took a cautious peek, the orc was fleeing, stuffing the amulet hastily inside his cloak as he tried to make his escape.

'Oh no you bloody don't.'

With a cry, he broke cover, closing the gap between him and Garaz as fast as he could. The orc flung several more fireballs at him, striking the snow on either side of his feet and throwing up clouds of steam.

He isn't trying to hit me. He just wants to discourage me...tough shit.

'Dammit, Nicolas,' Garaz said, finally stopping. The orc took a fighting stance, staff in hand. 'Do not make me do this.'

His answer was to scoop up a ball of snow and launch it. It hit Garaz right between the eyes. The orc staggered backwards, dropping his staff as he tried to clear the snow from his eyes. Then Nicolas was upon him.

He struck Garaz in the jaw once, twice, three times. The orc was already unsteady, and though he had the size and weight advantage, he stumbled backwards under the onslaught. Nicolas hooked the back of Garaz's ankle with his foot, and the orc fell backwards into the snow.

Leaping atop his former companion, Nicolas scrabbled inside the pockets of his cloak.

'Ah ha,' he exclaimed, grabbing the amulet.

Garaz's closed fist struck him in the side, knocking him to the floor. A clawed hand grabbed for the amulet he still held, but he rolled back and kicked the hand away.

On all fours, the orc scrambled towards him. Nicolas backed away, using his legs to keep Garaz at bay, before launching another snowball into his face. The orc growled ferally as he struck.

Nicolas jumped to his feet as Garaz thrust himself forward. He didn't dodge the orc's backhanded blow quickly enough, and the world blinked for a moment as he reeled back. The follow-up punch caught him right in the dwarven armour, which absorbed most of the impact.

My turn.

With a left, he cracked Garaz across the cheek, before driving his right palm under the orc's jaw. Before Garaz could recover, he kicked him in the shin, making him fall forwards into the oncoming chop, which hit its target under the jaw line. Clutching his neck, Garaz crumpled to the side.

'Yield,' Nicolas demanded, chest heaving.

Garaz's answer was a low growl. Nicolas found himself taking a step back as he sensed a change in the air. Slowly, the orc turned to him, fixing him with glaring red eyes.

Uh oh.

Garaz roared and leapt at him. Gripping Nicolas by the throat, the orc hauled him high into the air before slamming him into the ground. The force of it drove all the air from Nicolas's lungs, and the amulet slipped from his grasp. Roaring, the orc pummelled his armour then grabbed him by a single arm and hauled him into the air.

Dazed, Nicolas stared into the animalistic eyes glaring at him, filled with hatred and bloodlust. Slowly, Garaz took hold of his other arm, snarling with glee. The orc yanked both of his arms outwards, causing Nicolas to cry in pain as his shoulders became suddenly taut. Suddenly, Nicolas knew what was about to happen—the same thing that had happened to a toad creature on a freighter.

Oh shit.

Thinking quickly, Nicolas raised both his legs and kicked Garaz square in the face. The grip holding him vanished, and he fell to his feet. Not wasting his advantage, Nicolas dived in with a flurry of punches, none of which appeared to bother Garaz. The orc shrugged them off then lifted him up and slammed him to the ground again.

As Nicolas writhed on the floor, it took all his effort to roll away from the foot descending towards his head. Garaz's foot crashed into the snow with a heavy *whumph*. It would've turned Nicolas's head to mush. Grabbing a nearby rock, Nicolas drove himself from the floor, swinging it and catching the orc on the side of the head. Both fell to the floor, panting heavily.

Forcing his muscles into action, Nicolas got to his feet and did something he never thought he'd to do Garaz. Drawing his sword, he stood over the orc and put the blade to his throat.

'Yield,' he commanded again.

Sad yellow eyes looked into his. 'I cannot.'

The sword wavered slightly. 'We were *friends*. You betrayed me. All of us. Why? Make me understand.'

'I wish I had time to explain,' Garaz replied softly. 'Truly I do. But time is the one thing I do not have. I am sorry.'

Sorry?

Nicolas looked down. Garaz's hand was level with his stomach, fire trailing around his fingers.

No.

The force of the blast lifted him from the floor and launched him across the field and through the nearby fence. He was already unconscious when he hit the ground.

CHAPTER 47

Aware that his head was shaking slowly from side to side, Nicolas was sure he could hear voices. At the moment they were only whispers in the darkness.

What happened?

Wincing as someone poked him made Nicolas realise that his eyes were closed. He commanded them to open, but they didn't obey. Neither did his limbs. It was as if he was having a strange out of body experience. His consciousness wasn't quite connected to his physical form.

Why though?

The poking became insistent shaking as he searched his memory. Garaz. He remembered that much. There had been a fight. He'd been winning. Then he'd seen the orc's hand and...

'*Fire.*' Eyes shooting open, Nicolas uttered a panicked cry as he began to furiously pat down flames that weren't there. It was only when a hand slapped him across the face that he came to his senses and realised that he wasn't on fire.

'You're fine,' Shift said, hand already prepared to deliver a second slap, should the need arise. 'Thank the Deities. What happened? Was it Avin?'

'How did you find me?' His voice was more pained groan than...well...voice.

'We heard a boom and came running,' Auron told him.

'Only you cannot go for a run without getting blown up,' Silva said, looking down at him.

There's a terrible truth to that.

When he looked down at his armour, smoke was still rising from it, and there was some charring on it, but for the most part, it appeared unscathed. On the bright side, it was nice and warm.

'It was Garaz,' he said, propping himself up on his elbows. He scrunched his face up as he caught sight of the broken part of the fence his body had hurtled through.

It could've been much worse.

'There is blood in the snow over there and signs of a prolonged fight,' Silva said. 'I take it you gave as good as you got.'

'Damn right I did.' He gestured for the others to help him up, which they did. 'And I won. I had him under my blade, but he cheated and blasted me with a fire— Ow. What was that for?' He rubbed his head where Silva had hit him.

'In a real fight, there is no cheating,' the warrior snapped. 'There is victory and defeat.'

'Ow.'

'And you could've been killed going after him by yourself,' Shift growled, after hitting him on the other side of the head.

'I didn't have a choice. By the time I got to you guys he would've been long gone.' he protested. 'He should have just surrendered. Instead, he blew me right through that fence.' He gestured offhandedly to the ruined wood recently destroyed by his flying body.

'It would not have happened if you had not stayed your hand and given him a chance to yield. I told you we should just dispatch the turncoat.'

'I wasn't about to just kill him, Silva,' Nicolas retorted. 'I wanted to at least give him a chance to explain.'

'And did he?' Auron asked.

'He kept saying he couldn't. But that amulet is damned important to him.' His mind went back to the fight, to a very specific part of it.

'What is it?' Shift asked, searching his face.

'It's...about his eyes,' Nicolas answered once he'd collected his thoughts. 'They turned red during the fight. It was like he'd snapped. He became...'

'Like an orc?' Silva ventured.

Nicolas nodded. 'He was going to rip my arms off. I managed to subdue him, and he turned back.'

'That's a good job, too, kid,' Auron said. 'You realise he could've killed you, right? He could've roasted you in your armour. He could've melted your face with a fireball. He could've taken his staff and bas—'

'All right, I get it,' he interrupted quickly. 'I'm lucky to be alive, and he obviously still cares about us. I...didn't exactly give him much choice about fighting me,' he admitted reluctantly.

But Auron was, as usual, right. Garaz had spared him. Whatever was happening to him was powerful, but he wasn't lost yet.

'I take it you've got his trail?' he asked Auron.

'Of course.'

Nicolas shook himself. 'He can't have gotten far. Let's get our horses and gear and go after him.'

'Are you sure you do not need to recover?'

He answered Silva with a firm shake of the head.

I am not *going to lose him again.*

****

It hadn't taken long to resume their pursuit. Whilst he'd been off duking it out with Garaz, the others had already started getting their gear together ready to leave. Tallith and Dieter both insisted on continuing the journey with them. Nicolas found himself quite happy about that. Knowing now that his tales actually helped others, he began to tell them as they travelled. It was also a good way to take his mind off the worry that they'd potentially lost Garaz.

About an hour and a half into their journey, the group came to a landmark that brought them to a halt.

'There we are,' Auron said with a sweeping gesture. 'The Orc Wastelands. And the Great Wall that borders it.'

Shift screwed their face up in confusion. '*Great Wall*? That's barely a presentable fence.'

Their assessment was accurate. Going from one end of the horizon to the other was...a bit of a fence. Weathered wooden panels that didn't look like they'd hold back a half-assed breeze, never mind anything else. In fact, there were several breaks in it.

Beyond the—ahem—Great Wall was a harsh land of ashen ground, dead trees, and jagged peaks. He could even see where the snow ended and the wasteland began. It was as if nature itself was afraid of touching it. It was unnervingly reminiscent of the Underworld.

And we're going in there.

'I think I see how so many orc raiding parties get into Ivilar.' Silva snorted at the structure.

'The border is a long piece of ground to cover,' Dieter said as he gazed at the horizon. 'Building a wall the entire length and maintaining a standing army along it was considered financially unfeasible. Instead, there are guard towers at regular intervals and occasional patrols. It is more of a visible deterrent than anything else.'

'And not much of one either,' Tallith said, eyebrows raised high. 'I would think the orcs see it as a challenge more than anything else.'

'You'd think all the wealth that could have been saved over the years stopping orc raids by building a decent wall would have nicely offset the cost of building it in the first place,' Shift scoffed. 'It's a long-term investment.'

'Maybe if the raids were bigger.' Dieter shrugged. 'But the orc population has never really recovered since the Great Horde was eliminated a thousand years ago. Now they live in small tribes who are more likely to fight each other than us.'

Nicolas couldn't help but chuckle at the wonder in Dieter's voice. There was no way they could've left the writer and explorer behind. Even if Silva had chained him to Auron's statue, he would've undoubtedly managed to break the chains in his eagerness to join them. Somehow, it was quite infectious. Or would've been if they weren't about to enter a land known to claim the lives of any humans who entered it.

Hopefully, we can beat the odds on that one.

They'd done it before. *He'd* done it before. He'd escaped the Underworld. Was what was beyond the crappy fence any worse than the legions of the undead?

'Are they really as bad as they say?' he asked as he scanned the horizon. 'Orcs, that is.'

'Usually, they're angry, unintelligent brutes who see inflicting violence as a nice way to pass the time,' Shift answered. 'Garaz was the exception to the rule.'

'*Is* not *was*,' he corrected. 'Whatever's going on with him, he's still in there.'

'We all hope so kid,' Auron smiled sadly. 'Because there's only so many times we can beat him back to sanity before it stops working.'

That was something Nicolas didn't even want to consider. If that happened, then they'd truly lost him.

But we'll only know for sure once we find him.

'We are on the right track,' Silva said, narrowing her eyes. 'In fact, I am sure he passed through over there.'

When they rode over to where the warrior had pointed, one of the holes in the fence was charred around the edges. Silva approached and let her hand hover above it.

'Still slightly warm,' she told the others. 'He was here not that long ago.'

'Onward then,' Nicolas said with a hesitant nod. 'This isn't going to get saner any time soon.'

CHAPTER 48

The Wasteland had a strange aura to it. From the moment they set foot—hoof, actually—upon it, they all knew they were in danger. It was inevitable that at some point they would be attacked. It wasn't paranoia. It was simple fact.

None of the group looked at each other. Every one of them watched a different part of the bleak horizon, keeping their eyes peeled for the first sign of orcs. Ears were pricked for that first blow of the war horn. They most certainly kept their swords in their hands.

Aside from Dieter, who leaned over in his saddle, examining any rock of vague interest that they happened by. His enthusiasm in this blighted land was just plain odd.

Not odd for a professional explorer, I suppose. Just odd for me.

Would he be so eager without a group of warriors escorting him? Dieter had been in his fair share of scrapes—once he'd mentioned having his big toe bitten off by a troll—but this was way beyond that.

'What do you know of The Wasteland?' Nicolas was hoping to soothe himself with knowledge, even though he already knew it was a fool's hope.

The writer grinned at him with the excitement of Auron about to tell a story. 'Very little, really,' Dieter admitted. 'But I am aware of the myths and legends surrounding it. To be able to try to separate fact from fiction is an amazing opportunity.'

'I've been here once myself,' Auron muttered sourly. 'The novelty is going to wear off quickly. Trust me.'

'I heard a whisper of a rumour that this place was once a lavish land, before the orcs,' Dieter said. 'Back before the Great Horde descended on the Elven race, who had dominion over most of what we now know as the Nine Kingdoms. Back then, humankind was a small race, developing on the western coastlines. They say it was a time of peace. Any information about the orcs before they poured across the border in their thousands, scouring everything in sight, was lost. And once the attack began, no one cared anyway.'

'So it was that bad?' Nicolas asked, actually forgetting the impending danger in his curiosity.

'Terrible, according to historical records,' the writer replied. 'The elves had not fought a war themselves for centuries. They say that their society had become quite decadent. So, they were in the worst possible position to repel a sudden invasion of such magnitude. And they were hopelessly outmatched by their enemy's ferocity.' Dieter pursed his lips thoughtfully. 'By all accounts, the elven race was brought to the brink of extinction. Those last thousands made their final stand at Elendar. Invictria, as we renamed it once they left.'

'Seems tactically unsound to gather all your forces in one place against an overwhelming enemy force,' Silva mused.

'Here is where it gets interesting,' the writer said, waving his finger in the air. 'Humanity knew what was happening to the elves, and where the orcs would likely go once they were done with them. Our people were rallied into an army, which was sent to save the elves. It wasn't much, but it was enough to fight their way to the centre of the orc lines and kill their leaders.' Dieter allowed himself a slight dramatic pause. 'With their leaders dead, the main bulk of the horde became unfocused, wandering off in differing directions depending on whatever happened to grab their interest. The smaller chunks proved much easier to manage. It was long and bloody work, but historians believe that by the time the last of the orcs were driven back across the border, as much as eighty percent of their race had been culled.'

'And what of the elves?' Apparently, Shift was becoming as enthralled by the history lesson as he was.

'Interesting question,' Dieter said. 'Their people were nearly wiped out by the horde too. Accounts suggest they could have lost as much as seventy percent of their population. Their main cities were left in ruins. In the wake of such tragedy, their leaders decided to leave and start again.'

'Where did they go?' Nicolas asked.

The explorer shrugged. 'They never said. Apparently, the survivors departed on a fleet of ships on the eastern coast to find another isle on which to live. They gifted what was left of their kingdom to the humans. And so, over time, developed the Nine Kingdoms of man.'

'And the orcs?'

'They never came out in such force again,' Dieter replied. 'There have been armies and wars and raids, but never on the same scale.'

Funnily enough, there was a time when Nicolas cared little for the history of Etherius, but since leaving home he'd begun to see the wider world. He had to admit, learning about the events that shaped said world was fascinating.

'The only thing you really need to know, kid, is that orcs are bigger, stronger, and more ferocious than you,' Auron told him. 'Always go for the limbs and the neck. Even if the orc is down, don't assume it's no longer a threat. They're a tenacious lot.'

After fighting Garaz, I'm not likely to underestimate his kin.

'This land is quite intriguing,' Dieter said as he scrawled notes in a book. 'I wasn't expecting a measurable aura of…menace, I suppose would be the word.'

Please don't describe every horrible sensation we come across.

'I must confess,' the writer continued, 'I would be interested to meet the locals. Study their culture. See how the orcs actually live.'

'Would you also be interested about walking into a dragon's open mouth?' Shift asked with a smirk.

Dieter appeared to take no offence at the remark. 'A certain amount of danger is necessary for proper exploration,' he replied matter-of-factly.

'What about you?' Nicolas said, turning in his saddle to look at Tallith. 'How are you finding the exploration?'

'Dangerous,' the sergeant admitted. 'It's much colder and more bloody than the stories make out.'

'You hear that?' Nicolas grinned at Dieter. 'Make sure you accentuate the cold and bloodiness when you write my story.'

'But I can see why you do it.' Nicolas waited for the sergeant to continue. 'You're doing good. I suppose if you want to properly help people, a bit of danger is inevitable. Just like with exploration.'

'That is a fair point,' Nicolas conceded. 'Though I'd be happy to help people and not be in danger doing it.'

'Then you wouldn't be an example to others. A hero.' The awe in Tallith's voice made Nicolas fidget uncomfortably in his saddle. 'Not many people can do what you do.'

Are there many who want to?

This moment of camaraderie had the effect of taking all their minds off their surroundings for a short while. But fate wasn't about to let that stand.

Boom.

The entire party froze. Even their mounts appeared to know something was amiss.

Boom, boom.

Licking his lips nervously, Nicolas scanned the horizon with his peripheral vision, afraid that if he moved, he might give their position away.

A strange idea, considering they were sat on horses in the middle of a barren wasteland.

Boom, boom, boom.

'Drums,' he said quietly. 'War drums.'

'No,' Auron said, tilting one ear up as the drumming continued. 'I've heard orc war drums a few times. These are different.'

'How can you tell that?' Silva asked. 'It just sounds like someone beating a drum.'

'It's in the rhythm of it,' the spirit replied. 'So this one time—'

'Here?' Shift asked in surprise. 'Now? Right now?'

'You make a good point,' Auron conceded. 'But I think we need to go and look into it.' Everyone in the party who could hear Auron stared at him aghast. 'There's obviously a settlement nearby. We need to make sure they aren't on the move in case we accidentally bump into them.'

'You go and bloody check it,' Nicolas cried as the drumming continued. 'You can't die.'

The spirit stared at him levelly. 'Are you going to be sat on that horse worrying about some deadly fate befalling you the whole time I'm gone? Are you going to be watching the horizon nervously for my return until—?'

'You've made your point.' He sighed. 'Let's go and visit the orcs then.'

CHAPTER 49

The group moved slowly, shimmying up the slope on their bellies. Though the drumming still sounded far away, it didn't pay to be reckless.

'You don't need to hug the ground so tightly,' Auron remarked as he looked back at them from the lip of the rise.

'Will you get down?' Nicolas hissed. 'They could have a shaman, or a seer, and you're stood there with your hands on your bloody hips.'

The spirit held his hands in the air. 'Fair point.' Slowly, he got to the ground.

Rising just enough to see over the lip of their hiding place, Nicolas saw the settlement. It was far away, yet too close for comfort. The drumming, whatever it signified, had stopped. Nicolas had a moment of panic when he wondered if the drumming had been intended to lure them in. Glancing around, he saw no signs of an ambush. And he doubted orcs were the type to lay well thought out ambushes.

'We are definitely keeping our distance from that,' Silva said, nose wrinkling as she squinted towards the settlement.

Atop a small hill ahead of them, it sat like a giant growth on a cheek. To say it was ramshackle was an understatement. No two fence panels were the same length or width, which was so jarring part of him wanted to go over there and correct them, as suicidal as that would be. The smoke rising from campfires was matched by the sound of carousing. Whatever the orcs were up to, they were having a bloody good time doing it. A large totem rose from the centre of the settlement. Atop it was a grinning red face painted on a shield with crossed axes behind it.

'I assume that is the symbol of their tribe,' Dieter said excitedly.

Nicolas did a double take. The writer was actually drawing the sigil.

'You don't think they've seen us?' he asked, eyes fixed on the gateway to the township.

'We would know if they had,' Auron told him. 'Your average orc isn't a subtle creature. This seems to be more party than war party.'

Beyond the opening in the gate Nicolas could make out the vague shapes of tents and mud huts. The figures he could see appeared to be moving around leisurely. Certainly not the actions of people ready to grab their axes and charge down some foreign invaders.

Deities, please keep it that way.

'I'm going to ask the obvious question you all seem to be missing,' Shift said as they shuffled back slightly. 'How do we know Garaz didn't go in there? He has a red cloak, they have a red totem. Maybe the party is a welcome home one.'

'Shit,' Nicolas whispered. That actually made sense. It also potentially meant they would have to try to sneak in to find out for sure. The idea wasn't appealing. *Crazy* was more fitting to describe it. *Frightening* also worked.

'I don't think so,' Auron said after a moment's thought. 'We all know how particular Garaz is. Doesn't seem the type brought up surrounded by mud huts and tents.'

Nicolas liked that logic much better. But they still needed to check the camp. Garaz's trail passed close by, and the orc knew he was being pursued. He may have doubled back to throw them off.

'Auron, I think you need to go and have a look,' he said. 'Just in case.'

'I knew it was a tribal society, but I expected cave dwellers,' Dieter muttered to himself as he scribbled furiously. 'But they appear to have the ability to build dwellings, albeit rudimentary ones. There is evidence of defences and tribal symbolism. Fascinating.'

'If nothing else comes out of this,' Shift said, giving the writer a bemused look, 'at least we helped him write his next bestseller.'

'As long as he credits us,' Nicolas said, watching Dieter write. 'And maybe slips us some of the money he makes to compen— Yes?'

His gaze turned to Tallith, who'd tapped him on the shoulder, and he frowned. The sergeant was pale as he stared fixedly behind the group. With a sigh, Nicolas closed his eyes and turned around.

Oh bugger.

Along the next rise was a long line of shadowed shapes.

Tallith let out a single, frightened whisper, 'Orcs.'

Each orc appeared to be riding some form of giant wolf and was armed to the teeth. And looking directly at them.

'That's a lot of orcs.' Shift's comment was rather redundant, but he assumed it was from fear rather than the belief that the rest of the group couldn't count.

'At least thirty,' Silva informed them.

Nicolas's gaze flicked to their horses at the bottom of the hill. Though they were close by, they suddenly appeared to be miles away, as if the ground had stretched itself to create more distance between them and their mounts. And even if they got to them, where would they go? There was bleak landscape all around them with no obvious places in which to hide.

'We need to go toward the settlement.'

Nicolas's jaw dropped as he turned and stared at Dieter.

'We what?' Shift helpfully asked for him. 'Are you insane?'

'There is no time to explain. I just need you to trust me.' There was a resolution in Dieter's eyes that actually made Nicolas trust him. Whatever plan the writer had, it was better than anything he could come up with right now. And it was definitely better than fighting.

'Okay then,' he said, preparing himself. 'Everybody ready?'

'As we'll ever be,' Shift said.

Keeping his eyes fixed firmly on the line of orcs, Nicolas took a deep breath. 'Go.'

Quickly, Nicolas and his companions slid back down the slope. Apparently, that was exactly what the orcs had been waiting for. Their leader raised his sword, and they charged, mounts howling in glee along with their riders. A storm of dust was thrown up in their wake.

Nicolas slid faster, careful to keep his footing. Falling over now could be fatal. Reaching the bottom of the slope in time with the others, he jumped onto his horse and kicked it into action. As one, the group rode back up the slope, the orcs hot on their heels, having covered an impressive distance in that time.

The group crested the rise and rode down the other side. Within seconds, a angry cry rose from the settlement. A war drum banged, rallying the inhabitants to battle. Within moments, riders poured from the settlement, whooping and hollering as they waved their weapons in the air.

Please be right, Dieter. Please be right, Dieter. Please be right, Dieter.

Nicolas was so surprised when the writer came to a sudden stop that he nearly overshot him. Instead, he pulled his own mount to a stop.

'What are you doing?' he cried.

'Trust me.' Being sandwiched between two groups of orcs meant it was going to take more than the reassuring smile Dieter was giving him to calm him down.

'We cannot stay here,' Silva cried. 'You have led us to ruin, old man.'

'Have I?'

The orcs from the settlement slowed to a stop. Behind them, the second group had made it to the top of the slope and had also come to a halt.

'Don't make a sound,' Dieter whispered.

He didn't plan to. Though the way this was making his stomach churn, he wouldn't be surprised if he let out a fart that echoed across the plains.

Red eyes glared at them from either side.

Hang on. They aren't glaring at us.

Nicolas turned his head a few times to check that he was right. And he was. The two sets of orcs were glaring at each other. Now that he had the time to think, he noticed something different about the orcs on the slope. Their armour was covered in basic paint on which appeared to be a yellow claw of some sort. This was reflected on the banner the orc nearest the leader carried.

They're two different tribes.

Realisation hit him. These orcs hadn't stumbled on them. They were on their way to the settlement. To raid it.

'The only thing orcs like fighting more than humans is other orcs who trespass on their territory,' Auron said, smiling as he shook his head. 'Genius.'

Is it genius? Or has it made our situation worse?

'But we're still in the middle of a standoff,' Nicolas whispered.

'Oi,' the biggest of the orcs from the settlement—most likely the leader—bellowed. 'You gitz is on our turf. Fort you'd know better dan dat.'

The leader of the yellow claws laughed heartily. 'It's only yer turf whilst yer still alive, snotball.'

The settlement orcs didn't care for that insult one bit. 'Looks like we gets to bloody our blades on a weak mob today, ladz,' the leader roared.

Can they even see us? Now I know how Auron feels.

'And wot about deez humies?' the leader of the yellow claws asked.

Oh. They can see us just fine.

'Just some more skullz to display. Be a good warnin' to any other gitz who fink dey can challenge us.' The leader from the settlement raised his jagged, curved blade. 'Right, ladz?'

The *ladz* were in hearty agreement, beating their chests and snarling.

'Wen we dun bashin' yer skullz in,' yellow claw began, 'der won't be enuf to display anywhere.' Then it was his tribe's turn to snarl and beat their chests.

'I'm going to count to three then we go,' Silva whispered.

Go? Go where? I hope she doesn't mean towards the orcs.

'One...two...'

He tightened his grip on the reins, waiting for the inevitable number and hopefully the flight from death it would signify. Panicking wouldn't help right now, so he controlled his breathing, bringing his thumping heart back under control.

'Three.'

'*Ya.*' Spurring his horse to action, he followed the others as they galloped between the parallel lines of orcs. The hooves of his mount thundered as they made their escape. But over that sound came feral roars. Movement in his peripherals suggested the orcs were charging.

Let's hope they're more interested in fighting each other than us.

The two lines of combatants closed in on him, and each other, like the spiked walls Auron had once told him about in one of his adventures. He tried to keep his focus on the end of the lines. Their freedom. He urged his horse on faster and faster, but the gap began to close as weapon-waving orcs prepared to collide.

The two sides clashed just as Nicolas and the others broke into the open. Behind him, he heard feral shouts, the clashing of weapons, the howling of wolves, and cries of pain. Though he had no intention of stopping or slowing for a good long time, he did risk a glance back. Behind them, the battle had become a swirling dust cloud. He caught shadows of figures and blurs of movement. But he wasn't bothered about either.

He was more concerned with the eight orcs pursuing them.

CHAPTER 50

On their tails, the eight orcs charged after them, their mounts' legs working furiously as they bounded in pursuit. The wolves snapped and slobbered in anticipation of the kill. On their backs, their riders did the same.

Nicolas looked back at the oncoming attackers. Briefly, he considered using one of his throwing knives, but his aim could be shaky when he was stood still. His chances of hitting anything riding full pelt were negligible. Then he noticed something.

Their armour...

The eight orcs chasing them were split evenly between the two battling tribes. And it didn't take long for the enemies' bloodlust to cool enough for them to realise. Double taking as he realised who rode next to him, one of the orcs barrelled his wolf into the side of the orc beside him. Cutting with his sword, he caught the rider in the throat, dropping him from the saddle to bounce along the hard ground.

The orc didn't have time to savour his victory, as an axe struck him in the back of the head. Red eyes wide with surprise, he toppled from his wolf, to have his body trampled by its back legs as the remaining orcs attempted to either bash or slash each other from their mounts. Yet they never gave up the pursuit.

The axe thrower, who was of the yellow-claw tribe, died when an orc from the settlement pulled up alongside him. The yellow-claw orc swung his arm, trying to attack with a weapon he'd only just thrown away. He was still staring at his empty hand in shock as he was run through.

By the time they'd finished fighting amongst themselves, there were only three orcs left. But three could still be very deadly. And they were catching up.

Despite riding as hard as he could, Nicolas had somehow ended up at the back of his group, making him the first target for the orcs. Aware that someone was closing in on him, he swung the *Dawn Blade*. Even though he missed, it still discouraged the orc attacker—for a moment. Then he came in again, the wolf snapping at his horse's throat. Thrusting with his sword, he caught the wolf on the side of its face, leaving a long scratch along its snout. But it kept going. He managed to bring his blade up just in time to block a blow from the rider. As their swords locked, Nicolas circled his so it was in the dominant position. With a deft flick, he caught the orc across the throat, killing it.

Though it no longer had any rider, the wolf continued to attack, its blood up and anger too high to care about anything but the kill. It lunged at his horse's legs, but Nicolas managed to dodge it just in time.

I can't keep this up forever.

As the wolf came in again, he put some trust in his own aim. Drawing a knife from his belt, he launched it. At this distance, he couldn't really miss but hitting it directly in the eye was very welcome. With a yelp of pain, the wolf fell away, crashing to the ground in his wake.

'Die, humie.'

Urging his wolf towards Nicolas, the orc swung with his jagged sword. Moving quickly, Nicolas batted away the attack then cut the orc across the mid-section twice, before stabbing the tip of the *Dawn Blade* into the wolf's side. For a moment, he thought his sword was going to be yanked from his grasp but the flesh of the wolf gave, allowing him to keep hold of it.

He readied himself as the third orc bore down on him. Then it was dead. The creature's eyes rolled backwards as it slipped from its saddle, a knife stuck right between its eyes. As the orc hit the ground, its wolf decided that all this chasing had worked up an appetite. After slowing to a stop, it padded back around and began to eat its former rider.

'Thank you,' he shouted to Silva.

The warrior acknowledged him with a nod.

They rode hard for another half an hour, only slowing when they were sure there wasn't even the vaguest sign of pursuit. Coming to a halt within eyesight of a canyon, everyone took the opportunity to have a much-needed drink. Their flight had filled their mouths and eyes with dust. Nicolas took a small swig of his canteen then spat it back out on the ground before taking an actual drink.

'That was a good plan.' Shift looked as exhausted as Nicolas imagined he did.

'Well, I knew a little about the orc's tribal society, so I hoped for the best,' Dieter said, sagging slightly in his saddle.

Hoped?

Still, Nicolas wasn't about to call the writer out. The plan had worked. They were still alive. Though their horses would need a long rest before continuing any further.

'Hopefully, they all killed each other,' Silva remarked as she dismounted and fed her horse. 'Or the survivors are in no fit state to track us.'

'Either will do.' Nicolas sighed. 'I've seen enough orcs for a while.'

'We just need to find the one we're looking for,' Auron said, the sceptical way he looked around suggested what Nicolas already knew. They may have just ridden hard in completely the opposite direction to their wayward companion.

And there's another problem.

Nicolas stared back the way they'd come. Even if they didn't find Garaz, they would have to go back at some point. Which may lead to...

I'll worry about crossing that bridge when I get to it.

Now that the panic and adrenaline had receded, elation kicked in, and it kicked hard. Nicolas suddenly found himself light-headed as he enjoyed the fact that he was still alive.

'You alright?' he asked Tallith, who appeared quite pale.

'Yes.' The sergeant nodded after a moment. 'It's just...this is quite a lot to go through in a short space of time... How do you do it?'

Nicolas opened his mouth then closed it again. 'I really can't answer that, because I don't know. I'm sorry if that's disappointing, but I just keep doing things that need doing. Then other stuff...needs doing, I suppose.'

How do *I do it?*

'I'm certainly learning a lot.' Sadness took hold of Tallith. 'Like I may not be cut out for adventuring.'

'You've done fine so far,' Nicolas said quickly. 'You faced wolves, bandits, half-dragon men, orcs...that's a lot in one adventure, even by our standards. And you're still alive. Don't sell yourself short.'

'I... Thank you.' The sergeant smiled wearily. 'Coming from you, that means a lot.'

'I don't think this is for everyone.' *Myself especially.* 'But you'll be better for the experience when you return to Babylon.'

This seemed to hearten Tallith. 'It really isn't. I won't lie, there've been more than a few times when I wondered what in the Underworld possessed me to come with you. Hero stuff sounds great in a story, but the reality is a bit harsher. And yes, not for me. I suppose that's why you were chosen.'

Hmm.

'The tales you heard about me,' Nicolas began, 'what did they say about how I was chosen?'

'I heard you were making a delivery to the Oracle's cottage and suddenly he was possessed by a beam of pure light,' Tallith said, clearly struck by the imagery he was conjuring up. 'He became the voice of the Deities themselves, proclaiming you Etherius's new saviour.'

'Strange, I heard a different account,' Dieter remarked with pursed lips. 'I heard the Oracle found the *Dawn Blade* near Auron's body. You happened by, and the sword lit up in your presence, choosing you to be its new bearer.'

'I see,' Nicolas said dryly.

He was about to open his mouth and correct them, in detail, but he stopped himself. Both were so enthralled by his legend...which was apparently giving people hope. Nicolas remembered how disappointed he'd been when he'd seen the Tower of the Oracle. And he hadn't given a shit about going there. Shattering their illusions with the stupid reality of the choosing stick just felt wrong. Though it was interesting to note that not everyone had every detail of his life. People seemed to know specific events, but not what connected them. Namely, the Maestro.

'It wasn't quite like that,' he said finally. 'But near enough.'

Sudden awkwardness gripped him. It took Nicolas a moment to realise it was because Shift, Silva, and Auron were all staring at him with pride.

Looking at his companions, he gave a shrug...then something caught his eye.

'Hey,' he said, pointing past Auron and Silva. 'Hey.'

The others turned and saw what he was seeing. Near the entrance of the canyon was a red blob. A very familiar red blob.

'Found you,' Silva said, drawing her sword.

CHAPTER 51

Leaving their tired horses with Tallith and Dieter, the group jogged across the plain to the canyon entrance, closing the gap between themselves and Garaz quickly and quietly. The orc was making himself easy to catch. His path was erratic, as if he were drunk. The closer they got, the more Nicolas's chest tightened. He didn't want to fight Garaz again. He just hoped he had a choice in the matter.

Nicolas and Shift exchanged a glance as they closed in on their former companion. The orc was shambling, and Nicolas could've sworn he was muttering to himself. Briefly, he checked that the *Dawn Blade* would come out of its sheath smoothly if he needed it to.

It hurt him that he was approaching his former friend with his hand on the hilt of his blade. Garaz continued onward, blissfully unaware of the people behind him. Nicolas and the others spread out, and about twenty metres from Garaz, came to a halt. He shared looks of grim determination with the others. Tension wrapped around him like a constricting blanket. He didn't know what to expect. And he hated it. This was family.

Was.

His hand tightened on the hilt of the *Dawn Blade*.

How did it come to this?

'*Garaz.*' His voice echoed down the canyon, making Nicolas wince slightly. He'd only wanted to get Garaz's attention, not the attention of every orc within a mile.

Instantly, the red-cloaked figure stopped. Garaz just stood there, leaning on his staff.

'We need to talk,' Nicolas said.

Silence.

'You attacked me.'

Silence.

'You attacked me, stole the amulet, and stuffed me in a cupboard. You also shot me across a field with a fireball. And you *will* answer for it,' he shouted. 'Now, drop your staff, hand over the amulet, and yield. Then you can explain yourself.'

The harsh chuckle made the hairs on the back of Nicolas's neck tingle. Before them, the orc rose to his full, imposing height, his hood falling away. What was normally neatly tied back orange hair hung in matted clumps. Slowly, Garaz craned his neck around to look at them with blood-red eyes.

'Humies.' The orc's voice was a low growl.

'That...is Garaz, right?' Shift asked, clearly uncertain. 'It looks like him. But he doesn't talk like that.'

'Everything about him is off,' Auron said with narrowed eyes. 'His posture. His voice. It's all wrong.'

'Maybe he's possessed?' Nicolas ventured.

'Fleshy lil humies.' Garaz sneered at them. 'Comes to play wif old Garaz?'

'You all know exactly what he sounds like,' Silva said, taking a fighting stance. 'He sounds like an orc.'

He hated the fact that the warrior was right. 'Garaz, stand down,' he said, the authority in his voice waning slightly. 'Do not make us do this.'

'Oh,' the orc scoffed. 'Filthy humies tellin' me wot to do, is it? I fink yous gots a def wish.' A vicious smile crossed Garaz's lips, exposing his sharp teeth. 'I's happy to grant it.'

'Garaz, we just want to talk. This doesn't have to get violent,' Shift said, holding their hands away from the knives in their belt.

The orc scratched his chin theatrically. 'I finks it does,' he said after a moment, before raising his staff. 'Burns da humies.' With a swift movement, he swung his staff.

'Hey,' Auron shouted as the fireball exploded where he stood. The spirit glowed amongst the flames just before they dissipated, leaving a charred crater on the ground.

'Wos dis?' the orc shouted. 'Sorcery? I gots just da fing for dat.'

With a feral roar, the orc charged, brandishing his staff like a club and swinging it wildly. Despite the outward appearance, this was nothing like the orc Nicolas knew.

'Something's wrong with him,' Nicolas shouted as he drew his sword. 'This isn't right.'

Garaz swung the staff through Auron. It took several more swings before the orc realised nothing was going to come of it.

'It must be that demonic curse,' Nicolas said, as the others circled Garaz. 'Subdue him, and then we can work out how to help him.'

'If we can,' Silva shouted back. 'But I am not prepared to gamble your lives. If he gives us no choice, he dies.'

'I ain'ts the one doin' the dyin' here.'

As the warrior stepped towards the orc, Nicolas found himself breaking into a run. If he could get to Garaz first and just reason with him...

'Listen to me,' he said, ducking the swinging staff. 'It's me, Nicolas. You remember me. Whatever's happening, fight it. You did it before. I saw you.'

He stepped aside, and the staff missed him by inches, slamming into the ground where'd he'd been standing. Using the opening, he punched Garaz squarely on the jaw.

Uh oh.

With a furious shout, the orc backhanded him, sending him spinning through the air, until the ground sped towards him. With a crash, he landed in the dirt, disorientated. Controlling his ragged breathing, he spat blood onto the floor.

This isn't going as well as last time.

Whatever was possessing Garaz was making him feral. Giving him the fury to shrug off a punch that had worked well only recently.

A shadow fell over him. Looking up, he saw the orc towering above him, staff raised high, ready to hurtle down and crush his skull. Silva put a damper on that, barging into Garaz from the side and staggering him. Apparently, she wasn't as open to killing him as she'd first let on, as a sword to the side would've finished this easily.

Grabbing Silva's hand, he let the warrior haul him to his feet.

'Thank you.'

'Something *is* wrong with him,' Silva admitted. 'Despite what he's done...well, you gave me another chance.'

On the floor, Garaz was on all fours, breathing heavily.

'Do you yield?' Nicolas asked. 'Come on, Garaz. We're your family. Please don't make us do this.' He held his palm up in a gesture of peace. It was slightly undercut by the sword in his other hand, but he wasn't stupid.

The reply from beneath the hanging orange hair was slow and savage. 'Burn. The. Humies.'

From a kneeling position Garaz roared as he flung several fireballs, scattering the group. Even as the orc got to his feet, he was getting ready to cast more.

'Okay then,' Nicolas shouted after a sigh. 'Let's wear him out. Keep him distracted and firing in all directions until we exhaust him.'

'All we have to do is evade numerous fireballs.' For some reason, Silva didn't seem keen on the idea.

Rolling aside, Nicolas dodged an explosion nearby. The flakes of earth sprinkling over him told him it had been too close for comfort.

There was a flash of movement on his left. A cheetah sprinted past him, charging Garaz, who readied his staff to bat it away. At the last second, the cheetah changed direction, raking the orc's leg with its claws. Garaz howled in pain then launched fireball after fireball as he attempted to hit the cheetah.

But the animal was too fast. The ground behind it was torn up by numerous explosions. Garaz snarled with frustration as he kept missing.

'Hey, over here,' Nicolas shouted, diving behind a rock just as Garaz aimed his staff and fired.

'Here, here,' Silva called, waving her hands before throwing herself aside to dodge Garaz's barrage.

The group continued in this fashion, each drawing his fire until eventually the fireballs were less and less impressive, their heat less fierce. Then they stopped completely. Garaz stood shakily, panting hard, looking as if he might collapse at any moment.

'Now,' Nicolas cried as he and Silva rushed the orc.

But Garaz wasn't done. With a swing of his club, he caught Silva, knocking her aside, before he threw the weapon at Nicolas. Surprisingly, Nicolas batted the flying staff away. But it was just a distraction. The orc crashed into him like an avalanche, picking him up from the ground then slamming him back into it.

Pinning him to the floor, Garaz raised his huge fist, preparing to pummel Nicolas, but a stone hit him directly between the eyes. Seeing his chance, he threw several punches at the orc, who shook them all off before delivering one of his own. It was like a rock hitting him in the face. Garaz had been pulling his punches in their last fight.

For a moment Nicolas wasn't even sure what his name was, but he soon regained his wherewithal when the orc hauled him into the air, a single large green hand constricting his throat. Struggling to breathe, Nicolas threw more desperate punches at the orc's face, but it was for naught. Nicolas let out a choked cry as he fought against the grip, striking Garaz's thickly muscled arm. It was like trying to chop down a tree with a butter knife.

'Garaz...please...stop...' he said between strained breaths.

Already, spots floated in front of his eyes. No waking up in a cupboard this time.

If only there was some way to get through to him...but the person looking back at him wasn't Garaz. There was nothing in those eyes of the orc he knew. Feebly, he lashed out with a couple of kicks, to no effect.

Garaz roared as cheetah Shift landed on his back, biting his neck and raking his shoulder with their claws.

Nicolas dropped to the ground. His burning lungs fought for breath.

Swaying drunkenly on the spot, Nicolas tried to shake off the dizziness as he watched several Garazs and Shifts dance in front of him, brightly coloured spots pulsating in the air around them. The orc cursed and thrashed as he grabbed for the cheetah on his back, while Shift hung on stubbornly. Finally, Garaz's hand found something to take hold of. Snarling, he threw Shift off of his back just as Nicolas's vision cleared. Now he could only see the one orc. With a cry, he pushed off from the ground, large rock in hand and swinging upwards. With a mighty crack, he struck Garaz under the jaw. The orc took a single step back and Nicolas hit him again.

Dazed, blood running from his lips, the orc fell to his knees. Nicolas stood over him, rock at the ready. As he watched, the redness in Garaz's eyes waned then vanished, leaving behind the yellow eyes he knew so well.

'N...Nicolas?'

Nicolas smacked him with the rock again. Just to be on the safe side.

CHAPTER 52

A slight groan signalled that Garaz was coming round. Slowly, the cloaked figure stirred, his head rising slowly from where it'd been hung for a good hour. Considering his nose was still sore from the orc's punch—luckily, it hadn't been broken—it was hard for Nicolas to feel sympathetic as Garaz squinted then winced in pain...yet he still managed it.

'Sore head?' he asked. 'Sorry about that. But you weren't listening to reason. You had a harder job ignoring a rock to the head.'

Garaz blinked several times, staring first at Nicolas then at the camp-fire. It was only when he tried to bring his hands up to his face that he realised he was bound. Silva, Auron, and Shift had all checked the bindings. The orc was going nowhere.

'Oh no,' he whispered, deep shadows cast on his face by the fire. 'What did I do?'

'How far back would you like to go?' Nicolas couldn't keep the pettiness out of his tone. 'Do you remember stuffing me in a cupboard? You seemed quite lucid then. Just like when you fired me across a field. Did things become a little hazy after that? How about trying to choke me to death, does that ring a bell?'

'I am so sorry.' Garaz kept his head low, avoiding his gaze. 'I...did not want any of this.'

'Lobbing fireballs at us is a funny way of showing reluctance,' Shift scoffed from beside Nicolas.

When the yellow eyes did look at him, the regret in them made Nicolas want to forgive Garaz and untie him. But despite doing some daft things in his time, he wasn't *that* stupid.

Silva was less inclined to forgiveness. 'Give me one reason why we shouldn't kill you for betraying us?' she hissed, absentmindedly rubbing her jaw, which sported an angry bruise from its introduction to Garaz's staff.

'We said we'd give him a chance to explain,' Auron said levelly.

'Who is not doing that?' Silva snorted. 'I *said* give me one reason.'

'And it better be a damned good one,' Shift added venomously.

Dieter and Tallith had had the good sense to sit a little way off and leave the group to it. This was, after all, family business.

'The problem we have,' Auron said as he sort of leant against a rock, 'is that I suspect there's a reasonable, yet completely misguided, explanation for what you did. The kid can't quite make up his mind but wants to believe in you. Shift now distrusts you completely, and Silva wants to boot your disembodied head off the top of one of these hills.'

'That sums it up pretty nicely actually.' Nicolas nodded.

'It certainly does,' Silva said through bared teeth.

Garaz took a deep breath. 'I am so sorry to put you all through this, my—'

'Don't,' Shift warned, pointing at the orc. 'Don't say that word. You don't get to say it.'

'Until we decide you can again.' Shift looked less than impressed by Nicolas's addition, but the retort he expected never came.

Garaz opened his mouth to speak then stopped. He'd finally noticed the amulet around his neck. 'What is this doing here?'

Nicolas shrugged. 'Something's wrong with you, you have a healing amulet on you, so we thought we'd put it on you and see if it helped. At the moment, you aren't trying to burn us alive, so I think it's working.'

Frowning, Garaz took a moment to think. 'Nor am I inclined to try, so it is working.'

'It's lovely that it took you a moment to work out that you don't want to roast us alive,' Shift remarked dryly. 'Truly, I'm touched.'

'Now provide us with an explanation for your actions,' Silva demanded.

Garaz became silent. The orc's eyes darted from side to side, as if he was fighting some internal battle between wanting to tell them and whatever was keeping him from doing so.

'After all we've been through, you owe us that much,' Nicolas said. 'We've risked our lives for each other. I thought we were family. I've heard you say it yourself before now. So, you can't turn your back on us without some bloody good reason. What is it?'

'I...I cannot say,' the orc replied.

'Well, that's not acceptable.' Auron shook his head. 'So this one time, I was travelling with this group. We were off on an adventure together, but this one boy was a bit scared. He'd seen some stuff that frayed his nerves but decided not to tell anyone for...reasons. To him, they were good reasons. Anyway, we got into a bit of danger, and at a pivotal moment, he fell to his knees, weeping. We were captured and nearly killed.'

Hey.

'That's me you're talking about,' Nicolas snapped. 'In the Big Boss's arena. I did not fall to my knees weeping. I...passed out.'

'Fainted,' Shift corrected. 'And Auron's right, Garaz, you've nearly gotten us killed several times.'

'I did not expect you to come after me. I did not want that.'

'Oh, piss off,' Shift cried. 'You're the smart one of the group. Did you really think we wouldn't follow you? Do you know how many fights we've been in hunting down your stupid green ass? Nick got turned into a dog.'

'He did mention it,' the orc said, avoiding all their gazes.

'Perhaps you do not understand us *humies* at all.' Silva's barb was vicious but justified.

Garaz closed his eyes for a long time. Long enough that Nicolas began to wonder if he'd fallen asleep.

'You are right,' he said finally. 'I have made a huge mistake. I want to tell you why, but...it is better if I show you. Can I take you to where I was going?'

Both Shift and Silva let out a single, harsh laugh.

'If you think we are letting you lead us anywhere, you are gravely mistaken,' Silva said, shaking her head. 'The audacity to even suggest it—'

'I can explain, and I want to,' Garaz pleaded. 'But to really understand, you need to see with your own eyes. Without it, I fear my words will mean little to you. Please.'

Pushing himself up from the floor, Nicolas walked over and crouched in front of Garaz. Wordlessly, he stared into the orc's yellow eyes. This was the Garaz he knew, not the beast they'd fought earlier. It was the orc he knew and loved. But that had also been the orc who'd stuffed him in a cupboard.

So, what do I know?

'What do you think, kid?' Auron asked. 'Do you trust him?'

His mind was filled with conflicting voices. One screamed that Garaz was a traitor, that his good faith had been used up, and he was never to be trusted again. The other preached forgiveness. Told him that the orc was truly sorry. Both yelled equally loudly, but there was only one he listened to.

'Show us,' he said.

'Thank you.' Tears filled his yellow eyes.

'What?' Again, Silva and Shift were in perfect synch.

'How hard did he hit you?' Shift asked. 'Because there appears to be a concussion, at the very least.'

Nicolas thought back to how many times his mind had played tricks on him or directed him down the wrong path. Closing his eyes, he focused on his breathing, calming his thoughts and letting them drift away like leaves in a river. Just as Garaz had taught him, ironically enough. His answer was the same.

'You stay bound at all times,' he said firmly. 'You don't get your staff back. If you try anything, magic or otherwise, I won't hesitate to let Silva loose on you. If we get to where we're going and it's a trap, you die first.'

'That is fair.' The orc nodded.

'Too bloody right it is,' he said. 'And the amulet stays on. I can't believe you carried it around and didn't think to put it on.'

Garaz frowned at the amulet. 'The...what happened to me was already affecting my ability to think logically. All I could focus on was getting home.' The orc gave a sad smile. 'It is truly a dark day when I need you to teach me about magic.'

Nicolas rose, face set in a scowl. 'You don't get to try any levity with me. That is still back in the cupboard you stuffed me in. Now, unless you find the words to explain your actions, I don't want to hear from you again until morning. Understand?'

Garaz nodded again. Then he looked away, hopefully wallowing in shame.

Turning, he faced Silva and Shift. 'Are we going to have a problem with this?'

'I have some very strong opinions about it,' the shapeshifter answered. 'But I want to know why he betrayed us. And, on occasion, I trust your judgement.'

'Silva?'

'Where you go, I follow.' It wasn't exactly an answer, but he got the impression that was the best he was getting.

In his peripheral vision, Auron gave him an impressed nod.

Whatever this is better be bloody good.

CHAPTER 53

The sun had just risen, so the canyon they walked through was filled with shadowed crags. There was a chill in the air, but it was practically balmy compared to what they'd endured thus far.

Not even winter wants to touch this place.

Garaz shuffled ahead of them, hands still bound. Despite the necessity, guilt wracked him at seeing the orc on a leash like a dog. It was a sensible precaution, though, so he hadn't argued with Silva when she insisted on it. Nicolas kept half an eye on the orc and half an eye on the surroundings. The group's fear and tension were palpable. Save for Dieter, who was having a jolly old time collecting rock samples.

'This is the perfect place for an ambush.'

Inwardly, Nicolas sighed. This was the fourth time Silva had said that in an hour. She was starting to belabour the point now. And it wasn't like the threat wasn't blatantly obvious to everyone else.

'Does she have to keep saying that?' Tallith whispered in his ear. His voice was hoarse with fear.

'Apparently so.'

'We...we're going to be okay, though, right?'

Part of him wanted to lie, but he needed the sergeant prepared. 'I can't say for sure. I hope so. But be ready, just in case.'

'Please,' Garaz said, turning his head halfway back to face them. 'I have already told you. Generally, orcs do not come this way.'

'And that's because?' Shift asked.

'You will see soon enough,' came the sad reply.

'That's interesting.' Tallith's comment intrigued Nicolas, so he motioned for the sergeant to continue. 'He says *orcs* and not *my people*. It's almost as if he doesn't see himself in the same light as the others we met.'

Met? *That's a polite way of putting it.*

A tingle in his neck told him Shift was looking at him. Staring was a better word, their brow furrowed and mouth downturned in disapproval.

Though they weren't saying a word, the message was clear. *'Are we really doing this?'* Wanting to avoid an argument he simply looked in another direction...to find Silva doing exactly the same thing.

For Deities' sake.

He needed Auron for support, but the spirit was ahead of the group, scouting the direction Garaz had indicated for potential threats.

...at least he was...

Nicolas and the others came to a halt, drawing their weapons as the bouncing blob of light that was Auron galloped back towards them.

'How many are there?' he asked as the spirit reached them.

Auron frowned at him. 'Deities, kid, you're edgy.'

'You were supposed to come back if you saw danger.'

'I'm back because there's something interesting ahead.'

'Not danger?'

'No.'

'For Deities' sake.' Nicolas gasped. 'Don't scare me like that.'

'Settle down, kid.' The spirit smirked, shaking his head. 'If there was danger, I'd have ridden back screaming about it. I wouldn't have waited until I reached you to go, *'Excuse me, noble party. There appears to be a rather large force of uncouth orcs making their way to this position. I suggest we do not dally here and leave forthwith,'*

Nicolas pursed his lips in annoyance. 'So, what did you see then?'

'Something interesting.' Auron smiled, before turning to Garaz. 'I'm guessing it's where we're going. Right?'

'It is,' the orc confirmed.

'And that is?' Nicolas asked leadingly.

'Just follow me,' Auron said, nodding in the direction he'd come. 'You'll see.'

'Fantastic,' Shift exclaimed from their saddle. 'Everyone is being lovely and vague in orc country.'

Instead of sitting around arguing, the group carried on and soon left the canyon. Beyond it was a long plain. But unlike the rest of the orc territory, this one wasn't featureless. Ahead of them was a vast city. It had to be their destination.

'What is that place?' he asked.

'Golthorak.' The orc's voice was a sad whisper. 'My home.'

'Okay,' Shift cried aloud. 'That's enough. I kept my mouth shut through the canyon. But I am *not* going into that city. It's clearly a trap.'

'I'm inclined to agree,' Silva added instantly.

'But we must,' Dieter said. 'Who knows—'

Silva silenced him with a single raised finger.

'I can't lie,' Nicolas said, eyeing the city, 'I'm not too sure I fancy it myself.'

As much as he wanted to believe that Garaz wouldn't lead them into a trap, he wasn't always the greatest judge of character. Take Billy Bob-knobs, for example. He'd seemed decent enough, but turned out to be a nasty faun. Or the fact their formerly stalwart companion was now bound before them.

'Please,' Garaz said.

'*Please* enter the city so an orc war party can set upon us?' Shift suggested.

'They will not—'

With a growl, Silva yanked on Garaz's leash, pulling him to the floor. 'So, there *are* orcs in the city,' she snarled. 'Deceiver.'

'It's a trap then?' Auron asked.

Garaz let out a choked cry, his eyes pained. 'No...it is not like that...you must see. Please.'

'We're just supposed take your word for it that we aren't going to get hacked apart the minute we set foot in the city?' Silva clearly wasn't prepared to believe Garaz if he said no.

'No.' The orc was vehement, at least. 'There is no danger there for you. I swear it.'

Shift nodded sarcastically. 'Of course. Because you're so trustworthy now.'

This is getting us nowhere.

Staring at Garaz, he tried to discern some hint of betrayal. There was nothing obvious. He remembered the events of Babylon. And he remembered everything that had come before it. For them to go through so much together only for the orc to turn on them...there *had* to be a good reason for it.

'Look, I mean to go down there. None of the rest of you have to come, that's fine. But I'm going.' Nicolas held out his hand. 'Silva, give me the leash.' Silva and Shift were watching him with dumbfounded expressions. 'What?'

'Are you insane?' Silva asked bluntly. 'This—'

Nicolas held up a hand. 'Look. We've faced numerous dangers chasing this asshole down. I want to know why he betrayed us. All of it. The answer's in that city. So, I'm going in. The rest of you can wait here, and I'll call you when I'm sure it's safe.'

A piece of bread hit him in the side of the head. 'You're an idiot if you think we're staying here,' Shift told him. 'We can't even trust you to go for a piss by yourself.'

'And now you know firsthand what that's like,' he retorted quickly. The shapeshifter opened their mouth to deny his claim, then realised that they couldn't.

'We are going with you,' Silva said firmly.

Thank the Deities. I really didn't fancy going in there alone.

'That saddle must be getting mighty uncomfortable.' Auron's comment caused Nicolas to frown at the spirit. 'Because of those big hero balls you're growing,' Auron elaborated.

Lovely.

Dismounting, he walked over to Garaz. As set as he was on his decision, there was always a little uncertainty. Offering his hand, he helped the orc to his feet then pulled him close.

'We have fought together, laughed together, shed blood together,' he began. 'I can't believe you healed me all those times just to have me killed elsewhere. I really shouldn't trust you, but I can't help myself. So, I'm going to look you in the eye and ask you plainly...are we in danger in that city?'

Garaz's yellow eyes held his gaze. 'No,' he answered firmly.

Taking a deep breath, he remounted his horse. 'Let's go and visit the orcs then.'

CHAPTER 54

It took several hours to reach Golthorak. And with each one that passed, the realisation grew that the city was a ruin. The towers that rose above the city wall were either crumbled or looked as if they were on their last legs and might go at any moment. Even the city wall was ragged and holed, covered in old vines that had been allowed to grow unchallenged.

At least we won't have any trouble getting through the gates.

Because only one was left standing. The other lay on the plain, like a giant metal welcoming mat. Nicolas was sure he didn't need to point out that the gate appeared to have been knocked down from the inside. His companions were all seasoned enough to notice for themselves. Beyond the opening, the city was a wreck. The street he could see was covered in old rubble and overturned carts.

Even though there was a lot to look at, Nicolas found Garaz of the greatest interest. The orc's head seemed to hang lower the closer they got to the city. It was as if he physically couldn't bring himself to look at it.

'In you go then,' Shift said, nodding forwards. 'This was your daft idea, so you can go first.'

'I'll go first,' Dieter said, craning his neck as he shaded his eyes from the sun, lest it cause him to miss a detail. 'I haven't seen architecture of this style before. This is a true find.'

'Let's see if you're as excited once the orcs inside set upon us,' Silva said bitterly.

Nicolas didn't say anything. Instead, he drew his sword and spurred his horse onward, Garaz in tow. The clops of his mount's hooves on the metal gate seemed to echo everywhere.

Well, anyone who's here already knows we're coming. We rode across an open plain to get here.

Crossing the archway into the city, Nicolas shuddered. The aura of the place struck him fiercely. It was one of horror, mixed with sadness.

Tracking his gaze across the ruined buildings, it was almost as if he could hear the screams of the former residents. No building was in one piece as he tentatively advanced. The only thing he didn't see were the bones of the dead.

'Something terrible happened here, didn't it?'

'Truly,' Garaz whispered.

After a few moments, he saw no signs of an ambush, so he called the others in. As they crossed the threshold into the city he could see their reaction to the odd aura. His companions were visibly disconcerted by whatever hung over this place. The only one to quickly shake it off was Dieter, whose eyes darted everywhere, as if he were tracking a fly.

'Fascinating,' the writer said. 'A very practical architecture, where it is still standing. It appeared whoever lived here was a fan of columns.'

That was true enough. They were everywhere. In fact, the way ahead was lined with them, creating a path to an old plinth with a pile of broken rocks atop it that might've once been a statue.

Lingering here was making him uneasy. 'Which way?'

Raising his bound hands, Garaz pointed ahead.

Continuing, the only sound from the group was the furious scratching of Dieter's pencil on parchment as he noted down everything. Once, he asked to stop and take a rubbing of some writing on a wall. Silva's answer was quite unpleasant.

Following their guide, the group moved towards the centre of the city. Though the buildings were wrecks, Nicolas could picture how fine they'd once been, made of white stone with orange tiled roofs. Everything he saw spoke of a past civilisation.

'Here.'

Coming to a halt at Garaz's request, the group found themselves facing an old temple, whose side wall was missing, as was much of the roof. Even the stairs leading to it were cracked and holed. Beyond the open doors was a dark void, containing who knew what.

Raising his hands, Garaz approached Nicolas. 'I will need you to unbind me. They must see that you are no threat.'

'They?' he enquired quietly. Speaking any louder seemed disrespectful to those who'd dwelt here.

'You shall see.'

Well, we've followed him this far.

Silva made an outraged guffaw as Nicolas cut the orc's bindings. But whatever words came with it she thankfully kept to herself. Shift tutted loudly, just in case he was unsure about their displeasure.

Garaz rubbed his wrists as the rope fell away then undid the knot at the rope around his neck. Going to move, the orc stopped and turned back to him. 'Thank you,' he said. 'I truly appreciate this.'

Nicolas didn't answer. He wasn't sure if he was interested in Garaz's thanks. Clearly, that hurt the orc, but he said nothing. Instead, he turned away and approached the temple, arms outstretched.

'It is I, Garaz Galgrath,' he announced in a booming voice. 'I have returned home.'

Home? Here?

'This is getting more interesting by the second,' Auron remarked.

'These people with me are my friends,' the orc declared, gesturing to Nicolas and the others. 'They have come in peace. They have come to learn.'

For the longest time, there was only silence. But Nicolas knew there were people in the shadows beyond the door. He could feel their eyes appraising him. Slowly, he sheathed his sword. Looking at Silva, he nodded that she should do the same. When the warrior hesitated, he glared at the sword then her sheath. Jaw set indignantly, Silva finally sheathed her blade. Turning, he was happy to see that Shift and Tallith had already put their weapons away.

Deities, I hope I'm right about this. And if not, at least let me get struck down quickly, or I'll never hear the bloody end of it.

'If they are your friends, why did they bring you here bound like a dog?'

The voice raised a good question.

Garaz glanced back before he spoke. 'Because I betrayed them. I...thought they would not understand my quest. But they are good and true. They are...my family.'

Nicolas shot Shift a glare as they snorted.

Pairs of yellow eyes appeared in the darkness. Wanting to make it clear that they were no threat, Nicolas held his hand out to the side. Slowly, the eyes became figures, advancing cautiously into the light. A small party of orcs emerged onto the temple steps, brandishing spears. They didn't look like...well, orcs. Their bodies were wrapped in white robes, and their faces spoke of dignity and wisdom.

Just like Garaz.

There was also fear behind their eyes.

From the group, a single orc walked down the steps. Lines creased his green skin, which was closer to grey, and a long white beard hung from his chin.

'Garaz?' the orc said with a welcoming smile. 'It is you.'

'It is I.' Their former companion bowed.

'Is your quest complete?'

'I...I do not know.

The old orc frowned. 'You must have some idea or why return? And why risk bringing these people here?'

'I think I may have found an answer,' Garaz said. 'And I trust these people with my life.'

That's nice, because right now the feeling isn't mutual.

Stepping away from Garaz, he bowed low. 'I am Salrag, leader of our collective.'

Collective?

Dismounting, Nicolas approached the orc, bowed then offered his hand. 'Nicolas Percival Carnegie.'

As Salrag gripped his hand, the orc pulled him close.

Nicolas managed to keep calm as the orc put a hand on the side of his head and appraised him, his wizened eyes narrowed in concentration.

'You have a kind spirit,' the old orc said finally. 'I can feel it. But you have been through much. And not just to get here.' Salrag smiled at him. 'I can also feel your love for Garaz, even though you are upset with him.'

'You sensed all that from touching the side of my head?' he asked with a chuckle.

'It is a gift.' Salrag finally broke his grip. 'You are all welcome here,' he declared.

'These are my companions, Silva, Shift, Dieter, and Tallith,' Nicolas said, gesturing to each in turn.

'Don't bother introducing me then, kid,' Auron said tartly.

He hadn't really wanted to introduce Auron, just in case this new acquaintance thought him insane.

Still, what of this is sane?

'And we have a ghost with us, Auron of Tellmark.'

If he doesn't like being called a ghost, tough. Teach him for putting me in an awkward situation.

The spirit sucked his teeth in annoyance.

'Hmm.' Salrag stroked his beard thoughtfully. 'That name is known to our people.'

'Of course it is.' Auron grinned with no hint of modesty.

'In fact, he is so lamented by orc culture that his name has become a curse word for my people.'

Ha.

'So, for example, *'You just knocked over my wife, you absolute Auron?'*
Nice to see Shift perking up a bit.

'That is about the sum of it, yes.' Salrag nodded. 'It is akin to telling someone to go and fornicate with themselves.'

Nicolas dared a glance back at Auron; the spirit was seething.

But as much fun as this is… 'So, Garaz, are you going to tell us what's going on now?'

'Soon,' the orc promised. 'There is one more thing you should see first.'

'Of course,' Salrag said, gesturing towards the temple. 'This way, with haste, please. We are not used to being above ground for so long.'

Above ground? But underground's where the bad guys tend to live.

'Snarg and Gran will tend to your horses.'

As the group dismounted, a pair of orcs took the reins for their mounts. Auron's horse, Mare, simply vanished, ready to be summoned back when her master called.

Following Salrag, the group ascended the steps to the temple.

CHAPTER 55

Nicolas and the others were directed to a side room. At a guess, it used to be a shrine. Now it was just another nondescript pile of rocks. Salrag approached the pile and waved his hand across it. With a shimmer, the rocks vanished, revealing a stairway leading down.

Neat precaution.

'Follow me, please,' the orc said, leading the way down the stairs.

Whereas Garaz had been sad as they travelled through the city, he smiled as he saw the entrance. In fact, warmth radiated from him.

He is home.

Nicolas took a few steps down but hesitated when the rocks reappeared, blocking their exit. It didn't darken the place, though, as numerous torches ensured the way stayed well-lit. And it was wide and well-maintained, so there was no chance of slipping and going down the long staircase the fast way.

At the end of the stairway, which went deep into the earth, was a pair of formidable stone doors. They were all function, no form, designed only to block the way ahead. Evidently, the orcs took their security seriously. Normally, Nicolas would be wondering about what numerous horrors could be waiting beyond them, but he felt safe here. He couldn't put his finger on why, he just did.

'Welcome to Golthorak,' Garaz said as the doors opened.

Bright light penetrated the cracks in the door, growing more intense the wider it opened. Nicolas shielded his eyes as they opened completely. When he'd adjusted to the light, his jaw dropped.

Beyond the doors was a vast underground city. Stunned, he slowly walked onto the elevated walkway and gazed around him in awe. Several massive adjoining caverns were filled with farms and buildings of all sizes, made from sandstone in the same style as the ruined buildings above. There was so much to look at that his eyes could barely take it all in. He caught sight of lavish gardens, and large statues of dignified orcs in robes. Above it, a giant orb glowed brightly, bathing everything in warm light. He could see hundreds of orcs, all in various styles of robes or togas. The visible cavern walls gave it a slight feeling of being enclosed, but it was far superior to the ramshackle settlements of their brethren on the surface. Nicolas would've expected this place to smell of dirt and earth, but all his nose caught was the scent of fresh flowers. It was so serene here. Divine, almost.

'You are the first outsiders ever to set foot here,' Salrag said, looking at his home with pride. 'This is the city of the true orc.'

'True orc?' Dieter asked, pencil in hand.

Garaz turned to the others. 'Now you have seen for yourselves, I can explain.' Before he did so, he looked to Salrag for approval. The older orc nodded. 'What do you know of the history of my people?'

Nicolas winced internally in preparation for Dieter's long historical monologue.

'Beyond the Great Horde and the bloody history of your people since, nothing.' The simplicity of the answer surprised him. 'All records before then were lost.'

'When you are known for looting and pillaging, no one cares what you were before that.' Garaz closed his eyes. His lips were trembling slightly. It was so strange seeing someone so proud and powerful so vulnerable. 'What I am about to tell you has, to my knowledge, never been spoken about to non-orc ears. It is something we do not share.'

'If you're going to start a story, you need to preface it with, *'So this one time...'* Was Auron being glib to make Garaz feel more comfortable?

It worked. The orc allowed himself a smile before continuing. 'Long before the Great Horde, this is what we were.' With an open-armed gesture, he took in the city. 'A peace-loving people. A race of philosophers, healers, and poets. Many often mused on the irony of our gentle nature when we had such physically imposing forms. Golthorak was one of many cities dotted across our land, known as Oriseth. But Golthorak was the capital. The pinnacle of our people.'

'What happened?' Nicolas knew something terrible was coming. He wasn't sure he wanted to know, but he had to.

'Our history tells of a great storm that engulfed our lands. It came from nowhere. For a day and a night, it thundered, blocking the sun with swirling black clouds. Red rain fell upon the earth. And then it vanished as quickly as it had begun.' Garaz's fists balled in anger. 'And then the Regression began. That is our name for the disease that has haunted my people for generations. All around us, the land died, becoming infertile and harsh. As it did, our very minds were corrupted. The vast majority of our population became violent, the aggressive parts of their brain stimulated to insane proportions as their intellect and self-restraint diminished to nothing. Chaos engulfed our cities as our people tore down everything that reminded them of their past selves. Or maybe they were just giving into their destructive tendencies. Our cities scoured, my people sought to sate their urges elsewhere, moving south as one and setting upon the lands of the elves in an orgy of destruction.'

'The Great Horde,' Dieter whispered, so captivated by the tale he wasn't even taking notes.

'Indeed,' Garaz confirmed. 'Our lands emptied as the horde charged forth, leaving only a few who remembered who they were. Those who did gathered here, determined to try to survive, to rebuild. Which we did. But even generations later, the disease dogs us.' The orc turned away, rubbing his eyes.

'Those born on the plains suffer it from birth,' Salrag said, putting a hand on Garaz's shoulder. 'But even here we are not immune. Some may never suffer it, but many do. We can never predict who it will strike. But when it does, we must cast them out for the good of the community.'

'Deities,' Nicolas gasped. 'That's why you needed the amulet. That's why you were travelling, to try to find a way to heal your people.'

Garaz nodded. 'But the sickness began to take me too. Travelling with you, I have been exposed to quite a bit of violence. Although...I was suffering before that, truth be told. Meditation helped, but fighting stoked the disease.'

'Which is why your eyes go red...' Shift said, clicking their fingers.

'My fledgling healing magic helped those here, but only temporarily. Eventually, they would succumb. Like my brother Shagraz. He was a gardener, before he became a monster. He loved to nurture things, to coax them to grow, to blossom. And then he became that violent thing.' Garaz sighed heavily.

Shift paled. They had been there when Garaz fought his brother. Had watched him die.

'When he was exiled, I knew I had to try to find a cure, but I would not do so here. My hope was to travel Etherius, to find something to help my people, to end the disease once and for all. Or at the very least find an explanation for it. So, I joined the Academy of Magic and nurtured my healing gift, whilst searching their libraries for something. Anything. Then I walked Etherius, hoping to stumble on some kind of cure.'

'None of you know how it happened?' Nicolas asked.

'No,' Salrag answered. 'Once the storm dissipated, there was no trace left of how it had happened or why. And we were too busy trying to survive to investigate it properly.'

'Why have you not called out for help from the other races?' Silva asked. 'They may have knowledge that you do not possess.'

'Because no one wants to answer your pleas when your people are best known for driving the elves to near extinction and generally burning and pillaging anything they come across.' Garaz said bitterly.

A memory popped into Nicolas's head. He cursed himself again for not noticing the signs at the time. 'You thought you had the cure when you grabbed T'goth's staff?'

'Yes.' Garaz chuckled. 'It was right there, in my hand. But there was too much at stake. The Big Boss, T'goth, the monster. I had to let it go. I thought I might never get the chance again, and then Shagraz came for me, and I had to...' A single tear rolled down Garaz's green cheek. 'I could feel the disease taking me. I was running out of time. I knew I could not let the amulet slip through my fingers.'

'You could have explained.'

'I...'

'No.' Silva interrupted harshly. 'At any point in your time with us you could have told us this. Any point.'

'But instead you chose to attack Nick, abandon us and drag us across Etherius in winter,' Shift added, glaring at Garaz. 'We all nearly *died*. Just to find out something you could have told us pretty bloody easily.'

'For Deities' sake Garaz,' Nicolas cried. 'If you'd just talked to us we would've walked you here.'

'Good reason or not. It was a shitty way to treat people who care about you,' Auron added sternly.

'I...I...' Garaz stammered. 'I have been apart from the human race for so long that I did not think I could count on you in that way. I am not used to being welcome at places, as you may have noticed, so it is easy to keep parts of myself distant.' Sighing, the orc looked away. 'And as the curse has progressed I have been struggling to think rationally. When I realised Nicolas may not hand over the amulet...it wasn't the true me that reacted. Once I realised what I had done, I knew I was a danger to all of you. I thought if I left I would keep you safe.'

'We sympathise with your plight,' Shift said quietly. 'But that doesn't even begin to make amends for what you put us all through. Nick has done some stupid stuff that has gotten us into trouble in the past, but *you*...' They shook their head in disgust.

'I am sorry,' the orc pleaded. 'Please. You have to believe that.'

'We do, but we just don't accept it,' Silva replied cooly. 'The best I can offer right now is that you are no longer at risk of dying by my hand.'

Even Nicolas wasn't sure he could forgive Garaz. Yet the sadness in Garaz's eyes was making it very hard to stay angry with him. A tense silence descended on the group. Right now, Nicolas wanted to be anywhere else but on this walkway. Salrag, Tallith and Dieter, standing off to the side, seemed equally affected by the awkward situation.

'Are you going to show us around your home?' Nicolas asked finally. 'Dieter looks likes he's about to explode with anticipation.' His attempt to lighten the mood sounded hollow, and did nothing to affect the cloud that hung over them.

With a sad smile, Garaz gestured towards the stairway leading down into Golthorak. 'This way, please,' he said quietly.

CHAPTER 56

'**N**ick,' Shift hissed, elbowing him in the side.

Thank the Deities for my armour.

Nicolas held his hands up in apology. 'I was just asking. I didn't know.'

'You can't tell?'

Squinting, Nicolas checked the figure again. 'I...think so. But I'm not sure, and I don't want to put my foot in it. They're all...sort of green and muscly.'

'You're a fool,' the shapeshifter huffed, before lowering their voice. 'Yes, that is a female orc.'

'Okay, thank you.'

He doubted Shift's angry muttering included *You're welcome.'*

Continuing to shake their head, Shift walked alongside Nicolas as they were led down one of the main streets of the city. Golthorak had the dubious honour of being the nicest underground place Nicolas had ever visited. Considering the other—numerous—times he'd been underground, it wasn't stiff competition. But the orcs had done an amazing job of crafting this place into a home. There was a sense of contentment here. Not once did he get the sense they were a people in hiding...unless he looked up at the cavern roof.

Following a pillared path, the group came to a vast square. From the numerous benches, it was obvious this was a meeting place. One frequently used.

'Please,' Salrag said, gesturing for them to sit. 'We are preparing food and drink for you. It is only fitting that we give our first guests in centuries a proper welcome.'

Orcs turn out to be more welcoming than most of the humans we've encountered on this journey. How ironic.

And they were also very prompt. Within minutes of them arriving in the square, people began to file in, preparing tables and hanging garlands of flowers. Apparently, this was to be quite the event, though it was clear that having non-orcs in the city was going to take the citizens of Golthorak some getting used to. Salrag walked to and fro, overseeing preparations whilst simultaneously answering Dieter's numerous questions.

'What a place this is,' Nicolas said as he nodded thanks to the orc who brought him a cup of water.

'Wonderous indeed.' Garaz smiled into his own drink. 'You can see why I wanted to protect it so.' The orc hesitated for a moment. 'Part of my secret keeping was that I was not sure I could trust you all with this. One errant word, and the wrong kind of people could find this place.'

Shift put their tankard down and frowned at the orc. 'I notice when you said that your eyes were firmly on me and Nick. I can't speak for him, but I do know how to keep my mouth shut on occasion.'

Beside Shift, Silva frowned. 'It is not a skill you often demonstrate.'

'Shut up, Silva.'

'And you think that's the key?' Nicolas said, pointing to the amulet.

Garaz cradled it in his large hand. 'I hope so. In all my travels, it is the best thing I have come across. Save T'goth's staff. It obviously fights the effects. Since putting it on I haven't felt the aggressive urges that come with the Regression. The difficulty will be in replicating the effect for more than one person.'

'If anyone can do it, it's you, big guy,' Auron said. 'Right man for the job and all that.' The spirit grinned widely. 'So this one time, a lord had a bit of an issue with some kind of crab monster at the bottom of his lake. It would pop out every so often and kill the odd sheep. Or servant. He wanted it gone. He hired some cheap local muscle, but you can guess what happened to them.' Auron mimed a pincer-snipping motion with his hands. 'Coming to his senses, he finally hires me. Trouble was, this bastarding thing lived underwater. It would come up, feed, then bugger off. Three times I nearly had it, but every time it dived back into the depths just before I reached it.'

'So, you went down after it?' Nicolas asked.

'No, I realised I wasn't the right man for the job,' Auron said. 'I subcontracted it to one of the mer-folk, a renowned hunter. He went down and killed it when it slept, and we split the coin.'

'When he did the actual killing?' Shift asked.

Auron held his hands up. 'It was a sixty-forty split in his favour. I'm a fair man, but I had been working on this for several days. My time is worth something.'

'I wish someone would pay you to stop telling stories.'

The spirit maintained his glare aimed at Shift whilst he talked to Garaz. 'So, I guess once you cure this, you'll be getting your own statue. I think there's a nice space over there for it.'

'I will...take that under advisement.' The orc smiled.

'I hope when they do a bird shits on it,' Shift said, casting an angry glance at Garaz.

The orc sighed. 'Unfortunately, there are no birds down here.'

'There will be,' the shapeshifter said pointedly.

Nicolas was about to drink again when he realised they were leaving someone out. 'How are you doing?' he asked Tallith.

The sergeant gave him a thumbs-up. 'This place is amazing. I thought Babylon was wonderous, but...I see I've got a lot to learn.'

Nicolas narrowed his eyes. 'I think you're starting to get the adventuring bug now.'

Tallith chuckled. 'Maybe a little. I'm not keen on the danger. But the exploring is brilliant.'

'What you need to do is learn to manage the danger better.'

The sergeant stared at him quizzically.

'I can train you. Show you a thing or two to help you when you're fighting.'

From the look on Tallith's face, it was as if a herald of the Deities had appeared before him and told him he was to be imbued with untold powers. 'You would do that?'

'Yeah, I reckon so.' Nicolas smiled before taking a drink.

'Careful,' Shift warned. 'You're one step away from him calling you his squire.'

'I would be honoured if he did,' Tallith beamed.

Shift's lips curled in disgust. 'You're both as bad as each other.'

Trying to ignore the question *what have I become?* wafting leisurely across his brain, Nicolas grabbed an apple from a nearby dish and took a bite. It was one of the best things he'd eaten in weeks. For a hidden underground city, they knew how to make fresh produce.

'...you chose not to recolonise the city above?' he heard Dieter ask as Salrag approached, writer in tow.

There was a pleasant patience to the wizened orc's smile, but Nicolas got the impression he would very much like a break.

'Initially, we tried to rebuild above,' he told Dieter. 'But the others returned and tore it down. We got the message and decided to thrive in secret.'

And you certainly are thriving.

Though they'd suffered a terrible adversity, the orcs had adapted and survived. It was so impressive how they had rallied and built something new, instead of falling apart.

Then you have people like the Visitor, who are broken by what they've suffered.

'What do we do about Avin?' he asked the others.

'At the moment, nothing,' Silva answered. 'We barely survived travelling through Etherius in winter. Trying it again would be suicide. Though...'

'You can stay here and wait out the winter,' Garaz said quickly. 'This place has warmth and food. You would be most welcome.'

The orc looked to Salrag, who stared back at Garaz for a moment before nodding. 'You are more than welcome,' the old orc said finally. 'We will not turn away friends of one of our own. Especially after such a perilous journey to get here.'

Whilst Nicolas was grateful, he couldn't help but think of the consequences of them resting here. 'And how many people suffer between now and then?'

'Less than will suffer if we leave prematurely and die on the way,' Silva replied.

The logic of that left a nasty taste in Nicolas's mouth, so he bit into the apple again to cleanse it. But the warrior was right. Travelling in winter had proven much more dangerous than even he had thought. And maybe, if they waited, they could catch The Visitor when he hibernated. It'd certainly make the fight easier.

And the respite will give me time to train.

'Okay,' he said finally. 'We can wait out the winter here. Thank you for your hospitality, Salrag.'

The old orc bowed his head slightly. Looking around, Nicolas realised this would actually be a nice place to stay for a while. These peaceful and dignified folk were a far cry from the warlike orcs on the surface. Hopefully staying here would give Garaz the time he needed to find the cure. Then they could use the amulet to save those Avin had cursed.

But will he come with us when we leave? And do we even want him to?

'Excellent,' Auron said, looking around. 'I, for one, am looking forward to enjoying the orcs' hospitality. Because there looks to be a decent party on the horizon.'

CHAPTER 57

*D*ecent had been an understatement. When the orcs made merry, they made merry. Walking through the city, Nicolas had seen a people with a quiet dignity to them. Apparently, that lasted until they decided to let their hair down. And then it was all about fun. Perhaps that had been the best way for them to survive all these years, making the most of any chance they got to be jovial.

The square was filled with people. Nicolas had worried the orcs would be standoffish as they were outsiders, but apparently, he'd made at least six new friends for life during the course of the festivities. One, a lean fellow named Graul, had even composed a poem for him off the top of his head. Due to drink, it neither rhymed nor made a lick of sense, but Nicolas loved the enthusiasm.

'Right then, you,' Shift said, standing suddenly. 'Dance.'

'Dance?' Nicolas asked.

The shapeshifter offered him their hand. 'It wasn't a question. I'm not giving you the chance to say no this time.'

As if I would.

When he took their hand, Shift led him to the centre of the square where other orcs danced to the melodies provided by some very talented musicians.

As they reached the makeshift dancefloor, Shift turned to him and moved their hips suggestively. 'Come on,' they said. 'Loosen up.' Grabbing him around the waist, they made him copy their motion. 'See. This is how you dance.'

Shaking his head, Nicolas took Shift's arms and put them around his neck. 'I never said I couldn't dance,' he smiled playfully. 'I just get nervous sometimes when beautiful people ask me to.'

Shift laughed aloud. 'Someone has been taking charm lessons from Auron and needs to stop.'

'Fine,' he replied. 'I'll just focus on dancing.'

After a few moments, he was barely aware of the music. It was just him and Shift, moving as one. But he was very aware when it stopped. Frowning, he looked towards the musicians. Garaz was beside them, talking to them earnestly. Before Nicolas could wonder why, they struck up again, playing a slower, tenderer tune. Garaz caught his eye and winked at him at exactly the same moment Shift pulled him close.

'I'm really sorry we didn't do this on Ramirez's ship,' he said, gazing into their eyes.

'It's fine,' Shift replied. 'We're dancing now.'

'Yes we areeeeeeeee.' Nicolas nearly yelped in surprise as Shift dipped him. 'Aren't I supposed to be one who does that?'

'Bless you.' The shapeshifter smirked as they brought him back up. 'I can make you do whatever I want.'

'Oh, can you now?'

Shift tutted. 'You doubt me. I'm definitely going to make you say *yippee* again later.' Their smirk suggested he'd just flushed red.

Understandable, really.

'Well, I'll be the one making my own jests when I get you to shout out a random stupid word,' he replied.

Shift bit their lip playfully. 'Oh, Mr Carnegie, challenge accepted.'

This is going to be a bloody good night.

Except it wasn't. He knew that the moment Silva stood. The warrior was looking intently at the entrance to the square. Following her gaze, he saw a group of armed orcs talking urgently to Salrag, who rose quickly, his face stern.

'Dammit.' Shift sighed, seeing what he saw.

Jogging over to their table, Nicolas grabbed his armour from where he'd left it and put it on. Tallith stopped mid-drink and rose, though he was clearly unsure what to do.

'Trouble,' Auron said, at his side.

Nicolas caught Salrag's eye and motioned to the orc to wait for them. 'It appears so.'

'I assume it is due to our presence,' Silva said.

It has to be.

As Garaz joined them, the group hurried over to Salrag.

'What's going on?' Nicolas asked.

'There is something in the city,' the orc replied. 'My scouts do not know what, but something is here.'

I bet I know what.

'I'm sorry,' Nicolas said. 'Whatever it is, we'll lead it away.'

'If you keep it away from us, then no apology is necessary.'

Along with the armed orcs and Salrag, the group hurried through the city, leaving the festivities to continue in their absence. Nicolas calmed his mind and prepared it for a fight. He'd been drinking, but the thought of danger had sobered him instantly. Which was pretty handy, as he was sure he would need his wits about him soon enough.

The group made their way up the staircase hurriedly. Salrag waved away the barrier, and they slipped into the temple. There, a pair of orcs waited, watching the street outside.

'What have you seen?' Nicolas asked.

'I could not make it out,' the orc guard replied. 'There was a shadow, and a flapping of wings.'

Nicolas and the others exchanged knowing looks.

'Salrag, get all your people underground,' he told the orc.

'We can help,' the wizened orc replied.

'No,' Nicolas said firmly. 'He's here for us. Right now, he doesn't know about you, and I aim to keep it that way. Get back underground, and don't come out for a good long while.'

Though he was clearly conflicted, the orc complied, ushering the guards back down the stairs. He gave Nicolas a final nod for good luck before the rocks reappeared with a shimmer.

'Right,' he said as he approached the door and peeked outside. It was dark in the streets. There was no sign of life. 'We slip out and lead him away from here—at least a few streets—then make ourselves known and finish this.' He didn't wait for a response, but before he made to move, he stopped. 'He gets one chance to stand down,' he continued. 'Only one. I sympathise with what happened to him, but if he chooses a fight, he'll get one.'

'As it should be,' Silva replied.

Checking the way was clear one more time, Nicolas stepped out into the night. Forming a line, the group kept to the shadows as they progressed down the street. So far, all that was in the sky were stars. But it wouldn't stay that way for long.

Stopping at the corner, Nicolas peered around. Empty. He ushered the others on, and they carried on down the next street, and the next, and the one after that. Finally, they were on the edge of what appeared to have been a large park. Even in the dark, he could see how dead the patchy grass looked. Flowerbeds had long given way to weeds and brambles. It was enclosed by a pillared walkway that ran around its edge.

This'll do.

Looking back, he checked that the others were ready. Though he already knew they would be.

Taking a deep breath, he stepped out into the park. Keeping low, he gave the appearance that he was trying not to be seen but doing a poor job of not rustling every bush he came across. The others did the same.

The flapping of wings brought him to a halt. A breeze caressed his skin as the winged figure landed in the centre of the park.

'*Found you*,' Avin said with a snarl.

Here we go then.

CHAPTER 58

I t took Nicolas a moment to realise that Avin wasn't addressing them as a group. His eyes were only on Shift.

'How did you find us?' he asked loudly, wanting to draw The Visitor's attention.

'*Tether. Magic tether,*' Avin answered. '*Realised. The trader. He always found you. Tethered you he did. Followed it. Smart.*'

Apparently when Joe said he'd untether them later, he'd meant much later.

Too late, in fact.

'I will kill him,' Silva hissed.

You can beat him. But only when I'm done.

It wouldn't take long to find him either; he was bound to appear once this was over. Unless the lazy ass had finally done what he promised he would.

'Avin, we need to talk,' Nicolas said, raising an open palm and keeping his sword low.

'*Bark. Little dog barks. Woof, woof.*'

'Not about that,' he said, controlling his annoyance. 'But about you, who you were.'

Avin's uneven eyes narrowed. '*What do you know of me? Nothing. Nothing.*'

'Then educate me,' Nicolas replied. 'Answer me this, why did you learn the magic you did? Why did you want to join the Heroes Guild?'

The question clearly caught Avin unawares. It was something he was unlikely to have thought of in a good long time.

'*Wanted to help people.*'

'Are you doing that now?'

Avin's face darkened. '*Yes. Teach them. Inhospitable. Make them hospitable.*'

Nicolas shook his head. 'How? By leaving them cursed for months? Years? How are they learning anything if you never change them back?'

'He said…'

'What do *you* say?' Nicolas shouted. 'You once wanted to stand for something good, so you bloody well know the difference between right and wrong. So, tell me, is what you're doing right?'

'They treated me like a monster.'

'Can you blame them?' Nicolas asked with a sigh. 'You turn up at people's doors, in the dead of night, looking the way you do. How do you expect people to react? If you were home, with your children, how would you react?' He didn't wait for an answer. He could see Avin was confused, he had to keep pressing it. 'Badly. You trick people into being inhospitable towards you then punish them for it. What kind of twisted logic *is* that?' Holding up the sword, he angled it so Avin could catch his reflection in the blade. 'See?' he cried, pointing at the sword. 'Look at yourself? You're still half human. What would the human half want to do in that situation? You'd want to protect those you care about. How about Silva? Do you know how badly it affected her, not being there to protect you and the other people she loved?'

Lowering her blade, the warrior stepped forward. 'He's right. I lost you all, and it took me to a dark place. I hurt people. A lot of people. And I justified it to myself for a long time.' Silva's eyes lowered. 'That's why I must control my emotions so carefully now. Lest *she* comes out again.'

'I help—'

'No, you don't,' Silva interrupted. 'You hurt them. Do not pretend you are educating people. Deep down, you know you are hurting them. Think, Avin.'

'That…wasn't… I was…supposed…' Walking backwards, Avin clutched his head, as if wracked with pain. Coming a halt, he dropped his hands to his sides and his eyes widened. *'What have I done?'* With a sob, he fell to his knees. '*I* am *a monster.'*

Walking forwards, Nicolas crouched in front of Avin. 'You're only the monster you choose to be. Choose better.'

*'That…that…*that is easy for you to say. Have you seen my face?'

'Believe me, I've seen worse.'

Avin allowed himself a chuckle. 'You poor bastard.'

'Shift,' he said, indicating his companion. 'You took Shift because you thought their ability could help you.'

Avin nodded.

'You can still do that. As long as you swear not to hurt Shift, and to undo the curses, we will help restore you.'

'You would do that, after everything I've done?'

Nicolas nodded.

'He will be mad,' Avin said quietly. 'He was mad I would not hand your companion over to him. But then he changed. He said I should do whatever it takes to find you, to take Shift back so I could heal myself.'

Nicolas highly doubted the Maestro simply had a change of heart. 'Well, he can stick his orders up his ass, can't—'

Movement caught his eye. Something appeared on Avin's neck, the creature from the cave. It writhed as its tentacles circled his throat. Avin's eyes widened in surprise as he suddenly noticed it, but then it struck, digging into his skin. There was a single shriek of pain then Avin went silent.

Nicolas rose and backed away slowly. 'Avin? Avin?'

The instant the eyes opened, he knew he wasn't looking at Avin anymore.

Rising to his full height, The Visitor extended his wings as he let out a roar. Quickly, he grabbed for the mask hanging from his neck...but Nicolas was slightly quicker. Flicking a knife from his belt, he launched it. It embedded itself in the mask just as The Visitor raised it to his face. Caught by surprise by the sudden blade pointing at him, he dropped the mask.

'Garaz,' Nicolas yelled, diving aside. 'Curse mask.'

The orc didn't hesitate. As the string keeping the mask around The Visitor's neck pulled taught, the fireball struck it, immolating the damnable object.

'Nooooo.'

For a second, the earth seemed to hold its breath. Then the mask exploded. The Visitor disappeared in a plume of red flame, and Nicolas was caught in mid-air and launched across the park. Crashing into a bed of weeds, he rolled several times, just enough to entangle himself completely in the brambles.

Groaning, he looked up. From the burning flame, numerous trails of red energy emerged, winding into the sky before disappearing in different directions.

Does that mean the curses are broken? Please let that be the case.

Trying to rise, Nicolas soon found himself too caught to move. 'A little help, please?'

Silva came over and cut him free as Shift went and picked up his sword.

'You've still got work to do, kid,' Auron told him. 'You dropped your sword again.'

'I blame the teacher,' he said, finally pulling himself free and standing. 'There's been no class on holding my sword whilst being blown up.'

'*Yet,*' the spirit threatened.

'What happened?' Tallith asked. 'I thought you were getting through to him.'

'I was,' he replied, taking his sword from Shift. 'But then there was this *thing* on his shoulder. I saw the same thing on his back in the cave. It did something to him and then he went crazy.'

'Hopefully, a curse mask exploding in his face knocked the fight out of him,' Shift suggested, staring at the flames.

Nicolas side-eyed the thick smoke and flames where Avin had stood with concern. 'You don't think that finished him off completely then?' he asked nervously.

'Kid, even you've been on enough adventures now to know the answer to *that*,' Auron answered.

True enough. There's a fight coming.

Snarling, The Visitor stepped through the fire. At a glance, the worst he'd suffered was his clothes being burned away. Being half dragon probably gave you a certain amount of tolerance to fire.

Clutching his neck, The Visitor growled. As he did, small spurts of flame escaped from between his teeth. His insane eyes fixed on them with murderous glee.

Nicolas sighed. 'I think all we did was rile him up.'

CHAPTER 59

S preading out, the group formed a rough semicircle in front of The Visitor.

'Avin, we don't have to do this,' Nicolas cautioned.

'Avin is having a rest. I'm in control, at least for a while.'

'So, what are you?' he asked, realising he was addressing the tentacled creature, and not the person it was using as a puppet. 'Some kind of demon?'

The Visitor let out a harsh laugh. *'I am no low demonic creature. But it does not matter who I am. The only thing that matters is that I kill you and take the shapeshifter. It is what the Maestro wants.'*

'Why now?' Shift shouted. 'Why take control of him now?'

'Because he was wavering,' The Visitor answered. *'When you take control, people tend to fight back. That's why you wait until you really have to. Like now.'*

'Avin,' Nicolas shouted. 'Avin, fight it! I know you're in there.'

The stream of fire directed at him suggested otherwise. Rolling as he hit the ground, he looked up just in time to see The Visitor hurtling towards him. Grabbing his chest plate, The Visitor hauled him into the air, wings flapping fiercely as he gained speed. With a crash, he slammed Nicolas into the top of one of the pillars, the impact rocking his spine.

Dazed, and pinned to the pillar high above the ground, he saw his attacker turn and unleash his fire breath towards Silva, who stood beneath them. All he could do was watch in horror, letting out a wordless cry as the inferno from The Visitor's mouth bore down on his companion. At the very last second there was a flash of red. Garaz tackled Silva aside, saving her from immolation.

The Visitor snarled in frustration and let him go. Nicolas fell.

Luckily, The Visitor hadn't looked where he was dropping Nicolas, so he landed on a bush with a heavy thud, destroying the last few leaves that had been left on it.

Above him, The Visitor was a dark silhouette against the night sky. His body lit up as several fireballs struck him, with exactly zero effect.

'Hmm, that is annoying,' Garaz said, staff still pointed towards his target.

Laughing maniacally, The Visitor dived at them. As he did, Garaz struck his staff on the ground, throwing up a bright wall of flame that distracted the incoming creature and allowed them to scatter. Nicolas secured himself behind a pillar as The Visitor landed heavily in the centre of the park.

'Kid, knife,' Auron demanded, gesturing with his hand.

Nicolas gave Auron one of his knives and watched the spirit throw it. It pinged harmlessly off the green-scaled skin of The Visitor, who was still disorientated by Garaz's fire magic.

'The dragon side is tough,' the spirit told him. 'Focus your attack on the human half.'

Can do.

Nicolas ducked back behind cover as fire struck the pillar, throwing flaming droplets in all directions. The attack stopped abruptly with a shout of annoyance. When he peeked from his hiding spot, Silva was wading in, her sword blazing as she cut and stabbed at the half-human half-dragon creature. Using his armoured side to great effect, The Visitor fended off most of her attacks, until he used his fire breath again. Silva jumped aside, but as she did, he grabbed her leg, swinging her body into a nearby statue which was missing a large chunk of its torso. The sound of the crash made Nicolas wince. As the warrior fell to the ground, The Visitor reached down towards her unconscious body.

'Silva.'

Nicolas ran from cover, The Visitor watching his charge with glee. A clawed hand easily intercepted his sword swing, but that had been the point. With his free hand, he punched The Visitor in the human half of his face, before delivering a chop to the same side, just under the neck. Dazed, The Visitor took a step back, releasing his grip on the *Dawn Blade*, and giving Nicolas an opening. Aiming at The Visitor's human neck, he swung his blade with a cry.

Before the sword struck, a mighty flap of The Visitor's wings blew him back a few steps. He stumbled back more as the claws came at him, but they harmlessly caught his armour. The Visitor's follow-up attack might've been luckier had a fireball not hit him in the side of the head before he was able to land it.

Quickly, Nicolas retreated. As he did, he saw Tallith hiding behind a pillar. The sergeant was clearly gripped by fear so it was probably best he stayed put.

Discouraging any further attack from Garaz with his fire breath, The Visitor made to fly again. Until a giant eagle swooped down into his left wing. The beak and claws tore at the membrane, slashing it and rendering the wing useless. Spinning, The Visitor used his second wing to slap the bird from the sky. The eagle hit the ground, and a large foot rose, ready to stomp on it.

'*Shift*, no.'

The Visitor paused, realising who he was about to kill, then simply kicked Shift away before turning on Nicolas. In his peripheral vision, he saw Silva rising, but so did the creature. Leaning against the ruined statue, the warrior quickly ducked the fire breath aimed at her. But the attack was enough for the broken statue to finally collapse, it's stone head landing on Silva's, knocking her out cold.

'Rrraaagggggghhhhh.'

Garaz probably shouldn't have telegraphed his charge so much. Sweeping a rock from the floor, The Visitor threw it, and it struck the orc between the eyes, leaving him unconscious on the ground.

'*Just you and me.*' The Visitor smirked. '*As it should be. He wants you dead most of all.*'

Yay. I'm number one on the Maestro's to-kill list.

Determined to end this, Nicolas ran at the creature. The Visitor swung his wing to knock Nicolas down, but he rolled under it. As he did, he lashed out with his sword, cutting The Visitor's leg. Apparently, the *Dawn Blade* was better at penetrating dragon skin than a throwing knife. The Visitor roared in pain, swinging his clawed hand toward Nicolas, who cut a gash out of his forearm.

Seeing his chance, Nicolas thrust forward with his sword. The Visitor sidestepped the attack, wrapping his arm around Nicolas's and trapping it. But nowadays, he had a trick or two up his sleeve. Headbutting the human half of the face, he let go of his sword and struck The Visitor in the side of the neck with his elbow, following up with a backhand blow to the jaw. A fierce hook punch came after that. As The Visitor stumbled backwards, Nicolas grabbed his sword and took a chunk out of his torso.

With a mighty roar, The Visitor grabbed Nicolas by the rim of his armour. The dragon half of the face headbutted him, knocking Nicolas senseless for a moment. When he came to, he found himself being flung through the air to crash against a pillar. Again.

Blinking, he watched The Visitor smiling insanely, preparing to burn him alive. The half-human half-dragon mouth opened. Nicolas could see the glow of the fire, ready to be unleashed towards him.

This is it.

He couldn't move. At least not fast enough. And The Visitor had a clean shot. All of his companions were out of the fight. In his peripheral vision he could see the shock on Auron's face as the spirit realised what was about to happen, and that he could do nothing about it.

No. Not like this.

What would happen to the people of Hablock if he died here? He needed to live. To save them from whatever cruel punishment the Maestro had consigned them to. Using his elbows, he desperately began to try and crawl away. Even as he did, he let out a defeated gasp, knowing how futile his attempt to escape death was.

The Visitor thrust his head forward, unleashing the fire in his mouth.

Nicolas's eyes widened as time slowed. The column of fire hurtled towards him, signalling the end of his life. As it did, he caught sight of Sergeant Tallith, running desperately towards him. It took Nicolas a second to realise what the young sergeant was doing.

'*No*,' Nicolas cried, reaching out. 'Don't...'

At the last second, Tallith threw himself between Nicolas and the stream of fire, using his back as a shield. Numbly, Nicolas looked into the sergeant's eyes, knowing what was about to happen and unable to do a damned thing about it. There was a single moment of pure delight on Tallith's face as he realised that he'd succeeded in saving his hero. Then, as his body was framed by the licks of flame from the fire blasting his armour, his expression changed into one of pain and horror. His mouth opened and he screamed as his eyes bulged, his entire body clenched in pure agony. The fire dissipated and Tallith staggered a couple of steps towards Nicolas, his mouth hung open and his eyes unfocused, smoke rising from his back. Somehow, in an act Nicolas knew he would remember for all his days, Tallith reached down and picked up his sword. As he rose, he actually managed to smile at Nicolas, the smile of someone who was saying goodbye. Tears filled Tallith's eyes as he turned his shaking body to face The Visitor. Nicolas gasped as the sergeant's melted armour and the seared flesh of his back was revealed. Defiantly, arm trembling with effort, Tallith raised his sword, making his final stand.

The Visitor's fire breath struck him again.

Noooooooooooooooooo.

Knocked backwards, Sergeant Tallith fell to the ground, his body a smoking heap.

'No, no, no, no, no...' Nicolas crawled across the hard ground until he reached Tallith.

His skin was either blackened or red raw, with burnt flakes hanging limply from it. His hair was gone, and one eye was fused shut. The other stared back at him.

'You didn't have to do that. Why did you do that?' Nicolas cried, his hands hovering in the air as he desperately tried to think of something to do to make it better.

'Had…to…save…you… Too…much…good…left…to…do…'

'But you could have attacked him from behind, anything else but that. You didn't have to sacrifice yourself. Not for me. Never for me.'

'Yes, I did,' Tallith croaked weakly. 'It's been an honour. Thank you.'

'No,' Nicolas said, wiping the tears from his eyes. 'The honour was mine. People will hear how brave you were. I swear it.'

There wasn't much of a face left to smile. But he knew Tallith was happy as his eye shut for the very last time. Nicolas watched it for what seemed an eternity, waiting for it to open again, knowing it never would.

A light caught his eye. Beside the body stood the spirit of Sergeant Tallith. He looked down sadly at his own corpse, before his gaze rose to meet Nicolas's. Nicolas managed to force a smile and saluted Tallith. The sergeant returned it with pride before his spirit faded away.

Nicolas stared at where the spirit had stood for a moment, grief, guilt and anger all churning in his gut as one. Finally, he rose, dusting himself off. Walking a little way, he bent down and picked up the *Dawn Blade*.

'You should not have done that.' Nicolas's voice was a menacing growl.

For a single moment, Nicolas was sure he caught a glint of fear in The Visitor's eyes, but it was soon dismissed with a derisive chuckle. With an angry shout, Nicolas charged.

Fire breath blasted towards him, but he dodged it, not even breaking step as he closed the gap between himself and The Visitor at speed. Three times The Visitor launched a firestorm at him, and three times he wasn't there to receive it. Then Nicolas was finally in striking distance.

'*Die*,' Nicolas cried as he lunged forwards.

Ducking, diving and turning as his sword swung again and again, Nicolas unleashed a furious assault. Each time the *Dawn Blade* struck, another chunk of The Visitor's body was lost. The Visitor tried to step back, to block the attacks, to do anything to save himself. His efforts were fruitless against Nicolas's onslaught. By the time he'd finished, The Visitor was on his knees, covered in bloody wounds. With a cry, he struck down on the shoulder where the tentacled creature was. It exploded in a fountain of bright pink blood as the sword cut through it and deep into the shoulder. Using his foot, Nicolas dislodged his blade and kicked The Visitor to the ground.

Stepping on The Visitor's chest, he raised his sword.

But the eyes that looked up at him were Avin's. 'I think it's better this way,' Avin said, coughing blood. 'I let myself become a monster.'

Nicolas threw his sword aside. 'No. No more killing.'

Avin laughed. 'I am dead. These are just my last few gasps of life. Thank you for ending my misery.'

'I had no choice.'

'I did, before the creature took me,' Avin admitted. 'I knew I was doing wrong. I always did. But I deluded myself into pushing it away. It's time to pay for my sins.'

Avin's eyes didn't close like Tallith's. Instead, they slowly emptied. As they did, there was a glow over the body, and Avin's ghostly form shimmered into existence. Now Nicolas could see what he'd looked like as a man. Avin's spirit stared down at his monstrous body with shame. But there was also relief. He didn't have to be a monster anymore.

'I'm so sorry,' he said with feeling as he faded away. In the moment before he vanished, Avin frowned at the ground beside his body.

Wondering what had caught Avin's attention, Nicolas stared at his corpse. There was something in the dirt around his hand. Crouching, he tried to make out what it was, but it was too dark.

Auron appeared at his side, and the light from his aura chased the shadows away. It was writing. A single word, etched into the dirt with a fingernail before the last embers of life left his body. One last message.

Helstrum.

CHAPTER 60

The next day, the group gathered again in the park. This time, they weren't alone. Salrag and several other orcs had accompanied them to the surface, to help with their sorrowful task. Quietly, Nicolas stared at the open ground they'd chosen, beside what must've once been a water feature. He removed his armour. This wasn't work to be done wearing metal plate for, light or not.

'Shovel.' His voice was a whisper.

'You don't have to dig,' Shift said, hand on his shoulder. 'Salrag and the others said they would.'

'Yes, I do.'

He thrust the shovel into the earth. Putting his foot on it, he pushed the blade in deeper before hauling it upwards, creating a hole. Dirt fell from the shovel as he moved it aside and discarded what was on it. Then he did it again.

Around him, the others went to work. There were two graves to dig.

Even with a group, the work was hot and time-consuming. But it gave him a purpose, focusing him and stopping him from dwelling on what had happened. On what they'd lost. On what lay to the side, shrouded in white.

Avin Hipmuck and Sergeant Nathaniel Tallith both lay to the side, covered in thin shrouds. Ones that barely concealed the damage the battle had caused to each of their bodies.

Wordlessly, everyone worked until the holes were deep enough. Then they lifted the two dead men from the ground and carefully moved them towards their places of rest. Nicolas tried not to look at Talltih's body. Even with the shroud, he could see the terrible wounds that had caused his death. He didn't want to remember the sergeant that way. And then there was the guilt.

It should have been me.

Nicolas still couldn't wrap his head around Tallith's sacrifice. In his mind he replayed it, not for the first time, trying to discern if anything could have been done differently. Not that it mattered if he succeeded. He couldn't go back in time and change it. As much as he may wish he could.

Why should someone die in my place?

Angrily, he pushed the thought away. It should have been him. But he didn't want to devalue what Tallith had done. Right or not, the sergeant had done it for a reason. And Nicolas had to make sure he was worthy of it.

Finally, he cast a glance at the man he helped carry. Despite the horrific injuries, Tallith looked at peace.

I hope you are.

Sombrely, the two groups reached the graves. Standing on either side, they lowered the dead gently into their graves.

Part of Nicolas still balked at the idea that Avin should get a proper burial. But he knew it was the right thing to do. Avin had started out a good man and had been twisted by circumstance and outside influence into something worse.

It could've easily happened to me.

'We should say something,' Salrag said as they stepped back from the graves. 'Before we commit them to the earth.'

'I'll speak,' Nicolas said quickly. 'I want to talk about Nathaniel Tallith.'

For a moment, the words wouldn't come, emotion blocking his throat. Taking a deep breath, he forced himself to speak. 'I didn't know him as well as I would've liked. But I knew enough to know that he was a brave man. He wanted to make the world a better place. That's why he joined the city watch, that's why he loved stories about heroes, and that's why he followed me.' He took a moment to fight back his tears. 'He looked up to me. I don't get why. I don't feel like I deserve it. I certainly don't feel that someone should give up their life for mine. But he saw something in me that I don't see in myself. I swear to spend the rest of my days living up to that ideal.' Running his hands through his hair, he smiled and looked up to the sky. 'Don't worry, I'll give you plenty of adventures to watch. You won't be bored up there.'

As a tear ran down his cheek, Shift took him by the shoulders and pulled him into an embrace.

'I would like to speak about Avin.'

Until now, Silva had said nothing about his death. She'd barely reacted to it...which showed him just how much it had hurt her. The warrior stepped forwards.

'He was an idealist once,' Silva began. 'He wanted to make the world a better place, like Tallith. He had the power to do it, but he made a mistake. That mistake cursed him, driving him from everything he believed, to men who used him as a tool for their evil agendas.' Silva's knuckles whitened as she clenched her fists. 'But despite how he was twisted and warped, I believe he still wanted to help people, though he went about it the wrong way. I don't want to remember him like that. I want to remember the man he once was. So that is what I choose to do. I hope you are at peace now, Avin.'

Silva's jaw set as she closed her eyes. Nicolas went to her and put his arm around her. Staring at him, Silva placed her hand on his cheek and nodded her thanks before turning away.

All that was left to do was to bury the pair. This was done in silence. The only sound was the falling of dirt as it was shovelled into the graves. Finally, when it was done, Nicolas stuck Tallith's sword into the ground at the head of his grave. Avin had carried nothing on him, but Silva had carved a small marker for him, which she put into place.

For a long time, the group stared at the graves. How many good people had died already to get him to this point? Whatever the answer, it was too many.

'Thank you, Salrag,' Nicolas said finally. 'You and the others didn't have to help.'

'It was the right thing to do,' the orc replied. 'What are your plans now?'

'We were hoping to stay like we asked, until winter passes, then return to the kingdoms of man, if you don't mind?'

The orc smiled. 'Of course. You are all more than welcome here. I will have a house set aside for you.'

Nicolas shook the orc's outstretched hand then the group of orcs departed. Dieter, who had been stood in solemn silence throughout the whole thing, went with them.

Once they had left, Nicolas and his companions stood over the graves in silence for a long time.

'What happens when winter passes?' Shift asked finally.

Since the fight, there'd really been no time to breathe, to think about things. But they all knew about the writing in the dirt.

'We go back,' Nicolas said firmly, his fists clenching tightly. 'Because we have a job to do.'

'So, you believe it is true?' Garaz asked.

'It has to be,' he answered quickly. 'Why else go to the trouble of writing a name with your dying breath?'

'The kid is right.' Auron nodded. 'You don't just do that without a damned good reason.' Pointedly, the spirit looked at his companions. 'I take it we have all come to the same conclusion?'

'Tobias Helstrum is the Maestro.' Nicolas's voice came out as a low growl. 'He has to be. Why else would Avin write his name? It was one last good deed before he passed. Letting us know the name of the man who used him. Who turned him into a weapon.'

'And just so we're clear,' Shift began, 'what do we intend to do with that information?'

'When winter breaks, we are going to find him, and we are going to kill him,' Nicolas said firmly.

Garaz stroked his beard thoughtfully. 'He will not be an easy man to get to.'

'Good luck to anyone who tries standing between him and us,' Silva said, folding her arms defiantly.

'Looking at the kid's face, I think I feel a little sorry for the poor bastard,' Auron said with a half-smile. 'He won't know what hit him.'

'I'll make sure he knows.'

Nicolas stared at the sword marking Sergeant Tallith's grave. His eyes bored into the hilt, picturing all the carnage he'd seen. All of it because of one evil man. It was too much. Something needed to be done, and he was the one who was going to do it.

Tobias Helstrum dies.

EPILOGUE

After so much time being unable to comfort his family, Gerard wasn't going to be stopped now. However long he'd been petrified as a tree—a living nightmare for which he was awake the entire time—had caused his muscles to waste away. But a parent's determination was strong. Growling, he crawled through the dirt towards them, one hand at a time. With each movement he let out a grunt of effort. Ahead of him, his daughter Annabeth stared at him with hollow, tear-filled eyes.

How has this damaged her mind?

How had living in a waking nightmare damaged his? No. He couldn't think on that yet. Annabeth was there. She was more important. He had to get to her. Each movement wracked his body with pain, but anger and fear gave his arms the strength they needed. It seemed to take hours, but finally, he took her in his arms.

His daughter sobbed fiercely, finally coming to life. 'I can't move,' Annabeth wept. 'I can't move. My body hurts.' Suddenly, she began to struggle against his grip, her eyes darting this way and that. 'Where's the bad man? He must be near.'

Gerard held her close, rubbing her matted blond hair softly. 'Shhh, sweet bun. He's gone. He won't come back.'

Staring ahead as he comforted his child, his mind imposed a pair of red eyes on the horizon. Those eyes. The last thing he'd seen as a human. His breathing quickened as he stared directly into them, his skin prickling as if he were about to change again.

No.

Closing his eyes, he gritted his teeth and willed the image away. His family needed him. Steadying his breathing, he gently shushed his sobbing daughter, before looking to his wife.

'Alissa,' he called to her. 'Alissa, are you okay?'

She was right there, laid with her back to him, just out of arm's reach. As he focused, the terrible realisation set in that she wasn't breathing.

Deities, no.

'Mum?' Annabeth called, sensing something was wrong. 'Mummy?'

Judging by the anguished cries around him, his wife wasn't the only one not to come back. It didn't take his daughter long to realise what had happened. She let out a wail that no child should ever have to, pushing her head into his chest.

How had this happened? Gerard racked his brain. They were good people. They went to worship regularly. What had they done to deserve the terrible fate that had befallen them? His gaze went first to his wife, then to his daughter. His family. Torn asunder.

By the Deities, someone will pay for this.

'Over here.'

Gerard started as he heard the voice. With effort, he turned himself over, grabbing a nearby rock. He wasn't sure what good it would do when he couldn't even stand, but he would find a way. This time, he would defend his daughter to his last breath. He half-hoped it was the monster returning, that he might wreak vengeance upon it. At the sound of the voice Annabeth pushed herself against him more tightly, as if it may somehow help her vanish from sight.

Robed men appeared, walking amongst the bodies of his neighbours.

'They're alive,' one of the men shouted. 'Get the healers over here. *Now.*'

A single man stood over him then crouched. Instinctively, Gerard swung his rock. His hand was caught at the wrist and the rock removed and discarded.

'It's okay,' the man said gently. 'We are here to help.'

'Please,' he said, pointing to Alissa. 'My wife...'

Another man ran towards them, to be directed towards his wife. Gerard's heart fell a thousand leagues beneath the earth as the healer sat beside her and examined her, only to rise and shake his head a moment later. She was gone. How long had she been gone for? Since it happened? Or maybe just a few minutes before whatever magic had cursed them was lifted?

'I'm so sorry,' the robed man said. 'Was this The Visitor?'

'Yes.' Gerard was starting to realise how dry his throat was. The robed man seemed to pick up on this, giving first his daughter a long swig from a water skin and then him. His throat hadn't swallowed liquid in so long it almost hurt, and he coughed violently.

'Damned monsters.' The man shook his head. 'How can they do this to helpless villagers?'

Gerard looked back at his lost wife, his hands shaking in fury.

'I cannot bring back the dead,' the man said. 'But I will do my best to ensure you and your family are healed.'

'Who are you?' he asked, aware that other robed men were ministering to his neighbours in a similar fashion.

'I am a missionary.' The man smiled warmly. 'From the Custodians of Humanity.'

Gerard was vaguely aware of the name. If he remembered right, they were a small group who'd been preaching about the devilry of non-humans. At least, they were two years ago. Who knew how times had changed?

'Tobias Helstrum heard word of good people being attacked by this *Visitor* creature and sent us out to help.'

'How?' Gerard scoffed angrily. 'How can you help those who are already dead? Who can fight creatures that can turn skin to bark?'

The robed man smiled knowingly. 'Oh, we can fight.' He chuckled. 'We have the means and the motivation. We just need the manpower.'

Gerard looked at his daughter. Her lip trembled with fear as her eyes pleaded for salvation. No human could've done this to his family, that was damned sure. Monsters. There were too many monsters in the world.

I will not stand idly by and let others suffer as we have.

'If you need men, you have one here,' he growled, the resolution set in his mind.

'Focus on healing yourself and your daughter first.'

The man who'd spoken wore black, full-body armour, with a heart carved into the chest plate. His warm smile was surrounded by a neatly trimmed beard. There was a roguish twinkle in his eyes that reminded Gerard of his youth, sneaking into the wine cellars with his friends to drink whilst the adults slept.

'Who are you?' he asked. It was still difficult to speak.

The knight crouched. 'They call me Lord Blackheart. My men and I ensure these missionaries travel safely to do their job.' He looked around before dropping his voice low. 'And we make sure that those responsible for such things can't do them again.'

The man nodded back towards the road, and Gerard followed his prompt. He saw a group of wagons, guarded by warriors in masks. Each one was carved into a leering, almost-demonic looking face.

'Don't let the masks put you off.' Lord Blackheart grinned. 'They're supposed to put the fear of the Deities into the inhuman creatures who do things like this to good folk like you. They're dedicated to making sure people are protected, ensuring that chaos doesn't engulf our lands.'

'You aren't the king's men then?'

Blackheart shook his head. 'No. We aren't affiliated with any kingdom. Which is probably a good thing, as who knows how long you would've been left out here if you had to wait for your king?'

Our king.

He was supposed to keep the people safe. But they'd just been abandoned, trapped in a living horror. Was it days, weeks, months or even years they'd been left to suffer? No matter how long it was, no one had come. How was that even possible?

Bastards.

They had been left to the mercy of monsters.

'I want to fight,' Gerard said with passion. 'I want to help.'

Blackheart removed his gauntlet and put a hand on his shoulder. 'Of course you do. What right-minded father wouldn't want to protect his family?' He gave Annabeth a cheeky wink. 'But you rest for now. Grieve for your lost wife. Get strong again. Then come see me, and we will show you how to fight.'

This will never happen again. Never.

ACKNOWLEDGEMENTS

Phew. I think that pursuit exhausted me as much as it did Nicolas and his companions. Though that's probably a massive over exaggeration. I didn't have to fight a horde of barbarians, run from wolves...or get turned into a dog.

When I had the first idea for this book it was literally *'they're going to chase Garaz across Etherius in winter.'* That was the premise. I thought it was a bit basic. But by now, I'm learning to trust myself. I know that between the initial premise and the finished product, I will come up with plenty of crazy stuff. And I didn't disappoint myself.

I really enjoyed writing this seventh instalment in Nicolas's journey. Wow. Seven. That makes this book the halfway point of the series. That means you have seven more books to come, you lucky person you. Don't worry. I still have plenty of ideas. I'm sure by know you've noticed that each book has a slightly different flavour to it. This was, simply put, a chase.

It was strange not writing about Garaz until near the end of the book. I missed him. But it was a necessary evil. Though everything I do to Nicolas is a necessary evil.

The dog was quite a late addition to the plot, and one of those moments where I was just typing and it happened. And initially, Tallith was going to be the one with the tentacled creature on him. It would be the reason he kept messing up and getting the group caught out. But I changed that in the final draft. I wanted him to be an example to Nicolas of how he was when he first started out. Plus, I did the group travelling with an enemy in book 5.

One of the main notes Dani, my editor, gave me when she returned the manuscript, was that Tallith's death didn't have much emotional impact. So, I got to work on that. Now, this may be me being a sensitive guy, but I did tear up during the rewrite. I could vividly picture the scene. Nicolas about to die, the sergeant running towards him and Nicolas powerless to stop him...did you tear up too? If you did, it's okay to cry. I just hope you didn't laugh. That was one of the moments in the book I was *not* intending to be funny.

Once again, Dani worked her magic on this book. As always, I am massively grateful for her insights into how to make my books better so you, the reader, can enjoy them all the more. Thank you Dani.

And of course I have to thank my mum, Christine, who pursues those elusive spelling mistakes with all the determination Nicolas and the others used to pursue Garaz.

Then there are the Kickstarter backers. Each and every one of them is awesome for helping me fund the production of this book and continuing to make my dream of being an author a reality.

And being an author has been an amazing journey. There has been lots to learn. But I'm slowly getting there. And I'm getting fans. *Fans*. Can you believe it? Awesome people who are following my work and singing about it to anyone they can find. When I hear people talking about how much they love my books it affects me more than writing a certain death scene. My thanks go out to everyone who has followed the series. It's the reason I continue to write.

Speaking of which, you've just come to the end of the book. Fear not. There's plenty more to come. What have you got to look forward to next? Well...Nicolas has a man to kill! Sounds simple, doesn't it...

Until then,
Thank you for reading,
And keep adventuring,
Andrew

About the Author

Andrew Claydon has an imagination, one full of variety.
Sometimes it's funny, sometimes it's adventurous, sometimes it's shocking, and occasionally it's outright strange...but it's never boring!
Andrew is a UK author who grew up loving fantasy movies such as Conan, Krull, Beastmaster and Willow. The epic worlds and battles of swords and sorcery therein inspired him to create his own fantasy worlds, adding to them his own brand of irreverent humour; because sometimes it's good to chuckle in between sword fights!
He wants to inspire the imagination of others, just as he's been inspired; with dashing heroes, epic quests and vile villains.
So reader beware, you aren't just opening a book, but a doorway into Andrew's imagination. It'll be a strange journey, but an entertaining one!
When he isn't writing, he loves to read sci/fi and fantasy novels. It's one of the things that inspires him to write himself. He also enjoys playing Warhammer 40,000 and is a keen wrestling fan.
He has degrees in both history and psychology, as well as black belts in several martial arts.
When he isn't creating vast fantasy worlds and populating them with good guys and bad guys to run around fighting each other, he works as a supported employment coordinator, helping others to try and achieve their aspirations.
Subscribe to my newsletter for the latest publishing news (and a FREE prequel novella) at: www.andrewclaydonauthor.com
Or follow me on social media:
Facebook: Andrewclaydonauthor
Instagram: @authorandyc
Tiktok: @authorandyc
If you enjoyed the book, then please leave a review with your preferred retailer.
Reviews are really important to indie authors to help them get their work out there.
If you do take the time to leave a review, thank you.

ALSO BY

Chronicles of the Dawnblade Series
The Simple Delivery
Strange Companions
The Odd Sea
Wrath and Wraiths
Trail of Death
Demons and Disorder
The Pursuit

Novellas and short stories
A Grudge is Born
The Gathering
Don't you know who I am?
How I learned to hate adventuring
Refilling the Pot